Acknowledgements

GU00598686

To everyone who has given me help and support on this journey
so far I humbly extend to you my sincere thanks. I am especially
grateful to Angela, Helen and Benita, without whom this book
would not exist.

The Fatal Verse of the Valley

PART ONE OF
The Red Book

BY

Ben Wright

A CIP catalogue for this book is available
from the British Library.

ISBN 10. 0-900443-13-8

ISBN 13. 978-0-900443-13-8

Typeset in Times

Published by Headleys of Ashford
Printed by Headley Brothers (Digital) Ltd
The Invicta Press,
Queens Road, Ashford,
Kent TN24 8HH

www.headleysofashford.co.uk

Contents

Chapter 1

THE WALKING CHORD RETURNS

Behvyn's earliest memory was of his brother, Behleth, who was by some few moments the younger of the twin boys. It was of spotting him sat beneath the dinner table, steepling his small chubby hands to take up a sticky grip either side of the low overhanging tablecloth, upon which up above had been set a light evening supper for their uncle and surrogate sisters to enjoy. He watched on in astonishment as Behleth pulled it sharply downwards, as though he was plunging a sword into his chest.

The scraping of chair legs, cries of alarm from the girls and booming curses from uncle, the clatter of cutlery, bouncing of candlesticks and rolling of steel plates, sending their contents flying towards the large hounds who had moved from a dozing half-sleep to their clicking feet instantaneously, all of this Behvyn had foreseen, even as he had entered the room. What had surprised him, though, was the look in Behleth's eye as Uncle Grodel had reached his arm down to capture the delighted boy unerringly with one encompassing, heavily haired hand and to pluck him out and up by his shoulder. It was one of untethered glee.

It had expressed itself in a heaving of the chest, a glossy wideness of the stare, a broadening of the nostrils and a tilt of the head. Nothing to do with the mouth; it was all about the eyes. It had been a knowing look, accepting of consequence, and, Behvyn realised, his brother had been attuned to every noise, every spilt drop of wine, every pool of liquid wax to spot the floor or the tablecloth, every confused squeal and yelp as though it were the best payment for his daring. The only flitter of alarm to cross Behleth's face had come when Grodel had reached out for Behvyn too, and only then did he start to cry, to fight and to kick in his clutch.

Behvyn learned over time to spot these pending excitements that would infuse his brother at unpredictable moments and found that at such times he would be given a choice. He knew he could try to divert Behleth's attention, or make himself scarce, or join in.

But in a strange way, because he knew he had these options, each time he didn't avert his brother's mischief, he felt responsible. He took no satisfaction from seeing his brother take the punishments Grodel meted out, even if he had escaped them himself. In such a way as well, Behleth came to rely on Behvyn's decisions as the roll of the dice to decide his own fate, delegating his responsibility to Behvyn, accepting Grodel's wrath as nothing other than a barometer of wrong-doing, and looking to his own brother's choice as the true measurement of moral justice.

Now, years later, it was little different, though they were almost men. Behleth had calmed but would still get that same glint in his deep-set grey-blue eyes that Behvyn recognised from their early youth, and then it would be up to Behvyn to make the call. This time, though, at the end of a hard-worked day out in the wind-swept corn fields of the small village of Muscle Oaks, where they had lived all their lives, and where not another soul was known to be still toiling outside, the bonds of concern had momentarily slipped from Behvyn's shoulders as he and his brother grew more excited about the prospect of a special evening that lay ahead of them.

'You know, I think you stacked those sheaves wrong,' said Behleth, his face in and out of shadow as a light breeze messed his shorn dark brown hair. The oil lamp that he had hung from the barn door lintel now swung back and forth in winding circles. The late summer evening had finally drawn to a close.

'Rubbish,' replied Behvyn, not even cocking a look with his deep blue eyes through long black locks at his own piles of handiwork as he continued sweeping up his brother's end of the barn floor. He was now the taller of the two, which gave him an elegance Behleth's stocky frame would forever deny.

'Behvyn, they're going to fall down the moment we leave,' said Behleth, now stood nearer to the doorway, wiping the sweat off his neck with a rag that smelled of leather polish. He sniffed at it and then threw it away in disgust. It narrowly missed Behvyn.

'Cut it out. I'm nearly done and then we'll go.'

'We're late as it is,' replied Behleth. 'I bet they've already started.'

'They won't have, and it's not that late,' responded Behvyn without much thought, which then startled himself into wondering just what time it actually was.

He had never found it difficult to become absorbed in what he was doing down to the finest detail, whereas his brother would be fascinated with the ideas of things and urgently want to see them put into practice; but only for the first few times, after which his interest would soon wane. To elongate his brother's focus, Behvyn would develop challenges, competitions of strength, skill or endurance so that Behleth's lust for success over his accomplished brother would be sparked. That had always been the scary thing about Behleth, Behvyn mused at times. If only he had a consistent commitment, there was no knowing where his achievements would end.

Behvyn had challenged his brother that very day to see who could reap, bundle, carry and then stack the most corn in the barn by nightfall. His brother had seen through the ruse, but accepted; his passion ignited by the opportunity to wear down the advantage Behvyn had been given by fate – quite unfairly, to his mind – of being the eldest by only the amount of time it took to get someone pregnant.

Behleth had won, convincingly, his stack climbing to the roof some time before his brother's. He was a few inches shorter than Behvyn, who stood well over six feet tall, but was broader in the brow and in the shoulder. His physique had called him to the attention of Natch Fallwater, the village blacksmith, who was known at the time to be looking for a new stithium worker to allow him to pick up the trade of passing Royal Knights. These would regularly pass through Muscle Oaks on their way to or from the North Wall, sometimes with heavily notched blades from battle. As stithium was the hardest metal that could be worked it needed a strong man to wield the hammer and Fallwater had undoubtedly been earmarking Behleth for the job.

'Morning, Master Hahn,' he would say as Behleth passed by on his way to the fields, 'mind you keep your hands out of those threshers an' make sure you drop by the 'ouse every once in a while.' This from a man who barely spoke to anyone, Behvyn had noticed. Behleth would wave and glance at the man with his most

3

public face, one that spoke of assured charm, but one which also hid his discomfort. For all his overconfidence among friends and big groups, he still looked to his brother for the lead.

Behvyn finished sweeping the floor and slowly unfurled himself to his full height, enjoying how his back muscles flared and then quickly ceased their complaint. He finally allowed himself to look with lidded eyes at what Behleth had been telling him was a tower of straw waiting to collapse and then began to frown.

'What's going on?' Behvyn asked, noticing the regular shaking coming from the pyramidical stack as though it hid a strange, triangular heart within, or was being butted by an overly energetic cow from behind.

'I did say,' announced his brother in light despair as the stack continued its alarming sway. 'It must be the wind. You know how it gets from now on. It's all because of the Cloud Mount. But here, you're done. Let's go,' he continued. 'The "Walking Chord" is going to be here, at the Poacher's, tonight! I still can't believe it.'

'I know, you've said it a hundred times already today,' complained Behvyn.

'Well, I'm excited. And I'm starving!'

'Did you say it was the wind?' replied Behvyn, still watching the heaving bales, unconvinced, and rounded the door to examine what his brother was up to. The glint was back in Behleth's eye once again, as he saw his brother had been too slow.

'Ai! A gust!' cried Behleth, and scampered past Behvyn just in time. Behvyn had long enough to realise his folly. He noticed the pitchfork clang to the ground a moment before he was engulfed in a wave of toppling bundles of corn. A dust of husks, grass and dirt sprang into the air, billowing into a rising cloud as Behvyn, coughing, fought his way out of the straw prison he found himself in. Behleth was barely able to stand in his pristine half of the barn, convulsed as he was with an evil laughter that was so contagious, Behvyn could barely stop himself from laughing too.

'I'm not clearing this up in the morning,' said Behvyn, as straight laced as he could manage and casting his gaze around the place.

'Good,' replied Behleth heartily, wiping the tears from his eyes. 'I'm pleased to hear it. Now can we please go?'

4

'Yes,' answered Behvyn finally, who after ushering his brother outside, rescuing the lamp from its hook, and closing up the doors behind him, set off on the downhill wander towards the winking golden lights that shone out over the waving grey fields from the centre of the village.

Although Muscle Oaks nestled comfortably within the North Vale of the Shale Valley, the westernmost and richest of the Known Lands, its proximity to the ever-veiled white shoulders of Cloud Mountain, or the 'Cloud Mount' as it was referred to by the local inhabitants, caused a chill wind to run through the length of it once the sun had diminished whatever the season.

For that very reason the long-sighted village elders in days gone past had seen to it to grow two great circles of oak trees about the outskirts of the village, and in addition, have them line the straight edges of the central square as well. Huge and knarled they were by now, and close knit too. So much did they now define the place that the original name of the village had been lost in time to be replaced by 'Muscle Oaks', a name travellers had given to it that the locals, or 'Oaksters' as they became known, finally accepted for their own. The mighty trees did much to keep out the wind in the village, but out on the hills there was no such shelter. The twins walked quickly noticing as they did how there were much fewer lights about the main square than usual, but a great concentration of them still came through from one building.

'I'll bet everyone's in there tonight,' said Behvyn, breaking into a jog, and doing his best not to spill the oil from the lamp as he went.

'Thanks to you we've got no chance of getting a seat,' replied Behleth sourly, keeping up with his brother.

The Poacher's Inn comprised the entire eastern side of the main square. Its large size was a legacy from earlier days under previous Kings when travel had been common up and down the Great Shale Valley and the war with Mertos had yet to begin. Muscle Oaks sat on either side of the Great Shale Road, which was more commonly referred to as the 'Kingsway', and had been constantly busy with trade wagons, travellers, visitors from nearby villages, and guardsmen. The travellers were not brought by anything that was above Muscle Oaks; only King's Guards of the North Wall passed through. But they would be attracted up from the South Vale, and even on some rare occasions from as far afield as Khubron, to visit the tranquil beauty of Tieco Lake. As there was nothing else in Tieco, those unused to sleeping in anything other than a bed with soft sheets and a warm blanket would be found in Muscle Oaks looking for a room for the night, and the Poacher's warm glow would win their trade.

The regulars in the Poacher's spoke only cautiously to these intrepid travellers, however. It was a saying in the North Vale that if you kept your nose out of everyone else's business, you got to keep it yourself. One of the curious things about the Khubroni was that seldom few seemed to have kept theirs and they presented an alarming visage to the local children, many of whom burst into immediate tears thinking them monsters. The more cunning parents would then use this to their advantage and develop scare stories about how these deformities had happened to keep their offspring's behaviour in check. 'You just remember Khubby!' had become a favourite admonishment among those drawn to the end of their tether.

The travellers from near and far, however, had dried up many years ago with the onset of war and now it was a rarity indeed to have a new face – with or without a nose – within the regular crowd of the vast Assembly Room at the Poacher's. Not that they would be easy to spot; the atmosphere, as it was again this night, was traditionally thick with steam, smoke, heat and impassioned discussion.

As is always the case with communities that feel on the edge of things, the Oaksters had a strong sense of their own identity that they then used as the basis for their own perceived uniqueness. This was then contrasted with how everyone else from everywhere else, and most especially from the nearby surrounding area, simply did not possess this same blend of qualities. They would therefore be considered wanting and were criticised and pitied in equal and constant measure. Those who were less enamoured with such arguments, less dismissive of the positive traits of others and less firm in a conviction of their own superiority became a constant thorn in the side of those who sought to set in stone a definition of what an 'Oakster' was. As this was never to be achieved, it was the perfect source of conversation after a few heaving tankards of Old Scrappy, the potent North Vale brew, and readily joined in by the same familiar faces night after night.

This night was to be slightly different, however. As Behvyn and Behleth tumbled in through the door from the hallway, to excited gasps that then turned into low moans of disappointment, and pushed their way in past the immovable objects sat by the bar and waded over skinny dogs with long ears that slept incautiously under tables, the nature of the conversation inside the Poacher's that now picked up again was only about one thing: the visit of the Walking Chord.

'What will they sound like?' 'Will they play that one, you know, oh, now, how does it go?' 'When I heard they played at the Royal Court and Prince Idren himself compared their sound to the fairest memory he held dear…' and so on. As the chatter encased the twins, so the steam and the smoke filled nostrils with the combining scents of cooked meats, burnt tobacco, log fires and frothy beer. Their appetites made a sudden and demanding appearance.

'I have to sit down and eat!' complained Behleth. 'Where are the others? I can't see them.' Behvyn, keen eyed, searched about the gloomy room. He saw many faces he recognised but had never before seen either in or about the environs of the Poacher's at this time of day. Everyone in the village seemed to have turned up and as a reward had been crammed in almost on top of each other. Then he spotted them, waving madly over at them from some small distance away, and pointed them out to Behleth.

As he did so a voice boomed out across the room: 'Get off the stage, boys! Unless you want to sing us all a song?' A silence then fell, followed by a great laugh which emanated from somewhere within the huge barman's ferocious black beard.

'Very funny, Uncle Grodel,' replied Behvyn as the hubbub built once more, and continued to plough his way through the mass of bodies as nonchalantly as possible towards their friends, though both he and Behleth had been scared almost out of their wits. Grodel gave them a good-humoured and very knowing wink and urged them to 'find a place quick sharp!'

Uncle Grodel was not only Behvyn and Behleth's adopted father but also the most influential man in Muscle Oaks, partly on account of being the largest of its inhabitants but also on being the craftiest. It seemed that, judging by the sigh that otherwise now went around the place, Grodel had won again in guessing the number of logs the main fire would have combusted its way through once the brothers had decided to call it a day in the fields. Money exchanged hands in their tottering wake and not a few resentful glances were cast in their direction.

'Mandle, they're 'ere! Come on lads, dinner's comin'. Scoff it down fast!' bellowed Grodel as they finally reached their table. Sitting there with a mixture of embarrassment, impatience and relief on both their faces were the twins' two best friends, Kjerros and Feran.

'Mandle!' cried Grodel again in a blood-chilling roar, as Behvyn and Behleth took the weight off their feet and leaned back in the deep benches that had been saved for them.

'You decided to come along after all, then?' teased Kjerros, fully aware of Behvyn's habit of leaving everything to the last minute.

'You wouldn't believe how hard it's been to hold these seats for you two,' complained Feran. 'I had to turn away the entire Springthorn family, even Jaleffa, who is a much better looking – and smelling – sight than you two. They've all had to go and sit right next to the fire over there instead. The number of hateful looks I've had off her.'

'What would Tangle say if she heard you?' replied Behvyn, somewhat more brusquely than planned. Feran got the message and stopped grumbling. In that moment he resembled a dog threatened with a smack on the nose.

Then in dashed Mandle, the slip of a girl Grodel employed as kitchenhand, through the two-way door that was set off to the left of the long, high bar. She brought the twins' meals down heavily in front of them with a haughty: 'About time!' and then span away all in one move. She dashed off to collect tankards, plates, bowls and not a few knocks and bruises too from chair legs and doors in her flurry, all the while moving through the morass of bodies that clotted the room as though she was wading knee-high through a bog.

'What's up with her?' asked Behleth, sucking the spilt stew out of his cuff.

'Grodel gave her the rest of the night off from the kitchen, seeing as it's such a special night, but only once she'd served everyone,' sniggered Kjerros. 'You brothers have got to stop working so late, you never leave time to enjoy the end of the day!'

'Mmmfnnr shnnrrn hmmf hngg whmyyrrgh' said Behvyn, his mouth now full of spoon and stew.

'What on earth was that?' asked Feran.

'I said, we wanted to get everything done in time for tomorrow,' repeated Behvyn, after swallowing.

'No, you didn't,' corrected Behleth, 'I'm sure you said "in time for myyrrgh", which is, frankly, more than a month off!'

Kjerros set Behvyn laughing so that there was a risk of stew going flying once again. In order to calm things down, Feran moved the conversation onto the plans for the next day.

'It's been ages since we've seen them. But it's said they've been invited to the Mayor's office for a formal dinner instead. Are they going to come with us?' he asked, looking more at Behvyn than anyone else.

'It's been a while,' said Behvyn, 'but, come off it; of course they'll come with us,' he said, without betraying his own doubts. 'Anyway, how are the preparations going, guys? Is everything ready?'

'Ready as ever,' said Kjerros. 'And we have lamps, oil, blankets, mounds of food, and,' now speaking in an undertone, 'about a week's solid supply of rockflower, with plenty of gnastia to wash it all down with.'

Their faces lit up in devious eagerness at the prospect. At the same moment, however, a wave of excitement passed through the rest of the patrons squeezed into the Assembly Room of the Poacher's Inn. A head had briefly poked in from the hallway door and nodded to Grodel.

The assembled mass, still buzzing with chatter like a forest at dawn, turned expectantly to Grodel, who then took a dramatically long moment to organise himself. He placed both meaty hands, spread widely apart, onto the top of the bar behind which he always remained, unless there was a requirement to eject someone, and drew himself up to his full height of six and a half feet. He inhaled deeply and, seeing this, Behvyn clenched his jaw to deafen the boisterous sound he expected at any moment to fill the room. It would be the loudest announcement of the night.

'Right you lot: shut up!' Everything stilled and not a few ears rang. Grodel had never been one for pleasantries, Behvyn remembered. 'As most of you know, we've got something very special for Muscle Oaks tonight. We have visitors.' At this, the excited murmuring began again but Grodel decided his voice could carry over it. It did so in the way the crashing of a tree will cover the sound of a leaf falling to the ground. 'Not just any normal visitors, though, but famous performers no less, who have performed at His Majesty's Royal Court in Cambwall, to great acclaim.' Now everyone could detect the pride he had in saying it. Behvyn realised Grodel knew he had the biggest event in recent Oakster history taking place on his own premises and was making sure everyone realised it.

'My fellow Oaksters,' he continued to boom, 'you have constantly complained about the fact there's nothing happening here night after night,' at which there were several laughs and many fingers pointed at the most likely candidates for such protestation. 'You have accused me of being a lump-eared old fool who don't appreciate art. You have even,' Grodel paused, particularly agitated and arched his black eyebrows thunderously, 'criticized my beer.' A low murmur of disbelief swam around the room and the tension in the atmosphere creaked up a notch.

'But I do here tonight throw all that back in your ruddy faces,' he continued, now to the breaking out of laughter, '– ruddy from my own fire, I may add – and tell you to go and eat your words!' Some cheers and clapping. 'Why? Because tonight, and just for one night, mind, so make the most of it, I've got something here for you that, well, half of you in the room probably aren't good enough to be allowed to see.'

He gave the room a thorough scan and received back a few raised pints and meekly grateful nods of thanks. Assuaged, he narrowed his eyes and leaned back with crossed arms. 'Anyway, that's enough from me. Here now, performing just for you, at the Poacher's Inn in Muscle Oaks is the Walking Chord!'

His introduction rose to such a crescendo that the room resonated, which was then added to by copious amounts of clapping and cheering, whooping and not a few barks from the freshly woken dogs at their owner's feet, all as the door to the hallway slowly opened.

Then in walked the two most beautiful girls Behvyn and Behleth had ever seen.

No more than eighteen, they moved so gracefully between the closely packed tables that it was as though they floated in. They were wearing strange garments of light silk in crimson, blood-orange and burnished blue-green that flowed from their shoulders and waists as they passed through towards the small area that had been kept clear for their performance. The dim lamps and firelight inside the room highlighted their tanned brown faces, pitch-black raven hair and the subtle, filigree gold they wore about their foreheads and necks. As they passed, their motion drew from them strands of fine scent that intoxicated their audience.

Once in place, in the silence of stilled applause and hushed breathing, the taller of the two sat down on an awaiting stool. Her hair was perfectly straight and held back from her face by a delicate silver-threaded lattice, laced with small diamonds that scintillated in the low light. She reached down on her right side and brought up to her delicate jaw the instrument that had caused unending puzzlement. It had no moving parts that could be seen. No keys were apparent and there were no strings. Even this far north, villagers – even stubborn-minded Oaksters suspicious of anything imported from outside – knew something about music, but the object had kept all who had looked upon it mystified. About the size of a wine bottle, it was shell-white and honeycombed, tapered towards its top, and rippled with close-set ridges that ran horizontally the full way down its length.

The girl then looked out into the faces of everyone watching with large almond-shaped dark brown eyes and stopped their hearts for a moment as they felt a pang of recognition. Then, producing from her left side a slim white wand, she began to blow over the top of the instrument whilst simultaneously moving the wand along its side.

A tone of the strangest beauty lasted for each breath outwards and a complimentary tone then sounded in alternation for each breath inwards. The girl was able to generate many choral notes by changing the direction of her breathing and blowing over one or several of the many chambers within the honeycombed centre and so was able to describe a haunting melody that could be repeated without cease. As she held the wand higher or lower along the instrument the resonance would change so the sound would narrow or broaden to emphasise the emotions of the piece. The audience was held rapt. Behvyn and Behleth could not take their eyes off the girl's playing and Feran was tearful; the music's sweet power enchanting him and others with each soulfully spun note.

Then at the point at which it was impossible to imagine the sweetness of the music ever growing further the second girl, who had remained standing, lifted her head to the roof beams and raised her voice into a melancholy lyric that caught everyone by their very mettle.

She sang the tale of a wife who had rejoiced in the simple perfections of love, family and home and how they were for her the greatest gifts of a life lived well, but whose husband did not treasure them as she did. It told of how the husband, haunted by a yearning for the unknown, had decided to leave everything behind in search of the vision of distant happiness his restless dreams presented to him. The pleas of the wife were then repeated in hopeless opposition against the forces of doubt, curiosity and desire for new experience that she saw caused her home to be driven apart as her husband left her behind. Eventually, the husband realised his foolishness, his experiences leaving him a broken man, and determined to return home. But even as he had done so, and his young children had come running up to cling to his legs, he discovered his wife had killed herself only moments earlier in a sharp fit of broken-hearted despair.

Although an undoubtedly mournful story, it harkened to all who heard it and warmed them in the shared comfort of friends and family. As the lyrics ceased the music endured to become a sorrowful dirge that gently dwindled into a whisper until finally, like golden candlelight exposed to too strong a breeze, it was snuffed and silence fell, a silence none wanted to break, as rich as it was with the memory of so fulfilling a moment, and the girls were still.

Eventually Grodel, with his face twitching from suppressed emotion, turned and grinned about the room, and the spell was broken to be replaced by clapping; an applause that rang of bliss and contentment. Everyone was now wiping their faces, standing up, stamping their feet, cheering and smiling around at each other and especially at the two girls in the middle of the clearing by the fire. They beamed back charmingly and were forced to bow a great many times and were offered a large number of kind gestures, free drinks, offers of marriage and other accommodations along with thanks, though their eyes searched the room in growing concern until they found Behvyn's table.

'Now then, now then! That's enough I say!' boomed Grodel in an attempt to calm the sea of contagious merriment that had erupted around the place. Everyone wanted to shake the girls by the hand as they left and forged a path through towards the boys at the back by the kitchen doorway. A few people delicately re-examined the instrument that had been carefully replaced by the stool and one or two had a quick attempt at playing it but could make no noise come out of it. In such a way was the mythos for the girls' skill deepened.

'Erm, it looks like they're coming over here,' said Behleth awkwardly, looking around at Behvyn and then at Kjerros and Feran. They looked back at him, all slightly wild-eyed at the thrill of it, and promptly moved down the benches either side of the table to make room.

'Hello!' said the first girl who had played so captivatingly on the strange instrument.

'Wow, look at you four! Who am I going to kiss first?' said the second, and then they both ran around and hugged and kissed everyone. Still the boys were behaving oddly.

'What's up with you lot?' asked the first girl, now sitting down next to Behvyn and putting her hand onto his arm, talking light-heartedly enough but with a trace of disquiet in her voice. She flicked a glance over to the second girl, who had perched herself up by Feran.

'Speak!' she commanded, looking slightly hurt.

'Tig, that was fantastic!' 'Amazing!' 'What was that thing you were playing?' 'Tangle! You're so, so brown!' came the answers all at once.

'Thank you!' beamed Tig and Tangle again, their grins now wider than ever before.

'Hmm, well it has been a long time,' continued Tig after all the questions had filtered in, 'and it's a lot hotter in Cambwall.'

'We thought we'd play that one tonight as it seemed to suit our return,' said Tangle, placing her head on Feran's shoulder. 'You know, the way that you can spend your life exploring the world but only find happiness when you realise what you already have.' She gave Feran a hug.

'How long did we go on for? I always lose track of time; the sea-chelys makes me dizzy!' said Tig.

'Is that why you sit down?' asked Kjerros. Tig nodded and made a twirling motion by her head with her hand.

Feran let out a cry of distaste in the background. 'Urgh! My beer's gone flat!'

'The fire's reduced down, but that huge log was new on when you started,' said Behvyn. 'Amazing!' he said again. 'You completely bewitched us all for ages!' He looked to Tig who was so happy she was almost floating off the bench as Feran dashed off to get a fresh round of drinks in.

'Well, we have practiced a lot,' said Tangle, 'and they say that song was first created by a goddess. So, you know, we couldn't do it too badly.' Tangle removed the diamond-studded netting from her raven black hair and in the process caused it to spring back into its usual collection of untamable curls. From the same casual movement she melted Feran's heart who was now returning with arms full of frothy beer.

'Have you just arrived here or have you already unpacked?' asked Kjerros, simultaneously rolling his eyes at Feran's obvious incapacity.

'We've dumped our things upstairs; for one night only though, remember?' questioned Tig, excitedly.

'Oh yes, we're all ready for tomorrow,' confirmed Kjerros, contentedly.

'Tieco Lake! I can't wait!' squealed Tangle and the girls looked at each other and giggled mischievously.

At that moment, though, Mandle burst into the room again (she had remained steadfast in the kitchen during the girls' performance) and started gabbling a wild complaint to Grodel who eventually worked out what she was so agitated about. He looked over in the direction of their table and Behvyn's heart sank.

Grodel then boomed over at Tig and Tangle, though he gave a terse smile as he spoke. 'What are you two nattering about? Mandle says the dogs are going mad outside over something and trying to jump the fence in the yard. If you've nowt better to do, go and see if you can't shut them up for me.' With that he gave all six of them at the table a stiff look and turned back to his customers that were flooding the bar following the performance.

'Typical!' said Tangle. 'We come home for half an evening, and father's already got us doing chores again!'

'We'll come with you,' said Behvyn, draining his drink and getting ready to go.

'No, not just yet,' said Tig, wiping froth off Behvyn's nose. 'We've got to get out of these dresses first. I'm not having Half-Pint ruin this.'

'Well, we'll meet you outside once you've changed,' said Behvyn. 'Whilst you're doing that, we'll see if we can't calm them down ourselves.'

As the girls went off, back out the hallway door to a new round of applause, Behleth turned to Behvyn, a glint in his eye once again.

'So, what do you think?' he asked.

Behvyn looked to see Tig just leaving the room and turned back to his brother, a stupid look etched on his face.

'No comment necessary, I see,' said Behleth, and chunked Behvyn on the jaw.

Behvyn led them outside into the back yard he knew so well from having grown up at the Poacher's and was immediately hit by the cold. A strong wind curled around the courtyard, spinning up into the air early fallen yellow-green oak leaves and pulling out from within the hood of his cloak his shoulder cut hair so that it whipped into his face. Over the noise of rattling fence panels to his right and the squeaking weathercock set upon the roof of the stable ahead in which Glambard the carthorse stood around sheepishly, they could all hear the confused barking from Grodel's three dogs: Jigger, Jogger and Half-Pint.

Jigger and Jogger were both enormous wolfhounds, narrow backed and tall, with a springing gait that made them look half their weight, and both had coats of short white hair patterned with undefined grey-black splodges. Their extended muzzles and thin heads looked bird-like and they were almost identical to each other, but Jigger had half of one dark ear missing, lost many years ago in his youth in the thick pine forests westward of Muscle Oaks whilst out with Grodel hunting for boar. Now they both tore about the courtyard disturbing everything that lay about. Water buckets, bags of sand, wood chips, barrels, dead potted plants, Glambard's feeder, old bottles, old glasses, broken chairs left outside for mending, tables and benches for the good weather, used most nights through the summer until so recently, all were knocked, pinged, unsettled, dislodged, upended, scattered and dragged around in their chaos. Together, they were making a grand mess of everything, but were clearly spooked by something.

They were helped in creating this cacophony by Half-Pint, a soft-haired terrier with well-defined butterscotch patches across his back and ears, whose short white legs fitted with paws a size too big for him held his belly only half a foot off the ground. He had an intelligent, inquisitive face, within which were set two large shiny black eyes that had made him the girl's favourite. Completely unaware that he was not as large as Jigger and Jogger, he was usually adorably affectionate, effervescently busy and unceasingly noisy. But now, as he ran around the legs of Kjerros and Feran like a dervish, he flitted from issuing sharp barks of warning to giving winces of mortal fear.

'There! There! Why are you all so jumpy now, you silly doggies?' said Behleth, who knelt down and slapped his knees with his hands. He called again to the three dogs tearing their way about the cobbled yard, but without success.

'Why do people talk to dogs like they were babies?' wondered Behvyn openly, as Tig and Tangle rejoined them, now in heavy dresses, hooded cloaks and stout boots, arriving out of the back entrance to the kitchen and receiving a scowl off Mandle as they did so. The door was shut quickly and firmly behind them, much to the mirth of Kjerros.

'How's that for a warm welcome?' he said, smiling. The girls raised their hands, incredulous, then ran out over to the gate that was set in the middle of the back fence to check its fastness. Jigger and Jogger were standing with their front paws on top of the fence and barking into the night. At their fullest height, they were taller than Behvyn.

'It's locked,' confirmed Tig.

'Aw, they've made such a mess of things,' said Tangle, looking around.

'Don't worry, we'll get that,' said Feran dutifully, and he and Kjerros went about the business of collecting up the detritus that had been strewn about the yard by the dog's rampant behaviour. Unsure of where to gather it all into one place they chose to pile it up at the juncture of the fence and the kitchen wall.

Though they continued to try the dogs did not respond to the friend's attempts to calm them, but continued yelping, barking, darting around, running at the fence and reaching up for its top, standing on their hind legs and then hiding, tails between their legs, shivering against the cold, their moods taking such peculiar, pendulous turns first one way and then another.

'Its bizarre!' said Tangle dispiritedly. 'They won't even come to me. Jigger! Jogger! Half-Pint! Come here, come to me, come on, sillies, it's Tangle!' But they only kept barking maniacally into the night.

'It's like they're afraid of something,' added Kjerros, who after some struggle had now managed to get ahold of Jogger's scruff, but the wolfhound's strength nearly bore him to the floor. 'They won't stop shaking!'

Then Half-Pint took a nip at Feran, who jumped away into Kjerros. Kjerros' grasp of Jogger's scruff was broken and suddenly all three dogs made a jump for the gate. Jigger and Jogger both made an enormous bound and cleared the six-foot high barrier in one while Half-Pint sped up the pile Kjerros and Feran had organised moments earlier. He leapt over the fence from its peak, landing at a fevered run on the other side.

'Oh no!' cried Tig and Tangle in unison and were just about to open the gate and run off after them before Behvyn stopped them.

'Hang on a second!' he said. 'You won't catch them; they're too fast. Let's get organised. Feran, go and grab some lanterns from off the wall over there and light them up. Kjerros, they've headed off northwards up the Vale. They might get as far as Long Knoll. Have a look back inside and see who's in tonight from there. We don't want them to be alarmed when they come back to find six strangers wandering all over their land. Let them know we've gone to look for Grodel's dogs.'

He looked over to Tig and Tangle who he could see were desperate to begin the search. 'And Behleth, go and tell Grodel himself we're going off. We don't want him worrying over where these two are.' Tig and Tangle flicked a quick smile at Behvyn as Kjerros and Behleth went inside through to the kitchen.

'And you two,' said Behvyn, looking seriously at the sisters' once again impatient and concerned faces, 'look absolutely gorgeous.' They smiled graciously despite themselves and Tangle looked around to see where Feran was. He was over the other side of the courtyard, trying and failing to light the lanterns with tinder and flint.

'We have news,' said Tig, meaningfully. Behvyn remained quiet. 'I have something to tell you about your father. We can't talk about it here, there's no time to go through it properly, but I'll tell you tomorrow once we get to Tieco. And thank you for the compliment.' She kissed Behvyn's cheek, then drew her cloak up around her more tightly than before, and began to move off as she heard the approach once again of Kjerros and Behleth echoing through the kitchen. 'Come on, Tangle. The others can catch us up,' she said, as she unbolted and passed through the gate.

Behvyn watched them move off in a daze, his mind completely elsewhere until the wind swooped around the back of his neck and woke him to where he was.

'Feran!' he cried.

'I'm coming!' said Feran, finally able to get the wicks to light in the lanterns. He ran over to Behvyn carrying four of them, each glowing amber, layering the inside of the glass with a thin lacquer of black until the flames settled and began to radiate out a small pool of warmth. As he did so, Behleth and Kjerros joined them.

'Don't worry, Mandle, we can slam the door behind us ourselves!' said Kjerros, as he did indeed do just that, to the extent that the glass panel in the door nearly dislodged itself. 'I brought cakes for the journey,' he said, proudly holding up a bindle that smelled faintly of recent cooking and radiated its own warmth.

'Well done,' replied Behvyn. 'Now let's go. The girls have already gone on ahead.'

Kjerros and Feran then raced off to catch up with Tig and Tangle, but Behvyn did not immediately follow.

'What is it?' Behleth asked.

'It's nothing,' said Behvyn, choosing at that moment not to trouble Behleth with his own thoughts. 'It's just great seeing them again.'

'It really is,' replied Behleth, clapping him happily on the back as they strode out of the yard.

But as Behvyn passed through the gate and turned to latch it shut behind them, an odd sense descended upon him. Tig's words about his father still coursed through him and he thought about the strange behaviour of the dogs. He looked back at the Poacher's and at the high, star-lit sky looming overhead, hung with lofty traceries of wind-torn clouds that ran past like driftwood on a swift-flowing river. He wondered why it suddenly all looked so alien to him and then ran to catch up with his brother.

Chapter 2

THE LADY OF SORROW

As the moon continued to rise, steadily dimming the stars around it and lighting the high, thin clouds at first from below and then from above, Behvyn's eyes became so used to the darkness that he suffocated the flame in his lantern. But no amount of nocturnal vision seemed to help. Although the six of them had searched their way halfway into the night, voices as weary as feet, they had not yet seen anything of Grodel's spooked dogs.

Neither had they heard rumour of them. There had been no scampering or howling, barking or running, no growl or swish through the tall grass that lay between the edge of the Kingsway and the shivering blue pine forests on either side. Neither had there been a rattle of disturbed leaves among the low scrubby bushes that sealed the grassland and forest together. As they reached the northernmost village outpost of Long Knoll, appearing a full league past the furthest extent of Muscle Oaks proper, Behvyn's original enthusiasm had been replaced by a stolid determination instead. With ever sinking hopes he noticed how, save for the cold wind in the trees and the distant rush of the great river in the east, it was a lifeless night. All normal animation seemed stilled by the same fear he had seen descend upon the dogs.

Long Knoll comprised three large farmsteads whose main buildings overshadowed the climbing road, the most impressive of which they came to first. It was low but twin storied, made of brick and wood, and long, almost a match for the Poacher's façade. Through the leaded and soupily glazed windows shone a weak light as though from a dying fire and the white painted front door, heavily framed by thick grey-brown timbers studded with iron, glowed like a ghostly beacon in the silver moonlight.

'This is the Fallwater's land!' exclaimed Tig. She said it with such anxiety that the others stopped in their tracks, which then obliged her to explain. 'He once threatened me with a dead fish when I was young; said I'd killed it,' she muttered, as though still

21

confused by the ordeal. The others burst out laughing, especially Tangle who had all but forgotten the incident until then. The ring of laughter threw off much of the growing oppression that had been building since they had set out, but it sounded at once thin and harsh to Behvyn's ears. He wondered who else had heard it. He went to Tig and took hold of her hand.

'Don't worry; he's in the Poacher's this evening.'

'It's strange what memories come back to you after you've been away for a time,' said Tig, apologetically, as the others recommenced the hunt.

'I remember it's been a while since I held your hand,' he said, uncertainly, remaining back with her. In reaching for her he had acted purely out of pre-ingrained habit; he realised with a delayed tweak of concern that he didn't necessarily have the same permissions as before.

'Oh, Behvyn, it wasn't because of you we left,' said Tig, placing her other hand on top of his. 'That was the hardest thing for me. I've missed you so much. My heart leapt when I saw you again.' She gave him a diagonal glance as though with each word she was testing an unsure path. 'I know it was sudden, but tell me: you didn't think that, did you? Please tell me you didn't?'

'I didn't know what to think at first,' replied Behvyn, carefully. 'I didn't want to assume it wasn't me if there was something wrong. But then I couldn't think of anything, even from our childhood. I remembered you used to say you wanted to marry Kjerros when we were kids,' he said, smiling, 'but that was it. So then I assumed you were in trouble. I just didn't know how I could help.'

'You did understand!' said Tig, now greatly relieved as they walked on to meet up with the others who were stood near the exit off the road onto the rutted, rocky lane that ran down the length of the Fallwater property. 'It felt so wrong doing what we did, leaving suddenly like that. But at the time we felt like we didn't have any choice. I couldn't tell you, Behvyn, it was too hard and it happened so quickly. But between us, Tangle and I survived. We found our way when we needed to and we made it in Cambwall. I even learned to play the sea-chelys! And then, as soon as we could, we came back. I came back for you, Behvyn: nothing else.'

She turned to him and put her arms around his neck. 'Don't

ever let us be apart again,' she said, and kissed him properly.

It was better than he remembered it.

They continued their search between the dark angles of the Fallwater property, which comprised three decrepit barns of various size and employ that were sited behind the house and, even further back from the road, a short mews with several empty stables that were covered by an undulating and alarmingly warped roof. Kjerros and Feran took the stables, Tig and Tangle the house and Behvyn and Behleth the barns. They were separated for some time but rejoined, each unsuccessful, back at the western edge of the Kingsway opposite the beginnings of the knoll that now wound its way up for more than a mile northeastward in between two stout columns of pollarded larch.

At its tallest, adorned by patches of holly tree, rowan and thistle, the knoll would block out both the sight eastward of the far distant Mizzle Mountains and the closer sound of the Highborn River, and was so steeply sided that, though Behvyn had tried many times in his youth, it was impossible to run straight up it. A thin, deep and muddy pathway, overgrown like a ditch and stemming from the eastern edge of the road, was carved into its side in a meandering fashion so that it was possible to climb to the broad apex by youth and elder alike, and for both to be able to enjoy the view from the North Vale eastwards over towards the rushing river that spliced the Shale Valley in two. Here, where the knoll was low enough so that Behvyn, at almost a head taller than Feran and Tangle, could just see the path of the Highborn River from where they stood on the road, patience was finally running out.

'It's no use!' Feran moaned, openly. 'Even with the six of us, we haven't seen spit and now with that thing flowing past us making such a racket we can't hear anything.' He was referring to the Highborn River, which was starting to become noisy, though it still lay some distance off to their right. From here northwards the Highborn was edged along its eastern side by low-lying rocks that extended into its hasty flow, causing it to froth and flurry about them.

'I know, Feran, but we've got to carry on,' said Behvyn, although he doubted they would be successful. The dogs seemed to have disappeared completely.

'It's a bit strange, don't you think, that they would have run so far away from home and not stopped or felt they didn't need to keep running?' asked Kjerros, and the others agreed.

'I've never seen animals so afraid of something, and father's a butcher. Most of the time they're too stupid to realise they're in danger,' added Feran.

'All the more reason to find them quickly!' said Tig. 'I can't bear to think of them in such a state. It's cruel!' She turned to be comforted once more by Behvyn.

'Let's move on, then,' said Behleth, whose spirits alone seemed to be high, and showed the way for the rest towards the next dwelling. 'I bet they're no distance from us now.'

But they found no trace there either of the passage of the dogs, although they looked and listened more keenly than before. They could hear better now, as the rising knoll and a thin mist that had begun to twine up from the ground blocked out some of the river's clamour. Yet with this they could not now see so well as before.

They progressed with persistence, but with less patience. As they moved on, so they came to the beginnings of the wilderness in the North Vale. The gradient grew noticeably as they came towards the first steppes of the Cloud Mount and all about the North Vale closed upwards and in. Here, the trees that grew back in Muscle Oaks could not find sufficient air to breathe and failed, so that only fragrant pine and dark red cedar wreathed the growing hillsides ahead of them.

Finally, on the eastern side of the Kingsway as they fought against the slope that sapped them of all momentum, they saw the Mickleton farmhouse. It was low, ivy-covered and ancient and loomed through the mist like a ship breaking through a storm. Though it was classed as part of Long Knoll, the Mickleton farm was the northern-most of all homes in the Shale Valley. It was almost half a mile past the knoll's northward end and took some climb to reach. No one lived further into the shadow of the mountain than old Tuke Mickleton and he lived alone. A hermit of sorts, on seeing the skulls of various animals attached to the front of the house Behvyn remembered awkwardly how, when he and his brother had been children, they had made up terrifying stories about the man to explain what they saw, all about how Mickleton would turn into a different creature at night and go out and capture each new trophy by lulling it as a mate, before breaking its neck and draining its blood. About how he would only turn back into the shape of a man to drag its carcass back out of the forest.

As Behvyn approached the house he saw there was still candlelight in the windows but nothing was astir. They checked at the windows for sight of the farmer himself, Kjerros not having noticed him back the Poacher's, and they saw him sleeping through the glass with an empty ale jug hanging loose in one hand.

'Is it any use waking him, do you think?' asked Tig, as she came up next to Behvyn, her face lit by the light from the window.

'I shouldn't think he'd remember anything about tonight,' answered Behvyn. 'He's had a whole jug of Old Scrappy by the looks of it and that's some sleeping draught. Still, we won't disturb him by having a look around outside. He won't wake with that in his belly.'

'We should think about the time, though,' said Behleth, as he approached his brother from the road. 'Even if we did stay out all night, there's only the Winding Way to the North Wall ahead and to search up to there in the black of night is asking for trouble. The dogs could get past us easily enough as it is in this fog.'

'There's no need to go on any further after this, is there?' asked Feran. The girls gave him a hard look back in return. 'I mean to say, it's wilderness from here on and dangerous, even in daylight.'

Tangle was incensed. 'Kjerros, can you talk some courage into your cousin here. He seems to have lost what little he once had!'

'I agree with him, Tangle,' said Behvyn, cautiously. 'I think we should search Mickleton's place – and thoroughly – but then go back. Our hopes of finding the dogs dwindled once we went past the Knoll. You know what a hard place the North Vale is to go into. It's unlikely that they would have gone there, even in a craze. As Behleth says, they could have doubled back past us and be sitting at your back door again by now.'

Behvyn could see how thought of Jigger, Jogger and Half-Pint already back home worked to settle Tangle's mind. But her sister was now critical of them all.

'You'd just leave them out here?' Tig accused them. 'They're confused, they're lost and they need us! They're not wild; they're domesticated. They can't cope out here! We've looked everywhere along the way and the six of us haven't missed anything. They must be ahead of us! You go home if you want, but I'm going on! I'd sneak through the North Wall and go all the way to the Blackstone if I must!'

At mention of the Blackstone they all fell very silent and no one spoke for some time. They even stood still, as though a tutor had just scolded them. Only Behvyn did not divert his gaze from her challenging look.

Although there was not three years between all of them, most looked to Behvyn for a decision; whether to continue, or to return again at dawn. He didn't want to upset Tig but he thought she was being irresponsible. He tried to argue his point gently.

'I know you didn't speak the name of that place lightly, Tig,' he said. 'But please think about what you're saying. Where you go, we all go. Look around; none of us will leave you alone out here. So what you decide decides it for us all. That w-way is guarded by soldiers and y-you know the d-danger that lies behind it-'

As Behvyn spoke he began to falter and then tears rolled down his face.

Alarmed, he looked around at the faces of the others in Feran's low lamplight and they too looked in pain. His throat became so tight that he couldn't speak any more and, turning past his brother who was now sobbing, he saw each of his friends collapse to the grass in Mickleton's garden. Kjerros, Feran, Tig and Tangle: all of them suffering under the burden of some great grief. Tig wailed at the earth, and Tangle sat on her knees, her hands out in plea to no one. Kjerros lay on his side with his knees up and arms hugged about his chest. With his face buried he was lost to all but himself. Feran clawed blindly at the ground in a rage of woe. Staggering, Behvyn grasped for his brother – they were the only two left that were not wholly overcome – and shook him. Though he could not speak, Behvyn tried to send him the message with a look. Don't let it win. Fight it! But an instant later they both collapsed to the floor semi-conscious and lost themselves to misery.

How much later it was that Behvyn regained some sense of his surroundings he couldn't tell. Yet in the moment he awoke it seemed to him as though all the bad news he had ever heard in his life had just been suddenly told to him afresh for the first time. Disoriented and aimless, he found himself moving arm over arm towards the ditch by the side of the road as though to hide himself from the pain of his existence. He clambered in and fell onto his back. He stared upwards unblinking, with the walls of the ditch either side of him rising up like a valley.

But even as he lay there, utterly sad and with his spirit wounded, he sought and found a part of his mind that he turned to at his darkest moments. A memory of him and Behleth stirred and a picture built behind his open eyes. The thought to recover and force himself back up to reach his brother again swam to the forefront of his mind. He didn't know where his strength came from to resist the swell of sadness about him but, focused on Behleth through blurry eyes, he climbed out of the ditch and crawled towards him.

As he approached he saw he was still conscious, unlike their friends that were now lying awkwardly, as though they were held in a distraught asleep. 'No, mother,' Behvyn could hear Behleth pleading softly. 'Don't leave us! Don't leave us!'

'Behleth!' he called, and roused his brother away from his thoughts. 'Behleth! Look at me! There's something going on. We could be in danger. Come back to me, Behleth! Come back!'

'B-Behvyn? It was like I was there,' Behleth explained in confusion. 'W-When we were born, you know?'

'I know, Behleth. Now, can you stand with me?' With no idea how much time passed, they caught their breath, taking in gulps of air though they were still tight-chested from the heavy sorrow that still lay upon them, and used each other as a support to come to their feet.

In so doing they were the only two to see her approach.

Through the lifting fog she came. A Lady, dressed all in layered garments of white, came walking along the road from Muscle Oaks at a somber pace. As she came closer, with Behvyn and his brother still stood together in Tuke Mickleton's front yard, both noticed her long, light robes shine as though they captured the very light of the moon and contained it within. Behvyn saw that she had bound about her eyes a white scarf which was similarly luminous so that she couldn't possibly see the way although she strode confidently enough with her bare feet appearing and disappearing through the mist with each step. Around her neck she wore a fillet of silver set in the middle with a dark gem.

As she came closer the pain of suffering and hurt grew still further inside Behvyn so that he was at the brink of a black out, but against all he and his brother resisted, and so continued to behold her through a veil of bitterness.

Though it rent them, the twins watched and it was then that they noticed she held one arm by her side but the other bound across her chest, as though holding something to her. In addition, Behvyn suddenly felt that they were not the only two that were seeing this, as though some being on the edge of vision watched over her. As though in a dream she passed them by closely and made her steady way into the wilderness ahead.

Once she had continued up the road into the pine forests of the North Vale and out of sight, the intensity of Behvyn's sadness diminished, though it was still a struggle to speak to his brother who was similarly overcome.

'C-Can we wake them?' Behvyn asked. Their friends still lay in a mournful slumber around them. But though the twins tried, they would not stir.

'Who was she?' asked Behleth, in a small tight voice that was barely audible.

'I have no idea,' replied Behvyn, 'but I'm not interested in finding out if it means the memory of all the evils in my life are to haunt me again.'

Behleth nodded, understanding exactly what his brother spoke of.

'She was like a harpist that could play only mournful tunes on my heartstrings,' Behleth replied. 'I felt the death of our mother again as though I had just been told for the first time. But the Lady didn't look like she wished to harm anything, more like she had to get somewhere without being seen.'

'I sensed that, too,' agreed Behvyn. 'But what is she looking for? And if she causes this to all she passes and if she has walked up the Kingsway, she must have had this effect on everyone back in the village.' Behvyn again shook Feran and then Kjerros to see if they would come around now she was further distant. They remained still, as though stunned or in a deadly drunken sleep.

'They're probably all out like these four,' agreed Behleth, going over once more to Tig and Tangle, who were in deep sleep next to each other. 'But what should we do now if that's true? Wait for them to wake up or follow her and find out more?'

Behvyn hatred the idea of leaving them behind, but their minds were made up for them a moment later when they heard a cry of pain echoing from the direction they had seen the Lady go in.

'She's being attacked!' shouted Behleth, and he ran off after her without a second's thought. Behvyn threw down his lamp and chased after him.

It was not difficult to perceive the road as it was still lined even here on either side by chalk slabs brought up from the coast, far to the south. It had last been re-laid in the days before King Cuiron had been struck down and the local villagers had still been required to do their five years' service for him. As well as joining his armies, the citizens of the Shale Valley would perform other services for the crown, such as maintaining the look of the lands, and the Kingsway had been fair in its day. But much time had passed since then and nothing of the King's state, other than he yet persisted, had been reliably communicated this far northward for over a score of years.

Behvyn and Behleth, though footsore and tiring, and hampered as the mists of the Highborn came across thicker so that they couldn't see more than a few steps ahead, kept going. The fast pace they had established was soon diminished to little more than a jogging speed as they climbed the dark, steep, thickly wooded hillside. Ahead began to loom the North Wall although it was still some way off, framed by moonlight and set in front of the ghostly mountain. The Highborn became noisier again as the road came closer to it and the Vale sharpened into an adjoining point between two arms that swung from the lower reaches of the Cloud Mount.

And then they saw something. On the ground where their sight only just reached they saw footprints in soft earth leading no longer onwards but to the right, downhill, directly towards the river. 'These are the footprints of the Lady, I would guess' said Behvyn. 'They press the ground lightly and she also goes barefoot'.

Behleth did not respond. Even as he heard his brother, his throat swelled with a choke. Then Behvyn was similarly flushed with a sharp crack of guilt. They felt once again the despair of being close to the Lady.

Then they heard a woman's voice raised in confrontation, coming from the same direction in which the footsteps led. It was filled with imperious anger:

'You were wrong to call me,' it said, 'but now I see it was urgent that I came. I do not answer your plea, for they are not something to be given to mortals! Now, leave me! For every race's sake, I must remove them from this world!'

It was followed by a shriek and a loud splash that scared both the twins. As suddenly as it had arrived, their angst was gone. This time it was Behvyn who acted immediately and ran down the slope, calling his brother behind him to follow.

Fast he ran now, down past thick briar and under silver grey leaves lit by the shining moon that reached in through the shadows, with Behleth straining hard behind to catch up. Low thistles snapped and caught at his breeches as the sound of the river surrounded them. The soil underfoot became more giving until it was damp. The thickening mist parted into banks as they disturbed it in their rush. They both pelted down now, almost falling, past browning fern and under fragrant pine they went, well out of the sight of the road and alone in the wilderness. Darkness was everywhere save in the reflecting shards of the moon laid on the surface of the Highborn. And then they reached the riverside.

Without pausing to catch his breath, Behvyn sought the White Lady. He ran crouched along the embankment, leaning over the edge to see into the water. Behleth ran behind, scouting back up the bank and among the low trees around them.

Then Behvyn saw her and gave a shout. As Behleth approached, Behvyn looked around and thought he saw movement over on the other side of the river; but it was gone in an instant. 'A trick of the mist,' he muttered.

'Quick, Behleth!' said Behvyn. 'She's under the freezing water.' As Behleth looked over his brother's shoulder he saw her inside the river itself. She wasn't resisting as the current sought to move her southward and her face was down, still girt by the white blindfold.

But her cloak was caught on the branch of an overhanging bay willow and it held her back from floating away into mid-stream, though barely. Though there was no great sadness afflicting them as before, Behvyn worried for a moment that raising her would once again cripple his brother and himself with a further bout of melancholy.

But she was still and didn't struggle and the waters were cold enough to stop a heart in moments. Behvyn had no choice but to rescue her, and survive the consequences if at all possible. He bent down and reached in but had no stability. He nearly fell in himself.

'Behleth! Hold onto my other hand and set your feet. I need to lean in! And, brother,' he added, turning his head and speaking over his shoulder, 'steal your heart. She may still be dangerous.'

His brother did as he was told wordlessly and lowered Behvyn into the Highborn. But just as he did so ice flowed into his blood and he pulled Behvyn out quickly.

'What? What is it, Behleth?'

The noise came again; a cry came from the sky that scorched their ears. It threw them both into confusion.

'It sounded like a warning,' said Behvyn, 'but I can't see a thing: it's too dark!' He looked up into the sky but the fog obscured all. Then they both saw it.

A large white falcon, rarest of all birds such that they were legend in the histories of the Valley, came speeding out of the heights and swooped in one noble arc down to seize the Lady. But as it crashed into the waters, a blur of wings and motion, it perceived the folly of its efforts as the Lady was too much underwater. It was too small to reach in and lift her out and risked getting waterlogged itself. Whirling madly, it strove time and again to reach her until it was exhausted. Then it finally rose to the top of the willow beneath which the twins were grouped and gave a pitiful screech to the sky as it cursed itself for failing. It looked at Behvyn and Behleth as though acknowledging they had been there all along, and fixed them with a stare.

'I think it'll let us try now,' said Behleth. 'She must have been under the water for ages – hurry!'

Once more, Behleth held onto the bole of the willow that had the Lady caught and took in his other hand that of his brother's. Behvyn reached down into the swift-flowing waters, arm outstretched, head underwater, swiping for a grasp. Then, as the falcon surveyed all, Behvyn came into contact with her hand; slim and frozen and lifeless. He held onto it fast, sought a purchase underfoot and rocked himself backwards towards the bank. She came with him, her white cloak became disentangled and Behvyn sought his brother's aid to bring her up out of the river.

Behleth leaned into the water and reached under the Lady's shoulders to pull her out and over the pathway onto a bed of ferns that carpeted the rising bank side behind. It was as he lay her down that he saw bound to her left forearm, which she had previously kept folded under her cloak, was a gauntlet of leather inlaid with silver. His brother dragged himself out onto land, refusing aid, but shivering cruelly. By contrast, the Lady, whose clothes were strangely dry as though they had not just been in water, was still as stone.

Behleth placed his cloak around his brother as the falcon took flight from its perch and settled next to the Lady, though out of some kind of reverence it would not look at her as she lay. Its talons and beak, both a livid burnt yellow, and its black eyes stood out sharply against its pure white feathers.

'She's not moving!' lamented Behleth. 'Ah, she carries a nasty cut to her head! What can we do?' he asked. He looked at his brother hopelessly.

Behvyn, still shivering but with the warmth coming back into his bones, came up and crouched onto his knees next to the Lady. He took her right hand in his and held it to his heart.

'Take her blindfold and use it as a dressing to bind the wound. It's not bleeding; her heart must have stopped. The water is so cold,' said Behvyn.

Behleth gently lifted her head up from the fern bed upon which she lay and unwound the blindfold she wore. As he did the white falcon shuffled hesitantly next to them but remained silent. Her eyelids were closed so tightly that it gave her whole face a look of pain. It smote Behvyn at her side in almost the same way her passing by had, though it was a new sadness he felt as his brother covered the cut with the makeshift bandage.

'I don't know who you are,' Behvyn said into her oblivion, still holding her hand and not knowing where the words came from. 'I don't know why you have come through here on some way. But we will not cause you grieves in addition to those you carried, our Lady of Sorrow. And this land is fair although night and fog swathes its form. Won't you come back to it and let us help you? Your friend who watches over you from above is here. Let him no longer fear for you like this but have him fly up into the skies once again to your protection. Come back to us and let us help you, Lady. Do not leave.'

Then Behvyn rested his head onto her shoulder. Still he kept her hand in between his. Behleth sat down with his back to the rowan and put his head into his hands. The rushing of the Highborn continued unabated. The wind fell to a whisper and the darkness enshrouded them.

Then, imperceptibly, the moonlight seemed to grow and the Lady's garments once more seemed to capture its light. 'How is she now?' asked Behleth, as he noticed. 'It seems her clothes come to light once more.'

'It's a cruel illusion, though,' answered Behvyn, 'for she is dead.'

Behvyn then moved her hand down onto her chest. But at that moment her last breath expelled from her and she seemed to speak to Behvyn.

Find my surrogate.

He paused, wondering if he had indeed heard the words or if he had imagined them, like the movement he thought he had seen across the river. It unnerved him and then he remembered how they had overheard her before. She had been talking to someone else, someone who had attacked her. Behvyn's blood turned cold again. Perhaps they had stayed around to make sure she was dead.

'That is hard news,' responded Behleth. 'She seemed so ageless when she passed us. What shall we do with her? Take her back to the village or build a cairn for her here?'

'I don't think she is of this land, so it doesn't seem right to bury her here. And anyway, we have no tools and no time, Behleth. We don't know that whomever it was that took her life is not still around here. The only way to act as quickly as we must would be to let the water take her back to her home, wherever that may be.'

'It seems cruel to send her off like that, though, and there's been a terrible act committed here!' said Behleth. 'Who are we to decide what to do?'

'If we do nothing she will rot in the sun!' replied Behvyn, heatedly. 'What would you have someone do for you? I see no other choice! We can't leave her here, we cannot take her anywhere else and we can't bury her!'

'Then if we must act, let's act now.'

'If we live to regret this decision, Behleth, let the regret be all mine. You are not responsible for this if it's as unwise as it feels.'

Therefore, in grief for one they had not met or spoken to, the brothers lifted the White Lady upon their shoulders and walked with her back down the river bank. They trod haltingly and with shivering limbs into the icy flow of the Highborn, pressing their backs against the current. Once they were both waist-high and would not go any further in for fear of being caught off their balance and taken away themselves, they settled the Lady into the freezing grey-glass water. At a signal from Behvyn, they both released their hold and let the Highborn take her lifeless body out into the heart of its current to began a journey that would lead to the sea and beyond.

As they sought the bank side and dragged themselves out, wet again and numb, the moon played tricks on Behvyn's eyes as he sought to follow the Lady's path away with the river. He did not know for sure if he was watching her moving away from him or if they were the ripples that described about her form instead. As he returned his attention back to where he was, he noticed, among the ferns where they had laid the Lady, the moonlight catching on something. He muttered to his brother as he bent his shivering knees to get a closer look at it. He picked it up and held it out in front of him. It was the silver chain he had seen adorning the neck of the White Lady, unclasped with the black gem pendant still threaded upon it.

'Behleth, do you see? It is her necklace. It must have fallen from her when we lifted her up, though I don't know how. There is nothing beneath where she lay for it to have caught on.' His wonder grew as he studied the pendant in the ghost light. 'A shape is described on the gem. I recognise it for some reason. Does it remind you of anything?'

Behleth looked over his brother's shoulder and beheld the stone, as black and still as the eye of a predator.

'I don't recognise it,' he said, as his eyes followed its inscription, 'but the jewel itself looks like it's made of something familiar. I don't know why. Should we take it with us or throw it into the river? It's not ours to take, but this all seems like a dream to me now already, and I am still stood here. To keep it could be our way of remembering her and this night.'

'Or our way of getting into serious trouble,' replied Behvyn. 'It is as good a way as I can think of to make us look like the ones responsible for her death.'

'It's only small, though,' said Behleth. 'I can't see how it would do any harm and it is pretty. If we threw it away it would only be a waste. The Lady is gone. No one is here and we are not her killers. Maybe you could give it to Tig?'

Behvyn wondered at this momentarily but immediately thought better of it. No, he wouldn't give it to Tig. There were some things you should never do. But as he went to replace the necklace back down in the grass from where he had found it he had one more thought. What if the Lady had meant him to have it? His hand paused and his mind changed. Instead of letting it go he put it in his pocket. As he did so Behleth gave him a look of agreement and at the same time the first glimmerings of the new dawn edged the tops of the mountains with a purple glow. A great weariness descended upon them both and it was all they could do to clamber upwards towards the higher ground where it was dry, halfway back up towards the road. As they did, warmth grew in the ground and the remaining fog lifted, bringing a sharp clarity to the early day. The white falcon had risen into the night after it had seen the sending off of the Lady and had not come back. The brothers collapsed under the thick shade of a pine tree and slept long into the morning.

When they awoke, the clear air stung their eyes and the rattle of the Highborn rolling past below seemed loud. Behvyn was at first disoriented and, as he moved to get up once he realised where he was, he felt the twist of a root that he had slept on turn in the small of his back. He gave a sharp shout of pain which disturbed his brother from a doze.

'Wha'zit! Behvyn, are you all right?' asked Behleth, getting up himself and blinking into the daylight.

'I'm fine,' yawned Behvyn, now stretching and feeling his back. 'I just slept funny. Oh, it's day. And nearly mid-day,' he added with some alarm. He shaded his eyes and looked up into the high early autumn sky.

'I wonder if everyone else is up and about now like us' said Behleth. 'We have slept long!'

'Let's get back to them quickly,' agreed Behvyn. 'Today's when we're all going camping, after all. But let's keep our eyes peeled for the dogs; the girls won't want to come if they stay lost. And Behleth, I don't know that we want to tell them all of our story just yet.'

As Behvyn and Behleth made their way up the rest of the bank to the road and headed off downhill to Long Knoll they could hear their friends calling out their names. Once they were spotted they could see them running towards them.

'You fiends! Where've you been?' cried Tangle, as she ran up to hug Behvyn and then Behleth.

'We were just about to put a search party together for you two,' said Kjerros, looking at them accusingly but with a deal of relief. 'You're covered in mud!' he added. 'Did you sleep in a ditch or something?'

'They must have got lost in the night, the idiots,' said Tig. 'Couldn't find your way back to the road?'

'Lost it completely!' answered Behvyn. 'We thought we heard the dogs and went to follow them but, in the dark, we fell down off the road and, well, must've fallen asleep.'

'Oh, you don't need to look so sheepish about it,' piped Feran, 'we all nodded off too, it seems. No one can remember much about last night. It looks like we all needed the rest. It's nearly lunchtime already and we've only just woken up.'

'What about the dogs?' asked Behleth, but grudgingly so for, at Feran's mention of lunch, his stomach then regaled everyone with a loud chorus of its own.

36

'We saved you some cake as well. Sounds like you need it, too,' added Kjerros.

'Don't worry, they were in with Mickleton the whole time,' said Tig, and she called their names. The massive wolfhounds bounded and Half-Pint scampered over to her from where they had been sitting in the sun at the side of the house.

'We just found them dozing under his kitchen table,' said Kjerros. 'Although he's still out.'

'And what about our plans for later?' asked Behleth.

'Oh, we just need to collect up a few things back at home and then we can be off,' answered Tangle, skipping down the road, her hair a knotted mess.

They headed back apace, still hungry for food and a wash but increasingly puzzled by the night's events. Kjerros had grown particularly curious.

'What I don't understand is how we all fell asleep. I mean, one moment we're checking around old man Mickleton's farm for the dogs and the next we're on the floor.'

'I can barely remember anything. It's like I don't want to,' added Tangle.

They spent the rest of the walk home discussing all sorts of other things instead to keep their minds off it; the day was warming up and it made them glad. And not only them but, to their surprise when they reached Muscle Oaks, the whole village was in high spirits.

It seemed that the Mayor had been out early and, after touring the streets in a fine horse-driven carriage and listening to all the news of those folk that had by then woken up, he had now proclaimed that today was to become a public holiday. Not only that but it would be so for each and every year hence. His advisors that travelled with him added that the mass slumber had indeed been encountered everywhere they had yet been in the whole of the village.

As the day wore on the news fed in from surrounding villages that the phenomenon had hit them too, and the wonder of it all infused everyone now employed in arranging a sudden event fitting for a party. Food was found and cakes were made and flags were tied into bunting and banners went up. Extra barrels of ale were brought from the cellar of the Poacher's and lined up in the square on the back of carts. As the excitement for the evening's festivities grew, Behvyn began to forget most of the heavier concerns of the night and the friends decided to change their plans; they could delay things for one night. When Kjerros' father came over to them all with the plans for the event the twins went over and helped Grodel to build a great fire in the centre of the square by running to and from the woods. Kjerros went with his father to build a stage out of whatever they could find for the Mayor to make his speeches upon and the storytellers to spin their yarns from as Feran went with Tig and Tangle to help with putting up tables and sourcing chairs and then overseeing the food.

By mid-evening, and following plenty of work, Muscle Oaks had put together quite a festival for such an impromptu event. Grodel had even given it a name – Autumnfalls – and as is so often the way, the name stuck and does so to this day (though it is now generally abbreviated to either "Autumn" or "Fall" depending upon where you live). Once the great fire was made and lit it threw off the night and kept everyone warm. Music was performed of simple songs and was the cause of much fun and laughter. The Walking Chord did not perform because they were both too busy being given instructions of all the tasks that now awaited them at home by Grodel, but the food and drink aplenty held out the cold in its own way. And the Mayor warmed the hearts of all with a speech about how he had awoken that morning to find that he had slept in his best high hat – but that it was no longer as high as it should be, and so now marvelled to call such a 'low' hat a 'high' hat anymore.

Although they attended the festivities, Behvyn and Behleth longed for their small home that they had not seen since the previous morning. They saw the Lady's face in all they looked at and could not but be haunted by her passing.

'It is good to see everyone so happy,' said Behleth, though without much enthusiasm. 'There's no day around this time of year for months that gets everyone together like this.'

'I don't begrudge them a single moment of happiness,' his brother agreed. 'They've always shown us such kindness. We've been so lucky.' He stopped and looked at his brother.

'You know you're wrong to carry a single ounce of guilt, if you do,' Behvyn added. 'Mother was dying even as she gave birth to both of us. You can't think like that. It's something we couldn't have done a thing about ourselves.'

'Father thought there was reason enough, though,' replied Behleth.

Behvyn kept his eyes steady, looking out towards the flames as the village toiled in mirth.

'Did you see our mother in the face of the Lady last night, Behleth?' Behvyn asked gently after a while.

Behleth nodded slowly and sagged in despair. Behvyn put an arm around his brother's shoulders and looked up into the night sky. As he fixed his gaze every now and then on a different star the Lady's words came back to him: 'For every race's sake, I must remove them from this world!' He remembered how she had told him with her last breath to find her surrogate. He had no idea what it meant and not even the first idea how to begin understanding it all.

As the party came to a close the boys noticed Tangle had got the whole village dancing around the fire to an exhausting jig that Feran was seemingly making up on the spot with his fiddle, whilst Tig skipped round in a circle. Even the Mayor joined in for one chorus and wine and ale went flying at the crescendo with one final hoot at the evening's close. Everyone that was except Behvyn and Behleth, Tangle noticed. She watched them wander off homeward while the last song still echoed in her ears and couldn't guess the reason for their low spirits.

The vast fire in the centre of the square was now ash, though still glowing hot. Tig, irritable now and wanting sleep, was employed grudgingly to fetch water for Grodel so he could dampen it down, but Tangle found herself faced by an animated Kjerros. Noticing Feran, she gratefully waved him over.

'Feran, you played wonderfully!' and she gave him a kiss on his cheek for his pains.

Feran grimaced in mock horror but blushed all the same. He'd always been uncomfortable with public shows of affection, something which Tangle had no concept of.

'Glad you enjoyed the show,' he said. 'I didn't know I still had it in me. Now, then. What are you two talking about?'

'The brothers!' said Kjerros.

'He's off on one of his wandering theories again; don't listen to him, Feran,' said Tangle.

'It's not made up!' defended Kjerros. 'I was just telling Tangle that I reckon Behvyn and Behleth got up to something last night that they're not telling us.'

'Where'd you get that idea from?' asked Feran, but seemed to recall something he remembered from earlier as though turning it around in the different light cast by Kjerros' words.

'I noticed Behvyn was covered in mud, didn't I?' asked Kjerros.

'So what?' snorted Tangle. 'They must have been disorientated by the same thing everyone else was and fallen in a puddle. That's not a theory, that's a wild stab in the dark!'

'Well, what about tonight?' asked Kjerros, rallying swiftly. 'They've not said two words to anyone after helping put everything together. That's not like them at all.'

'Behvyn hasn't said a word to Tig all night,' added Feran.

Tangle was surprised to hear Feran had noticed. Maybe there's hope for him yet, she thought to herself.

'So!' she accused Feran, nevertheless. 'You're supporting Kjerros in this then, eh? Honestly, you two are as bad as each other.'

Tig had finally finished and came over to get Tangle. She was half-asleep as she wordlessly dragged her sister off towards the rear of the Poacher's Inn with Jigger, Jogger and Half-Pint dancing around their legs.

'Oh, maybe she's right,' Tangle heard Kjerros admit as they waved goodnight to each other. The cousins walked off home and Tig began to mumble. Tangle knew how she felt; nothing had changed here. They wouldn't be able to endure it for long.

Chapter 3

THE MIRRORHORN

It was still dark when Behvyn woke. For one disorientated moment he thought he was still in his bed but couldn't understand what was causing the sound of ceaselessly rushing water. He then felt hard wood underneath him and opened his eyes. He tried to get up but couldn't and saw though bleary eyes that rope held his legs tied together. He then felt a cord about his wrists which were held fast behind his back. His head swam with nausea and his senses were dull. He looked upwards as he lay on his back and wondered why the sky swung so, left and right, before guessing that he was on some form of boat. He looked to his left and saw Behleth lying still. He attempted a shout. But the gag in his mouth kept him quiet, though it amused a group of men whose voices Behvyn heard from a space further behind him. He coughed and struggled for breath as the cry was stifled; his body twisting and seizing through cramps and asphyxiation. He was nearly sick.

'Be silent,' said a voice nearer to. It was not aimed at him, for the men he had heard sniggering muttered a swift apology under their breath. The commanding voice did not sound evil but tired by decades of trial.

'One of them is awake,' sounded the voice again. 'Gilliant! Torkeden! Wake the other and sit them both up. Keep 'em aft. Remove their gags.'

Two men came over, jerked Behvyn from off his side and shook Behleth out of his drowse. They had on the uniforms of the King's Guards: black leather gloves with long gauntlets woven with bronze and dark maroon tunics over the chest of which was clasped a tough leather cuirass. About their waists they were girt with a sword and a dagger, both with worn-looking handles. Over all they wore a black cloak of a heavy and luxurious fabric that dusted the floor even when they stood tall. Their boots were worn and mud-caked from riding; they didn't have the wind-cracked, sun-blanched look of seamen about them. Their hair was short, almost shaved bald and they had stubble on their jaws. If they didn't have the bearing of trained men and the expensive uniform Behvyn would have sworn they were thugs.

Silently the bonds on their hands were untied but then they were re-tied to where they were moved to and asked to sit, upon an uncomfortably thin lateral beam in the wide stern. As soon as their gags were removed Behvyn started shouting into the night for help. As his captors seemed duly unconcerned at this they let him carry on until he was hoarse. Behvyn realised they held no fear he would be heard and stopped shouting. Bitterly, he tried to focus his eyes, as Behleth still seemed to be in a haze, unaware of their situation.

Behvyn took the brief opportunity he sensed he had to look around. Below and in front of him was the cloaked crew of a long, wide, flat-bottomed vessel. The sail barge had no majesty about it; indeed, it looked shabby. It also looked recently borrowed as though this was not her usual crew. The majority of her sailing equipment was left untouched or was being inquisitively turned over by gloved pairs of hands as though parts were recognised to have some use but quite what no one knew. Most of the men stood at a loss about the edges of the deck, their dark silhouettes just readable against the blue-black night, but there were four figures busy tying down the main sail and setting the barge steady in the current with twin anchors to stop it turning broadside into the mainstream. As it lurched heavily, Behvyn guessed it had a very shallow hull for its size. The anchors then did their job and they stilled on the river.

As Behvyn noticed this, a fierce wind tore down from behind them and he felt his neck freeze, so exposed were he and his brother where they sat high in the stern. As he hunched he looked along the deck, which was some thirty feet wide amidships, with a small cabin before it and behind which raised up another level that led off to the bow. Grab rails ringed the gunwales that surrounded a deck dominated in the middle by a tall mainmast from which jutted a long, low boom. Both mast and boom were of a grey wood that blurred into the background, the same shade as the rest of the craft that seemed to exist only on the borders of sight, so well did it blend in with its surroundings despite its size.

Looking further distant, Behvyn could almost be sure of the shapes of the Valley, east and south and west, but it couldn't be right, he thought. That would place them more than twenty miles north, well inside the North Wall. No, he reasoned, I must be wrong.

But try as he might to fool himself, Behvyn couldn't forget being taught as a child by Uncle Grodel about the geography of the Valley they lived in. He became more and more concerned that the distant sound of crashing water behind him was the Cold Falls, filling the Gathering.

A sudden alarm flooded his mind as he realised what also sat behind him and his brother. It couldn't be more than a mile away. At that thought he shivered with dread.

'Behleth!' he said under his breath. 'Whatever you do, don't look behind you. Keep your head down! Don't look around! Only ahead! Do you hear?'

Then the door to the cabin opened and all the men Behvyn had noticed up until now moved silently to the bow. One figure alone moved aft towards them but it kept its face hidden as it approached. Behvyn guessed it was the man who had spoken earlier.

He nudged his brother in the side hoping he'd heard him. 'I won't let anything happen to you Behleth. Just stay quiet. We'll be all right.'

Behvyn lifted his gaze enough to see the figure approach. It was a man clad in a dark green cloak underneath which, held to his side by a wide leather belt with an ornate silver buckle, was a long black sheath. The pommel of the sword it contained caught the light of the moon only in places, as one of the man's ungloved hands was upon it. His other followed the course of the gunwale as he moved slowly, sideways on, towards them.

With each pace, the man's boots rang out on the deck, interspersed with a repetitive creaking sound that came from behind Behleth from one of the two anchor rodes holding the vessel back in the flurrying waters. Once the figure reached within two paces of the brothers he sat down and stayed motionless for some moments. He faced east, to Behvyn's left, and kept up his hood. He said nothing for a long time before speaking, which made Behvyn wonder if he had fallen asleep or hope he had forgotten what he was going to do. It was a hope soon dashed.

'You are due to be executed for murder before the dawn,' the figure said finally, in the deep, worn voice of a man who had seen too much in life. 'I am the Captain of these men.' Then in an undertone he added: 'Do as I say and the two of you may yet live.'

'Murder?' cried Behvyn, still stunned by the man's first words. 'That's ridiculous!' But the man seemed uninterested in his protestations.

'Do you know where you are?' he continued aloud once more.

'I think so,' shivered Behvyn.

'Then you know what lies behind you. Do you know the story of the Blackstone?' he asked.

Behvyn shuddered again, but this time not from the wind.

'Of course not,' he responded. 'No one does. It's ancient.'

'Correct, Master Behvyn,' answered the man, startling Behvyn with the use of his own name. 'You are right, in part. It is ancient; its power is older than the Cloud Mount. But its story is not completely lost. I know the tale and will tell you a little of it while we have time.'

Behvyn was caught between a gut-wrenching fear from the man's first blatant words and a fascination of what he might reveal about the object that had overshadowed the lives of all Oaksters. He remained quiet.

'No doubt your silent brother sat next to you would confirm he doesn't believe a word of myth and legend, but would he chance to look at the Stone itself? Is not the one consistency in every campfire tale that the Blackstone will blind any man who perceives it? Is not history still as full of heroes as villages were full of the incautious that had been tempted – and then cursed – by the challenge such tales presented to them? That was the case before King Charion outlawed approaching to within a league of the Stone in all directions. Hence the North Wall that has stood for over a thousand years. I trust I've told you nothing yet that you don't already know?'

Behvyn was forced to swallow the same retort by the man's perceptiveness.

'"Blackstone" men call it,' continued the man, 'but "Arleghan canu Tovatum" is its real name, which means in your tongue "The

Mirror'd Horn of the Sightless," or "Mirrorhorn" as it was once more commonly known. What you call the "Shale Valley" has a much deeper past than you would expect, O' son of Breve.'

At mention of their father's name, Behleth stirred and Behvyn looked more quizzically at the figure sitting in front of him, still obscured by his cloak and hood, wondering what he knew and how he knew it.

'The name given to the Stone that lies in the very centre of the Gathering may change over time but it itself does not,' said the man, his voice now cold as steel. 'It has never altered in size nor has it altered in shape save for during the earliest age of this world when the craft of those that lived here before was great and the stone held no peril greater than its awesome splendour. It was they that first named it for they could see it without harm, though it did then drive them blind at the end. For too much did one of them look upon its mirrored facets and praise its fell beauty that it enraptured him. And so it was that his family was smote by a tragedy he could have avoided had he not been so transfixed. A man of great power, he then cursed the stone such that no man could look upon it thereafter or else turn blind. He did this to remove his own temptation and to save others from his own tragic fate, or so he judged. But he was unthinking and in his fit he made this whole area a danger to anyone that came across it by luck or foolhardiness.

'Yet before he did so it had been crafted. It has remained adamant against all nature or man could throw at it before and since save for the cunning of this race of people. The Mandulians, they were called. It is said they were a race descended from Mandulous the Changeling. Although originally a God, Mandulous had fallen in love with one of Alcabell's first-born mortals, a girl of such poetic beauty that he chose to become a mortal also, that they could spend a long lifetime together as equals. But after much time and leaving many children they both passed from this world forever. Yet though Mandulous lost his control over death he was able to inspire his offspring to become great learners who could overcome many challenges. The waters that swell around the Mirrorhorn in the Gathering have not worn it though they forged this entire valley. But his people crafted the Stone and forged in its dark side a case of deep steps leading up to its very top. They made there a plateau upon which they would leave offerings of thanks to Mandulous, whom they believed, after he had passed out of this world at a great age, had returned to the side of his father as a God once more. But our only clue to this is that each stair is described differently to the next with a representation that would have expressed something deeply telling about them.'

'How could you know any of this,' asked Behvyn in an exasperated tone. 'You would've had to go there yourself but no one would do such a thing, not unless they were mad.'

'And I won't listen to another word,' shouted Behleth, suddenly, 'from a man who doesn't introduce himself with his first words but instead accuses us of a crime we know nothing about and holds us in ropes.'

At the sound of Behleth's raised voice three figures came running towards them from the prow, one in front brandishing a whip and two behind with daggers drawn. With a wave of his hand the hooded man stopped them from coming any closer.

'You upbraid me,' he said in a voice loud enough for all to hear, 'but are right to do so. My name is Rumé, son of Rothé, Captain of the Royal King's Guards of the North March. These are my men. Together we keep the North Wall for His Majesty and it is my undertaking to keep all who would from approaching the Mirrorhorn. You say you are not guilty of murder so why do you think you are here?'

'It's not for us to give you an excuse to continue our abduction,' answered Behvyn, as bravely as he could say it, stopping his mind from reaching the memory of the Lady.

'Fetlock, what is the charge?' asked Rumé of the one holding the whip.

'That you killed the White Lady,' Fetlock answered with zealous vigour.

'We did NOT! She was dead when we found her!' shouted Behleth, instinctively.

'So, you know to whom Fetlock is referring to?' Rumé asked, quickly.

Behvyn and Behleth said nothing.

'She had a task that you interrupted,' said Rumé. 'You will

finish it for her. I myself have tried once already, but failed.'

With that he stood up, turned to face the brothers and brought down his hood. They gasped as they saw through the moonlight that his eyes were entirely blank, as though turned to milky glass.

'I doubted the power of the Mirrorhorn as you still do, young Masters, and thought earlier this night that in darkness I could attempt the task the Lady came here to achieve, now she is passed. It stung my eyes at the first glance even though thick night lay between and I am blinded. I know not if I will ever see again but cannot abandon my goal. So, I must now use her killers as my proxy.'

'There is no other way, my Lord,' added Fetlock. 'They did for the Lady, there's no doubt, and now that you have lost your own sight we must use these two to complete her task. Guards!'

With that, Fetlock barked his orders, first to have Behleth untied and then to have him moved down to the stem. There, held in the iron grip of the guards, a rope was tied about his waist and the other end was tied to the grab rail. One of the men then threw Behleth into the water and the current brought him out eastward, towards the middle of its passage.

'What are you doing to him?' cried Behvyn, full of concern. 'The water's freezing!'

'Quite the point, young man,' said Fetlock.

Rumé then had another of his men release Behvyn from his bonds and take him at knifepoint over to the port side where he could see his brother and, hard against the side of the barge, a very small rowing boat.

'Your brother is strong, Behvyn,' said Rumé, 'but his life will be taken by the cold of the mountain's water. He will not last forever. However long he can survive is the time you now have left to save him.'

'What must I do?' Behvyn asked desperately, as he was thrown bodily into the rowboat. He had only just sat upright again and dug out from under his tangled feet the short oars when Rumé's absent gaze appeared above him and explained.

'Here is a bond for your eyes,' he said, and another guardsman threw in a wrap of material that Behvyn was asked to wind around his head. 'You will not be able to look where you go but you don't have to end up like me. Only if you want to.' Behvyn put on the bind about his eyes. 'I myself do not require such a measure,' said Rumé, as he swung a leg confidently over the side and dropped into the same small boat.

'Master?' asked Fetlock, full of concern. 'You're going as well? I do not think it wise!'

'I leave the barge and the other boy to your care,' answered Rumé. 'We will go to the Mirrorhorn and Behvyn will take from its peak that which we will find there. I go to see it done. Either we will be back in time or out of it! It is time for Master Behvyn to choose!'

'You expect me to take this boat blindfolded and find the way to the Blackstone? You're mad!' Behvyn was afraid but also angry. 'That's impossible! I can't even row!'

'You won't have to. Put the oars down. As I went there earlier this fateful night I took with me a rope that has one end tethered to this barge. Here is the other end,' he said, placing a thick plaited cord into Behvyn's hands after searching out his wrists. 'Don't let it go. This rope is looped about the base of the Mirrorhorn. All you need to do is pull us along the length of this side of the rope and it will take us straight back to the rock. If you let it go, Fetlock will let your brother go. If you attack me, Fetlock will run your brother through. If you do not complete this task or if I sense you are even thinking about dropping this rope,' Rumé paused for effect and then spoke loudly enough for the entire crew to hear, 'I will run you through.'

Rumé then put his hands out to feel for Behvyn's face and was only satisfied again once he had felt the blindfold in place.

'Good,' he said. 'Keep it on at all times. It will save your sight as you face the Mirrorhorn, or if it is reflected into your eyes.' Rumé held on tightly to another tether that held the boat beside the barge. 'You only have to draw us northward; feel your way there. The rope leads straight to the Gathering. You will know when we are close, the Stone can be heard for the flow of the waters around it. It is very distinctive and is closer than the sound of the Falls. Once there, feel your way westwards round to the steps in the Mirrorhorn's left side and go up them. Bring me back whatever you find at the top! I will hold the boat in place for you while you leave it, for there is no way to tie a craft to the rock. But let us go now and be quick about it. Your brother will not last long. You have until then to get what I need and then come back for him or he loses his life!'

'You just want to kill us both so why don't I give you the excuse now?' said Behvyn, distraught.

'Behleth is running out of time,' replied Rumé, smartly.

With that, Rumé pulled from his right side a stout knife and slammed it down on to the mooring rope to release the shallow-hulled boat into the swift-flowing waters of the Highborn. Immediately, Behvyn felt the rope between his hands slip through, sodden wet and heavy but burning with friction. Rumé shouted at Behvyn to take up a firm grip as they coasted southwards.

It was dark and Behvyn could not see. He was very cold and had been hurt from the fall into the boat. The last thing he had seen was his brother's shoulders and head only just above the water level at the side of the barge as he put on his blindfold. He caught hold of the rope until it stopped slipping and then slowly pulled on it. Being strong, he was able to propel both himself and Rumé steadily northwards, though the current resisted his progress.

He found a rhythm and it was calming for now. His task was simple: to save his brother. He imagined wildly heroic escapes, strangling Rumé with the rope and then rescuing Behleth from the cold of the river, dragging him up into the boat and drifting off to safety whilst disarray stalled their enemies. He didn't like his chances.

'Have you worked out how you will kill me yet?' asked Rumé, after Behvyn had moved them upstream sufficiently for all rumour of the river barge to be lost.

Behvyn said nothing.

'Come now, I have a knife; you could steal it off me and plunge it into my heart. I do not wear chain mail. Or you could throw me off the boat and make sure I drown. Come on! What are you waiting for?'

'If I did that and did not rescue my brother, he would die.'

'And you would too, young master.'

'But don't believe I wouldn't do it if I thought I could.'

'There's where we'll have to disagree, Behvyn Hahn.'

They progressed in silence. Behvyn worked on the rope and on his mind. He knew he wasn't thinking clearly; his mind was filled with rage. He wanted to cast off everything that stood between him and his brother and their freedom. He wanted to click his fingers and for all the problems to disappear. He knew it would take more. He knew he had to think. Rumé was a silent unmoving weight in front of him. Behvyn remembered how he had said they were now linked to the goal of the Lady.

'You said earlier that you had tried to complete the task of the Lady. How did you know her intent?'

'It was long marked that she would return to this land,' replied Rumé. 'And her path yesterday led all through the Shale Valley from south to north. If you extend the route she took onward, there is only the Mirrorhorn in its way.'

'So you're coming this way again because you now don't have anything to lose? Or you don't trust me not to leave my brother to die so that I could keep whatever it is that awaits us?'

'Both. Keep going.'

As Behvyn pulled through the rope he guessed they were moving past more steeply sided banks. The sounds of the river cascading through it echoed loudly above him on both sides. They were getting towards the southern end of the Gathering. He thought of how the men might be too frightened to look ahead for him and watch his progress in case they accidentally glimpsed the Blackstone for themselves. In that case, mused Behvyn, he was definitely not being watched anymore. The thought flashed across his mind that if he was quick he could seize Rumé and hold him hostage for his brother. However, would he himself take that chance? Would his men care for their Captain over the justice they wanted to mete out to him and his brother? He could not risk Behleth recklessly. He thought of his own position. He wondered if he could be more reckless, though driven by the direst need. It was the most foolish of all actions to attempt an approach to the Blackstone whilst blindfolded. For all he knew he would retrieve whatever awaited them only then to be murdered himself by Rumé.

He continued pulling, his fears growing. His back began to tire, then his shoulders, so that each surge they made through the river became shorter and less urgent. He was not moving forward as fast as before but he could keep going at the same pace for longer. Rumé said nothing.

When Behvyn made the Gathering suddenly they were out of the concentrated flurry of the Highborn. The more languid flows held within the Gathering's large basin allowed him to progress more easily. He could feel the tumble and crash of the Cold Falls in front of him as he faced northwards and they were indeed deafening. He had never seen a map of the Gathering but if it was at all circular the Falls sounded as though they were half a mile away, making the Stone about half that distance again.

"The Cold Falls are the coming together of numerous streams and smaller mountain rivers sourced by Cloud Mountain,' said Rumé. 'It is these at their birth that gave the mountain its deeply riven look, most weather beaten of all peaks in the land. Once they combine as the Falls they make a great and steady thunder.'

'I have heard them as a distant rumble once or twice before,' said Behvyn, 'when in the wilderness hunting with my uncle. But I never knew they were this loud up close.'

It was a physical noise that resulted from the great drop down icy rocks, landing far below in the Gathering. It was disorientating, and as Behvyn came closer still, the sound encircled him, so that he knew no longer where north and south lay. His mind raced as he realised this new danger and the impossibility of hearing a subtle movement from Rumé should he wish to attack him. The wind was now swirling around Behvyn, carrying on it the dense vapour of the Cold Falls that slowly drenched his hair, face and clothes, freezing him almost as efficiently as if he was in the Highborn with Behleth. Here he sat, in a boat becoming ever more affected by waves and still he pulled himself towards his doom, imagining to be pierced by steel each time one hand went over the other. Eventually, he took a risk.

'I cannot do it!' he cried, and released the rope.

'If you do not do this…' started Rumé.

'I won't spend my life to get you what you want so you can just kill me and then my brother when you return!'

'Think what you want but time passes and my men are well trained. They will not disobey orders, especially when it comes to murderers such as they believe you and your brother to be,' answered Rumé, as they drifted backwards.

'Yet you don't believe it.'

'Why do you say that?'

Rumé's answer gave him his first hope.

'You have no proof,' said Behvyn, over the thunderous noise from the Falls. He reached for the coil of rope that sat behind him and halted their lapse back towards the Highborn. 'And you have seen more things than they have to make you know they're mistaken.'

'Have I?'

'You've placed yourself in danger by getting into this boat with me and if I were a murderer then you would put at risk all that you have. But you know that is not the case. So, I ask: how do you know?'

'The Lady was an immortal,' Rumé answered, much to Behvyn's relief, with a degree of respect in his voice. 'Immortal in the sense that her spirit is permanent, but her body was not immune to all forms of death. All who live can die; the body of an immortal can be killed. Yet taking the life from their body so that another must be found is a terrible thing. To extinguish a light that could shine on indefinitely carries a heavy burden all of itself. In so doing, Master Behvyn, you remove from the world acts of kindness and far-sighted benevolence for many long ages to come. For that spirit, when it returns, is never quite the same. It is a crime so extreme that it leaves an indelible mark on the heart of all that have committed such an act. But I know that mark and I do not see it on you or on your brother.'

'Then why persist in forcing me to this task or in torturing Behleth?' lamented Behvyn, his anger now rising and his breath coming in gasps from the effort of propelling them back into the heart of the Gathering.

'Because this now must be done by another since the passing of the Lady and a justice found for her,' answered Rumé, with not a little anxiety in his deep, tired voice. 'And I came into this boat because you and your brother are the only people I can now trust and I need to be away from that barge. If Fetlock has his way all three of us will soon be dead.'

Behvyn did not know what to make of this. He stayed quiet as they moved back towards where he thought they had been before he let go of the rope and let Rumé make the next move. There had been nothing in this man's behaviour back on the sail barge to betray this information. He wondered if Rumé was in some way trying to coax him towards an admission of guilt, setting him a trap. But it somehow didn't fit with a quality about him that Behvyn found profound.

'Although my men are loyal to the authorities of the land, they are not all loyal to me,' Rumé finally continued, as though by saying something that had been closely guarded for a long time he was finally exposing himself to fatal forces. His voice barely carried over the roar there was in the heart of the Gathering. 'Many factions have grown up in the Cambwall court since King Cuiron was taken ill. They're all involved in a dance of politics between those that resist attempts to have His Majesty formally abdicate and those that either seek for him to be replaced by his son, Prince Idren, who is upon the brink of manhood himself, and those who would end the monarchy and have the country run once again as separate smaller Princedoms. I have no doubt this latter path would ruin the Valley and leave it open to attack from terrible forces that most are ignorant of. For that reason alone it must not be so. Those who promote this idea are not yet influential and have little credit in the eyes of the Royal Executive. Yet the faction that seeks to have Idren on the throne is gaining in potency. Its influence is now far-reaching, and Fetlock is testament to it.'

'Fetlock? Isn't that your man back there in charge over my brother?'

'Indeed. Though we are two hundred of leagues north of Cambwall, the northern borders of this land, the North Vale, the North Wall and the protection it gives from the Mirrorhorn are matters they control there, not here. I serve the King but Fetlock was placed with me by order of the Executive. Prince Kinithor it was that sold the idea to them on the basis of Fetlock's military background, which I concede is most flattering to him. But Kinithor's real motive is more sinister and yet perfectly obvious to those that have wit enough to see it. He wants the throne again for his line to which it once belonged for more than twelve generations. He will see Idren replace his father at too impressionable an age and has been insinuating himself into his young confidence for many years already. And all the while preparing an army in secret under the protection of Fetlock's patrol inside the North Wall.'

Behvyn stopped but kept hold of the rope. 'Rumé, that's ridiculous. The idea that someone could build an army and then hide it behind a wall and nobody find out!'

'Keep going. If you think this is all baseless,' continued Rumé, 'then I concede I hoped it was nothing more than a hunch I had. But there are two legions of troops already on the western side of the Gathering; two on the east and another, smaller one albeit, north of the Falls, none of which I have commissioned or been told about. Indeed, if I did not have spies of my own, I would not even know of their existence. But they have come and been billeted by Fetlock, all under the pretense of my command. But I asked for no one. And then the arrival of the Lady, completely unanticipated, has served to stir up everything.'

'How so?' questioned Behvyn. 'How can she have such an impact?'

'Because now Fetlock is again reminded of the higher forces that can still yet influence this world and operate in ways that cannot be controlled by intrigue and political manipulation. He seeks to move forward more quickly now for he knows Kinithor must move closer to his goal shortly or see his opportunity move forever away from him. You see, Behvyn, our fates are not all without design. Yet the purpose of the Lady can only now be known by uncovering what is on top of the Mirrorhorn. Fetlock greatly desires to have this article for his Master, to give Kinithor another advantage over the young Prince Idren, to persuade him closer to his total control.

'But he must not have that advantage. I have no intention of ever getting back on that barge. I must keep this secret from him for the future of the land, for the King that yet may wake, should grace bless us all, and for the safety of his only son. And you and your brother are my only remaining hope of that.

'Surely,' said Behvyn, now pulling them much faster towards their dark destination, 'a soldier couldn't kill his Captain so blatantly and hope to live to see another day?'

'In other circumstances I would agree with you, Behvyn. But not only am I blind since yesterday eve, but also, by seeking to reach the Blackstone, I go against the very law the King whom I protect laid down. It is a capital offense to approach it! I therefore lay myself open to such justice by my very actions and cannot deny them lest I go against the King himself.

'As for you and your brother,' Rumé continued, 'Fetlock has already assumed your guilt. He will be poisoning the men's minds with the idea of the murder of the white Lady to the point where they will be unable to bare the thought of your existence. They are men of high morals and can therefore be played quite easily by someone like Fetlock, as long as he can make them believe in your guilt.'

'The thought of it makes my blood boil! We didn't do anything wrong!' cried Behvyn. 'But we heard her. There was someone else there. She spoke to them; warned them. She said that what they asked for was not to be given.'

'You heard her, Behvyn?'

'Yes. In an ageless voice I heard her cry: "For every race's sake, I must remove them from this world!" It was then she was killed, though it sounded more like she slipped and fell.'

'"I must remove them from this world"? Those were her words?'

'Yes.'

'Don't believe it was an accident. An Immortal One doesn't just lose her footing and die, Master Hahn,' replied Rumé. 'No, even as I fear for the King, I fear that events greater than I can yet perceive are being set in motion. But we must get to the Mirrorhorn to find out what was not to be given! Now I dread our course too.'

Behvyn felt even more unsure in the company of Rumé as they closed towards their goal. Although less threatened by the man, he was more bewildered by the prospects the future presented to him. He wondered if he was Rumé's captive any more. If he didn't do as he said there seemed very little Rumé would do about it. In addition, he started to panic over time; it had surely run down. At any moment his brother could sink into deadly unconsciousness and drown in the waters. Then his own blood froze.

'The rope!' he cried. 'It is undone!' Rumé had felt it too.

They slipped backwards, away from the Blackstone, towards their enemies, the Lady's words ringing in their ears.

'What fate is this?' said Behvyn, a surge of fear upon him.

'Our own, and let us decide it!' commanded Rumé. 'The rope in the boat. Seize it now!'

Behvyn did so, and reeled in from the Gathering the remains of what would have taken them to the Stone.

'Its end is cut!' said Behvyn.

'Sheared on the side of the rock,' said Rumé, after feeling it himself. 'The oars! Put them in place and turn the boat around. We must stop moving away!'

Behvyn reached for them with hands numbed as though in gloves, and then remembered he would not know in which direction they faced, or in which to row.

'How, Rumé? What will find us the rock?'

'The water sounds different at the base of the Mirrorhorn, for it asks that the Gathering flows around it. We will listen for that. If we get drenched, we have gone too far, for it is separate to the Falls.'

Behvyn began to row, filled with misgivings, and his heart burning with hate. The world seemed against him. He remembered bitterly the previous night when his brother and he had found the Lady and cursed their misfortune in seeing her. Yet it then set him wondering how she had seen the way, though she was blindfolded herself.

'The Lady could see the road with her eyes bound, but I cannot see the Stone even with my eyes open!' he thought, ruefully. 'What was it that had shown her the way through darkness and danger?'

As he powered them both forwards into the Gathering, without a clue in which direction they went, he remembered the white falcon and how it had been bound to the Lady through some means. But he had seen it himself and it had flown away. 'It must be long gone now,' he guessed. Again he shivered from the cold; the mists about the Cold Falls were beginning to wreath them both in an icy layer of water once again.

'We are gone too far!' He took in the oars, put his hands in his pockets at a loss and let despair finally well up inside of him. Behvyn's misery had finally overwhelmed him.

If Rumé sensed his dejection, he said nothing, but allowed the craft to slip steadily southwards as his own dark thoughts unravelled inside his mind.

But there, inside his coat pocket, Behvyn felt something. He extended his fingers and caught it, and pulled it out so he could feel it better. It was the necklace they had found where the Lady had lain. He ran his fingers over the smooth chain and came to the dark gem set about the middle of its length. He recalled it was black. A black stone: Blackstone! From nowhere, his hopes rose again and filled his heart once more.

'This may be the answer!' he thought excitedly to himself. 'But has it a use? The Lady still needed a bond about her eyes, so I cannot take mine off. But what if I wear both?'

Behvyn, taking great care to be quiet, suspecting Fetlock and his men would use it as the proof they looked for of his and his brother's guilt should Rumé's story turn out to be just that, placed the necklace over his head and tucked it inside his jerkin so that it touched his skin.

Immediately he grasped the sides of the boat as the world changed for him.

No longer was he in the boat, it seemed, but flying high above the land, weightless and free. He could see again but it was as though his eyes were above him. Then he saw himself, shaking, the size of an ant in a tiny boat, facing the hooded figure of Rumé. He was looking down on himself. Then his perspective came lower as it dived and shot through thin low clouds to emerge at the height of the treetops and skim around the Gathering before hovering above his own shape. Now, even in the lowering moonlight, he could see where he was clearly. He could see the empty look of Rumé and the southern entrance to the Gathering. Then his view turned about and he saw the Cold Falls that lay behind him.

These were great and no dim remembrance of the mighty tributary that had gorged the valley in ages past. Wide the waters were as they sprang down from their height and crashed onto the dark rocks below. As they filled out into the Gathering, inky black and depthless, before feeding their way down out of the North Vale as the Highborn River, they slowed almost to a stop and churned, heavy and regal, like marble forming.

In the centre of the Gathering, Behvyn finally saw the great rock: the Blackstone. Smooth it was and shiny, polished as a gem, and vast. Forty feet at least it towered dark and adamant, from water level to peak, and the same distance around its middle, with only a slight narrowing towards its top. Unworn by the waters, it remained steadfast and caused the Gathering to pass around it on its way outward. Because of its curse and glistening menace, Behvyn even now barely dared to perceive it, though he saw it not with his own eyes. He was awed by how the Blackstone stared back at all that encircled it, ever watchful. He understood why so many had craved to see it, though they all suffered the same consequence.

In the westward side of the Blackstone, coming into view as he picked up a stroke and approached it as fast as he could now time was perilously short, were hewn the many steps that Rumé had mentioned. Behvyn saw them clearly, lit by the thin pre-dawn light, as they led to the top of its height but also down past the point at which the water levelled; for how deep he couldn't see. Even Rumé's story gave no hint as to how they had been created, or for what reason.

On through the dark water he moved, against the undercurrent that would have him away southward. Rumé noticed their progress was now targeted and became suspicious.

'Have you heard the sound of the waters against the Mirrorhorn?' he asked.

'I-I think I heard it, off to the right and just ahead, for just a brief second,' Behvyn answered, coolly. 'I must try for it.'

Rumé seemed satisfied, though Behvyn then watched from above as Rumé leaned over to the side of the boat and turned his head to try to catch the sound himself.

Behvyn then fixed his sight on the Blackstone and kept going, though sleep would have him despite the peril his brother was in. On he rowed as his legs, back and shoulders screamed their exhaustion at him. Still he moved, and slowly but inexorably came towards his goal. Lighter now he perceived the night. Time had moved on. He could hear clearly the higher-pitched boil of water around the base of the rock and Rumé's posture softened.

Finally, Behvyn reached out for the steps that led up the side of the Blackstone and he made for the one that was at his head height. His view was from above and therefore he found it difficult to judge distances. As if this mere thought commanded it, his angle of observation moved around so that it was just behind and above him and hovered there. He thrust out an outstretched right hand and was able to grasp the ice-cold stair firmly. Even though water had constantly splashed it for eons, the sharpness of the step edge still nearly cut into his cold skin.

Yet now here, Behvyn felt most endangered. As far as he could guess his time had already run out, so slow had he been to discover the function of the necklace. Five enemies beset him, as he saw it. Rumé, who could leave him marooned here or send him to a watery grave; Fetlock, if he was to believe Rumé; the Blackstone, that could still steal his sight; time, enough to save his brother; and fear, of what lay at the top of the steps.

But he could not remain on the water much longer, for his brother's strength was weakening and there was no debate. With much regret Behvyn moved onto the stair and trusted to hope that Rumé would still be there when he came back.

As Behvyn began the climb of the Blackstone steps, watching himself from behind, he noticed in their design a shape of something drawn on their tops, as Rumé had predicted. They were incomprehensible to him. As he forced his tired body onward he noticed that each step bore a different symbol to the next and that no device was repeated. The markings appeared as letters of a written language, but he couldn't understand their message. Each stair seemed to read as another part of a sentence that continued all the way up to the very peak of the stone. But if he sensed anything, it read like a warning.

As he reached the last step, pulling himself up with his hands, his point of view showed him what rested on top. He crawled the few paces over to it, commanded his sight over, and stared at the object he found there in wonder.

It was circular in shape and elliptical in width so that it tapered towards its outer edges from a wider middle. It was larger than a coin but smaller than a plate and fashioned out of a bronze-coloured metal. There were markings on the exposed side. Behvyn moved to take it in his hurry but even as his hand went towards it, the first light of morning fired its rays down past the eastern shoulders of the Cloud Mount, down past the brim of the Cold Falls, and straight onto the heart of the discus itself to illuminate it brightly.

Behvyn paused in his motion, caught off guard, and watched in wonder as great arcs of sunlight were suddenly re-directed from off of the shiny surface of the discus away into the distance. He looked along the light shards to their ends and saw three dots of brilliant light formed on either side of the great eastward pass out of the Shale Valley. The Twin Mountains of Ithed and Antheon were ignited, two great peaks that sat at the ends of long ranges, at a place some one hundred leagues southward from where he knelt. So bright were these beams that they stood out in the landscape unmistakably. Behvyn felt sure Fetlock and his men would have seen this but hoped it had gone unnoticed.

He quickly picked up the discus. It was light and seemed very old. He noticed it had a passage of text written on the back of it in some language he didn't recognize as he folded it under his cloak.

His thoughts now turned to getting back to Behleth as quickly as possible. He had surely exceeded the time Rumé had given his brother to live. He cursed the stone for being so far away and then cast his remote gaze around for Rumé.

He looked but could not immediately see the boat. His stomach churned in panic. His worst fear had been realized. Then he got control of himself once more and commanded his view to rise upwards and fly out over the southern edge of the rock. From there, he beheld a sight that cheered his hopes once again. For there, swaying like a cork, was the boat. Rumé sat inside with the oars withdrawn. He saw that it was held against the rock by the two competing arms of water as they swung around the Blackstone and raced back to meet each other, where they created a small whirl that did not conform to the rest of the flow. And there it had held the vessel fast.

He cried out to Rumé that he had completed his task. He saw

Rumé start and then row determinedly back to where he believed the steps to be, feeling his way around the southward, then westward sides of the Mirrorhorn until he came again to the staircase. Behvyn stepped backwards down the steps with great care and then cautiously maneuvered into the boat. As soon as he was in, he took the oars back from Rumé and began to row as fast as he could southwards.

'Behvyn,' said Rumé, as they left the Gathering, 'I do not know what it is that you hold, but keep it secret. Now you have it, you must do two things. Firstly, no matter what happens, Fetlock must never have it. Secondly, you must trust me that I will do all I can to help you escape.'

Behvyn watched them both from above as a deep frown and look of sorrow appeared on Rumé's brow. He certainly behaved honorably, but Rumé seemed to have such depths to his personality that Behleth guessed he knew nearly nothing about him. It was this he feared, but the urgency of the situation brooked no further delay.

'Save me and my brother and we will both trust you,' answered Behvyn.

'Then let us save Behleth with all speed. We have little time left, if time there still be.'

The new sun had already warmed the air enough to cure his chill but by now Behvyn could feel his senses dimming as he pulled on the oars with every effort he had remaining. He had slept little between the two nights since the Lady passed through the Shale Valley. But this time the flow of the Gathering, and then the drive of the Highborn southward, was with him, and the journey that had taken him an age to make in one direction took him only a tenth of the time in the other.

As he made fast progress and Rumé remained silent, Behvyn wondered at the sight he had gained and compared it to the view a bird might have of the lands below it. Of course! He realised with a degree of embarrassment at not having concluded it immediately; it was the view of the white falcon itself. It must be linked to the stone in the necklace, and not flown from these lands as he had assumed. That explained how the Lady had planned to reach the Blackstone without harm. He now speculated whether Rumé had guessed any of this.

But just then he rounded the final curve in the Highborn that lay between them and Fetlock and saw Behleth immediately, waving to him, from the deck of the river barge! Waving, waving like the captain of a ship, standing at the railing and shouting at them. He watched himself wave back from over his shoulder, his heart suddenly warm again with relief, and let himself smile. His brother was alive, he was waving to them, and he was saved. He continued to row on and the gap between them narrowed to less than a furlong. But Behvyn also felt Rumé tense up, alert for something.

'Give me the necklace, Behvyn,' Rumé said quickly.

Behvyn was speechless. How could he know about it?

'Behvyn, there's no time! You must give it to me, and take off your blindfold. We are in great danger.'

'Y-You're not blind?' asked Behvyn, incredulous, unwrapping the binding from his eyes.

'I am blind but you are no expert at deception. How many times did I hear the sound of a large bird hovering around our craft at the Mirrorhorn, or before it the tinkling of a chain? And why did the Lady wear a gauntlet? Yes, I saw her body as it passed south. But enough explanations! I am blind but can only help you if sighted. You must trust me, Behvyn. Lend it to me, now!'

Behvyn could not refuse his command. He removed the necklace and placed it in Rumé's hands. As he did so Behvyn's point of view switched to his own eyes. He was disoriented for a quick moment, before he adapted and swung his head around to see his brother again.

Now that he was much closer he could hear some of the words Behleth was saying.

"Stay back! Stay back, don't c-"

Suddenly, the barge exploded.

Chapter 4

ALCABELL'S GIFT

Tangle would look back on the day she first became a mother with a concoction of bittersweet emotions, but always, for herself at the very moment she woke up, with frustration and annoyance at her own innocence. At times she would want to shout through the past at her younger self, or shake into her at that point what she would know later. It was a regret that stemmed from remembering that, as she swam into consciousness, mid-morning after the Autumnfalls celebration, waking in a once-familiar bed, she had heard a voice that sounded like her own, coming from elsewhere, as though she had split in two during the night and left only what was weary behind.

As the voice filtered in through the window and slowly registered with her, Tangle rubbed the top of her brow where it met the pillow and noticed the smell of the bonfire was still in her hair. Horrified at her own laziness, she commanded herself to go and wash immediately, and almost listened to herself, but remained there, frozen in warm comfort. Then another thought bubbled up from memory. Today was the day of their trip to Tieco Lake. She sprang out of bed, but it was miscalculated, taking no account of the disorder that lay in waiting about the bedside. She ended up face down in the middle of the room, tripped by the clutter of travel cases, strewn clothes, leather boots hinging double over themselves, boxed up possessions untouched for years and the excitable entrance at that very moment of Half-Pint, who, sensing the time had been right to bark his 'Good mornings' to his returned mistress, had stormed in, yapping excitedly, with legs ablur. He ran rings around her, even as she fell.

'Get off me, you fool!' she said, more out of embarrassment than anger, and pulled herself up off the floor, out of the door at an odd angle and away down the corridor, clinging to one wall as she went.

'It that you up?' came the voice she had heard earlier, now

rising from the bottom of the stairs. It was Tig.

Tangle murmured something in reply that didn't consist of words, but was a sufficient enough amount of noise to answer her sister's question.

'I'll get Mandle to make your breakfast,' she heard Tig say. 'We're not that late yet.'

After a particularly spiteful attempt from Mandle to provide Tangle with a scorched and unrecognisable meal of eggs, bacon and sausage, that backfired tremendously when Tangle took Mangle's plate instead, and following a dull ten minutes eating it, looking at the same four things in front of her from where she sat at the table, she went outside into the rear courtyard to find Tig.

She found her grooming Glambard, the carthorse, in his stable. When Tig saw her, she came outside and stood half-in and half-out of the shade cast by the sun reaching towards its apex in the crisp sky. The shadows were a foot longer now at this time than they had been a month ago. Tig gave her sister a look.

'There's no harm in a lie-in, is there?' yawned Tangle in reply, her mind still bleary but the light breeze working to sharpen her up for the day. 'And anyway, I was awake when you got up; I just didn't want to leave the bed, it was so comfortable. There's no great rush, though; we're not leaving with the boys until the afternoon, right?'

'That's almost right,' confirmed Tig. 'But I told Feran and Kjerros last night that we'd go round to theirs first and then make our way over to the twin's place.'

Tangle took in the plan and reshuffled her expectation of the day ahead accordingly. 'I can't wait to get going, now I'm up! It feels odd being here again, like we've outgrown the place. I had a hunch, but I see now how I could never come back to live here again.'

'Hmm, well. Maybe,' smiled Tig. 'You seemed used to your old bed already, at least! But I know what you mean. It would be like trying to put on an old skin you'd once shed.'

'Are you saying I look like a lizard?'

'I'm saying it's best to look to the future.' At this, Tig broke off from her grooming. Glambard stomped impatiently. 'Well, I let you lie there,' Tig said, combing the looming Shire horse's sides again, 'but I really shouldn't have done.'

'Why, what's up?' asked Tangle.

'I'm not sure. Something was found on our doorstep this morning when father left to go,' Tig replied. She finished with Glambard, stroked his broad mane, and took her sister round to the barn. As she went, she explained further. 'It gave him quite a shock, I think; I heard him cursing as he walked down the road. So I sneaked downstairs to find out what all the fuss was about.'

Once there, and after fighting away Jigger and Jogger who had remained interested in the new object since it had been placed there, Tig showed Tangle a sorry pile of straw and clothing that had once passed for a scarecrow.

'It's the one we made with Behvyn and Behleth last year, before we left,' explained Tig, as they both stared at it. 'It used to be in the Gardener's field behind their house. I can't guess what it's doing here, but it's in a real mess.'

'Yes, I recognise it!' said Tangle, warmed by the memories it brought back. 'Some kind of 'welcome home' prank by the boys, I guess.' She bent down to have a closer look. 'It looks like it's been attacked by the dogs,' she said, staring around accusingly at Jigger and Jogger, who, noticing her look, played around innocently but moved away back outside, disturbing Glambard in the process with their sudden suspicious adoption of nonchalant slinkery.

'No,' said Tig, 'they haven't been at it; look at these cuts in the jacket, and here in the trousers. You can only imagine a knife doing those.'

'Well, what can it mean?' asked Tangle, honestly puzzled. 'That's not very nice! Why would they do something like that?' She thought back to the party and how introspective the brothers had been. 'They didn't say 'goodnight', but there's no way they'd do something like this. I can't believe it. Maybe it's a message instead. We should see if they're safe. The twins I mean. Let's visit them now, Tig.'

But then Tangle stopped, put her hand on Tig's arm and paused. She stood still and listened out again.

'Can you hear that?'

'Hear what?' answered Tig, shrugging off her sister and

walking out across the courtyard again.

'I just heard a, well. I'm not sure. It sounded like a moan,' said Tangle, in a whisper.

'It's Glambard, the dogs have always been more playful than he likes,' said Tig, moving towards the carthorse and smoothing his nose as his head came over the lower half of the stable door.

'It's not coming from there,' said Tangle in an inquiring tone. 'It's in here, in the barn with me.'

'You sure it's not your breakfast? What did Mandle get for you?' teased Tig.

But just then they both heard something, and Tig came back to her sister. She put her hand on Tangle's shoulder as they both stood fixed to the spot and looked around, but there was nothing to catch the eye in the barn. Just a pile of split fence panels over in a corner, empty ale barrels with bent lids stacked up along one wall, disparate collections of iron tools with dry, cracked wooden handles hanging idle, dark glass bottles filled with layered cobwebs, an oil drum punctured by rusty holes, a few dislocated chairs from a recent brawl heaped into a confused pile that resembled a root system, the broken scarecrow, and the sturdy oak wagon Grodel used for deliveries.

Then they heard it again. It was a mournful sound like the rustle of long reeds in a strong wind, but sharper in tone. It was definitely in the barn. Tig moved backwards but as she did so Tangle thought she could make out words.

'Not safe,' the voice seemed to say in very quiet, slow breaths.

'Who said that?' asked Tig. Glambard's nose disappeared deep into the stable. But before Tangle could answer her sister there was no doubt any more.

'Not safe!' came the voice again, as loud as the buzz of a blade of grass blown as an instrument.

Tangle felt the excitement of fear slide down her back before, as suddenly as a twist of fate, the scarecrow jerked up from where it lay and began shaking itself so that all the seeds in the ears of corn it contained rattled in concert. Straw flew around the barn as it jumped on the spot, lifted its arms above its head, tilted back its neck, and cried out its warning once more towards the roof.

'NOT SAFE!' it blasted, and then collapsed on its knees,

seemingly exhausted, at Tangle's feet, and began to sob in a sorrowful dirge.

'I hoped it was the scarecrow!' said Tangle, as she gave her sister a wide-eyed look of glee.

'So, you came all the way over to here on your own last night?' asked Tangle, without betraying any hint of fear or surprise, once she had soothed and coddled their strange visitor. All three of them were sitting on a bale of hay removed from Glambard's stable next door. The scarecrow nodded, and as it did so, Tangle could see how the straw behaved like a skin, pulsing and stretching, instead of snapping and breaking. She and Tig had swept around the floor together and picked up all the straw they could find that had flown off the figure as he gave them his warning and then Tangle had watched transfixed as it was re-introduced. At once it went from being dry and stiff to become life-like and flexible so that it glowed a healthy gold and the mend could no longer be seen.

'Do you have a name?' Tig asked, less confidently than Tangle, but smiling reassuringly.

'A name?' answered the scarecrow slowly.

'Well, we can't just call you 'Scarecrow', can we? You need a proper name,' said Tig.

'"Scarecrow"?' asked the scarecrow.

'Yes, it's what you are, but I think we can do better than that,' answered Tangle.

'Don't want to scare,' said the scarecrow, unhappily.

'No. Well then, we'll call you something else, like I say,' said Tig, getting into the line of thought with some seriousness. She had always been the one to officially name their pets and dolls and toys, recalled Tangle, so she was happy to see her sister take the familiar responsibility upon herself. It also gave Tig's mind something to do, at least for a little time, whilst it became used to the idea of a living scarecrow.

Tangle, however, was more concerned with how it had come into being, and more interested in what it had to say for itself.

'Do you want me to get you some better clothes?' she asked. 'Those ones you have on, well, I'm not trying to seem rude, I promise, but they are in a bit of a mess. They've got tears all over them and they're a little tatty. Will you wait there, just a moment?'

The scarecrow seemed quite against the idea, judging by his look of concern, but Tangle ran off to come back quickly with armfuls of different shirts and vests, coats and cloaks, breeches and shorts, handkerchiefs and hats, scarves and boots, many of which were Grodel's and many of which were new. She also brought out with her Tig's sea-chelys.

'You should play a song to calm him down,' she suggested, passing the instrument to her sister as she sat down in front of the scarecrow. 'Here, we can find something for you from this little lot,' Tangle explained. 'We'll have you looking very dapper once again, and then we'll think of a song to celebrate your new outfit.'

As Tangle began undressing and re-dressing the scarecrow, which now seemed utterly embarrassed and kept emitting hoots of worry, Tig came up with her name.

'Tangle, I have arrived at a name for our friend here. Can I check it with you first, to see if you agree?'

Tangle had also brushed his hair of very fine, very long golden straw away from his face and was busy fashioning a tie from a red spotted scarf as her sister spoke. Tangle stood up and held a brief meeting with Tig away from their new friend.

Afterwards, Tig approached the scarecrow with Tangle following closely behind, smiling. The scarecrow felt obliged to stand up.

'It is our pleasure,' said Tig, proudly, 'to announce that from now on your full name, as given to you by two of those that created you, on the event of what would near enough be your first birthday, shall be: Paequat of the Golden Fields!'

'We'll just call you Paequat, though,' added Tangle from behind her sister's shoulder.

'It means "Child of Four",' explained Tig, still smiling.

The tall scarecrow looked down blankly at them, then down still further at his trousers, one leg of which was hanging off empty, and pulled them all the way on. He then stood up and repeated the word. It sounded like "Pecat".

'We can go and take you to see your other makers this morning, if you like?' suggested Tangle.

Paequat walked forwards, held out his arms to the girls and stared at them with his vacant sockets.

'Not safe,' he said.

But Tangle didn't see the harm in visiting the boys.

They reached so far before Paequat would not go any further. Although Tangle could see no one else from where all three of them now crouched, Paequat repeated his warning. So they settled down in the long yellow grass that defined the end of Behvyn and Behleth's back garden with the Gardener's west field and waited.

They had approached the house away from the road because Paequat had told them that there were still "bad people" inside, and even though Tangle's imagination thrilled to the idea that she could go walking through the middle of the village next to a live scarecrow, she saw the wisdom of some degree of secrecy if there really were villains in town. Although she couldn't take the risk seriously herself, she pretended to be concerned so that she didn't hurt Paequat's feelings. Tig, she could see, was enlivened by the opportunity to be justifiably concerned at something definite, spending so much of her time, in her opinion, concerned by fatuous ennui, such as what other people might think of something should a certain possible event ever come to pass.

The grass hid them, but the longer they stayed there even Tangle felt the sense of danger grow, and she felt more exposed. She was not sure why this was. They had seen no movement inside the house. It was now past midday and she was getting impatient. However, she tried to cover it up by asking Paequat more about what he had seen the night before.

'It was dark,' he began. 'Then came small lights, carried by men wearing black, like the night; faces covered so Paequat not see them. Then Paequat hear noises like breaking and afterwards see men come out. Two men carried over shoulders. The men then went away with them, but they did not struggle, the ones over the shoulders. They were still. Like they were Paequat, before Paequat was awake.'

Tig stifled a sob. Paequat looked alarmed.

'No, it's not you Paequat,' said Tangle, putting an arm around her sister. 'Tig is worried about the ones you saw, held over those men's shoulders. About Behvyn and Behleth, who live here. They are our friends, and they made you as well. They are your other makers I wanted to show you. They are our friends, and we're worried about them.'

'Why people take them?'

'We need to find out, Paequat,' said Tangle. 'We will, though. Now, can you help us again?'

'Paequat helps,' said the scarecrow.

'Did you see which way they went?' asked Tig.

'They went to Paequat.'

'They walked up to you?'

'Yes.'

'Were they the ones who, who cut you?' asked Tangle, her face full of concern.

'Yes,' Paequat shivered, his seeds rattling again.

'I'm sorry, Paequat,' said Tig, and patted his arm.

'Paequat better now,' he said.

'Did they have the boys with them as they went past you?' asked Tangle. Paequat nodded, and then pointed towards the river.

'They went east with them!' said Tangle.

'That's where we're going, then,' said Tig, determinedly, beginning to get up.

'No, stay down!' hissed Tangle, a pang of fear striking through her.

But it was too late. There was movement inside the house at last.

As fast as a battle charge, three men in black cloaks with black hoods covering their faces came out from the back door of the twin's house and ran straight towards the spot where the three of them lay, swords drawn in the bright sunshine. They were on top of the girls before they had chance to react. One attacker jumped on Tangle where she lay and another caught up with Tig who had belatedly thought to run, but didn't want to leave her sister. The third strode up to Paequat, who had remained still, and unblinkingly ran his sword through him. He then looked back down as though in brief recognition.

'We have them, sir,' said the one bringing Tig back to the group.

'Good, it's as the Captain predicted,' said the one who had stabbed Paequat. 'We'll be able to meet with the others before mid-week.' The man looked at the two girls as though they were nothing. 'Let's gag the prisoners and be on our way.'

'But why?' shouted Tangle in a flush of frustrated anger.

'Insurance, to make sure your friends don't misbehave,' replied the one holding her, before forcing her back to the ground and taking out a long handkerchief. As the other guard holding Tig did the same, the leader casually wandered over to the scarecrow and took aim with his sword to chop off his head. 'I could've sworn I saw this thing last night in the field over there,' he said. He placed his foot on Paequat's prone chest and swung his sword back.

As he did so, however, Paequat brought his arms up to grab a hold of the foot stood upon him. He then thrust his arms above his head and in so doing the returning sword stroke cleaved off the soldier's own leg. In a shower of crimson and with a cry of shock, the man fell to the floor, dropping the sword and clinging onto the gory stump of his abbreviated limb. In one fast movement, Paequat grasped the sword, rose up and spun around. Caught off guard, and transfixed by the blood-spattered scarecrow, the two men holding Tig and Tangle failed to react. In the same instant Paequat had beheaded one, freeing Tangle. The other man holding Tig then took the extra moment to move up from his hostage and attack the man of straw.

The scarecrow and the man met in a high parry that blew Paequat, much the lighter of the two, back into the springy swales of deep yellow grass. His sword flew from his hand as he landed and the man approached quickly. Once on top of Paequat, he hewed off the scarecrow's left leg and sent straw sailing into the air. Then he hewed off the right leg. Paequat looked upon his own ruination silently as the man held both legs up as trophies and then tossed them aside. Paequat didn't move.

Tangle was still stunned by the death of the man that had been holding her and the way Paequat had so coldly killed him. The man who had defeated Paequat then completed his accomplice's task of gagging Tangle and then went over to Tig, who had still not moved from where she stood.

But it was his undoing, for Paequat was not nearly so much as wounded: only enraged. He reached up slowly to his legs and sunk them back into his being silently, all the while hidden by the tall grass. Again, all life returned to the straw and he was whole again. He rolled for the sword and, coming to a stand in one fluid motion, caught the man off his guard. With one tall drive, he skewered his foe even as the man slavered in his attempts to gag Tig, and the dead man fell away ashen faced and frozen, a sword buried down through his shoulder into his heart. Tig had not been looking and did not see his life extinguish. Paequat saved her the sight and rolled the man onto his front before removing his sword and rousing her. Tangle came up gently to her sister, as Paequat returned to the mutilated captain, his face white, his lips blue from the loss of his leg, his mind spinning toothlessly, aimlessly with images of the slaughter of his guards and the nearness of his own inevitable death. He was nearly out of blood and almost asleep from the pain.

Paequat stood over him and drew his dripping sword down the man's body. 'Where to?' Paequat asked steadily of him.

With his last breath, Tangle saw the captain speak a single word to the straw man, and she watched as his eyes turned to glass as he slipped away from this world.

Paequat picked up the three dead bodies and piled them together along with the leader's leg and the other guard's severed head. As he did so, the blood that covered his clothes and skin grew dark and rusty brown. The sight of the bodies cowed Tig. She had seen the purposeful slaughter of livestock before, and had comforted herself that their deaths, although unpleasant, had been for a purpose. But she had little comfort in these deaths, and was now very concerned about Paequat's capacity for violence.

Paequat paced back and forth, collecting up swords as Tig and Tangle spoke.

'He doesn't mean us any harm,' said Tangle.

'I can see that, but he certainly did mean harm to those others and now look at them,' responded Tig.

They watched him amusing himself by picking off the boots of one of the carcasses and trying them on for size.

'He seems very innocent, like a child,' added Tangle. 'He doesn't know what's right and wrong. We could teach him, though.'

'We could try, but he's dangerous!' said Tig.

'Not to us, though!' Tangle cried. 'He wouldn't hurt one of us. We're his mothers, and he's our child. He's just saved us from three attackers. If it wasn't for him, we'd be kidnapped by now! We don't have a scratch on us, and they're all dead! Maybe he didn't have to kill them all, but maybe he did. Who is the innocent one here, I'm not sure. But knowing there are people like that out there that took Behvyn and Behleth, we need someone like Paequat. We need him, Tig! We couldn't take on people like that ourselves, and we have to see if we can help the twins, don't we?'

'Of course we do, but Tangle, I don't know. For instance, we might have made Paequat, but I don't remember putting life into him. I mean, it's just a creation, something we made. How did he, I mean; he's walking around for goodness' sake!' They both looked over at him, in the process of tying up the laces of his new boots, with little success. 'He doesn't have a brain and he speaks and moves. What happened?'

'What does that matter? Paequat is ours, Tig; we can't disown him. And now he can help us save our friends.'

'Who did this to him, though?'

'I don't know, maybe he can tell us. But do you think we have all day to sit around? There are three dead bodies over there. If nothing else, we have to get out of here quickly.'

At that, Tig nodded in agreement.

'Paequat?' said Tangle.

He walked over awkwardly to the girls and reached down. They let him pull them up to their feet.

'Paequat, where were they going to take us? Did you find out?' asked Tangle.

'Man say: "Netheign",' answered Paequat.

'He must mean the Fords of Netheign,' said Tig.

'They're some way from here! I've only ever been there once,' recalled Tangle, tying Paequat's shoelaces for him. 'Thinking about it, though, it's an obvious place to meet. There's nothing for leagues in any direction. It's in the middle of nowhere.'

'How long a journey would it be, do you think?' asked Tig.

'I went there once with father, when we were much younger. It took us two days in the carriage, going along the roads. It was a few years ago, back when it wasn't a cruelty to raise Glambard above a trot. But if we don't want to risk running into any more of these men, I would estimate a week on foot, walking cross-country away from the road, with few stops along the way.'

'Then let's get prepared. I don't want to waste any more time.'

Tangle was itching to set out. 'We can take food and preparations from here,' she said, gazing through the overgrown grass to Behvyn and Behleth's house. 'They won't mind.'

'What about Grodel?' asked Tig. 'He knows we're going off to the lake for a week, but if he finds these bodies and we're gone for longer, what will he do then?'

'Oh, don't be silly,' answered Tangle. 'He'll not be surprised if we were to go off again.'

They made their way cautiously into Behvyn and Behleth's house and gasped at the state it was in. It wasn't that everything had been gone through, but that it had all been destroyed as well. It was as though, in looking for something and in not finding it, the invaders had used it as justification for wreaking a thorough havoc on anything that had the temerity to present itself to view. Pictures had been torn into small pieces, every single article of crockery was smashed, glasses were crushed into fragments, each joint of furniture disconnected, draws ripped into component parts, tables cracked and splintered. Chair seats were sliced open and the horsehair strewn as entrails over their own snapped backs, plants had been torn into shreds and the compost trodden into the floorboards and tiles. In fact, the only things at first sight to look undamaged were the still-drawn curtains and shutters that had facilitated everything to have been so utterly masticated in secret.

And then they all saw it. The only article in the place left by Behvyn and Behleth's mother, her tapestry, had been torn into four pieces and was now in place as wicks stopping the tops of four glass bottles, each filled with lamp oil. Perhaps their arrival had averted the ultimate desecration in the burning of the boys' home, but Tig and Tangle could not imagine, gorged as their eyes were on the total destruction of their friend's belongings, how it could have possibly been worse had it all gone up in flames.

'Oh, Tig! It's horrible!' said Tangle finally, and started to cry.

Tig said nothing, but went over to the bottles and removed the pieces of tapestry. She placed them in a wrap of chair fabric and put them in her pocket.

They went through to the pantry as far as they could reach among the detritus to search for any food that was untouched. Among the ruined eggs and cheese gone to spoil they were surprised to find a supply in a low cupboard that had gone unnoticed and salvaged what they could. Miraculously, there were fragrant seeded breads and sweet firm cakes, dried cured meat and hardy fruit. They wrapped the provisions in waxed paper and placed it in a sturdy canvas bag that Paequat found underneath an upturned coat stand that had itself been snapped in two.

Tangle decided she couldn't leave without having a last look around the rest of the house.

'Perhaps, if we do find them, we could give them something brought from home to cheer them up,' she said to her sister.

They went through to the simple bedroom that led off a short corridor from the main room. It was low-ceilinged but large and contained two thin beds wrapped in white sheets and a table upon which were folded the brother's clothes. Then, over by the window, they saw two sights that struck fear into them. The first was the phrase: "Murderers must pay!" that had been scorched into the wall with a lit candle. It had left thick brown stains that smelled of burned paint.

The second was the sight of Kjerros and Feran struggling in the far corner, bound, gagged and beaten.

'We just came to visit the twins this morning,' said Kjerros through cracked lips, now released and sitting on the bed closest to the window. Tangle had made a specific point of keeping Paequat outside the room to avoid any further shock for the time being. 'We knocked on the door, waited a moment and then went round the back.'

'Then these two huge guys jumped on us and clubbed us in the guts,' added Feran with injured gusto, enjoying the attention from Tangle. The moment she had seen him, she had dashed to get water and a cloth. Once she had cleaned a nasty cut he had above his brow, she focused on cooling a bruise that was swelling over the joint of his jaw and left cheekbone. She didn't like the way he took such an obvious pride in surviving what to her sounded like a simple beating, especially in the light of what she had just witnessed from Paequat. But she turned it inside her mind into relief and pushed any negative thoughts away.

'We tried to get up and fight, but there were loads of them,' continued Kjerros, encouraged by Tig, who seemed similarly keen to assist in his comfort, but didn't know what precisely to do. She ended up sitting next to him and settled her features into a look of astonished concern. 'In no time, they'd tied our hands together and thrown us in here. They didn't gag us at first, though. They kept asking us questions, although they never let us see their faces.'

'What did they ask you?' said Tig, as though on tenterhooks.

'They wanted to know the strangest of things,' answered Kjerros. 'We couldn't understand it. They kept asking if we knew about 'the beams'. They kept going on and on asking about the beams. We were so confused by it. I kept saying I didn't know what they meant, but it made them angry. They shouted at us then. Shouted us to tell them about 'the beams', but we just had no idea; it was almost funny. I nearly laughed, but then they beat us for ages. And they kept saying the people who lived here were murderers.'

'They wouldn't stop with that,' added Feran. 'They said we were friends with murderers, that Behvyn and Behleth had killed someone very important, like a woman or, or a lady.'

'Yeah, that they had killed this lady,' added Kjerros. 'They seemed so sure of it. They told us that they had already caught them both and that they were going to kill them anyway, but that they couldn't until their old Captain was got out of the way or something. But that they were as good as dead already and therefore that we should tell them if they had left anything of the lady's here.'

'What did you say?' asked Tangle, removing her hand from Feran's face and looking straight into his eyes.

'We said they weren't murderers and that they had the wrong

people,' said Feran. 'They were so insistent, though. We kept saying they were wrong, and each time they hit us and they told us we were wrong. They just kept on saying they had them and that they had confessed. It was only a matter of time and there was nothing we could do to rescue them.'

'They just didn't want to hear the truth,' said Kjerros.

'What if it wasn't the truth?'

At this, everyone stopped and looked at Tig.

'What on earth do you mean by that?' charged Tangle, hotly.

'I mean, what if they did kill this lady,' said Tig, unblinking.

'How can you even think such a thing?' accused Kjerros. 'We've just been tortured by a load of maniacs and not once did either of us ever think they were right.'

'I can't believe what you said, Tig,' added Feran.

'Just think for a moment,' said Tig. 'Bear with me. I'm saying that it seems that over the past few days the unthinkable has started to become possible. I don't suspect Behvyn or Behleth in the least of doing anything wrong. Of course not, they're too kind-hearted and courageous. But what if killing someone wasn't wrong? Tangle, what did we just see? Kjerros; Feran: your kidnappers are dead. At least, those that were left this morning. They're lying in the field at the top of the garden, piled one on top of the other.'

The cousins looked at each other, but before they could speak Tig carried on.

'Two nights ago, we all fell asleep suddenly in the middle of our search to get back our dogs, or had you forgotten? I wouldn't be surprised if you had. No one seems to remember, but I tried really hard and can just recall it. We all crumbled to the ground in agony and I don't know why. But we know Behvyn and Behleth had been somewhere else, like they had been awake while we had been asleep. Do you remember?'

'Well, maybe,' said Feran, 'but I still don't believe Behvyn and Behleth could have killed someone, and I also don't believe those men are dead. In fact, I'm more worried that they're going to come straight back in here and capture us all again, you included.'

'Would you like to meet their assassin?' asked Tig firmly. 'Paequat, can you come in here please?'

Paequat walked into the room and looked at Kjerros and Feran, who stared back in wonder at the blood-spattered clothes he wore, and how he carried his appropriated sword by sheathing it straight through his own thigh.

'This is Paequat,' added Tangle, delightedly. 'Paequat, please meet our friends: Kjerros and Feran.'

Paequat leaned down and gave them both a wide, rictus grin.

'Friends,' he said, and held out his hand.

'You'd better shake it, gentlemen,' said Tig. 'You don't want to be his enemy.'

Kjerros and Feran climbed over each other to shake Paequat's hand and stumbled to their feet. There was quite a height discrepancy, for Paequat towered over Kjerros, who was the tallest among the others. The urgency in their handshakes almost knocked Paequat off his feet. Although he was tall they all noticed he was light, even in his newly appropriated boots.

'We may have to weigh you down, Paequat,' giggled Tig.

Paequat smiled again, but then became grim.

'We have to go now. Friends not safe.' He turned to Kjerros and Feran. 'The beams were seen. They show the way. Must follow quickly. Go to the Fords of Netheign. Meet friends, help them.' Paequat paused and then became afraid. 'They are coming,' he said. 'She was lost and now they come.'

'Who, Paequat? Who are coming?' asked Tangle.

'They are coming,' he answered more forcefully, as though he was frustrated he didn't quite know why he knew that little which he did already.

'Who was "She", Paequat? Do you know?' asked Tig.

'She was the one that woke me,' he said, gently. 'She spoke to me. I became and then she spoke again. She said the things I know and the things I will know.'

'When was this, Master Paequat?' asked Feran, deferentially.

'Two darks ago.'

'Do we know where this "She" is?' asked Kjerros. 'Perhaps if we look for her instead of Behvyn and Behleth, we could resolve this quicker; you know, get those people or whoever they are that are coming here to turn around and go back without causing any trouble. And maybe we can get to the end of where these "beams" point to and use what's there in no time.'

'She's dead now,' Paequat said simply.

'Dead? Oh, we are sorry Paequat, so sorry,' said Tig. She went over to Paequat and gave him a big hug and smoothed down his crumpled jacket. Paequat sighed.

'She tell me she be killed,' the straw man said.

'What was her name, Paequat?' asked Feran.

'Alcabell,' he answered. 'She said she was Alcabell. She says she will be killed. She told me she knew twins would kill her.'

At that they all looked at each other, startled. But they were not given any time for it to sink in for Paequat was now urging them to leave. 'Must go now,' he kept saying, as Feran assessed the food rations with Tangle and then limped determinedly into the ruined pantry to double them with the declaration: 'We're going to need more than just a snack!'

'What will they think once we're gone?' asked Tig, as they closed the door and began their walk up to the top of the garden.

'When they find the inside here ripped to pieces and the three dead soldiers in the back garden, they'll think the worst,' answered Tangle. 'But we have more important things to think about now. We have to try to save Behvyn and Behleth.' She looked around. 'Where's he gone now?' she asked, annoyed, looking for Feran.

'Wait up!' Feran cried, emerging through the brambles from the yard next door, in his hand a posy of small blooms, which he presented graciously to Tangle, calling her his 'beautiful nurse-maid'.

'You are a soppy sod,' replied Tangle. She looked around at them all. 'And so it is, with bags loaded with food, and what looks like just about every other serviceable possession of the twins,' she added, raising an eyebrow to Kjerros, himself weighed down by four bags, 'that we begin our break in the countryside. Not in the way that we would have thought!'

The others flashed brief smiles, but they faded quickly like drawings in soup. Their plan to race off into the countryside and get out of their heads had been the plotting of idle children. But now Tangle saw they were racing out of the village with another, more vital, role to play. With two acts of kidnap and four deaths already, she knew their plan was ill conceived, perhaps even more

79

foolish than their earlier idea, but she welcomed the purpose it gave to her. She could think of none higher than that of saving her friends, and she determined to bend all of her being into doing so, with the will of a mother searching for her lost children.

Chapter 5

THE HOARD OF THE VULTURE KING

The first explosion took out the prow of the sail barge and spread fires among the sails and the rigging. As it did so, it brought Behleth flying backward onto the deck from where he stood at the stern and the sudden rush of water into the hull forced the prow down and into the river. Debris flew in every direction and Behvyn and Rumé stood no chance to avoid it. By luck, Rumé was not hit, although his cloak caught on fire and had to be removed, but Behvyn was knocked into the water.

The stern of the barge then reared up out of the water, before the hull snapped in half from the pressure built up by the invading torrents. This caused the stern to crash back down onto the river once more and for the craft to re-balance, but Rumé saw it would be sucked down in no time. As Behvyn slowly made his way back to their small boat, in pain and confused by it, he watched Rumé dive into the water and swim to the remains of the barge to find Behleth, whom he saw surrounded by flaming canvas and clinging to the mainmast.

'Behleth, come to me!' Behvyn heard Rumé say through ringing ears, and saw him hold his hand to his face to ward off the heat from the flames once topside. 'It's going down and there will be more explosive inside the cabin. The fires are around it. You must come with me. Your brother needs you.'

However, Behvyn could see Behleth was utterly frightened and clung to the mast like a lifeline.

'Master Hahn, you must come with me, it is not safe!' said Rumé again, but he could see Behleth was not going to move willingly.

Then Rumé stepped into the flames that separated them and unpicked Behleth's hands from the mast to transfer them to his own neck, so that he could carry him across his back, back through the flames and into the water again.

Back in the boat, Behvyn realised the cause of much of his pain; a bolt of wood from the deck had torn its way into his left forearm; but all he could do was watch Rumé with his brother coming towards him. Light-headedly, he propelled the small boat over towards them, one-handed.

Rumé from below and Behvyn from within were together able to bundle Behleth into the boat, and then Rumé took up the oars. They had put a little distance between them and the barge as a second explosion obliterated its remains. The fires had reached whatever it was in the cabin Rumé knew of before the water from beneath had wetted it. Although all three were now further away than when the first detonation occurred, the force of the blast drew great waves over the edge of the little boat. Rumé was forced immediately to look for land on the eastern side of the river, lest they all sank beneath the hungry currents of the Highborn.

The cold light of a new day crested the mountains in the east and swam down into the North Vale, borne on a sweetly chilled wind that drew off the damp of the pre-dawn and rippled the spider webs that hung heavy with dew among the scrawny shrubs. Behvyn tried to put a brave face on things as Rumé pressed the dressing hard onto his wounded forearm, but he was woozy from the pain and loss of blood, and couldn't help but wince in front of his brother. Although he didn't hold Behleth one part responsible, he saw that he blamed himself for what had happened. The thought of it cut him deeper than any flaming shard of wood could possibly have done. This made Behvyn doubly angry at Fetlock, the man who had left them all to die. Another knot was tied tightly and the arm placed in a sling. Rumé indicated that he had finished. Now back on dry land, on the eastern side of the Highborn, Behvyn saw that Rumé was keen to be off.

'I can go on if need be, Rumé. But to where?' Behvyn asked.

Rumé smiled. 'I believe you could, young Master Hahn. But we shall not move yet, though it's still dawn. That injury of yours needs rest to heal all the quicker and I can hurry it along still further if I find the right treatments. Stay here. I will not be gone long.'

With that, Rumé was away, the white falcon on his shoulder, moving off into the dank rich green thickets of hawthorn and wild cherry, his shoulders accosted by the drape of wide-splayed sycamore leaves bearing their seeds like twin resting dragonfly. Left together alone for the first time in what seemed like an age, sharing with the birds the dewberries that swarmed upon the brambles around them, the brothers waited until Rumé was out of earshot before talking.

'Quick!' said Behleth.

'What?' replied Behvyn.

'Let's go! Before he comes back!' Behleth had already gone on several paces before he realised his brother wasn't going anywhere. 'What's wrong? Come on!'

'I'm not leaving him,' said Behvyn.

'Are you mad?' cried Behleth. 'He'll be back any moment; now's our best chance!'

'To do what? Go home?'

'Of course! Now, will you come on? Hurry!'

'We're wanted men, Behleth.'

'We're dead men, so we're in the clear!'

'Oh come ON, Behleth! Use your head. Yes, we did well to survive the explosion, but it's hardly a reliable way of killing someone, is it? It was a getaway, so Fetlock could get ahead of us for some reason. But they'll have our house staked out, our friends watched and everyone looking for us, just in case we survived.'

'How would you know?'

'Rumé told me that would be their procedure.'

'Rumé told you. And you trust him?' asked Behleth.

'No,' replied Behvyn. 'Not completely. But we are alive.' He looked down to his arm. 'He also mentioned to me that they normally would have set many traps before departing but that only one went off. You must have stopped several of them. If you hadn't, who knows what else could have happened.'

'I couldn't get to them all, though,' responded Behleth, quickly flushed with remorse. 'I tried, I really tried, but I couldn't get to the last one in time!'

'You did fine, Behleth,' assured his brother. 'We're both here. That's all that matters. We're fine. It's all right now.'

'We're not on our own though, are we? I mean, who is he, that Rumé fellow? Isn't he the one that had us kidnapped and tied up? How are we going to get away from him as well? And he doesn't even seem blind anymore!'

'I know I can't back it up with much proof, Behleth, but I think he's a lot different to the others. He told me a few things as we went to the Blackstone, things I sensed he'd not told another soul. He needs to trust us, Behleth, for some reason. We were captured because we were suspects, but Rumé explained why he knew, once he had seen us both, we hadn't done anything wrong. Only that other one, Fetlock, was the one that couldn't see it and plotted not just to kill us but also Rumé as well. The trap was left for us all; he wanted us all dead, including his Captain. And as for Rumé's sight, well, it's the Lady's necklace and the white falcon, Behleth! They connect when you wear the necklace so you can see through the eyes of the bird. I only found out because I put the necklace on in desperation. The next thing I knew, I was looking down on myself from the sky. It was the strangest and most wonderful sensation, like I was as light as a wish. It was the only way I was able to reach the Blackstone and complete the task. Once I was hit in the arm, though, and Rumé needed to save you, I had to give the necklace to him.'

This partially satisfied Behleth, who kept his peace as Behvyn looked over to the Highborn and followed the course of the barge's last remains southward, until all detritus had disappeared from view. The sun rose higher and the morning came and went. Behleth put his cloak down and let the warmth fill him after his trials in the river, and Behvyn absorbed the heat onto his aching shoulders. They seemed stretched after such an amount of heaving and rowing the previous night.

'Then we'll wait for him,' said Behleth.

As they lounged about with fading cares they began to doze and fell into an exhausted sleep, even as Rumé returned carrying pockets full of roots.

He saw the brothers lying there and chose to sit apart from them. He sought rest but little would come to him.

As the sun began to wester behind the range of the Uspheron and to swathe the land in deep oranges and purples, the twins woke almost together. The warmth had bled from the air and insects frothed in tall clouds within the remaining rays of light. Rumé was preparing a meal that smelled wholesome. Behvyn's good hand went to his chest to feel if the discus was still there. It was. His other hand and arm now pained him only if he tried to move them from within the sling, and as he had slept, the bloody mark had stopped growing beneath his bandage. Behleth confirmed everything he had was still there with a nod to his brother, although the suggestion was that the blind captain wouldn't win his trust by failing to pickpocket him as he slept. Behvyn reminded his brother that Rumé had rescued him from the sail barge, but Behleth still blamed Rumé for putting them all at risk in the first place.

After a cursory wash in the river they both went over to Rumé, where he dished them out hot portions of lotty. Then he removed the canister he had hung above the small cooking fire and replaced it with a kettle of sorts.

'I thought everything was lost when the barge went down!' exclaimed Behleth.

'Yes, much was lost. But some things float.' He pointed to a wooden barrel braced by iron hoops. Now broken open and lain on its side, they could see it was full of food, military issue uniforms, boots, weapons and torches and carried the crest of the King upon the side. Rumé tapped on the lid of a small metal canister, one of many spilled from the barrel. 'These are Kings' Guard rations, packed in Cambwall and unopened until now. Whilst you two dozed the day away I searched the banks and now we have enough to keep us going for the next two weeks, with care.'

'To what end, Captain Rumé?' asked Behleth, pointedly. 'If we are no longer captives of yours, why should we accompany you?'

'Although I know you are innocent of the crime you stand accused of,' replied Rumé, 'you are both unable to prove it yet. But all of us have an advantage. Fetlock guesses us to be dead, and if not he knows me to be blind at the very least. In addition, he is wrong to assume you two are guilty of the murder of the Lady. Therefore, we will not chase down that dead end ourselves. We owe it to the Immortals to find the Lady's truthful killer.

'So, we must prove your innocence, and to do that we must find the guilty, or your pursuers will never stop. She was a Great One, was the Lady, and my heart mourns for her heavily. But more than that, we must complete what she travelled for an age to do. You do not, I guess, know too much about the Undying Ones and their history here.' Behvyn and Behleth looked at Rumé with a new sense of interest. 'Aye, this used to be their home, Master Behvyn. But maybe you know something of where they are said to be now. Only then can you begin to imagine how large a need would have to exist to draw one back here. The last time it happened the land was rent and the seas were delved such that the world was re-shaped anew. They have a beauty and love of things, but terrible power as well. If the Lady's work is not finished it may sow the seed of destruction for this world. I fear it would be so if we do nothing to stay it.'

'Well, that is a pretty story, Rumé, and quite beyond the point,' said Behleth. 'Let's go, Behvyn. If all we receive in response to questions is riddles, we're better off on our own.'

They both got up and started to walk off.

'Wait!' said Rumé, and stopped the boys in their tracks. 'Here.' He held out the necklace to Behleth.

'Put this on, young master.'

Behleth did so reluctantly. Then his face changed.

'I-I am passing over the river!' said Behleth.

Behvyn looked out and saw the falcon skimming low over the Highborn, heading off in the direction of Muscle Oaks.

'You see through the falcon,' said Rumé.

'It is the North Wall. Now it is Long Knoll, but from high. And I can see the Kingsway wind for miles. There! There are the Oaks already! She flies so fast! The lights are on in the square. Now we're going to our house, Behvyn. I can see it!'

'What do you see?' asked Rumé, with considerable interest.

'It cannot be! No! There are guards outside it, dressed in black. They are fending off the villagers who carry torches! It looks like they want to burn down our house! That's Middleton, and Fallwater and the Springthorns! They're shouting at them to let them do it. Now where? We're moving around to the back. It's our garden. There's a load of rubbish piled up at the top end of it, like, like…no!'

'What is it, Behleth?' asked Behvyn.

'Dead bodies. They're dead.' With that he took off the necklace and placed it back into Rumé's grasp.

'More guardsmen, but attacked and killed,' replied Rumé, after having placed the necklace over his own head once again. 'This is strange.'

'Our place is under attack, Behvyn. The villagers have been turned against us.' He sank to the ground and looked at Rumé, whose milky white eyes glowed eerily in the dusk. 'You were right, Rumé. Behvyn, we can't go back.'

It was a terrible moment for Behvyn and his brother. Until that point, Behvyn had been able to make a choice in what he believed, but now he felt trapped. Taken by circumstances away from his home and now, it seemed, permanently so. He wasn't alone, but suddenly his whole world diminished into what they had about them there and then, and his reliance on Rumé, once based on a matter of trust, would now have to be based on need.

'Did you see Tig or anyone else?' Behvyn asked his brother.

'What? No. No, they weren't there.'

'What do you think, Behvyn?' asked Rumé, as the falcon returned to his side.

'I think that if we have no option but to play a role in this, then we'd better eat this first.'

'There speaks a practical man,' responded Rumé, as he poured them a hot drink. They ate for a long while in silence; they were hungrier than ever once they broke their fast and went through two servings, the second gone cold, to sate it.

After they had eaten, the boys lay down again, but Rumé looked focused. The falcon rose into the air and held itself low over the river.

'He must be looking at the falcon, from the reflection in the water,' nudged Behleth.

'With my mistake at the Mirrorhorn yesterday,' said Rumé, 'I had resigned myself to the fact I would never see again, but only a short time afterward the most unlikely of chances has restored it.'

'Rumé, you spoke earlier as though you knew the Lady. Was it so?' asked Behvyn.

'Know her? Yes, in a way,' replied Rumé, the falcon returning to his side. 'I feel I knew her, through tales and poems and such learning as I have gained. Her name was "Alcabell" and I cannot guess why she came back. But it intrigues me greatly, and not without much concern. Before, in the times when the Great Ones and men lived together, before the Sundering at the dawn of our memory as a people, there was division among them that threatened our existence. Alcabell brought peace where none was seen to be possible; she was our saviour. You will have heard of her, Behleth?'

'It is the name of our brightest star.'

'Yes. Not only did she save all men from their doom, but she united her own kind, too. You maybe begin to see some of the size of things now, although I do not claim to grasp it fully yet. There is a depth to this that suddenly grows the more I look at it, as though I was walking on rock only for the ground to melt away with the next step.'

'You have answered our questions so far, Captain, but there is at least one more I would know the answer to,' said Behleth.

'If I answer it, may I ask your brother a question of my own?' said Rumé, flicking a glance at Behvyn.

'That seems fair,' replied Behleth. 'So, what is Fetlock's story? What is he up to, and why did he hate you so much?'

'Well now,' laughed Rumé openly, 'that is three questions or I am a fool! I will answer the first question only, Behleth, but if I were to answer them all we would be here until tomorrow. You will then be able to guess the answer to your last question from it, but what he is up to, I must yet learn.' He smiled at Behleth, who smiled back for the first time, but still with an eager look in his eye.

'He is my sworn enemy now,' said Behleth. 'I want to know all I can of him.'

'Very well, we shall settle down for the evening and you will hear his tale,' Rumé began.

'Fetlock grew up in the South Vale near to Cambwall as a child. It is where I was born as well. I can recall fondly the chatter and play of sea gulls and I miss them when inland as we are now. I liked the way they monitored the skies in armies and I count them still among the augers of my own safety. They would only calm and disperse when a truly violent storm was coming so that I had enough warning to stop what I was doing and get inside before it hit. The weather can be deadly along the coastline. But though Fetlock lived by the sea as well, it is said he would not venture as his friends did onto its iron-grey waves in their fishing vessels or as later in their military berths. Rather he found all the enjoyment he wanted in the pure air at its shores and the discreet coves and hollows it had fashioned in the cliff-face over the course of thousands of years.

'The coastline of the South Vale is notorious because there's only one safe passage inland along its entire stretch, and the Governor of Cambwall taxes it heavily. Any ship making port in Cambwall has to pay a keen percentage of profits from its trade, but the taxes are set with some cunning so that it is never enough to deter sea-fairing entrepreneurs and company tradesmen alike. In such a way, businessmen are able to find rich profit despite this, and Cambwall has grown in culture and society a great degree since I have known it. The taxes are enough, however, to discourage poor fishermen, pirates, privateers and corsairs from coming into Cambwall, heavily defended as it is and expensive to attempt to attack. Almost everyone has paid with his or her lives that have tried. Public crowds momentarily congratulate anyone that survives to land before they are summarily executed for their enjoyment.

'Those that have no choice but to attempt a landing elsewhere chance their luck against the towering rocks and high overhanging cliffs that are pounded incessantly by tall waves. These can either bear a broken vessel up with their foaming fingers to a perilous perch atop a sharp, slimy outcrop that is showered by salty rains, or just as easily smother a crew and its cargo to the depths of their doom in a wide unthinking fury. And it all happens in a cacophony that thunders on relentlessly, as each bank of water hits land and breaks reluctantly to diminish into spray and reform once again. Wiser men quail at the sight and yet they are foreboded of it by the tremor of its great squalls even before they sight land. Their need drives them and their fortunes are gifted to the mercurial judgement of those waves that men justly call the wreckers.

'It was along there, along the coastline, that Fetlock spent his early days, spying on the seas and waiting for those that chose the wrong path, the path of the desperate. And he would wait for them, watching as they ran into danger, seeing the ruin of another ship below, and then, when there were no survivors, hunting through the flotsam and jetsam that found its way ashore. Much did he retrieve from the hands of the wreckers, and so it became his income. He came to know each crag and cave and how they linked, above and below sea level. He stored his bounty here and the only remuneration he gave in return to those that had unwittingly delivered it unto him was that whatever he couldn't use as wealth or entertainment was cast back into their living grave.'

'He grew up in a cave? That's pathetic,' interjected Behleth.

'He spent more and more time there,' continued Rumé, 'able to live off his findings instead of spending time at home with his family. They were never told of his secret hoard and did not know where he spent his time. They would send out for Fetlock and searches would never glimpse him, so capable was he in hiding and confusing by rumour. No one ever guessed where he went and soon his family tired of his deviousness. They seldom saw him, but knew he wanted them not, and so they became disaffected until they came to disown him. No more would he be admitted to his father's home, the fine abode of a well-respected aide to the Governor. His formal education, always poorly attended, became forgotten, and his friends lost their own curiosity for his whereabouts. This curiosity he replaced with mistrust so that they stopped looking for him and instead felt distaste if they ever caught a brief sight of him in Cambwall.

'Fetlock, it seems, had no qualms about what he was becoming. He saw old friends flinch if he looked at them directly and felt a growing power each time busy streets parted in studied ignorance of his presence. As he grew more maligned he grew more content and with it more wealthy. So much did he collect as the rocks continued to take their toll by his stretch of the coastline that it almost matched the income of the Cambwall quayside masters themselves. However, this did not incline him to share it. Instead, he coveted it jealously.

'On one occasion, when a slim trading vessel had been beached upon a slimy shelf, before the wreckers grew again, a crew member about his own age, and about yours too, Behleth, had managed to struggle to the relative safety of a broad step leading into one of the hundreds of caves. The next moment the ship was gone again, torn into many parts, along with the rest of its crew.

'Unhappily for Fetlock, the very cave in which his fortune was stored was the one in which the young survivor found himself in. After much wandering, the man saw he was wringing out his clothes in a round-ceilinged trove that held more than ten bound crates brimming with jewels and gold. But that was not all. There were also innumerable barrels of the finest wines and spirits and packets of fine spices and fragrant powders. Along one curving wall, hidden behind columns of rock, were collections of animal skins and plates of hard timbers, smooth to the touch and polished as mirrors. There were clothes, shoes of all kinds, weapons of recent fashion, ornaments of personal value and tapestries in rich decorative colours that the young man had never seen the likes of before. It was as though all the riches due to decorate the finest homes in Cambwall were dammed up in once place. It was all presented about the edges of the main floor of the cave for stuffed animals and rare birds in gilt cages encircled the haunting centre-piece.

'This was a throne of curious design, hewn from the trunk of some goliath tree and fashioned as a hand, with gnarled fingers forming the back and the palm being the seat. The web between thumb and first finger was formed to provide an arm for resting on and the whole was a deep fibrous orange-brown that took the light that shafted down from one solitary source high above and refracted it internally in ripples of amber and burnt carmine.

'"I see you have found your way into my home," said Fetlock, stood behind the chair, to the man, who was taller than he, even though Fetlock probably guessed he was a year or two younger than him. Surprised but unworried, the young man turned to look at Fetlock, who was walking slowly around him, so that the man had to keep turning on the spot to keep track of him. "Yes, I suppose so. I'm Rothé, from the crew of the *April*. It has just been sunk off these shores. We were sorely lost by the gale that has swept us up the shore. I am afraid I am its only survivor. I've just lost everything. Could you help me?"

'"Lost everything? That's terrible," replied Fetlock. "Let me know what you would have of me and I will see what I can do for you." Fetlock continued to circle. He moved towards his stash of weapons upon the left of the exit to the cave. Fetlock took down from off the wall a light, single edged sword.

'"Perhaps I can give you this," he said, studying its length and balance. "It is a great treasure. The pommel is inset with ivory and silver, and the blade is crafted in triple-forged stithium. It must be worth something to the right buyer. You could take it to market and sell it for lodgings and fresh clothes, if you like."'

Rothé said nothing but smiled as politely as he could as Fetlock approached with the sword pointed at him.

'"It was made by the finest sword smith that ever lived, or so they say," continued Fetlock. "To the stories of Hameld the Forger I give little credence. All that about making the stars and hanging them in the sky seems rather far-fetched, to my mind. But the way he armed the Gods and their kin to fight off the attacks of the Gulkrylith and his hoards from the Outside, well maybe this sword imparts some truth in that child's tale."'

'"I have never known anyone that dared speak of the greatest evils of this world with such lightheartedness," answered Rothé, horrified by the words of Fetlock and now fully aware of his intent. "You see I am unarmed and happy only to have survived a terrible ordeal. I ask for assistance, yet you advance upon me sword in hand, masking your purpose with careless words." He began to circle as well and desperately sought an object to grasp. He seized upon something. "I thank you for your offer, but would not wish to burden myself with your aid," Rothé concluded. "I will leave you to your fool's gold and cause you to suffer my presence no longer in your ill-gotten kingdom!"

'With that, Rothé threw that which he had in his hands at Fetlock. The weighty object turned out to be a heavy bronze candlestick and it made a sickening thump against Fetlock's back as he tried to duck out of the way. As Rothé seized his opportunity to make a dash for the exit, Fetlock flashed his sword wildly but re-gathered himself enough to know he still held the advantage.

'Rothé scrambled through the entranceway and headed down the most familiar corridor to him, but became uncertain where he was headed. He realised that he could not stop and hope to fend off an attack empty-handedly. Therefore, he kept running and tried to put as much distance between himself and his pursuer as he could.

'Yet Fetlock's presence of mind meant that he was able to catch up quickly, for although all paths led back out to the coast, as he had learned from his years of exploration, some took further to reach it than others. In addition, all of them were very dark and Rothé had no firm idea where he was going. Fetlock picked up a torch and took the shortest path to the exit. It was here that he laid his trap.

'Rothé ran still onwards through the tunnels that abutted the shoreline and felt his way through tight twists and squirmed through sections where the walls would suddenly narrow. He skirted around deep pools of water that seeped through the limestone cliffs and around sharp stalactites that leaned up out of the floors. His progress could have been slower but he was strong and each time he fell he rose up again to carry on, losing no time. His dash finally took him to the same cave mouth he had entered in by. With it only a few yards ahead of him he fell still and looked around. There was the opening and through that he knew lay the shallow, slimy platform and then the roar and fizz of the sea. He moved closer until he was stood in the frame of the entrance. As his eyes adjusted to the brightness of the daylight he heard a sound behind him, which made him look around.

'But he was fooled, for Fetlock was already outside the opening. As Rothé turned his back to the outside, Fetlock sprang out from the side and, sword raised to strike in protection of everything he had become and everything he possessed, yelled a cry of deep satisfaction that he had outwitted his prey. "He that dares to come and raid shall fall upon this mythic blade!" he sang with glee.

'But it was too soon. For in a twist of fate that Fetlock must forever curse, it was then that Rothé slipped and fell backwards awkwardly. He held his arms out behind him to stop his fall, but landed straight onto Fetlock. Although the ledge by the opening was wide enough for one, it could not hold two. Abruptly, Fetlock felt his feet drag over the edge and he fell fifty feet to the bottom, flailing helplessly at thin air all the way and cursing as he dropped.

'Rothé looked down and saw Fetlock land into a deep pool of water that saved his life with no injury. He watched as Fetlock struggled out of the pool, still bemoaning his ill fortune, and caught a murderous stare back up to where he was lying. Knowing Fetlock would use the fastest way back up from where he had landed, Rothé looked around and saw the sword that Fetlock had 'offered' him. He took it and climbed away, up the treacherous face of the cliff and found his way to the top. Once there, and without looking back, Rothé ran to complete his escape and so lived to tell the tale of the ill luck of the *April*. But only to one did he tell of his escape from the dark-minded boy that haunted the cliffs as a vulture king.

'Even now, Fetlock knows not why he had befallen to such an ignominious defeat, at the hands of such an inexperienced foe. But he knows who the boy grew into. He saw him progress in Cambwall over the decades. He saw him start his young family and watched his son grow up while Fetlock himself re-entered society. With his own help, Fetlock managed to entwine himself into His Majesty's court, once King Cuiron had been taken ill. From there, he built his support but did not reveal his own ambition. I believe we're the first to begin to learn it here, so secret is he.

'He was included in my detail to spy on me; I know that now, and also that I do not know where he has gone. I can only guess at a question that may help us. So, Behleth, if I have answered your question satisfactorily, may I ask my own?'

'Yes,' said Behleth.

'You don't need to, Rumé,' said Behvyn. 'I know what you'd ask of me. But I give it to you now and will tell you what I saw.'

With that, Behvyn removed the discus he carried from inside his jerkin and gave it to Rumé.

No larger than the span of his hand in diameter, Rumé was awed and held it gently as though it was a new life, not a metal object he had in his hands.

'As I reached for it at the top the Blackstone,' continued Behvyn, 'this gave off six rays that cast their light over to those mountains away there.' Behvyn pointed to the two great peaks on the eastern side of the Valley. They were on the edge of visibility. 'Does this help solve the riddle?'

With the falcon sat on his shoulder, Rumé moved the discus around in the dwindling light and read its faces: first the front with its strange array of golden spots. Then he turned it over and gasped when he saw the writing that lay upon it. As though stung, he flinched and nearly dropped it. He covered it with a cloth and took some moments to recover.

'What is it, Rumé?' asked Behleth, similarly intrigued, seeing the discus for the first time himself. 'It's just writing, isn't it? How is it dangerous?'

'I'm sorry, Behleth, I will not speak of it much here,' replied Rumé, sounding as though a great weight suddenly pressed on his shoulders. 'It is a fearful token, one of six that were believed destroyed or lost many thousands of years ago. The words on the back have a power we should all dread. We must go where Behvyn pointed us, as soon as we can. That reminds me. I must tend to your arm again, Behvyn, before we move on. There were medical stashes in the barrel. It will heal fully in only a few days if I treat it now. And then, by first dawn, we must begin our journey. Fetlock must never possess this disc!'

Behvyn and Behleth were unsettled by Rumé's sudden reaction to the discus but did not ask why. They readied themselves for their early departure the next morning and kept their own council. As they lay down for a last rest before what would be a long march through the day they avoided looking at Rumé's eyes. For although they were milky-white and sightless they had a haunted look about them.

Using the sight of the falcon, Rumé set off at first light and led the twins through an unfamiliar country, moving southeastward out of the North Vale, accompanied by the constant babble of the Highborn at their right.

Never before had Behvyn been on this side of the river and although there was nothing too dissimilar to his own environs to begin with, as is always the way when somewhere new, his senses picked up everything afresh so that even the smallest difference was noticed. As they progressed the day grew cool but the air stayed moist. Broad white clouds neatly clogged the light blue sky, unmoving like benign celestial observers of their progress.

As their lofty vigilance continued and the sun rose, the river parted gently from their course, finally exposing the underlying sounds of the country they moved through; the swish of leaves cycling the bases of the trees; the skeletal clamour of denuded branches roused by a leaden wind; the drunken, belligerent buzz of wasps about the last of the year's fruit. It all fought with the muted sound of his footsteps for attention.

Whereas the upper North Vale behind him was all rock and crag, moss and pine, the lower hills ahead of Behvyn were rich in growth. Rolling folds of open land glimmered emerald green and opened the view to a broad horizon that was framed by the Eruna to the left and the Uspheron to the right. In between lay the vastness of the Shale Valley, stretching onward and downhill, severely so in parts, past sight to the sea; that view blocked by the smudge of distant forests and the trailing limbs of the mountains at the 'waist' of the valley. At this point, where the Uspheron encroached eastwards, the land and the sky described a perfect 'v' shape, so that only a narrow passage existed to the Southern Steppes. Few took it now, but it was a route taken, Behvyn knew, by the Highborn's silver band that coursed ever away from them, past Artua, the second city, and onward still to Cambwall, though he had been to neither. Yet it was not the only river they could see from there. For crossing their path a few days' march away was the first of three rivers that would divide them from their way.

Then Behvyn noticed a curious thing that he long doubted he saw, until he caught his brother staring out in the same way he had. Eventually, he couldn't go any further without asking Rumé about it. It had become something of a habit now that, when they would stop, Behvyn would actively encourage Rumé to tell them about events they had only ever heard in rumour, or ask about things he didn't understand. In turn he was enthralled by the answers they received. Sometimes Rumé denied them, for he was always at once both leading and protecting them, but as often as not he would sate Behvyn's inquisitiveness.

Grodel had not been one to tell them stories as they grew up and such as Behvyn had learned had been gathered from the range of characters he saw in the Poacher's Pocket of an evening, and specifically Kewyn, Kjerros' father. Kewyn would entwine even the most simple of stories into an evening's entertainment, full of jokes and gossip, much to the delight of his son and his friends. Sometimes old Farmer Dogwood would turn up at the Inn looking wild with excitement at some close scrape he had had with a mad animal or stranger that had become lost. But nearly always they turned out to be quite innocent events that spoke only of Muscle Oaks and conveyed to Behvyn no more enlightenment than that.

'Of the Mizzle Mountains, or the "Tothian Range" as it is also called,' replied Rumé, in the indirect manner which Behvyn was now becoming used to, 'which extends down from the Cloud Mount in the very North and along the east of the Valley, you will not be ignorant, as you will have grown up seeing it from afar. It is from its peaks that most of the storms that happen in the North Vale originate. But if you have not travelled so far south before upon this side of the river, you will never have seen the "Eruna", also known as the "Green Mountains", although it may be that you have heard of them?'

'Yes,' said Behvyn, 'I had heard of them, but never believed that what was said was true. And yet, now I see it, I doubt my eyes! But they move! They send their shape out ahead of them into the Valley, and turn all the air green!'

'Do you see the same, Behleth?' asked Rumé, clearly enjoying the others' wonder.

'I don't know if I see it or dream it,' replied Behleth, 'but there's something far ahead that isn't there!'

'Can you answer for it, Behvyn?' asked Rumé.

'I cannot,' he replied. 'It's like the spirit of the mountains sits over the heads of those who live in their shadow.'

'That is true, in its way,' said Rumé. 'Do you see the sky is clear down there? Then you will notice how the sun shines brightly upon the mountainsides. They are clothed in trees that only grow in the soil of the Eruna and will not grow anywhere else. These are called lannian trees and have thick, oily leaves that are dark green in colour. They like the sun, they soak it up and they love the waters inside the Eruna and they drink of them deeply. And in their moment of happiness, when in the full gaze of the sun, they release the oil from their leaves and send it out into the atmosphere around them, where it hangs in the air and seems to turn the sunlight green. It is best not to rest in that area at dusk as I have learned over the years, for any man who does will wake covered by a film of oil! At night it drops from the air like dew and you will smell of the lannian tree for many days afterwards! Come now, we should make to move on.'

The twins found themselves laughing as they collected together their packs and set off once again. As they did so, Behvyn noticed that they had now come far enough to see some detail of the two peaks they approached, though still far distant.

'What of where we travel to, Rumé?' he asked. 'They are not clothed in green. They stand in grey. Are they of the Eruna, too?'

'No!' replied Rumé. 'Mighty Ithed and Antheon are neither Tothian nor Eruna. They would be very offended if you suggested it to them.'

Behleth gave Behvyn a funny look, but let Rumé's odd comment pass.

As they progressed and found a rhythm in the passing of the days, Behvyn's thoughts seemed always to end up back in Muscle Oaks. In the time that had passed following Fetlock's attack their diversions had been few. But, like the drip of blood through gauze, the wound of their sudden separation from home had caused a lake of concern to pool. Following behind the idea of never going back came the realisation that he and Behleth were not only sundered from their friends but that their house was lost along with all their possessions. This meant they had lost every last legacy of their parents. Also, Behvyn had noticed that Behleth was becoming very quiet: something that concerned him most of all.

'Do you remember what we agreed to do after the harvest this year?' asked Behvyn, when the two of them were trailing a little way behind Rumé.

'Wasn't it to lose all our friends, become outlaws and leave the country?' Behleth replied, sourly.

'That was plan B. It wasn't the original idea,' said Behvyn.

'Well, I wasn't about to become a stithium worker,' Behleth eventually conceded. 'But weren't you going to talk to Tig about something?'

'Yes,' replied Behvyn. 'We didn't get much of a chance before all of this happened, but she mentioned we needed to talk, like she had found out something.'

'She did?' asked Behleth, surprised. 'And you didn't tell me until now?'

'I don't know what it is,' said Behvyn.

'But it could be something?' urged Behleth. 'Something about father?'

'We were chasing after the dogs, Behleth. We didn't have time to talk.'

'Yes, because finding Half-Pint is more important than learning about our parents!'

'It didn't sound like much! I didn't press her on it, Behleth. It wasn't the right time!'

'It sounds like it was the only time!' said Behleth, angrily. 'Now they'll never speak to us again! They probably think we're murderers!'

'Don't think like that, Behleth! Of course we'll see them again, and they'll be fine.'

'How? How can you say that? You don't know what is going to happen!'

'No, I don't!' replied Behvyn. 'So why don't we just assume now that on the other side of this rill there's a corps of guardsmen waiting to take us off to Cambwall so we can be tried and hanged and that we'll live on in infamy; that no-one will ever know the truth, that we'll never see our friends again or learn any more about our parents!'

'Well, there's no need to get snippy,' replied Behleth.

At the sound of their raised voices, Rumé had stopped up ahead at the top of next crest. He waited as they found their way through the grass and the gorse among the rocks of the hill.

'What can you see, Rumé?' asked Behvyn as they approached, short of breath from the steep gradient.

'I can't see a corps of guardsmen, if that's what you expected,' he replied. 'I think we might just have to carry on ourselves.'

On the tenth day out, Rumé was unusually close lipped and the twins were edgy. From glances at each other neither were sure why but it felt like there was more reason for caution than there had been since they had begun. Now they spoke more among themselves but only about trivial matters such as small discomforts or hunger, or they spoke about Behvyn's arm and how it was mending.

'Yes, it's a lot better,' Behvyn replied. 'It's repairing itself so quickly. I doubt there'll be much of a mark there. It's almost hard to remember now that less than two weeks ago there was a flaming bolt of wood in it.'

'Rumé's herb-lore is a wonder,' agreed Behleth. 'It would have taken months for it to clear using one of the remedies Mandle would have concocted and no doubt you would have had a grizzly scar to show the girls too.'

'How's your head? You haven't spoken of it since the explosion,' asked Behvyn.

'How do you mean?' questioned Behleth in return, blushing slightly. 'I'm fine, I don't need to be nursed like you,' he said, taunting his brother playfully.

'Will you tell me what happened?'

'Very well,' replied Behleth, seriously. 'I will tell you, just once. You may like to invite Rumé to hear as well. Perhaps what I overheard would be useful to us.'

Rumé came over at their bidding and thanked them. He broke out some dry bread as Behleth began his story.

'After you had left with Rumé to go to the Blackstone, I heard a voice. "They're taking a long time, master, and this one looks nearly dead. Shall I cut him lose?" My body was numb with the cold of the river; I had stopped moving.

'"We don't need three anchors, you're right," I heard Fetlock say in an offhand manner. "But then that wouldn't be showing much faith in our Captain now, would it? If he wants this one to live, he'll see things go well at the Stone. Back to your post, Guardsman." And then I heard the retreating footsteps of the man who had spoken to Fetlock. But then I also heard Fetlock muttering down to me once he had been left alone. I kept as still as death.

'"Cut you lose?" he said. "That would be too easy, my murderous friend, wouldn't it? As you float in the waters of the mountain river, in isolation from everything about you, playing dead and ignorant of your destiny. That fool Rumé with his broken eyes and high-minded principals will be dashing your brother to his doom as we speak, if he hasn't already put a knife in his side. Their task is hopeless. But what would you know? Grodel won't have told you anything, would he? That fat oaf, his mind addled by beer and rich food. He would have wanted to forget much of it. But a simple release from bonds and the possibility to be washed up back to land, to be brought around with a blanket and a fire by some meddlesome folk? No, my friend, I think I can offer you something far more dramatic."

'You remember it as clear as day,' said Behvyn.

'It's how I always beat you at cards. But, if you interrupt once more, I shall forget it all instantly,' reprimanded Behleth. His brother stayed quiet as Behleth continued.

'I heard nothing else but stayed perfectly still for a long time until I was sure I could risk a glance. I opened my eyes slowly and saw the dawn. My muscles were cramped and I could barely breathe. I saw Fetlock moving away from the rails and going into the cabin. His men were busy readying the barge in some fashion, but I couldn't make out what they were doing. It was getting lighter, but my vision was blurred.

'I dropped in and out of consciousness. I focused on moving my hands, curling my fingers into a fist and then opening my hands again. My only proof of this was seeing it happen. I couldn't feel a thing anymore. I took in mouthfuls of water and sank entirely below the surface on occasion. It had seemed like forever since I had seen you leave. Still time went by and no sighting of you came. Tiredness came on me then, and my eyelids shut. My thoughts stopped and my head became really heavy. I'm ashamed to say it but I began to welcome death. But then a picture of you came to mind. I wrenched open my eyes to see the world about me for one last time and took as full a gasp of air as I could. I didn't care if they saw me then.

As I did, just then the world came alive and the sky burst into light. I thought I saw six vast circles streak over to the mountains in the distance. I thought I'd imagined them, but then I heard Fetlock dash to the side of the barge at cries from his men.

"'The token. The sign! Ha!" he cried. "Pull in the boy and get him warmed. I need him alive. Do it! Do it now!"

'So it was, I was reeled back in to the barge like a stunned fish and dragged up on board. I was taken into a dark cabin, dressed in the black clothing of the guards and draped in blankets that smelled of horses. Fetlock gave me several sips of a stinging drink and, although my head was still thick and senseless, I felt my limbs stir again.

'"Leave him there and set these up," said Fetlock to his men. They were passed three bundles of cloth from within a trunk that he opened and then locked afterward with a key; although what they contained I didn't know. Only, the men handled them with great care and they seemed weighty.

'"Where do you want them, master?" one asked, not without looking at me in disgust.

'"Fore, aft and under!" Fetlock spat back at the man, and spun off to check for the coming of you and Rumé after locking the cabin door behind him.

'I was left alone inside, but then I started to worry about you. I hope you're safe with that Rumé, I thought. All I knew was that it was him who had ordered me into the water. But Fetlock wanted control of everyone. He didn't seem to care for his commander anymore. Well, all I could do was hope to stay alive and not catch my death. If I could do that, maybe I could do more to help you.

'There was a lot of activity outside the cabin by now. I cursed that I couldn't see out of my prison. I'll not be useless, I thought; I'll learn to stand again, at least.

'I struggled to move my legs, but eventually reached a kneeling position. I brought my arms out from under the blankets and flailed for a hold onto the side of the bunk. Eventually, I managed an uneasy stagger and begin to flex my muscles back into wakefulness.

'Then I heard more voices. "I see the Captain! I see the Captain!" shouted one of the guards and Fetlock was heard above the sound of what I later saw was a gangplank being moved over the edge of the railings. "A distance, Guardsman?" answered Fetlock. "Quarter-mile, master," the man responded.

'"Very well, we will have to say goodbye to our guest and wish them all a very welcome reunion. Our illustrious Captain has disgraced himself again, and knows his fate as prescribed by the King. No one is allowed to go to the Mirrorhorn and live. Set the acids and light the wicks, then disembark. Our path now shines in front of us!"

'Now I heard the hurried footsteps of the men and horses leaving the barge; as each one ran down onto dry land the whole vessel juddered.

'"Farewell, master murderer," came Fetlock's voice from close by. He was at the door of the cabin. 'You, your brother and Captain Rumé are all hereby condemned to death, by the laws of His Slumbering Majesty, King Cuiron!"

'With that, he shoved the key to the cabin door underneath so that it flew across the deck and hit my foot, and then he walked off the barge with slow stride. My hopes rose as I heard the sound of the gangplank being pulled off the edge and tossed into the water and the departure of Fetlock and his company on horseback.

'On closer inspection I saw his trick. The cabin could not be locked shut from the inside. There was no keyhole inside and now no way to open it from the outside. As well as a cabin it doubled as a cell, I realised. I would have to try breaking down the door with what strength I had.

'At first I ran at the door, charging my shoulder against the lock, but to no avail. The door opened inwards, and I would have had to batter out the frame, which would have taken too long. Then I stopped and looked around instead for a lever to insert in the gap between the frame and door. As I searched, I tripped over a loose board in the deck and struck my chest on the side of the bunk, winding myself. As I lay on the floor, I noticed the loose board could be removed and that even though it was too broad and thick to be used to pry open the door there was a space below where it had been. A shallow existed that was covered by a further loose board.

'I put my head down into the void and saw that it opened into a small area that was suspended above the insides of the hull, but below the level of the deck. I dropped down onto it and from there saw a sliding door, large enough to crawl through. I pushed it aside and found myself looking right down into the hull. The area was deserted. I allowed myself to drop the five feet or so onto the hard wood and landed safely. Hope at last came to me as I realised that from this bay led a short flight of stairs back up to the deck, and, once over the side, a short swim and escape!

'I made the stairs and was about to dash up them when I heard a fast 'drip, drip, drip' sound coming from somewhere behind. I turned and saw the flicker of a light warming a far corner of the hull. I went up to it. The drops were coming from a raised bottle with a small hole at the edge of its base aimed at the rope below it. The rope was tied to a lighted lamp that was suspended at an angle so that the rope in the process of being dissolved would eventually release it and swing the flame into – well, Behvyn, I did not know what it was. It looked like a sack of black gravel.

'But it smelled bad and the odour sickened me. The rope was at least half destroyed and a full strand unwound as I watched. I didn't waste another moment. I blew out the flame. For good measure, I moved the bottle away.

'Now I remembered what Fetlock had ordered. Light the wicks? There had been three bundles handed out. Did this mean three traps? "Fore, aft and under!" he had said. With no time to spare, I tore up the stairs and into the sunlight. "Fore and aft!" I shouted, and ran to the back of the barge where I saw another one of the things set up. I kicked the lamp into the river, but the rope was nearly burned through. I had barely any time to find the third when I noticed the shape of your boat coming towards me.

'I felt a twist in my stomach. You were alive but you were coming right here! I had to warn you to keep your distance. I could see you take off your blindfold, so I started waving and shouting at you.

'I wasn't sure if you'd heard me, so I climbed onto the very edge of the barge and waved as I shouted. This time I knew you'd heard me, but you waved back and pulled harder on your oars.

'"Stay back!" I screamed, but you kept coming. Now you were only twenty yards away. "Please stop rowing, Behvyn,' I said to myself as I looked around for the third lamp. "Stay back!" I shouted again, and then I saw you finally stop rowing, but all too late.'

'I know the rest,' Behvyn finished and looked at his brother. 'You nearly died of drowning, but you managed to unfreeze your body, discover a plot, escape from a prison and foil it enough to keep all of us alive, all in great danger to yourself.'

'Well,' said Behleth.

'Don't ever look apologetic for that again, brother,' said Behvyn. Behleth smiled and looked like a great weight had been taken from off his shoulders. Rumé gave Behleth a clutch on the shoulder and walked away wordlessly.

'I wonder how he is,' said Behleth, after some consideration. 'He's gone from being a Captain of the King's Guard to losing his sight and the command of all his men. He must feel abandoned. I don't suppose he could have predicted he'd be on the run with us two about his heals. Fetlock's behaviour must burn him inside, that vulture king.'

'It must burn,' agreed Behvyn, 'but Rumé has sight once more, and of the most fabulous kind. He can see twice as far as before if the white falcon sits upon his shoulder. And yet if he should chose, he can see the world from above with only a thought to do so. There are few that could have been so fortuitous in such disaster. And he has us as well!'

'Indeed he does,' laughed Behleth, and Behvyn laughed as well. The falcon turned its head around to see them from its perch on Rumé's shoulder, and cocked its head to one side before turning back again.

'And, what's more,' added Behleth, more conspiratorially this time, 'I think you fetched him something off that, that B-Blackstone – there I said it – that I get the sense was only a fool's hope for him to have. And now that he has it, it seems to be a weight on his mind. He has given us some idea of what it is, but I'm sure he hasn't let on anywhere near as much as he really knows about all this yet.'

'I wonder if we would want to know?' Behvyn mused.

Rumé moved them on apace but they all found the going harder once the ground began to swell and wrinkle into severe ruts as the plains broke up into rocky channels. They entered a field of scattered boulders that rose to twice head height and their smooth dark grey flanks formed an almost unbroken barrier between them and the river. Their voices echoed as they went and they stayed close together. A day later they emerged into easier terrain once again. Rumé advised them that they were walking through the remains of an ancient orchard that had once been harvested by a primitive people who'd left little but this legacy. In a handful of places the twins could see, twisting like ropes grown from the ground, a few ruined trees that had stood for over two thousand years. Their trunks were wide and short and in most cases hollowed. Their branches were few but at their base all had small collections of olives that had been dropped that year. In one or two places where they had lain unmolested by wildlife, their stones had found a way to the good soil and become young saplings so that the trees stood a chance of well outlasting not only their original farmers but Behvyn and Behleth's day too.

But though the way was easier, it was uphill and was unremittingly tiring. Behvyn and Behleth began to stumble and slow much earlier than in previous days. Rumé seemed unaffected by the difficulty but slowed his progress so as to keep the boys close by. The falcon would make numerous forays into the skies as Rumé paused for the twins, and as they made a lunch of bread and dried salted meat under the thin shading of the wise old trees, the bird flew off for its own meal. At such times Rumé would remove the necklace and give the creature its own time. He would stare into nothingness once more and focus on his other senses. Now he lifted his head and turned towards the forest.

'Do you smell it yet, Behvyn? Behleth?' asked Rumé, filling his lungs.

'I can't catch anything,' replied Behleth.

'It is the scent of the Lightwater,' said Rumé. 'We approach it even now and should make it by tomorrow. The river has nectar of its own that is unlike anything else in the Valley. It is said that its fragrance comes from underwater flowers that are there at the river's birth high in the mountains and that it carries the aroma down with it as it falls through the foothills and forests on its way to meet the Highborn. I can just catch its sweet perfume hanging on the wind, though it is still five leagues or more away. I cannot wait to inhale it more deeply. With one breath it can wash the troubles of the world from you like a deep sleep.'

With this news, Behvyn and his brother were enlivened by the prospect of making the Lightwater as soon as they could. They finished their lunch with fresh determination to walk ceaselessly if they needed to. Even when the sun went in behind a bank of slow-rolling cloud that had come in from the northeast they did not think it ill. But Rumé seemed changed upon the return of the falcon and fell into a more concerned mood than they had seen him before. For a long while, once he had put on the necklace again, he sent out his sight about them. Reluctantly, he allowed them to progress, but the twins set off in good spirits for the first time in several days.

Chapter 6

LAKE AND LEAF

Tangle struggled with a potent sense of déjà vu as they moved
southward, away from the road but following its line at a distance
of around a quarter of a mile. With the days of warm weather
gently fading into memory and autumn taking up the palette,
rejecting the fanciful gold and blue of summer for the red, yellow
and brown of flourishing decay, all was just as it had been when
she and her sister had left the year before. Only, this time, the
circumstances were very different. For one thing, they were not
alone. She had Feran at her side, and Tig had Kjerros to bother
her, and Paequat loomed over all four of them in paternal silence.
And this time they weren't escaping; they were chasing.

Even so, the first two days had been torture. Kjerros had complained about the heat as though he was being paid to do so and
Tig had been mithered to distraction by the flies that, at dusk, had
gathered at head height in urgent clouds. In order not to exacer-
bate the situation, Tangle had kept herself unusually muted and
strode the majority of the day in the comfort of Feran's company,
where she could also keep his normal tendency to talk endlessly
in close check. But this had, in turn, seemed to make it difficult
for anyone else to speak. Now, however, the third day brought
soft cooling mists and low white skies suited to their walking and
their spirits lifted. After they had eaten and got underway once
again, slightly more hardened to the rigours of travel in the wild
than complete novices, there was plenty of discussion and debate,
story-telling and gossiping.

For a long while, Tangle was happy to listen rather than take
part, but over time she realised that there were certain topics no
one wanted to raise directly and would, with deftness or clumsi-
ness, pass over them. As she thought about the sadness of this and
counted it as a cost of doing what they had done the previous year,
Paequat scouted the way ahead. After the initial shock and fascination of meeting him, the friends had grown to take Paequat's

109

presence for granted quickly, although they did not speak to him as readily as to each other. As natural as he behaved, Paequat was still feared. Tangle knew Feran and Kjerros saw him as an indestructible swordsman, a mighty ally to have with them, but one over whom they had no control. She felt safe in his company but was uncertain if he had the same moral limits as she had herself.

It was whilst Tangle was determining to take it upon herself to begin his teaching that Tig spoke.

'You know, we were both bloody nervous just before we saw you all again the other day,' she admitted to Kjerros, who was walking beside her. Feran and Tangle behind were close enough to overhear. They were ploughing through the last of the long heath-carpet that led towards the basin of Lake Tieco.

They looked around at her, even Tangle, for this was quite an admission from the normally stoic Tig.

'Well, we'd been away from here for over a year,' Tig explained. 'I don't think either of us knew exactly what to expect. There might have been a lot of changes to catch up on.'

'Fat chance of that,' humphed Kjerros, despondently. 'The only thing that changed in Muscle Oaks was the weather.'

'That's true enough,' enjoined Feran. 'You don't get many surprises there.'

'What gets me, though,' continued Kjerros, passionately enough to turn even Paequat's head, 'is that everyone there likes to be stuck in their rut! It's as though the idea of there being a whole world out there offends them. Everyone just seems to want to live their parent's lives over and over again in the same place. They marry the same type of women, have the same number of children, work at the same crafts and live in the same house, their whole lives a repeat of those that came before them. It's exasperating; nothing progresses! I was so pleased you two managed to get out; at least it gives me some hope.'

Tangle smiled and glanced forward sympathetically at Kjerros. She was intrigued to hear his outburst.

'I wouldn't romanticise it, Kjerros,' protested Tig at his side. 'We just ran away! It was hardly the most mature thing to do in hindsight. If we'd known what we were letting ourselves in for! Well, let's just say the minstrels won't be writing any songs about it. Not the ones who want to scratch a living, anyway.'

'Oh, I don't know,' answered Tangle, keen to preserve her own and now others' blossoming enthusiasm for the journey ahead, 'I feel twice the person I was back then. Grodel used to ask me: "What do you want your life to be about, young lady?" I used to answer that I wanted it to be about having as much fun as I could, just to annoy him. But now I think it's more about getting in as many experiences as I can.'

'It would be comfort, for me,' said Feran. 'I'd just want to be really comfortable, for ever.'

'Comfortable like this?' asked Tangle, and hugged him with both arms tight about his waist as they walked. She buried her head in his chest.

'Er, yes, that's about right,' he blushed, eventually plucking up the gumption to put his arm around her shoulders. Tangle felt him kiss her hair and saw Tig and Kjerros give each other an amused glance.

'Sme hpe fmwr ht?' asked Tangle from among the leather of Feran's jerkin.

'Huh?' responded Tig, turning around. 'Did you just try to say something from in there?'

'Kjerros, some hope for what?' Tangle asked again, emerging from Feran. She had become serious. She fixed Kjerros with a level stare.

'For doing – something,' answered Kjerros, somewhat put off balance by the directness of Tangle's question. 'You know, something big! Making a difference.'

'You want to change the world?' asked Tig, unconvinced by his potential.

'Change something,' responded Kjerros, 'although I don't know exactly what, yet. It's just, I don't know, there are a lot of things that I think are wrong. I just can't reconcile spending my whole life in some nowhere village making up the numbers; it's just a waste to me. Shouldn't every day be an opportunity for the extraordinary? Oh, I guess I must sound like an idiot.'

Tangle could sense Feran was surprised by how animated Kjerros became as he tried to explain his thoughts. He'd clearly not known this side of his cousin before. But Tangle was pleased with the response.

'That's just how I was,' she murmured quietly to Feran, and remembered how she used to feel.

'Well, yes you do sound like an idiot Kjerros,' said Tig, leading the conversation away from another topic with which she was now uncomfortable. 'But you never know. You just might get what you wish for. We're not in Muscle Oaks now.'

As Tig spoke, her words could not have been timed any better. For, opening up in front of them, clearing suddenly of all mist, was the first sighting of Tieco Lake itself. It brought everyone to a halt to admire its beauty. The ground dropped away sharply from where they stood and, over Paequat's shoulders to their left, they could all see clearly the horse-shoe shaped sweep of the north side steppes that layered down to the lake's edge. From their north-western approach, they could see how these steppes sheltered the lake and its surroundings from the cold winds of the north, and formed a natural viewing point from which to appreciate one of the most poetic sights in the Shale Valley. The northern rock flung out two broad-backed arms along the eastern and western sides of the lake. These tapered and diminished the further they continued away south until they merged with ground level about half a mile past the far end of the lake. These arms allowed much more gentle varieties of plant life to succeed here than for many long miles southwards; and indeed, from all the bright-hot colours that lay about in abundance, rainbowing upwards from the brink of the water, it was as though here was an oasis of perpetual summer.

As they progressed gently downwards, sideward to the gradient, Tangle noticed how, to begin with, each tier was covered in the same heather and gorse as found at the top. Then, about the midway point of the descent, the lower ground coverings were replaced by tree-sized rhododendron, red-orange maple and thick-leafed thickets of laurel. As they watched, the sun's pale silver rays broke through the cloud cover briefly and ignited the heart-shaped lake, highlighting the patterns the breeze drew across its rippling surface, before the clouds came in and cut them off again. The lake itself was dressed about its edge by sprawling water lilies and tall grasses that stirred in unison, and was framed in the east by the wandering path of the Eloquand and the growing proximity of the Mizzle Mountains. Although they had travelled only twenty leagues from Muscle Oaks, the mountains were nearly five leagues closer to, for the Valley closed in the nearer they approached its middle.

As the Highborn burst over the northern steppes and tumbled down into the lake, the rock could be seen to end, sheer and dark and mighty. For southward from Tieco lay only shallow folds and open landscape, save for where the mountains pinched in, as it was built upon the same fibre of the sea-beds of old, and here was betrayed most clearly the rest of the Shale Valley's slow construction over the eons that had raked the world into being. The rills and runs of the view downhill to the sea resembled most closely a deep sandy shore at low tide, save only for being clothed in swathes of green and engraved by silver arteries.

'Tieco is "The Joining",' chorded Paequat as they descended further down the western side of the steppes, until they were almost level to the water's edge. For having not spoken for so long, this quite astounded the others.

'How do you know that, Paequat?' asked Feran, intrigued, but Paequat seemed as surprised as anyone that he had spoken.

'Don't know,' he piped, with a hint of fear. 'Someone else makes me know.'

'That's nothing to be worried about, Paequat,' soothed Tig. 'You just get us past the lake. We've got to be careful around here.' She looked at the others. 'Until we're into the deep grasses of the flat ahead, there must be plenty of places about the top of the slopes that someone can scout us from without being seen themselves.'

This made sense to them all and they quickly became conscious of the danger they faced in being spotted by King's guards in the employ of Fetlock. But it was with some reluctance that they moved on so quickly within the landscape, in amongst the trees about the western arm and blurring past the lakeside. Paequat led the party, followed by Tig and Kjerros, and Tangle and Feran brought up the rear.

'Is this what you mean by experience?' Feran asked Tangle, scampering about awkwardly at her side. He was walking almost sideways, still buoyed by the majesty of the view they had just enjoyed, and trying to catch as many glimpses of the lake as he still could. His shadow would briefly emerge and loom over the brink.

'What? Oh, yes,' Tangle answered, absent-mindedly. She was concentrating on keeping up with Paequat and the others, without leaving Feran entirely behind. 'Although, I've seen it before. Do you think you could be comfortable somewhere like this?' she teased. She regretted it instantly as she saw Feran blush, unsettled. He didn't answer, but smiled as warmly as he could, and walked properly once more.

'It's a shame we can't have a swim in the lake,' sighed Tig, ahead of them. 'If you look very closely,' she said, turning to Kjerros, 'you can see a thin mist lies just above the waterline. That's because the water is so warm; it's heated underneath by vapours that come out of the rocks. They bubble up to the surface. It's a natural spa.' Kjerros nodded, both fascinated and disappointed.

'I guess we can't go jumping in,' he said. 'We could be seen, or Paequat would probably come after us for our own good. And given the diet we're on, and all that dried fruit? Well, it wouldn't just be vapours rising up from the rocks below that would disturb the surface of the water.'

For some reason Tig found this unstoppably funny and snorted in continuing fits that disturbed Paequat and eventually annoyed Tangle and Feran. Kjerros carried on walking, slightly more upright than before.

'It can't have been that funny,' muttered Feran.

'At least she's smiling,' answered Tangle, grasping Feran's hand. 'She's been through a lot recently.'

Tig eventually managed to bring herself under control and linked her arm through Kjerros' for a little time as they carried on forward.

At leaving the beauty of the lake behind, the lowering sun finally burst through underneath the clouds and layered everything with a deepening orange-red blaze. But as the slow darkness swung up and they began to look for somewhere to set up for the night, Tangle couldn't stop the trite riposte she had made to Feran earlier from ringing around her mind.

They progressed through the same terrain for the next few days, finding little difference in the environment, and gradually made their way southwards by another twenty leagues, always between the road to their right and the Highborn to their left. But on the fourth day from Tieco Lake, and the seventh day out from Muscle Oaks, Paequat needed to change their course.

'Must go to the road,' he said. 'No way to cross river here.'

'Which river is that, Paequat?' asked Feran, but it was Tangle who told him.

'Ah, we must be coming up to Rhal Springs. It's just a river that flows into the Highborn further down but if we continue on here we'd go past the bridge and then have to double-back on ourselves. If we go to the road, we can get over that way. But, well. Tig? Tig!'

Tangle ran up to her sister. They spoke rapidly. Then she went to speak with Paequat.

'What are they on about?' asked Kjerros, walking with Feran up to Paequat as well.

'I think she's thought of a problem, but I guess we'll find out.'

After some time, during which it seemed Paequat was deciding upon something, Tangle saw him nod, and then she turned to the boys.

'What was all that about?' asked Feran.

'Oh, don't ask silly questions now,' she snapped. 'I need you to come on a mission with me!' She decided to beam at them both delightfully until they said they'd do it.

'Fruit picking, honestly! This is embarrassing, Feran,' Kjerros moaned.

'Hush, you two!' warned Tangle. 'We're close to the road here. And it's not fruit. They're buds, like this one. Hurry up and get as many as you can.'

'But what do you need them for?' continued Kjerros. 'It doesn't make any sense.'

'Here are those leaves you asked for as well.' Feran's pockets were burgeoning with the thick, broad leaves, rubbery to the touch, that Tangle had told him to harvest after she had found a patch of what she had been seeking. They had been hunting around for half the night before she had come across them and tempers had frayed long ago.

'I can't see us sewing those into wings that'll fly us across the river,' said Kjerros. 'What does your missus need these for, Feran? And why are you so happy?'

'Because I'm actually doing something instead of walking about,' responded Feran in a whisper, 'and if this will help us, at least I feel useful for a change.'

The whisper carried to Tangle and it troubled her but she couldn't let it stop her concentrating. She was stood flat against the trunk of a birch tree within a small copse of trees close to the Great Shale Road itself, on the lookout for anyone coming. Feran and Kjerros were exposed. They had approached the road on their knees, and now crouched down in the ever-thinning grass, fearing being seen should anyone be watching. The ground rose to meet the road so that there was a steep side to climb of some forty yards. Apart from the copse, there was no means of cover within that distance on either side of the road, save for a drainage ditch, just outside the white stones that were cut skillfully to line the roadside here as in Muscle Oaks, and also for the odd clump of scrubby briars where a thin sapling might grow. But there was no shelter from even the most casual gaze of a passer-by whose point of view was at such an advantage on the road. This was not by chance but through design, for the safety of travellers so that they might not be approached without warning by bands of outlaws.

Time after time, Tangle imagined she heard noises of men approaching, or the sound of a horse neighing. Then she would call out to the cousins and they would scamper back to the comparative shelter of the copse before they agreed it was safe again. She couldn't believe their bad luck in the location of the very plants she had them looking for. She had remembered just the point at which she had found them the previous year, but now they seemed so much closer to the road. They had looked elsewhere, further away from possible danger, but found nothing. Then the moon had come out like a sun and sat fat and round gazing down at them, lighting them up so that she could not imagine anyone could pass along the road and not notice them.

They had left Tig and Paequat behind with the promise that they wouldn't be long. Now Tangle worried not just about their own safety but whether or not her sister would be wondering if something had happened, and might come looking for them. If she did, it could attract attention. But time had moved on and there was nothing Tangle could do about it. From where she watched, she continued to scan the road and, every so often, she would allow herself a glimpse back the way they had come to see if her fears proved true. But she saw nothing. Then, with a growing sense of alarm, she saw that Kjerros seemed to be becoming more blasé about the precautions they had been taking. She observed him closely for a few more moments until he had finally had enough. Then she watched in dread as he stood up.

'Right, that's all I'm doing,' she heard him say aloud.

'Kjerros, get down or you'll blow the mission!' Feran said, frantically.

'Mission? Ha! I don't know if you've noticed, but it's dark and there's no one here except for your jumpy girlfriend, who is at this moment probably having a heart attack over a leaf moving beside her.'

'Get down, you fool! I think I can hear something!' Feran froze where he lay, but Kjerros was unimpressed.

'Rubbish, it's probably just-'

But at that moment, Tangle watched as Kjerros was thrown backwards by the sudden thunder of hooves and the speeding of horses, which appeared from nowhere racing along the road at a full gallop. It was fortunate that he landed harmlessly, out of sight of the three riders that pounded past. They raised such a cloud of dust in their wake that, even though Tangle could see one of them glance over his shoulder in their direction, she doubted he could see anything. Feran and Kjerros both looked at each other open-mouthed, stunned by the suddenness of the riders' appearance. As they lay motionless among the all too thin cover of the tall grass and amidst the dust cloud, Tangle began to hear following hoof falls, along with the rattle of a carriage travelling somewhat slower. As it rounded the bend in the road at the edge of which the boys hid, Tangle watched the arrival of a similar-looking rider to those that had raced past. He reined his mount to a smart trot ahead of a solid-looking mare that pulled a simple carriage. Two further riders covered the rear. All wore dark cloaks with the hoods down. They all had short hair and were un-shaven.

They floated past in a dream for Tangle, slowing all the time, until they seemed almost to be at a walking pace, and their disappearance southwards took forever. Then the dust settled, silence fell once again and Kjerros and Feran crawled arm over arm back to the copse and Tangle.

'Those other three that went on ahead must be his vanguard,' said Kjerros, patting his clothes and swiping grass off his cloak.

'But who was it inside?' asked Feran. 'Fetlock, do you think?'

'It looked like his men, from what I saw,' said Kjerros. 'I can't be sure, but I think I recognised the first one as I fell back.'

'I'll tell you something we do know, Feran,' said Tangle, as though in a trance. 'That was Grodel's carriage.'

The silence was overpowering. 'Let's not talk about it here,' continued Tangle once it looked like Kjerros and Feran both had enough questions to keep them going the rest of the night. They picked up the leaves and buds they'd collected and returned, wordlessly and with more caution than ever, back to Tig and Paequat. Paequat seemed to be resting; at least, he had his tall hat over his eyes. But Tig was wide-awake. She made to rise but Feran told her to stay low.

'Where have you been!' she hissed, staying down. 'I've been jumping at every noise since you left. You've been gone ages!' she accused, but she was looking at them less in anger and more in wide eyed gratefulness. Their return had clearly delivered her from an anguish she'd not endured well.

'We're sorry, Tig,' answered Kjerros, 'but we've brought you back what we went for.'

Feran and Kjerros then spent some time emptying out various pockets and made quite a pile. Tig seemed placated and smiled at Tangle.

'Well, that's more than enough,' she quipped, and began separating out the leaves from the buds.

'And there's something else, too,' mentioned Feran, less easily. Kjerros looked at his cousin sharply, and Tig noticed.

'What?' she asked, suspiciously.

'We saw a group of riders go past us, on the road,' Feran said, neutrally, avoiding eye contact with her.

'Oh my goodness, were you seen? They didn't see you did they?' Tig was now very concerned.

'They didn't see us, I'm sure,' said Tangle, 'but we saw them clearly enough. They were dressed the same way as the men who were at Behvyn and Behleth's house. There were at least seven of them including one in a carriage, whose face we didn't see. Three of them went on well ahead of the rest.'

'Did they have any prisoners? Did you see the twins?' asked Tig, now desperate for more information. She nudged Paequat awake. 'Did you, Kjerros?'

'I didn't see them, but we couldn't see inside the carriage,' he replied.

'What did the carriage look like?' asked Tig.

Feran didn't answer. He looked at Kjerros. Kjerros looked at Tangle.

'Tangle?' Tig asked. As she did, a silence came over everyone as the importance of the question sank in.

'It was very dark and we only saw it for a second or two,' said Tangle. 'But it didn't look big enough to hold more than one or two people. I don't think Behvyn and Behleth could have been in there.'

'Are you sure?' asked Tig. 'And you didn't see anything else?' she quizzed again.

'Nothing,' answered Tangle steadily, as Feran opened his mouth only to close it quickly again.

'Well, it sounds like we have some choices to make,' said Tig, her voice thick with emotion.

'You can't think –' began Feran, before Tangle hushed him up with a jerk on his arm.

'Come on, Feran! You do remember why we're out here?' asked Tig. 'We're going to the Fords of Netheign because that's where the guard told Paequat the twins were being taken. If this is the same lot that took them and they don't have them with then, then even without thinking the worst, this could prove our information was wrong. Behvyn and Behleth might be behind us now, and we could be going in the wrong direction.'

'But it might not be the same people; it could be another group?

Or we might have been wrong about how big the carriage was?' added Feran.

'Exactly. But which way do we go now?' asked Tig.

'We can't turn back yet!' said Kjerros determinedly, after more discussion had gone over the same ground. 'We have to be sure about the carriage first. I really don't think it was big enough, but I can't be sure. The way those first three riders went on ahead, it was as though they were an advance team to arrange lodgings for the rest of the night, and in Rhal, I would suppose. Do you two remember from your previous travels if there was much about the crossing? Any buildings, houses?'

'Rhal's only a little place,' replied Tangle, 'but either side of the road on the approach there are a number of large estates and the river crossing isn't just a little bridge. It's unique, to say the least. There's an enormous grey castle that people stay in that spans the entire river. Rhal Springs runs underneath through an archway about its foundations and the traffic across the water has to go through the castle. You have to go through the equivalent of the basement, given how high the rest of the building is. By the time you get to the end of it, you're on the other side.'

'That's right,' added Tig, 'but there's a gate at the far end, and a toll to be paid to be allowed into the gallery. It's free if you have a boat of course, but the road goes through the castle, from keep to keep. It used to be free when it was a royal residence, but since King Cuiron's curse a merchant's family has run it as though it was an Inn. It could be these men are staying the night there, or in one of the large houses about it.'

'If they're staying the night there,' said Tangle, 'we might be able to get there before dawn, find them and listen in to what they're saying before they move off.'

'So we have to decide now,' said Tig, 'if it's worth making a dash for Rhal, probably along the road, or whether it's too dangerous. We're making a lot of assumptions.'

'I don't see how we could turn back, without trying to find out more if it's only just up ahead,' said Tangle, desperately worried about the twins and sick with the thought that they may have wasted their time journeying for a week in the wrong direction.

'Are we agreed?' Tig asked. Then everyone nodded one by one

and Tig asked Paequat to lead them as fast as they could onto the road for the first time, to reach Rhal Castle before dawn.

'In case you were wondering boys,' said Tangle, 'we now need that plant life you collected more than ever. It will come in very handy.'

'How exactly?' asked Kjerros.

'You'll see,' Tangle replied, evasively.

They made their way towards Rhal as cautiously as possible, but ran along the road all the same to make up time. Night was already passing. Once Feran had pointed out to them the top of the hulking castle, illuminated by burning torches that glimmered red through the play of long tapering banners in front of them, it loomed ahead for a very long time before they reached anywhere near it. Tangle felt that every footstep they made was being watched.

As soon as they came within the last furlong of the approach, the roadway was lit by oil lanterns. These were hung on ornate brackets attached to the wide trunks of trees that stretched onwards towards the castle in twin columns. Each tree was set at a large interval apart from the next, but so vast were they that their lowest branches still touched those of their neighbour. The cover of the trees provided a canopy over the road that now partially sheltered the travellers from the red gaze at the top of the castle, but gave the Gatemen, clearly standing guard up ahead, early rumour of their arrival. Between each set of trees was a pathway that led up to a large house that was typically set on great stilts or surrounded by a deep trench or moat. Within the grounds of each garden were numerous, less noticeable and far smaller homes that acted as servants' quarters to service the gentry that lived in the shadow of the castle.

'Why the stilts, I wonder?' asked Kjerros, curious.

'I think it's because the area floods a lot,' replied Tig. 'The waters in the mountains off to the right are frozen up much of the time, but when there's a thaw, a lot of the rivers in the west valley flood.'

'Where did you-' began Feran, when he suddenly spotted the Gatemen for the first time. 'Those guards can see us!' he whispered in astonished alarm.

'Of course they can,' responded Tangle, calmly. 'We won't be able to do this without their help. And we'd look far too suspicious if we dove in and out of the shadows.'

'But what if they alert the riders we saw? How can you be sure they won't?' asked Kjerros, also concerned.

'Because you don't get to stay a Gateman long in the service of powerful people if you forget their names or jump to conclusions too early,' replied Tangle. 'Also, you tend to miss out on added benefits. Now, just behave as though you three are our servants and everything will go well. And keep your eyes peeled for that carriage we saw. It may be the riders are staying at one of the homes before the castle pass.'

Chapter 7

BEFORE THE LIGHTWATER

'We will make camp early tonight,' said Rumé, his voice particularly tired and stony. The twins did not disagree.

Their earlier high spirits had been sapped from them as the ground had continued to fold and trough. 'We will make for that coppice and settle in,' he said, and pointed over to a further ridge that lay below their feet from where they now stood, upon the highest vantage point that lay for several miles around. They had made for it as a way of defining their progress that day and, now they had reached its peak, they could see how far they had come. Not nearly so far as Behvyn had guessed, he thought disappointedly. For as the crow flies the distance they had to the Lightwater was but half a day's journey, yet they had taken one full day and closed only half the gap. They had not been able to walk in a straight line to it for the Mizzle Mountains sent out their roots far into the heart of the valley and caused them to round them one by one. Now there was another drop in the ground to climb down and rise up from before reaching what looked like an animal trail or possibly a pathway that finally led the way to the coppice. But they forced their weary legs into motion once more and with a last effort made their resting place for the night.

There, Rumé sent the white falcon up into the higher branches of the trees above them and around the dark airs of the early night to scan for danger, but it returned to his shoulder without having seen anything to alarm him.

Time after time the falcon had issued into the skies during that day to scan the district. But whether it was friend or foe Rumé sensed, the bird's sharp eyes had seen nothing to satisfy his inquest. Behvyn could tell that this was causing frustration to grow in the man, though he hid it well. But all the while that Rumé's feeling of being pursued or watched was just that, Behvyn couldn't get himself too agitated by it. It was beginning to dawn on him that he was enjoying the excitement of their predicament, and though there were many long hours spent trudging through boggy turf, between cold walls of rock and underneath the scratching branches of trees, he felt comfort in the simplicity of their purpose, a liberation from the unnecessary aspects of larger community existence and a peace within himself that came from knowing that what he was doing now was the only thing he should be doing.

After eating, and as a way to pass the time before sleep took them, Behvyn asked Rumé something he dearly desired to know.

'Why is there a curse on the King?' he asked.

Behvyn did not think he would get an answer. Seldom had Rumé spoken that day and did not make any gesture of being pleased to hear Behvyn's request. Behvyn mouthed an apology and set himself down with his back to everyone else under a large horse chestnut tree that had scattered about its base mounds of conkers. He picked up a handful and began whittling away at them idly with a thin stone. Behleth showed little interest but sat opposite Rumé, the pair divided by the low red flames of their cooking fire. Without anyone noticing when he started, suddenly Rumé was speaking.

'When Prince Cuiron was four years old,' he began, 'there arrived at the Royal Court two men dressed from head to foot all in blue. Even their wide-brimmed hats and clay-caked boots were blue. They had the demeanour of old men, but seemed as sharp as the youngest or most ambitious courtier. They explained they had come to offer urgent council to the reigning King; Cuiron's own father, Xiomes. But they were refused. The blue-clothed men were insistent and claimed to know a great many things about the King that would prove to him their value, yet he deemed them unworthy of attending him. Despite this show of strong-mindedness from His Majesty, the men did not lose heart and remained about Cambwall, staying in lodgings with the family of a courtier that was sensitive to their case.

'It so happened that, at that time, Xiomes was unpopular for having committed more troops into battle, removing of the Shale Valley some more of its sons and men, out into the westward reaches of Khubron and lower Mertos. The 'Endless War' that lasts unabated to this day was begun a long time ago. During Xiomes reign, he did not want to be the one that risked the efforts that so many of his forbears had waged before him, paying dearly with their lives. But not everyone was happy, even if they did not say so to his face. And so it was suggested in the brief snatches of conversation among the courtiers that these two men should be heard out. Xiomes was a just and decisive ruler but had no way with people. He saw them as subjects and ruled for his own, rather than for the common, good. But so it was, as the whispers grew stronger and less kind, that Xiomes' chief advisor, who was called Knival, came to his King and sued for him to receive the two blue-clothed men. Xiomes was swayed by his words only when Knival gave a promise upon his own life that the two men would not ask the King to stop the war.

'Xiomes finally granted them an audience, some eleven months after they had first arrived in Cambwall, but it was not to be in the council room, which Xiomes had publicly promised would never happen. It was arranged instead to meet outside in the palatial gardens as Xiomes took his daily turn about them before his evening feast. This was as clear a message as the King could send that he did not value their council even before they spoke to him. But at the same time, the rumour that he had met with them would be undeniable. In such a way Knival saved his master's face.

'"Your Majesty", began the first man when the time arrived for the meeting, "my name is Caeghin, and this is Peridous. May we speak plainly with you?" Caeghin had an authoritative voice that was at odds with Xiomes' own.

'"That would make a nice change", replied Xiomes, focusing on keeping a steady stride and forcing the two men to keep apace with him. "Usually, one is spoken to with such noncommittal words as carefully pick'd as steps o'er a creaking bridge. Pray continue."

'"In that case, Your Majesty", continued Caeghin, "you do not have long to live, unless you follow our council."

'"You do speak straightly! Wherefore do you have the gal to threaten your King?" asked Xiomes, increasing his pace still further.

'"Your Highness", spoke Caeghin again, "we are not from these lands. We have travelled a very great distance to be with you here. We are come from Laummeth."

'Xiomes was furious. "First you seek to intimidate me. Then

you say you are from a land summoned up by imagination! Yet you have remained here for the best part of a year to tell me such things. It is a long time to propagate only one jest and an unfunny one at that. Your time is running out, gentlemen."

"'Are you aware", spoke Peridous this time, "upon whose authority you hold the seat of this Kingdom?" Now Xiomes stopped walking.

"'Completely!" he responded, infuriated. "And you are to preface each time you speak to me with "Your Majesty". But come now," he continued walking once again, "the Gods shine on my reign no more or less than all others preceding it, save Charion himself. You cannot tell me they are especially displeased with anything I may have done? And even so, what of it? The histories tell us they left this world an age ago."

"'You are right. The Gods chose the first King of this world," continued Peridous, as patiently as ever, "and you will know they saw to it personally that the reign of King Charion was enduring, much honoured and highly prosperous for everyone. But although they did then leave this land they never promised to leave it forever."

"'You mean to say you bring tidings of the return of the Gods?" laughed Xiomes now, so taken by the frivolity of their topic that he could not resist a jest of his own. "Well, in that case, I should have the maids prepare more quarters!"

"'Fool of a man!" stormed Caeghin, his voice growing in power. Xiomes froze in his tracks. The sun fell behind a bank of cloud, a wind rose up from the north and all about turned dark and cold. Caeghin seemed to have grown in height and loomed over the King. "Your rule is doomed to end in but one month, beginning from the setting of this sun today until the thirtieth rising of the moon, unless you cease your war in Mertos immediately. The Gods will not allow it! Will you defy them, Xiomes son of Cassimes, and bring disaster on yourself and on your line? The fates of all who follow you, from your own son Cuiron onwards, rest on your decision."

'Yet Xiomes did not react well to this threat, as he saw it. He had his bodyguards arrest the two strangers and had them thrown into jail to await a trial that he had no intention of calling. Then

Xiomes doubled the security of the palace and saw to it that no one came near him by keeping to his living quarters. He allowed only his wife, young son Cuiron and his chief protector around him. Then he had Knival, his chief advisor, privately hanged for his earlier deception; for the two men had sued him for peace. After that the only strange tiding during the remainder of the month came once he had sent Caeghin and Peridous to their cells. A report came to him only hours after he had given the command that they had broken out of their bondage as though held in cages of paper and left the palace without being seen. Xiomes cursed his jailers, but pretended to think little of it. Yet, although he rubbished the message of the visitors, every action he then took was designed to defend himself against the very possibility they had spoken of.

'The time slipped away as time will when one does not want it to pass. Weeks went past like days and days went past like moments. And so it came to the last few moments before the time appointed by the men who claimed to come from Laummeth, and Xiomes was jubilant. Here he was in his palace fortress, surrounded by family and protectors, infallible to attack. He rejoiced at his ingenuity at outwitting the Gods and sought a glass of wine to celebrate. He went to the cabinet and poured himself a drink into a goblet and walked to the window so as better to breathe the coastal sea air, to watch the sun sink and see the moon rise for its thirtieth time. Then he took a mighty swig of wine, but at the last possible moment he changed his mind over swallowing it for sudden fear it could be poisoned. What he didn't spit out again went 'down the wrong way', as one says.

'He began to choke and cough, struggling for breath, unable to breathe in. He moved around wildly, attempting to grasp anything that came to hand. He dropped the goblet on the ground. He bent down and thumped himself on his back, but the coughing would not let him fill his lungs. Then, he slipped on the wine that lay about his feet and fell, with deadly accuracy, through the open window, down onto the fountains that lay beneath him. One fountain impaled his body straight through the chest, ending him instantly, and turned the gushing waters red in front of everyone that had seen him fall.'

'That's ridiculous!' said Behleth, although quite enamoured by the gruesome tale. 'He fell out of his own window, choking on poisoned wine?'

'It was later concurred by the Physicians General that the wine had not been tampered with and would in no way have killed King Xiomes,' Rumé added, straight faced.

Behleth laughed at the idea of the foolish King's arrogance and stood up and staggered about clutching his throat.

'The Gods cannot hurt me – I am invincible!' he mimicked, and then fell over backwards, clutching his stomach as he giggled heartily.

Behvyn laughed too, but also looked at Rumé, who was now smiling at the sound of Behleth's antics.

'What happened to Cuiron?' he asked, as Behleth eventually controlled himself.

The fire was getting lower. Apart from the occasional giggle, Behleth was drifting off to sleep as Rumé finished his telling of the tale, but Behvyn was now fascinated.

'At the moment of his father's death, the curse of the Gods was laid. It was not to affect Cuiron for the next seventeen years, but as his twenty-first birthday dawned he never woke from that night's rest, and so he remains.' Rumé's blank eyes grew red with remorse for his King's fate and his voice was tighter as he continued.

'That boy who saw his father die in front of him and his mother crumble from being a beautiful queen to a shadow of herself, grew up as Prince Regent of this country from the age of four. From the age of four, the weight of a nation has lain across his shoulders. I saw him grow into a young man as I grew myself, only five years older than he. I saw him walk into the council room for the first time at the age of twelve, and how he had to face down a hundred imposters to his throne and see off handfuls of false advisers. I saw a fine young King with all that a man of his brilliance promised. I saw him grow to weight judgement with maturity, wisdom with understanding, mercy with the need for justice. I saw the best chance this nation has of having a King Charion for the present day. I saw the people fall in love with him. And I saw him fall in love, too.'

Rumé looked at Behvyn who was transfixed despite the soft

snores that now emitted from Behleth. 'Of course,' said Behvyn, quietly. 'He has a son that lives on. Prince Idren.'

'Cuiron lives on too, Behvyn; never forget that. But yes, you are right. He married the most beautiful girl in the kingdom and they had a son together. They named him "Idren" after the phase of the moon in which they first met. It is a while since I saw him,' Rumé recalled. 'He must be about twenty years old now.'

'What can they do for Cuiron, though?' asked Behvyn, now desperate to understand his King's plight.

'He is doomed to his father's fate unless the request of the Gods can be met. We must end the war with Mertos and Khubron, but I had tried to read its significance to the Immortals otherwise. Wars occur all the time; it is the way of men. Such a small thing would not be enough on its own. It was to find out this other reason that I ventured from the court, to help my King not just in the control of his realm, but to restore him to health.'

'Is that why you know so much of the healing powers of plants?' asked Behvyn.

'Master Behvyn, you read me well. Aye, I did spend long years trying to discover an antidote for his condition. I thought if I could I might find my way back to his welcome; we did not speak to each other last as friends, alas. But there is nothing "wrong" with him that can be "mended". So I then looked to achieve that which would break the wrath of the Gods elsewhere. And now, with your help, I think I have it!'

Rumé became animated. His momentary delight showed to Behvyn how, underneath his many layers of concern, there beat the heart of a man recognizable to him.

'Yes! It never made sense that the Gods would notice a war between lands. But now it is clear. Xiomes was looking for the tokens of Mertos and Khubron. By some learning he must have heard rumour of them and sent his men out to find them under the cloak of a war. It all makes sense now I have thought about it! Behvyn, the discus was the missing link I needed. Although I do not know exactly what they do, they are the reason Alcabell will have made her journey – to protect them from being found and used! That alone makes them out to be perilous. It must be what Fetlock pursues for Kinithor. But they must not have them!'

'Them? The there is more than one?' asked Behvyn.

'Certainly, or we would not be alone now.'

As Rumé finished, Behvyn could think of nothing to say, yet he burned inside with great fear and excitement. He yawned and the air stilled.

'It will grow cooler tomorrow, I think,' added Rumé.

Then Behvyn tried to settle down to rest like his brother, but only an uneasy sleep would come to him. When he shut his eyes, he saw the shapes of two men in long blue cloaks and wide-brimmed hats moving towards him. He woke several times in the night and each time he felt an unease that he could not place. He would glimpse Rumé sitting still, open-eyed and unmoving before he fell back into a shallow drowse once more.

Rumé's guess about the weather proved true. The next day it dawned a chill and foggy morning for the three travellers who woke to find their cloaks and bags covered in a thick layer of dew. The cold east wind brought forth a new air that lifted the cloying mantle of summer but blew against the wet skin of hand and face to make both raw. They could not see more than twenty paces ahead. The Mizzle Mountains were well named. Behvyn and his brother drew the hoods of their guard-issue cloaks up to keep warm, but it was not too unpleasant as autumn's first foreboding took root. Carried on the wind was the first rumour Behvyn smelled of the Lightwater. Rumé had not been wrong to praise its fragrance; it was a scent that spoke of happiness and sent his spirits rising once more.

As the day progressed the cracks that had been baked in August's oven now filled with rain. The ground softened into planes of mud from which grew green grass once again. Their boots splashed through shallow puddles resting on the hard earth of animal trails that lent their way southward. Rumé determined to follow these where he found them as being the most sure-footed way into the forest and to the Lightwater's edge. Behvyn and Behleth followed closely after, not wanting to be separated in the fog. Whereas before a cracking twig could reverberate across a quarter of a league, now every noise was dulled in the soupy air. Thin strands of vapour were drawn from their mouths when they spoke in this reduced world. As they moved further towards the canopy of the trees, they spotted squirrels, rabbits and foxes, all making plans for the bad weather to come.

'And so we move to the shelter of the forest following the wisdom of the animals and the birds,' mused Rumé outwardly. 'But be wary!' he said, turning towards the brothers. 'The Lightwater is possessed of sweet scent but by its banks we must not tarry. There may still be Daymen about it.'

'Daymen!' burst Behleth. 'But they're the stuff of child's tales! You can't be serious, Rumé?'

'I only said "may"; we might not see any and let us hope we do not,' replied Rumé. 'Now pick it up, both of you. We must go at no less than the speed we have maintained till now.'

Rumé marched off at a swift pace and Behvyn and Behleth struggled to keep up. It was therefore quickly that their surroundings changed from being open to closed. In what light there was Behvyn could see they were moving through tall clusters of young trees to begin with, that were skirted by saplings bent with the weight of the rain where there were gaps above to feed them with sunlight. Then, as they went further inside, the way was more blocked. Hungry ivies and lurid green mosses absorbed fallen trees. Skeletal structures ran up dark tree trunks and put out small leaves. Lichen hung down from above like curtains in an abandoned house and the floor was a mulch of bark, fresh fallen yellow leaves and slippery branches.

In between gasps for breath, Behleth's face lit up at the prospect of Daymen, but Behvyn was less pleased.

'I don't like the idea of us staying in here tonight, Behleth. I can't see much in this fog and in the dark, and it's going to get darker still. What if we're being followed by some of Fetlock's men? You've seen how Rumé's been lately. The falcon has been up and around twice as often as before. He feels we're not alone, but whatever it is he senses he can't see it. And now it has the perfect cover. It's dryer here and maybe we can cross this river more easily this way, but I don't think we're safer here than outside.'

'Your imagination is working well on this short diet, brother. But give it a rest, please. You're beginning to sound like Rumé. But think. If it were Fetlock or his men following us, the falcon would have seen them coming. There can't be anyone behind us. So what else is there apart from the chance to experience seeing Daymen?'

'I can't remember the stories of them,' replied Behvyn. 'They're not meant to be very nice though, are they?'

'They only live for a day so they don't have to be, I suppose. But if I see one of them I'll be made up. It'd be like a piece of my imagination just walked out of my head to stand in front of me.'

'We will see; that's if the light ever gets better here to see anything in,' said Behvyn, acquiescing to his brother's enthusiasm. 'Although, if we do see any, I doubt they would have such manners. Come on, I can barely see Rumé!'

Once they had continued on without a break for the remainder of the afternoon the complaints of the twins eventually forced Rumé to stop. They chose to settle on the crest of a small hill that was less wooded, had much drier ground and gave the clearest view around them. The fog had not lifted but was much thinner for being exposed to a stronger breeze and the rain had stopped. Rumé took the opportunity to release the falcon to scout their location. As it sped off, Rumé grasped for the ground, still unused to how disorienting it could be to be both in one place and move through somewhere completely different at the same time.

With little else to do for the moment except catch their breaths, the twins stood around looking for the river. They could now hear it close by.

'We have walked far today, boys,' said Rumé, pleased with the progress. 'We will be able to make the Lightwater very soon. In the meantime, have something to eat. I am trying to find rumour of Fetlock and the men away to the other side of the Highborn.'

Rumé looked like he was in a daze as he took in what he could see from the sight of the falcon. Every now and again he would comment on progress to the twins.

'He looks like he's on rockflower,' muttered Behleth to his brother.

'Yes, but without the incoherent rambling,' answered Behvyn knowingly.

'I can see rumours of the progress of others,' said Rumé, after some time, 'although it's difficult with the low clouds. I must fly the falcon beneath them. Away southwestward there are smokes rising from small fires that are in places people do not live. I would hazard a guess it is where Fetlock and the men are camped. Yes, yes I can see their horses. Ah, but they have made fast progress!' Rumé lamented. 'They must be twenty leagues ahead of us. The only thing to our advantage is that they are not in this side of the Highborn. This is Fetlock's next challenge. He could take the longer way to the Fords of Netheign, but he could lose much time. Or does he think to cross it by boat? It would save him time, but there are at least ten of them with much equipment and horses. Maybe he looks to find a vessel, but that would take time too.'

For a long time Rumé said nothing more, and then he became alert to something else.

'Ah, there are other fires a little way further south, in the midst of the same quiet lands. These are not far from the Fords. How strange that is. Maybe I can get a better look.'

Rumé was silent for a few moments but suddenly he cried out in pain.

'Ai! The falcon! By the mercy of Charion, no!'

'What? What is it, Rumé?' asked Behvyn, and he and Behleth came crowding around him.

'The falcon, she is attacked. I have lost her sight and now I fear for her,' Rumé said.

'How is this?' asked Behleth. 'Did you see who it was? Was it Fetlock?'

'No,' answered Rumé. 'I had the falcon follow away south from him, and came upon a second group. It was a strange sight. Two girls and two boys about your age dancing around the flames of a large fire, drinking from bottles; and then they dispersed and some went into the woods about and in them I saw a tall figure, standing still, that was holding a weapon.'

Behvyn and Behleth looked at each other in wonderment. For an extending moment there was silence. Then Behvyn broke it.

'Rumé, of the two girls, did one, the shorter of the two, have wild long black hair; and the other, was she tall and beautiful with straight black hair?'

'Aye, you have described them both as I saw them. And the two boys, they both had very short hair and looked to be friends with the girls. One was a lot taller than the other.'

'Tig and Tangle and Kjerros and Feran! They're trying to find us!' said Behleth.

''And they are in the company of a tall figure, you said, Rumé?' questioned Behvyn.

'Strangely dressed but with a deadly shot on him,' replied Rumé, in wrath at his own mistake.

Whereas before Behvyn and Behleth were drained by the day's efforts and sought only sleep, the impact this new information had on them changed things entirely. Behvyn started speaking quickly.

'They must be following the same beacon we are. In that case, we're going to the same place. But they have Fetlock on their tail! They might know about him, but they'll not know where he is. Rumé, you said they were south of him and his men, near the Fords of Netheign? But that's probably not much more than half a day's horse-ride away.'

'How can we get there first?' asked Behleth. 'Fetlock's leagues ahead of us, and we're on foot. There's no way we can warn them by getting to them before he does.'

'Yes, you're right,' replied Behvyn, 'but the falcon may wake. We don't know its condition. Rumé may be sightless for now, but it could return once more. But there's also another problem,' he added in an undertone. 'If your sense of foreboding is to be trusted, Rumé, then we really might be being followed as well.'

'We'll just have to take as much care as possible,' answered Behleth.

Much later, once Rumé had settled down and appeared to be resting, Behvyn and Behleth convened again to see if either had any new thoughts on how they could contact their friends and warn them of the approaching danger. They had not been able to think of anything else and sleep was impossible.

'The only things I could come up with were the falcon and the discus,' said Behvyn. 'If the tall stranger didn't kill the falcon, if it's just stunned, then maybe we could communicate with them. And maybe there's something we could do with the discus.'

Behleth agreed, and Behvyn removed the bundle from inside his jerkin. He had not found himself curious of the discus before.

Yet now they were in great need he removed it from its wrappings and they studied it for the first time. Rumé's reaction to it had been such that they treated it with great care. It seemed like an object of great power. Behvyn looked at the edging on the decorated side of the disc, which was in gold and ran about the rim as wide as his thumb. It was smooth and reflective and cold to the touch. The edging was rounded, almost tubular. He noticed how it was perforated at one point about a quarter of its circumference around. Near to there away from the edge were clustered six smooth indentations in two groups of three, gilded in gold.

'These must be what caught the light and threw the beams out to the mountains,' said Behvyn.

About the lower half of the discus was an engraved design showing a setting sun with wide rays. It was gathering to itself a long boat with a high sail. Behvyn could not see its significance.

'What's that, do you think?' asked Behleth, pointing to the last of the designs opposite the indentations.

'It reminds me of something,' replied Behvyn, 'although I don't know why. These five shapes speak to me of something big, but what exactly I don't know. Although it is odd how this one is going black when it is made of the same substance as the others; silver or stithium, I think. It's polished like the rest but will catch no light.'

'Let's have a look at the other side; there are words on there. Maybe they can tell us more,' urged Behleth.

'I think Rumé was most shocked by them,' said Behvyn, 'so let's be careful.' Behvyn turned the discus over and ran his hand around the edge once more; this time with the perforation in its top left half. The brothers stared at four lines of words inscribed within a square.

'I can't read it. The words won't let my eyes settle on them!' complained Behleth. 'They seem to keep moving!'

'What? It must be the light,' suggested Behvyn. 'Here, let me have a closer look.' Behvyn then moved his face nearer and nearer to the words in order to read them. Eventually his nose was almost up against the discus.

'I think I can make the first few words out,' he said, 'but they're not Shalean. I recognise some parts of words, but it's a different language. Let me see.' Behvyn then tried to pronounce them but couldn't shape his mouth to fit them. Each time that he strove to speak the words nothing came out. It was as though he was mute.

'See what I mean?' asked Behleth.

Panting from the attempt, Behvyn put down the discus, confused and annoyed. 'I can see them with effort but when I try to say them it's like they can't be said. They keep changing in my mind so that I can't be sure what sound to make!'

'And yet they don't change on the discus,' added his brother, taking it back from Behvyn. 'They are written into the surface. What language is this, I wonder?'

'Well, I won't be made a fool of by them!' announced Behvyn, and, as though smarting from a blow, he snatched the discus back from Behleth. 'I don't wonder at their language; I wonder at their gal! I'll make them behave or else I'll break their page to teach them!'

With that, Behvyn brought the discus close to his eyes once more, only this time with a fire in his temper like nothing his brother had seen before. Behvyn was enraged. His face turned livid purple and his mouth into a cruel sneer. He started trying to shout the words as though to force them out, but still he could not pronounce them. He struggled in silence, forming them in his mouth, his forehead becoming sweaty and hands shaking in torment, when Behleth suggested that he gave it a break and try again in the morning.

'No, we must help our friends!' roared Behvyn, and he struck Behleth with his fist. Then he ran over to the other side of the hill to continue his duel with the words that would not form. His face contorted and pulled into hideous, unnatural shapes. Spittle flew from his lips and he emitted bursts of snarling as he stared into the text.

Behleth was shaken by the change that had come over his brother. He was tearful from the shock of being hit. He didn't try to wrest the discus from him again. Instead, he went over to where Rumé was entranced, searching for the connection with the falcon and bent to rouse him.

But Behleth could not do anything else. For at that moment

came a terrible resonating sound that shook the ground and the air.

A metallic force buzzed between all things and fear rained down upon Behleth. He dropped to the ground. On the edge of his sight, Behvyn could see Behleth roll in agony as a hateful oppression spun his mind into thoughts of chaos, destruction and hopelessness. The world seemed as a cesspool of black and decaying green, repeating whichever way he looked. Suddenly all life appeared repugnant, underneath whose sweet façade there lived one abhorrent and disgusting truth; that it was always rotting, always doomed and always in the process of being digested by Death in His tireless compassion to give release from the fetid misery of existence.

Behvyn could only watch in horror as he continued to articulate the words, each sound causing anguish and unbearable pain to his brother. A force compelled him not to stop. He looked away from the disc but the words floated in front of him. He was shaking violently and sweating, with tears falling down his cheeks in wild rage as the strange words flew from his mouth and reverberated carrying an awesome power that made him quail. Trees aged to black skeletons and then turned into powder as the grass died beneath him and stone broke from the side of the hill. He felt he would break his own jaw in the effort to expel the sounds, and was cruelly twisting his face to do so when Rumé appeared. He moved unwaveringly up to Behvyn, who was in the midst of a ring of low flames, and removed the discus from his hands in one swift motion.

'I'll take that for now, young man,' Rumé said, and then walked back calmly over to where he had sat before.

At the moment Rumé took the discus, Behvyn felt an urge to kill him that was gone as soon as it arrived. He flushed in guilt and scanned the skies for sight of the falcon but he was confused. It was nowhere to be seen. He rose painfully and would not have moved had it not been for his desire to comfort his brother who now lay exhausted away from him. He saw him shivering with cold. When he reached him, he saw there was blood in his mouth.

'Behleth, are you all right?' he asked, full of concern. 'I'm sorry, I didn't mean to hurt you. Behleth!'

Behleth could do nothing except continue to fill his lungs, desperate to grab hold of as much air as possible.

'It's over, Behleth. Rumé has the discus now. Everything's going to be fine,' he added, but doubted his words even as he said them. He stayed with Behleth until he slept, and then he went over to Rumé. He was now angry.

'I will not let you break the discus,' Rumé said as he approached.

'But that thing nearly killed us!' shouted Behvyn.

'It will also save you,' answered Rumé simply. 'You cannot destroy it without destroying your brother, yourself, your friends and everyone else you care about. I understand more of this token now that you have read of it. But I will not discuss it here, save only to say that it makes finding the second token even more vital. If we are to make it to Ithed and Antheon, then you may find further answers there, as well as your friends.'

'Then I will swallow my questions until we are at that Pass,' answered Behvyn, 'as an act of a friend who trusts the other, though he does not know why he should do so. But one other question I can't withhold.'

'Ask it of me, Behvyn,' said Rumé.

'How did you see to take it off me? The falcon is gone.'

'I have no sight, but I still have my hearing,' answered Rumé. 'You are still unconvinced? I admit to you, I myself am not certain. Let me put it this way. In that moment, I knew I would be able to reach you because the consequences if I hadn't would have been too fearsome to contemplate.'

'You mean you were guided by chance?' asked Behvyn, jittery at the thought.

'Call it blind luck,' responded Rumé, giving a sour grin.

Chapter 8

A FIT OF COURAGE

Tangle noticed Kjerros and Feran's growing apprehension as they followed her confident lead. The two sisters adopted an extravagant, queenly stride as they flowed together from one pool of light to the next towards the guards in front of Rhal Castle.

One sturdy-looking man stood out from a small gatehouse and barred their direct path to the tall vaulted gate. He carried a functional pike staff in his hands that had a cleaving edge on one side of the blade and a hooked spike on the other. It was pointed at the top. The tassel that hung from it did not diminish its threat one iota in Tangle's mind. Two further guards patrolled the gate itself. She saw that one was very tall but less authoritative in his movements. He looked harshly at them as if to make up for the shortcomings of his youth. His face was pale and thin and his neck raw where the uniform had rubbed him.

The other guard was at least twice his colleague's age and did not deign to wear the helmet that seemed part of the uniform. He was weathered and olive skinned, with large knotty hands and shocks of white-grey hair at his temples that contrasted with his otherwise black hair. Although he affected a casual demeanour it was as the mark of an expert in his field. Tangle made eye contact at one point only to be held in a quick stare that calculated her threat. Once the guard had made his assessment, he let her off with a wink.

As the girls set foot into the last pool of light before the gate, the front Gateman spoke. He was young, though older than the tall guard, and he was wearing the helmet.

'Halt, in the name of the King!' he said, and held his pike out horizontally.

The two girls kept walking at their steady pace as Kjerros and Feran froze. Paequat nearly walked into the back of them.

'Hello, Canderwood,' said Tangle, still walking towards him, her sister alongside. She dropped something as he involuntarily moved aside and gaped at her in surprise.

'Our apologies! Good morning, Lady Tangly! Lady Mandle!' Canderwood adopted a deep bow, and as he did so he collected the bundle of leaves that now lay at his feet. In one smooth movement, he swept them up and hid them inside his uniform. Then, still on the rise from out of his bow, he barked out an order. 'Guardsmen! The gates!'

'Oh, and could you possibly advise our entourage to kindly follow us in, there's a clever fellow,' commanded Tangle, sweetly.

Another order was barked in the direction of Paequat, Feran and Kjerros to 'hurry along now!' as the gates swung open just in time so that the two 'ladies' needn't break their stride. The 'entourage', with Paequat causing some looks of wonder from among the Gatemen, followed the sisters inside as Canderwood watched them pass. As calmly as they could manage, they began the walk through the long gallery underneath Rhal Castle. With a glance behind, Tangle saw Canderwood remove the leaves from under his breast and study them.

'Before you say anything, boys,' spoke Tig, once they were all through the gate and their eyes had adjusted to the torch-lit darkness, 'look above you. Do you see the rope that's hung along the left side of the ceiling?'

'Yes, just about,' answered Kjerros. 'It hangs through those brass rings set in the stonework. What of it?'

'It runs the full length of the gallery,' Tig explained. 'Attached at either end is a bell that hangs down outside the gates. A Gateman at one end will dampen his bell and pull on the rope it is connected to during the passage of travellers through the room. If it rings once at the far end, the gates will open and we will be through, no questions asked.'

'What if it rings twice?' asked Feran, unable to hold back the question.

'It means they didn't like our bribe and we will be taken prisoner,' answered Tangle, matter-of-factly.

Feran's face turned ashen as he considered such a fate and stared around the gallery room intensely in an attempt to bleach his mind of the thought. He noticed their steps made no sound as they walked. On looking down, Feran noticed the corridor was carpeted, with a patchwork of sizeable rugs providing a luxurious covering to rough cobbles underneath. He also noticed how the way first inclined from the entrance up towards the halfway point and then reached a plateau that extended for fifty feet or so, underneath which, he assumed, the river then ran.

Feran saw how thick, heavy arches supported the roof and that the ceiling itself was curved to take the weight of the castle above. As they approached the plateau, with the sound of Rhal Springs flowing beneath, he was even calm enough to see that in between the arches hung upon the walls there were paintings and tapestries depicting great leaders and scenes from ancient battles. He could see emblazoned on the breastplates of the soldiers the crest of the Shale Royal Household, established by Charion, of a new living sun emerging from a dying star.

Stout iron railings tipped with sharp points to discourage close inspection defended these artworks. Not that they were particularly fine examples, being for the most part dully coloured or tatty, and every now or then obscured by molding flags and torn pennants of war. But they served to remind him how this had once been a house of the King for many long ages of man; and that one day, should Cuiron return to health, or Prince Idren survive the curse of his forebears, it could be again.

'It should be,' Feran breathed aloud.

'What?' asked Kjerros.

'What a place, Kjerros,' said Feran. 'Did you see those great houses back there on our approach to the gates? Full of lackeys to the castle owners, I'll guess. This whole area is getting fat off the traffic that has to pass through whilst King Cuiron sleeps. Well, I can't wait to see their faces if he awakens!'

Feran's courage built as he thought about the great deeds of those celebrated in the old pictures. Once his eyes had fully adjusted to the dark, he could see the depictions more clearly.

'That's the Earl of Ambror, The Sharp-Toothed!' he said to Kjerros. 'I remember him. He always used to scare me when stories told of his deeds. They said he feasted on the still living bodies of the enemy during battle.'

'I preferred King Mixo,' his cousin replied. 'Look, there he is. The Fair, they called him. He was an enchanter of animals who could tame anything to his purpose. He was supposed to have vanquished Ambror after a long intrigue. There he is, on this one over here. That's him. The artist has him riding a zebra, clothed all in striped armour! Ha! That's my Mixo!'

'Hey, look at the one on this side,' added Feran. 'It says down here it's 'Of the demise of the terrible Lord Wrey, a thorn in the side of three successive rulers in the days of the First House, as they sought to establish the extent of their rule in the Shale Valley.'

'Catchy title,' said Kjerros.

'Your father told us one night in the Poacher's how he met his end. Not the easiest thing to accomplish, either. He was the one who could use fear to turn whole armies against themselves.'

'He fended off everything thrown at him for over forty years, didn't he?' asked Tig, from up ahead.

'That's right,' replied Feran. 'But it was Prince Thosiah Firebrand, son of King Tautilus, who ultimately overcame Wrey. Look, the tapestry depicts it. There's Lord Wrey, standing on an outcrop by the Pinch looking out over his army of women and children. He put them through a hideous process to train them up to kill; a devious move because most armies wouldn't fight them. He sent them to meet the advance of the King's men head on, but Thosiah had led a single division along a different route. You can see him emerging here in white battle dress from the snow-covered mountains above Wrey's position. At the moment Lord Wrey fell to his death, the entire north half of the Shale Valley was free for people to move into once again.'

'You always did like your military history,' said Kjerros.

'I've studied everything I could,' replied Feran, 'from Cassimes' opening battles in this war to those of the Second House and before, even as far back as Charion's day. I enjoy it, casting my imagination back to the times of the great Kings, to the days of daring and reckless ambition. But what is that noise that grows? It sounds strange.'

He listened more intently and then clutched at Kjerros.

'What is it?' his cousin asked.

'More than strange! It is the armies of old! They are come, come for us! We are caught like rabbits in a fox hole!' Feran turned about madly, an unshakeable feeling of pursuit upon him.

Surrounding them all was a low, complex chord that hung in the air.

'Keep your courage up, Feran!' chided Kjerros next to him, jerking him on his arm to settle him down again. 'It's just the wind; this tunnel is channelling it across the brickwork. See those holes in the buttresses? They're acting like reeds in an instrument; that's what's making the sound. It's just a piece of cunning.'

'That footman is right,' added 'Lady Tangly', taking full advantage of her sudden rise to royalty. 'There are several places where the Kings of old used the winds in their defence of the Valley. The catacombs underneath Cambwall Castle, at the Gates of Manton and, as I understand it, on the eastward pass out to Khubron. I wouldn't let them worry you Feran, they're just to scare off the weak-minded.'

'Now, come on,' added Kjerros in an undertone. 'The last thing Tangle needs is to see you panicking like one of her dogs the other week. Don't you realise what a chance she and Tig are taking? Get yourself under control. We're more than half way and we haven't heard a bell yet, but if the guards at the far end take one look at you in this state, we'll be sure to hear it twice.'

On they walked, now beginning the down gradient and still they heard nothing. Feran flushed in embarrassment, an apology on his lips to Tangle he daren't speak for fear of angering her. Kjerros, feeling disappointed about having to upbraid his cousin, took his attention off towards anything else that would keep it and let it rest on the dance and flow of Tangle's hair in front of him. It picked up more as a wind grew in strength towards them. They were getting closer, but still no bell came.

Paequat, moving behind them all, mimicked the chord of the Rhal Castle gallery in his high reedy voice. Tangle then joined him, holding a note lower down the same chord and Tig added a third note that fluctuated up and down an octave to define a sweeter sound, backed by the broad bass of the tunnel itself. But still there came no sound of a bell.

There were only thirty paces to go. Paequat stopped singing. Twenty paces were left. Tig and Tangle ceased their notes. Fifteen paces left and the gate remained resolutely closed. Feran grasped

Kjerros' shoulder again. Kjerros barely noticed. Ten paces. Nine. Then it came. A single ring on the bell and the Gatemen in front of them swung into view from out of their small gatehouse.

All three of them, carrying pikes and looking annoyed at being disturbed at such an early hour, walked up to the entrance to the gallery and looked through the gate to watch the travellers approach. Eight paces. As the 'Ladies' and their entourage came closer and closer it seemed they were less and less likely to move, especially when Paequat came into view. Six paces. Eventually a guardsman took out from his coat a large ring of keys and inserted the longest of these into the lock. He paused and looked up to the bell expecting a second ring, but it never came.

Two paces. The large iron gates swung open silently and the Gatemen formed up in a short line along the left side of the road that now sang with the steps of the five wanderers as they left the haunting chord of Rhal Castle behind. Feran could barely hide his relief as one of the Gatemen quickly offered a "Good morning, sir," before efficiently returning to the gate, locking it and then filtering back inside the small guardhouse.

'Unbelievable,' said Feran. 'How did you do it?' he asked the sisters, once they had turned a curve in the road. They were now out of sight of the men.

'They liked our bribe,' offered Tig, tension flowing out from her in waves of smiles.

'But what was it?' asked Kjerros, now overcome with joyous curiosity.

'It was your leaves, didn't you see?' responded Tangle, aglow. They were all buzzing from their encounter with the Gatemen.

'I saw that, but how did leaves get us past those castle guardsmen?' Kjerros was clearly desperate to know.

'Well, those are just leaves at the moment, I'll grant you that,' said Tangle. 'But if they then dry them out and crush them, and grind into fine flour,' and here she laid stress on the word flour, 'they'll be something else. Any guesses?'

'Rockflower!' answered Feran. 'So that's what you had us picking!'

Kjerros was impressed. 'You knew all the time we'd need it to get through the gates. But how do you know which plant to use?

That's a big secret to know!'

'And there are some secrets that we won't reveal so lightly,' answered Tig, still flushed with success.

'Well, you two 'ladies' were majestic!' announced Kjerros, and gave them both a big hug.

'Wait!' cried Feran, suddenly. 'There's the carriage!'

There was an awkward moment as Tig tried to see the carriage. The pre-dawn light showed it to be drawn up the pathway of a great house set upon stilts on the left side of the road. It was no further than fifty yards away and only the towering boles of the tall trees that repeated their boulevard on this side of the castle obscured them from it. It could be glimpsed to the right of a well-occupied stable that was full of horses, like those that Tangle, Kjerros and Feran had seen from the side of the road earlier that night. They were not tended but they could hear voices, even at this distance, just inside the house.

'We need to get closer; I can't really see it!' said Tig, but Kjerros was more cautious.

'We need to be very careful,' he said. 'That place is full of those riders and it sounds like they'll be getting up soon to move on.'

'But we need to know where Behvyn and Behleth are!' urged Tig. 'Otherwise, we'll not know if we should turn back or carry on!'

'But those riders in there could raise an alarm, or attack us,' said Feran. 'They didn't look friendly.'

'Thank you for pointing out the obvious,' admonished Tig, 'but I think we need to do this, with care. We must get to the side of the house and see if we can hear their conversations. Let's just make sure we're not seen.'

It was Paequat that led the way as Feran fumed.

'That's twice I've been called an idiot today,' he complained as they hushed him again.

They crossed over the road, from right to left, between two trees diagonally opposite each other that were in line with the stable and so screened their approach. Then, from behind the vast trunk nearest to the house, they were able to peer out relatively well hidden and see the carriage clearly. Tig took one look and returned behind the tree, her chest heaving with surprise and confusion.

'It can't be,' she mouthed.

'It's Grodel's,' answered Tangle. 'I didn't want to tell you unless it was necessary, Tig. But it could mean anything!'

'You didn't think this was important enough to share?' Tig replied. 'That our father might be helping the very people who tried to kill us?'

'Girls, girls!' hushed Kjerros. 'Not here! They'll hear you!'

'I don't understand,' said Feran. 'Does that mean Grodel's in there?'

'Oh, come on, don't make me call you one, too,' said Kjerros, rolling his eyes.

'Listen petal, either it's stolen, or he's here, or he's lent it to somebody,' said Tig, patiently. 'But anyway. Looking at it, I don't think you could fit the twins in there if anyone else was in it. It's just not big enough.'

'We can do two things,' said Kjerros. 'Either we stay here, hope we're not seen and wait until they ride off again to see who gets in the carriage, or we go round the far side of the place and see if we can hear the conversation of those inside.' He pointed to the right wing of the great house.

'If we wait, we might see them but they'll ride off and we'll be behind,' said Tig. 'We might never catch them up and there's no guarantee we'll find out about Behvyn and Behleth. They could easily spot us from here if we hang around too long as well.'

'But if we try to get closer, it's very risky,' added Tangle.

'I could do it,' said Feran.

'Yeah, right,' said Kjerros.

'It's easy; wait here,' said Feran, and without warning he sped up to the side of the great house. He flew like a spark from a fire until he was away down the right side and was lost to the view of the others, who sat there dumbfounded.

'That dangerous,' said Paequat. The others nodded concernedly.

'What an idiot!' said Kjerros, furious.

'I don't see you rushing to his side,' responded Tangle. Kjerros returned a blameless look.

'Well, I'll be. Now that was the last thing I expected,' said Tig.

146

'I wonder if that daredevil of yours can hear anything, sis?'

In fact, Feran couldn't hear anything for several moments. Even though he had stopped running and had landed up beneath the sill of a kitchen window, the thunder of blood rushing through his ears and clatter of his panicking heart drowned out all else until he had calmed down. He found himself several feet below the window due to the place being on stilts.

'What am I thinking?' he asked himself. He looked back down the side of the house and dimly saw the road, some way ahead of where the others now hid. 'I'm no Firebrand! Maybe I've been stung into action, but at least some good should come from this recklessness. I'll show them what the idiot can do!'

He stood up gently to bring his head up to the base of the open window, standing up straight against one of the stilts. With great control he kept perfectly still, and simply listened for anything he could overhear. After a while he made out several voices, although it was difficult to separate them from the other sounds of a meal being had. The riders were seemingly having their breakfast.

'That's not the point!' one husky voice croaked. 'You can't just turn up here unannounced and expect us to have everything in!'

'Rest yourself, Captain Sirephus,' answered another voice, sweetened but under cold control. 'We'll be out of your way before daybreak.'

'As you say, sir,' responded Sirephus, 'and don't think I'm not honoured to have you and your men under my roof, but I could have put on a better spread had you called ahead, is all I'm saying.'

'As I say, we're just going,' replied the cunning voice. 'All we needs is our victuals, eh lads?'

There was a chorus of approval and the clinking of bowls grew louder. Feran's stomach rumbled with sudden hunger. 'Ow, shush. Now's not the time,' he commanded it, as he continued listening.

'So, where to then, sir?' asked Sirephus. 'I see you're travelling fast and light. Might you tell me your task?'

'Same as ever, Sirephus; it hasn't changed since you retired from the Guard,' answered the cunning voice. 'The recovery of the King and the defence of his realm!' At this, everyone in the room laughed. 'But in all seriousness, we're on the way over to the Pass of Khubron. Fancy having a dip into foreign parts once again, to see how our investments are and how the war goes. And this old fella, here? Well, we just found us a pair of murderers didn't we, lads? So he's going down to claim their execution for us whilst we're busy, along with the sad news of the death of our devious old Captain Rumé.'

'Rumé, dead?' Sirephus sounded shocked. 'Well, that is a bit of news. Really, sir? But I've not seen any of these others you mentioned. They're not travelling bound with your company?'

'No, but they are following us,' said the cunning voice, 'floating down the Highborn in fact.'

'In a riverboat?' asked Sirephus in his croaky old voice.

'In pieces!' cracked the cunning voiced man, gleefully. At this, there was uproarious laughter and the banging of mugs on tables.

'Careful,' said a different voice. This one was more authoritative and was very deep, but obscured, as though he had a mouthful of food. Feran found it familiar.

'We'll be fine,' said the sly voice again. 'Let the men have their fun, Grodel, and they'll find your daughters all the more quickly.'

From beating like a swallow's wings, Feran's heart almost stopped. Grodel was there? He knew these people?

'And you don't know that for sure, Fetlock,' continued Grodel. 'Rumé was clever; he may have rescued himself and the twins. And he will have seen the beams if they survived. There is every chance we race each other to the same place for now. You would be wrong to under-estimate him. He was never a normal man, you know.'

'Peace, Grodel,' replied the sly voiced man again; whom Feran now realised was Fetlock. 'I didn't tell you yet, did I, but he was blinded before he died. Looked at the Blackstone, didn't he, men? As blind as a baby rat he was when he came back. No, my friend, he would not have been able to save himself, let alone those two red-handed yokels.'

Grodel seemed content; he said nothing else at least, and for a while, there was just the sound of the men finishing their food. This was then followed by the sound of chairs moving backwards, heavy steps on a wooden floor and the banging of doors off towards the opposite side of the house. They were readying to move out.

Feran made to fly back to the road once again, but his legs had cramped from where he had stood for so long stock still under the window and he found he could barely move. He stumbled to the corner of the house from where he could signal to the others behind their tree. He waved at them frantically to come across, but had no idea if they could see him.

'Now what's he doing?' asked Kjerros.

'It looks like he wants us to come over to him,' answered Tangle. 'They must be coming outside.'

'We'll be found if we stay here,' said Tig. 'There are only the trees for cover and we'll be surrounded. It looks like our only choice.'

'But how do we know we'll not be seen?' asked Kjerros, staring around vigorously at the pathway, the carriage and the gate that led through to the stables from where there now came the sounds of horses being mounted. 'If we get caught, that's it!'

'I know,' said Tig, 'but none of our options are very good.'

'Come on everyone!' said Tangle. 'We just have to be brave like Feran. Quick! Run!'

They all stood up and ran as quickly as they could diagonally across the front of the lawn, from the road to the far corner of the house, as the stables filled with riders mounting up. They had almost reached safety when the gate burst open and the flood of riders poured through. Tig and Tangle, running behind Kjerros who was now at the corner and ducking behind it, looked left and glimpsed three guards gallop down the pathway and onto the road. Paequat was behind them as they noticed Grodel climbing into the carriage after another man. The girls almost stopped before Paequat came crashing into them, his hat flying off and onto the ground, before they recovered their wits and together dashed around the side of Sirephus' house.

'G-Grodel?' mourned Tig, as she was dragged around the corner of the house by an arm from Kjerros.

'Oh, no!' cried Tangle, once they had all reached Feran, upon noticing Paequat's hat sitting there on the lawn.

'Let's just hope no one sees it!' replied Kjerros, as another group of riders flew out of the stables and, upon reaching the road, dashed along it at full speed. Then the sound of the carriage moving could be heard and Tig and Tangle were reminded of what they had just seen.

'That bastard!' seethed Tangle, as she hid down low against one of the stilts. Feran came and tried to hold her. She elbowed him in the ribs.

'Ow! What was that for?' cried Feran.

'For running off without me!' answered Tangle, pushing him away.

'Shush!' reminded Tig. 'Keep very still.'

They could see three riders on the road waiting impatiently for the carriage to reach them. Suddenly one turned his restless mount and looked exactly at them. All five huddled friends froze and stopped breathing. Time stretched out enough for them to realise their own foolishness. What had they been thinking? They would be found. They would be caught. There was no way they had not been seen. But the rider then looked away and made no motion towards them. They only let themselves breathe again once the sound of the carriage, with its squeaking springs and iron-bound wheels crunching over the stone chippings of the driveway, drew further away; and they could watch its passing leftward along the road, to the south, attended by the remaining three riders. Once it had left, everything was silent once again.

'I heard them talking,' said Feran. He looked so burdened by this that no one spoke. Tangle stayed apart from him, unsettled by the array of different feelings she now had. Tig, Paequat and Kjerros rose to their feet and looked further along the side of the house. Cautiously, they went a few paces towards the rear grounds and established as far as they dared that they were alone. Then they came back and sat once more with Feran and let him tell them what he had heard.

'A man called Fetlock just bragged to your father he'd killed Behvyn and Behleth,' said Feran. 'He said that they were floating down the river in pieces.'

There was horrified silence as they each took in the full meaning of Feran's words. Kjerros looked defiant as though they were lies. Tig, unblinking, shed tears of pain.

'I then heard Grodel speak,' Feran carried on. His voice did not waver but it was only through effort that he kept it steady. 'He didn't sound disturbed by the news. He continued eating his food. Then Fetlock mentioned a man called "Rumé". He spoke of him in contempt but you could tell he had respected him or at least feared him of old. Grodel had heard of him. He seemed to think a lot of this man. It sounded like the grudging admiration someone could have for an old adversary. He thought Fetlock's claim unlikely if Rumé had been around to stop him. But Fetlock then told Grodel that Rumé was made blind, and your father's doubt drained from him.'

'They are truly thought to be gone?' asked Kjerros, in shock.

'Fetlock didn't say he'd seen them dead. Grodel wondered if they might still be alive,' said Feran. 'It was said Rumé would follow the beams if they survived.'

'Then that becomes our only task, too,' determined Tangle, 'and to hold on to hope in the face of all the words of our enemies.'

Chapter 9

UNDERWATERWAY

Behvyn tended to Behleth throughout the next day, following their ordeal with the malevolent words released from the discus. Huddled together atop the small hill in the midst of the forest of the Lightwater, he would talk to him or sing him songs to ease his recovery.

His brother had a deep fever and for a long time did not recognise Behvyn's face. It was as though he was held by a delusion that a dangerous force pursued him. He struggled desperately to escape it. Then he would be at rest only for another wave of fear to strike him. Behvyn felt a heavy guilt lie upon him for bringing the sinister object back from the peak of the Mirrorhorn. Rumé sought to reassure Behvyn that his brother would be well in time, but Behvyn knew he didn't know it for sure.

The first waters of health only sprang inside Behleth once the sun had begun to hide itself behind the Uspheron. As the darkness grew, he raised Behvyn's spirits by eating and speaking a few words before falling into an unmoving sleep. It was an improvement from that morning when Behvyn had been woken by his brother calling out senseless words.

'Fie! I'll not have thee at my feet!' snarled Behleth as Behvyn had come to, wondering who was speaking. 'No little manling's request shall avail me to make my collection when 'tis not ripe! Or is't that you would have me attend to you? I'll hold thee to a bargain you'll wish not to've made!'

'Behleth!' he had cried, and ran to his side. 'What are you saying?'

But Behleth had no idea. He had still been reliving his conflict with the dark words, struck as though in a trance.

Later he had been able to explain it to his brother. 'My mind resounded with their echoes, echoes of the words, I mean, if that's what they were. They are like spirits of death, which shape themselves as words to trick you into saying them. The memory of each syllable I heard still writhes through my mind. They left these echoing, diseased trails. I thought I was going mad. And then I heard your voice – you in your normal voice, I mean – and your touch on my brow; it gave me a direction to focus on. As though another being controlled them, the trails of those words took on a personality. They didn't want to leave my head! But I fought them with your help.'

Now that sleep had again taken his brother, Behvyn could think on for a while. He wanted to take him back to their home, but knew it was no longer possible. They had no option but to carry on, to find the second token before Fetlock. He spoke to his brother as he slept.

'They are so far in advance of us still. I don't know how we can close up to them. I wish I could think of something to offer Rumé as a way.'

Behvyn also knew that Rumé was thinking through alternatives, with similar levels of success. The grim man could be heard every now and again dismissing them one after the other with a disgusted sigh of contempt.

Even still, it wasn't just how far away the pass of Ithed and Antheon was, or his brother's health that dominated Behvyn's concerns. There was also Rumé's condition. The man was utterly blind, no longer able to view the world through the white falcon's eyes, now it had been lost. In which case, he knew Rumé would not be able to continue his journey to the pass alone, and that responsibility weighed on Behvyn's brow.

It had taken some time for Behvyn to believe much of Rumé's predictions about Fetlock and his master Prince Kinithor's plans to overthrow the King. Rumé's intimations of the larger consequences had seemed out of all proportion to events when he had first heard them. But in his mind, Behvyn was now becoming more convinced.

'We have seen the White Lady,' he spoke to Behleth as he lay. 'We've seen the Lady Alcabell herself, and mourned at her death. We saw her to into her grave. It's dizzying to think she was there at the making of our eldest legends. She spoke to me. She asked me to find her surrogate, which I still don't know what it means. But I don't think I've missed it yet. We've not met anyone since then who hasn't wanted to blow us up or drown us or blind us or have us hanged.'

Behvyn looked down to his lap and saw his brother's face with closed eyes and imagined the struggle within.

'The power of the discus is real, too. I fear it now, as we should have from the start,' Behvyn said, loud enough for Rumé to hear. 'I've seen the beams it cast and how it used me. I have no more curiosity for it. I feel sorry for Rumé that he must now look after it. It is a tool of evil. I don't know what we'll find at the pass, Behleth, but if it's another discus then I only want it so that others can't have it. We must get there first, before him. If only I can think of a way!'

He put Behleth down gently and walked without direction to the edge of their clearing.

'You know, Behvyn,' said Rumé, speaking for the first time that day though it was now nearly dark, 'the Lightwater's fragrance has been valued as a health-giving source for thousands of years. King Cuiron's apothecary always kept bottles of it in the royal apartments. Its scent is stronger at the river-side.'

'Can we take him?' asked Behvyn, knowing he would have to talk Rumé through each step from the little raised hilltop they were upon down to the riverside.

'Of course,' Rumé replied. 'I will carry him on my back. Guide me.'

The going was very slow in the failed light. Behvyn carried all their packs and walked forward deliberately with Rumé's left hand on his shoulder. Rumé's right hand held Behleth's dangling arms clutched at his chest, as he supported his sleeping form across the width of his shoulders.

After passing the scorched trees, turned black from the events of the previous night, they entered down through the canopy into the interior of the wood. Then it was only a short while before they felt the gradient of the land leading them downward towards the riverbank.

The noises of the forest were building up as the business of the night got underway in burrows, hollows and nests; all under a swift-moving cloudscape that flew on a warmer breeze come up to meet them from the southeast. It brought with it the scent of the river and rattled the first dying leaves still on the twig. By the time they had reached the very brink of the Lightwater, taking tentative steps so as not to stumble on the damp undergrowth that bordered it, they had breathed many a great lungful of its heady fragrance. Behvyn's cares, if not washed away, were pushed from the forefront of his mind as they stood by the languidly flowing water. He hoped the same was true for Behleth, who still rested.

Although dark, their new surrounds seemed pretty. There were feisty tufted grasses rising up from the dank earth, threaded with dropped, sinuous branches. Through the thin layer of soil shone hulking networks of luminous white tree roots, bursting proudly above ground level like bulbous icebergs in a black sea. Nestled among them were families of shiny toadstools, glossy red and white. Dustings of campion, swathes of heavy-headed foxglove and rich tapestries of dark green ivy contested to clothe the floor from which emerged the smooth trunks of elegant trees that cast their broad-leafed roofs high overhead. These trees were mighty on both sides of the river yet they were much fewer along the waterside than only a stone's throw further back. It lent those that were there a rather superior air, as though they had been specifically planted by man's hand rather than by the caprice of nature. It gave the bank an artistically pleasing but curiously manufactured look.

With care, Rumé lay Behleth down and covered him in his own cloak as Behvyn returned to his brother's side, coming back from the waterside having filled his lungs with several deep inhalations.

'With luck he should sleep through tonight undisturbed,' said Rumé, feeling around for one of the long branches that dotted the ground, trying them out as a staff and rejecting one after another until he settled upon one that would suit him. As he sat down he took out his hunting knife and began shaving off the twigs along its length that would otherwise catch against his cloak as he walked.

'Rumé, you were not affected by the words my brother spoke,' said Behvyn, after he had assured himself that Behleth was as comfortable and asleep as he could be. The moon had risen and cast everything in a grey-silver glow. 'Why was that?'

'It scares me to think of it, Behvyn,' answered Rumé, 'more

than the idea of what if I had been affected by it as well as you both and you had been able to complete the passage aloud.' He let the thought sink in. 'You know what effect it had on your brother and the ground about us from just a few words. Although it may have seemed to you that you had nearly completed the incantation, you had but merely begun to utter the third word inscribed on the discus. Now consider the power of this language! It holds the power of creation and destruction. They are the words of your creation! But, it seems, not mine.

'It means I cannot be Shalean, though I may have thought I was until now. But I know my father was washed inland from the sea. It is just I was always told it was a return journey.'

Rumé fell silent and it did not dawn on Behvyn for some short moments what had been revealed, until he thought of who his father might be.

'You are Rothé's son!' exclaimed Behvyn. Rumé nodded. 'Then you are alive only through your father's cunning over the very man that tried to kill the three of us! The same man who you had assigned to you. Oh, how cruel! I am sorry Rumé. To have to see him each day, to listen to him speaking, see him building up his lies and maneuvering around you in his plotting circles, when all you could see was the man that – I'm surprised you didn't kill him.'

'Where would that have got anyone?' responded Rumé. 'I would have been sentenced to death myself and my sons and wife would have lost me to the grave. And Fetlock did not kill my father, so such revenge would not be equal to his crime. I do not harbour any desire to see Fetlock hanged over his past wrongs, strange as that may sound. I would instead have him understand the sanctity of life, the wisdom in accepting that others think differently and that I want him to live.

'He does not understand why I don't want to kill him,' continued Rumé, 'and it riles him. It does not fit with the simple ideas by which he runs his thoughts. If something is a lose end, have away at it, so goes his mind. Throw away the difficult, keep only the straightforward. He would dispense of me at the first opportunity, as he tried, because it makes sense to him. He does not accommdate that which is a possible risk to him, does not allow those he disagrees with to run free and does not look to mend things that are broken.'

'Then he is dangerous until he is stopped!' responded Behvyn.

'But that is looking to control nature and you cannot control it,' replied Rumé. 'I would have him learn it. If he and those he works for believe they can take complete control of this kingdom, they will fail. Even as he would grasp the reign of power, it would turn to dust within his hand. You see, he seeks power through fear, a fear that comes of not having the power to defend himself against the forces he perceives threaten him. Think! Why would any great force focus its attention on one quite ordinary man if he does not want to do wrong? There is no reason in this world at all. Therefore, I would rather have Fetlock see this than the steel of my blade, for that would not add to the good of this world; only its woes.'

Behvyn considered this from Rumé, and found in all truth such magnanimity and responsibility hard to reconcile with the fact Fetlock had tried to kill them both. But the thought that Fetlock was motivated through fear rather than hate he found made him less a force of evil and more a weak man.

'If I were to have the opportunity to kill Fetlock,' said Behvyn, 'I don't know if I would be able to control myself as you.'

But before Rumé could reply, there was a sharp crack from behind them that startled them both.

Rumé was the first to react.

'Get down, Behvyn!' he urged, and they both lay flat on the ground.

Rumé then unclasped the handle of his hunting knife from its sheath and passed it under his body over to Behvyn who he could feel lying next to him.

'Take it, don't be alarmed,' he said.

Behvyn looked down to see what it was being offered to him. He saw the handle of the knife and took a sharp intake of breath.

'You don't think it's someone, do you?' Behvyn asked, as he reluctantly took the knife.

'I don't know, but don't move. No creature less than half your weight could snap a branch that big with a footfall. If I can hear it move again, maybe I can understand what it is.'

Behvyn strained his eyes in the dark, looking from trunk to trunk, and Rumé listened for any telltale sound that he could interpret.

'Be very careful,' Rumé said, whispering. 'It may only have been an animal but something tells me otherwise. Now, rise up a little from where you are and have a quick glance around, then get straight back down again.'

Behvyn did so, feeling very exposed, then lay down flat again to report he had seen nothing. Behleth, still asleep just behind them by the bank of the river, was making most of the sound they could hear as he rested.

'Should I wake him?' asked Behvyn. 'What if someone is out there? Two pairs of eyes would be better than one?'

'No, he must rest,' answered Rumé.

So it was that Behvyn kept up their vigil himself, letting Behleth sleep on and letting himself be guided by Rumé who would sense the odd movement through the ground, or pick up on a sound that raised his suspicions and alert Behvyn to look to his left or ahead or to his right. Into the night Behvyn followed Rumé's instruction, during which he scanned every sound they heard. At times Behvyn thought he had seen something only never to spot it again. A rustle here, the disturbance of a sleeping bird there, sounds confused by the lolloping wallow of the river, Behleth's breathing behind them and the living chatter of the leaves on the towering trees above. As time wore on with no sightings of anything obvious enough to report, Behvyn began to tire.

'Do you think-' Behvyn began, looking over towards Rumé, when there was a clear noise heard off towards their left, westward towards the edge of the woods nearest to the Highborn.

Behvyn turned his glance sharply towards the noise but saw nothing. Then he heard two distinct sounds come from another direction completely – from the river behind him and to his right. But once he had turned and looked into the Lightwater there were only the ripples left on the surface to confirm the two splashes; he could see nothing else on the river's surface.

He explained it all to Rumé who understood what had happened instinctively.

'I heard the splashes too, Behvyn,' said Rumé. 'Two creatures diverted your attention by throwing a stone in another direction to that in which they were going. Do not be hard on yourself that you did not see them. It lets us know several things. Firstly, that the noises were not those of animals but other men. They saw us and did not want us to see them; they threw a rock; they dived into a river. And I can say the sense I have had of being pursued since we escaped from that doomed vessel in the North Vale is now suddenly gone. Our pursuers are now only yards ahead of us! The question now is: when and where will they surface?'

This time, knowing all he had to do was watch the waters for a few long moments at the most, Behvyn stood up and openly scanned the riverside looking for bubbles rising to the surface. He expected to see two bedraggled figures climb out of the stream and crawl up the bank opposite. He guessed how far they could swim under water before needing to come up again for air and worked out they would not be able to go so far upstream as downstream because of the current. There were no turns in the path of the Lightwater as far as his eyes could reach through the dark of the night. Though the moon was lowering, it was far enough up in the western sky to cast its silvery grey light along the length of the river. Behvyn knew he would see anything trying to get out of the water.

But though he looked, he still saw nothing. The motion of the flow smoothed the ripples and soon they had disappeared. The memory of the sound of the splashes was lost. He began to doubt that he had heard anything and after finally losing all hope, eventually threw himself down on the ground in complete frustration.

'Outwitted by a couple of children, no doubt!' he derided himself. 'Some pursuer I am! I'm sorry Rumé, I'm so sorry. I couldn't see anything. They must have drowned or turned into fish!' At the thought, Behvyn found the idea a little funny and began to chuckle ironically.

'Don't be so hard on yourself,' advised Rumé. 'No one can see into a river at nighttime as though it were day. If they didn't come out, then they must have stayed in.'

'Stayed in? But how? They wouldn't be able to breathe!' responded Behvyn, still offended by how they had escaped his notice on land and now in water.

'Maybe we should find out,' answered Rumé, as the wind flowed faster out over the river than through the wood bringing along with it the scent of the mythical flowers that enlivened the atmosphere. 'Jump in.'

'What?' asked Behvyn, confused.

'I don't know what you'll discover, but jump in the river. I know you swim well.'

'Yes, I can swim,' answered Behvyn, 'but isn't this a – it's a river; a river's a river's a river. Isn't it?'

'Stay close to this side of the bank and get out quickly,' Rumé commanded. It was a tone that could not be disobeyed but also filled Behvyn with confidence that even though he was facing an unknown, Rumé would know what to do in any circumstance that might stem from it. He removed his cloak and dived into the slow rolling Lightwater.

Behvyn expected to make more of a splash at entry. He expected his ears to fill with water. He expected to get wet. Instead, he had the greatest surprise of his life: he could breathe!

The sensation was unlike any he had experienced in the past. He was swimming, but not through water. It had the texture of water; it was colourless and transparent in the shallows by the banks and blue and opaque in the depths. But it wasn't water. The moment he noticed them, he couldn't believe he hadn't seen them from above as he had gazed into the river. But now he was face to face with them, he saw more as he looked. Up, down, near, far. Millions upon millions of eyes were looking at him, tiny points of light with each capturing only a pinprick of moonlight, but each holding a steady intelligence behind it. A billion glances in his direction, as they crossed each other in different directions. With curiosity overcoming his concern of descending further into the morass, Behvyn swam his way down lower, further away from the surface, until he could perceive the lowest depths of the river. He saw the riverbed and pulled himself through to touch it. As he turned and looked up to see the flows describe themselves above him he was staggered by what he saw.

An entire system of rotating currents revealed themselves. Nearer to, the eyes moved past him off towards the mountains, whereas the minute particles flowed away, out towards the

Highborn, nearer to the surface. But in between the surface and the riverbed, huge cycles of astonishing beauty formed complicated patterns in the flows, linking great vertical swirls into each other, wheel upon wheel moving in opposite directions. Each torpid structure created plunging or rising vortices that caused both the rolls and ripples on the surface and the current that now worked on Behvyn, looking to draw him back up from the riverbed.

Before he let it take him, he looked around inquiringly, trying to see if there was anywhere to hide inside the river. He was still close to the northern bank and remembered Rumé's caution about staying close to it, but saw nothing dangerous in trying to see if there was any cover offered by the southern bank. He swam strongly over to it and began to search, but could see little. There were a few submerged overhangs but they offered no real shelter, and there were no plants offering a canopy to shield a person from watchers above. In fact, there were no plants or weeds or fish at all. It was as Behvyn was discovering this that he heard Rumé call his name, and turned around to look up at him when he saw what he had been looking for all along.

It was the start of a tunnel, deeply delved into the side of the northern bank, obscured by clouds of eyes whirling in their creative dance to speak to the world above: "I am a river". It was six or seven feet across. Satisfied, he rose to the surface and swam to the northern bank.

'I'm here! I've found it, I've found it!' Behvyn cried, as he climbed out. As he did so, he noticed the river did not cling to his clothes, but instead drained from him back into itself as oil will from an iron stirring rod. 'And I am quite dry!' he announced in wonderment.

Behvyn quickly explained everything he had seen and experienced to Rumé.

'Well, if I had guessed at it I would have never believed it,' Rumé said eventually. 'The finest inquisitive minds in the entire Valley would be astounded by your discovery, Behvyn; and some no doubt would then set out to prove you wrong as well. So, our path of action is now clear to us. We must explore the tunnel, but do so warily. Whoever it was that went in before you could be down there still. Also,' he added more delicately, 'we'll need to wake Behleth now.'

Behvyn had been worried about Behleth's reaction to being disturbed, but he needn't have been. Behleth was slow to wake, but once he had opened his eyes, his face creased into a shallow smile and Behvyn saw that his brother had returned.

'I thought it was too much to ask to get away with a good night's sleep with you around,' Behleth said, as he sat up and took in his surroundings.

'There's only so much of your snoring I can take,' replied Behvyn, exuding relief and pulling his brother up to his feet.

'My tongue feels weird,' said Behleth, and he tasted the blood inside his mouth.

'You've been talking in your sleep,' answered Behvyn.

'About what?'

'About why your head is so fat and why you aren't as good at everything as I am.'

'I was obviously just saying that to make you feel better,' said Behleth, rubbing his eyes and stretching his limbs.

Once Behvyn had explained what they had to do, his biggest problem was stopping Behleth from jumping straight into the river, so excited was he by the prospect. In the end, Behvyn simply gave up and watched as Behleth performed a running jump into the heart of the Lightwater and didn't see him for quite some time, knowing exactly the stages of discovery he was going through. When Behleth finally resurfaced, Rumé and Behvyn were ready to leave.

'Stay in!' said Rumé to Behleth, as his brother threw in their packs.

'It's amazing, Rumé,' said Behleth, as he watched the others join the river. Behvyn grabbed Rumé's shoulder and guided him down to the tunnel entrance. As they arrived, Behleth swam straight in, only to fall from midway up from the tunnel floor suddenly down to meet it. Behvyn and Rumé heard an embarrassed thud resound from within.

'Ah, when you swim in, swim in near the bottom of the tunnel,' advised Behleth, distantly.

Behvyn found out why instantly. Instead of the tunnel being filled with the same river of life as the Lightwater, it was entirely empty. Behleth had dropped to the ground like a ripe fruit.

'Don't worry, I'm fine,' Behleth grinned before his brother could ask.

'You landed on your head, then?' responded Behvyn.

'I didn't expect that,' added Rumé, as he too emerged from the river into the tunnel, all the while holding on to Behvyn.

The twins noticed the river was held back from flowing into the tunnel by a skin over the entrance, through which they had passed. This same skin then coated the sides of the round tunnel, which was large enough in height to let the three of them walk fully up-right along it. The membrane sent out faint rings of blue light that pulsed slowly away from where they stood and disappeared away ahead of them, as though indicating the direction they should now go. The scent was strongest here as Behleth lead them on, through the gently curving route and up a small gradient that grew steadily with every few hundred paces.

'The climb rises. We must be approaching the mountains,' said Rumé.

'Do we want to go there?' asked Behvyn. 'Shouldn't we return and make for the Highborn instead?'

'We can't turn back now!' answered Behleth. 'We just found a secret tunnel! I want to know where it goes! Unless, of course, you're scared?'

'Of course I'm not,' responded Behvyn, piqued. 'But this might not get us any closer to where we want to go.'

Rumé held a steady silence and did not stop, forcing Behvyn to guide him forwards as Behleth forayed enthusiastically ahead. If he had any inkling of where they were heading, he did not let on.

They had travelled long enough to expect dawn's rise, had they been outside, when Behleth stopped up ahead.

'We're here!' he said, surprise and excitement in his voice. 'Wherever "here" is.'

'I can see an exit!' remarked Behvyn, equally pleased to have some real progress at last.

'It is like the entrance we came in, only it's set into the roof. We'll have to rise up and out of it,' explained Behvyn to Rumé. 'The tunnel flattens out below it.'

Rumé was relieved. At this point in their journey, the inclination of the tunnel had grown so steep that he had feared they would not be able to advance much further. The softly glowing gelatinous lining gave little grip and they had each slipped not a few times before reaching this point.

They gathered together around the end of the tunnel. Then the twins held their breath and raised their heads up and through the membrane to see where they might be.

They emerged out of what transpired was a hole in a flooring that was seeded with pools and inlets, trap-routes, chutes, flumes, other tunnels and holes of all shapes and sizes. Some were filled with water; others had light steams rising from them. Some had fountains, and others supported bouquets of wheeling plants upon their surface.

Behvyn could see they were at the base of one side of an enormous chasm that stretched away to their left and right without seeming to end and that rising up in front and behind were sheer black walls that lead to a narrow stripe of sky. From a glance upwards he could see it was already well into the day, although little light reached this far down. But slender networks of rivers that pooled, divided and ran off lengthwise, and those that rolled down into other tunnels similar to their own, were only a prelude to what rose in front of them. It was a stranger sight still and Behvyn felt obliged to describe it to Rumé once he and Behleth had pulled him out of the tunnel and onto the hard wet rock next to it.

'It is a, well, it's a kingdom!' Behvyn glanced at Behleth questioningly at Behleth, who nodded acceptance of the word. 'There is a horn of rock that spirals itself upwards, as you would imagine upon the brow of a sperm whale. It's colossal at the ground, the size of the whole of Muscle Oaks. It must be a league about the base to walk around it. As it climbs, it tapers to a point above, but it is incredibly high, its apex is among the clouds. The rock is white, unlike the dark sides of the chasm that face each other; but there is life all about it that makes the vast tower a garden and it is wild and green but blue as well. A river runs around it, but – it cannot be! It flows upwards! And there are birds that encircle it. They flock and feed from the rivers that clothe it from peak to root. Ah – hear how their song echoes off the faces of the chasm.

The rock hosts hardy trees with their roots above their branches, so steep does it climb, and they hang on as lichen and drink in the mist. Yes, there is a mist about it too in places, and it sends coloured shimmers into the air around it where the sunlight reaches.'

'And about it all,' continued Behleth, keen to complete the picture for Rumé, 'up to its furthest reaches, there are rich carpets of a flower I have never seen the likes of before. It's a fierce blue as the eyes of a God might be, and its bloom must be the work of many summers. The petals are small at the centre and thickly knit, and at the edges are long fingers that take the breeze and reshape it. They look like the souls of the stars set in the ground. And Behvyn describes it well. It is a view I wish long to hold in my memory.'

'Now, that is kind,' said a distant voice that echoed around the chasm.

Behvyn and Behleth looked around, startled. Rumé tensed.

'What was that?' asked Behleth, unable to gauge the direction of the sound and looking frantically back down the tunnel as Behvyn stared over at the forests on the White Horn.

'A compliment, I would say,' came the voice again, now clearly originating close by. But its speaker did not reveal itself. The voice sounded pleasant enough but the words seemed strained through a boiling noise that obscured some of the pronunciation.

'Well, thank you,' responded Behleth cautiously, roughly towards where he thought the words came from.

'You really like it? Tell me what you think of the hanging trees?' came the voice again, speaking excitedly, still with the bubbling sound behind the words.

Behleth noticed ripples appear in a large pond ahead of them that stood among others about the foot of the mighty rock.

'I wonder the most at them,' he hazarded. 'I can't imagine what clever fashioning would be needed to grow them so.' Rumé squeezed Behleth's shoulder in approval. As the ripples grew larger on the surface of the pond, Behvyn wondered if Behleth's answer would be appreciated in the same way as his earlier comment had been.

'Do you see? There, in the pond ahead!' whispered Behvyn. 'I thought I just saw a foot.'

'I can show you a leg, if you like,' came the response back from within the rippling surface as both brothers caught a brief glimpse of a svelte leg, crowned with a pointed foot, appearing out of the water. For a moment, they thought it was transparent. Then, at what sounded like giggling, it dived back under and the ripples on the pond changed into a swirl. The swirl was slow to begin with, then it gained in speed and magnitude; the centre of the pond lowered as the water was spun out to its sides.

The twins moved forward unconsciously. They lost all sense of danger and became fascinated in the display that seemed to be being put on for their arrival. As the pond spun ever faster, the centre of it went lower until they couldn't see all the way down it. They stepped still closer, right to the very edge of what had been a pond and was now a whirlpool, when suddenly the spout rose up from the middle, inverting itself entirely so that the pond parodied a miniature version of the white rock in whose shadowy bulk they stood. Then, with the dizzying vortex still revolving upwards, sending out a fine rain around them, a figure of great beauty emerged high above them from its spindly centre, as though born from its fibre. A water-person, she was entirely transparent but could be perceived because of how her body refracted what light there was. Then she dived gracefully from its summit, far above their heads, back towards the pond to enter without a noticeable splash by the feet of the twins. Immediately, the pond collapsed back down following the figure, and the surface splashed only momentarily against the sides before being entirely calmed.

Behvyn and Behleth, gasping in awe, were then presented with the re-emergence of the beautiful figure. She swam up out of the centre of the pond and walked across its very surface towards them, clearly smiling in delight. As though it was the most natural thing in the world, they both started clapping applause. Although the twins could not explain why, they both found her to be more alluring than anything they had yet experienced in their lives. Each step she took was deliberate and under a feminine control that sent warm shivers through them. Her figure, though transparent as the air, was of real substance and had weight and strength. After her efforts to make her show, her body heaved heavily to restore its equilibrium. As she reached the brink of the pond and stood in front of the boys they couldn't help noticing the fullness of her blue-tinged figure, and as a consequence they stood there for a short while unable to think what to say. All the while the figure stood in front of them in gleaming happiness, her eyes the colour of the warmest ocean.

'My name is Behleth, Water-Princess,' Behleth finally spoke, wild-eyed, following a nudge from Behvyn.

'And this is my brother, Behvyn,' prompted his brother, looking at Behleth, but failing to elicit anything further.

'I am Yinko, Behleth and Behvyn,' she replied. She spoke in the same youthful lightly burbling voice the brothers had heard earlier. 'I am very pleased and excited to meet you both. Could you help me out?' She extended her hands towards them.

Behvyn and Behleth met this with some mild alarm, but took one of her hands each in theirs. To their great surprise she was not wet to the touch but dry and warm and clearly as solid as they were themselves. Yinko noticed their reaction and delighted in it.

'You are very kind to call me a princess,' she said with amusement in her voice, staring deeply at Behleth as she passed.

The brothers turned to look once again at the surface of the pond in the vain hope of understanding how someone of their equivalent presence could walk upon it. She moved onto the bedrock and her swaying hips bewitched them again as she strode unerringly towards Rumé. From behind, they noticed how she had a waterfall of hair that fell down her back to the base of her waist.

'You are he that cannot see; I am tasked to guide you to our Citadel,' she spoke to Rumé.

'You are kind, lady,' answered Rumé, and let his arm be taken by Yinko.

'You younger manlings may take the main flume yourselves, or I can send for others to help you, if it is too much for you?' she asked, as she walked over to the base of the White Horn and showed the boys what she meant. They saw the main 'flume' rising and flowing up from where they stood, cycling around the kingdom several times on its journey to the peak.

'The Citadel of your people is at the top of the flume?' asked Behvyn.

She nodded.

'We can do this ourselves, Yinko!' responded Behleth, bravely, but upon looking up at the full height of the horn, felt some of his confidence waver.

'Very well, brave boys,' replied Yinko, smiling. 'We will see you at the top. Will you race each other for us? We enjoy sports and competition here.'

'Of course!' announced Behleth, seeing the perfect opportunity to challenge his brother to a feat of strength for the first time in a long while, and also keen to show Behvyn that he really was recovering well.

Yinko then wished them both the best of luck and with a wink entered into the current with Rumé. She began to swim up and around the sides of the lower horn, with her arm around the man's chest, and pulled him through the ascending river effortlessly.

Chapter 10

MOTHMAGS

It was one thing to talk bravely about hope, Tangle realised, but it was quite another to try to conjure it within her breast, as the light of the morning grew. She had been confronted by the idea that her own father was out searching for them in the company of their enemies. She thought back to a year before and wondered if Grodel had looked for his daughters in the same way then. He hadn't discovered them until they had wanted to be found, so Tangle wasn't particularly alarmed at this news. But the fact he knew these men had shocked her. She felt embarrassed, foolish for never having known this before, and wondered if Tig felt the same. But she also knew there were more urgent matters to be dealt with first.

'How can we get ahead of the riders?' asked Kjerros. 'We have to find out the truth, so we know if the twins are alive. Or if not, then we have to avenge them!'

'We need to find a faster method of transport than our own legs,' said Tig.

'But the stables must be emptied now,' added Feran.

'Most likely,' said Tangle, 'but we should look in any case.'

They had just plucked up the courage to walk round to the front of the house to investigate when, suddenly, an old man appeared. Not seeing them, he bent down, reaching for what he had just found.

'Well, well,' the old man said. 'Whose is this?' His narrow eyes, crowned by long bushy grey eyebrows, studied the tall black hat in the early dawn light. His silhouette showed him to be short, but much of his lack of height was due to how his back had hunched through age. His head was stuck out well ahead of his shoulders, and with his sallow grey skin and overbite, this gave him the look of a tortoise. He held the hat up to catch it in the low light and to watch the play of dew that had settled on it. Then a figure loomed at his side.

'Mine,' the figure said in a high, reedy voice.

The man, startled out of his mind, collapsed to the floor in shock. Then, as Paequat, with a rictus grin spread across his face, reached his straw hand into his own chest and produced one of his swords from within, the old man's face contorted in sheer terror.

'No!' cried Tangle, running up to them, and Paequat halted in the process of swinging back the blade.

'Don't hurt him, Paequat; sweetie,' added Tig, walking towards them, with Feran and Kjerros following more cautiously behind. 'We could see if he can help us.'

Paequat, slightly deflated, cocked his head to one side and reached down. He plucked his hat from the old man's clasp and gestured to him to lead them towards the stables, but the old man stayed put.

'P-P-Please don't hurt me,' stammered the man as Paequat, running out of patience, pulled him up onto his feet. He jittered nervously like a monkey on a rope in Paequat's grasp. Then, at swordpoint, he led them to the gate into the stable yard. He struggled clumsily to open it, yelping pathetically in panicked frustration with each failed attempt, so much so that Kjerros came forward to help him. The man flashed him a look of immense thanks, but Kjerros thought he caught a glimpse of mischief behind those old eyes. He wondered if it was his imagination, but extended his hand towards Paequat who passed into it the pommel of his other sword, just to be on the safe side.

Eventually Kjerros opened the gate and they filed into the square of the stable-yard. Kjerros cast around for somewhere to move the man to and saw that the first stable had both lower and upper doors open and, inside amongst the straw-laden floor, there was a stool.

'Go on,' motioned Kjerros.

'Can I sit?' the old man asked, once Paequat had led him to the stool. The room smelled strongly of horse, leather, wax and damp hay. The others held back by the door as Kjerros considered the suggested accommodation.

'If you will,' he answered.

'T-t-thank you,' said the old man, moving to sit.

It was upon hearing the old man speak that Feran recognised the croaky voice.

'You're Sirephus!' he said.

172

'What?' The man paused in his motion. Crouching, he twisted his face in a brief anguish, as though a plan had failed. 'Oh, yes, I'm Sirephus, Sirephus Oakridge,' he answered, and gave Feran a sideward look of confusion. 'But I'm retired, see. I wouldn't hurt no-one.' He moved to sit down on the three-legged stool but Kjerros kicked it away before he could reach for it and levelled his sword at him.

'Exactly,' replied Tangle. 'You wouldn't hurt no-one,' she mimicked. 'Now could you possibly tell me how you know Grodel?'

'G-Grodel?' asked Sirephus, incautiously. Paequat brandished his sword flamboyantly again. It spun around like a sycamore seed falling towards the ground, only stopping an inch from the man's chin. 'Oh,' continued the man, suddenly with perfect recall. He launched into a nervous tirade. 'You mean old M-Marshall Lodger. 'Course, you're supposed to call 'im 'Grodel' these days, I know, but old Lodger, well, 'e hasn't changed much since he left the forces if 'e's changed at all, no 'e hasn't. 'E might've mixed the letters up in 'is name, but no, 'e's just the same; though it's been twenty year if it's been a day since 'e left. Few things might've gone over time, but my memory's still there and no mistaking, young lady. You'd never forget a man like that; top o' the pile in the Kings Guards. No matter what name 'e goes by; once you've served under a leader of men as demands as much as Lodger from every man, and your every effort I mean, you don't forget 'im, not in a hurry, not in a hundred years.'

'Hmm,' he broke off, suddenly, looking up at Paequat. 'I see you still have me under your sword, old feller, but mightn't you not do me a favour and just give me a bit of room to breathe here, and I'll 'elp you out, so I will.'

Paequat gave the man another deathly smile, retracted his sword from Sirephus' chin, but moved it to under his jaw where it touched the skin. Sirephus winced.

'Don't understand much Shalean, eh?' muttered Sirephus. 'There's a good lad. Easy now.'

'You worked for him?' blurted Tangle, surprised.

'Aye, miss, thousands of us, so we did,' replied Sirephus vehemently. 'You'll not find us thin on the ground. Lodger kept us out o' much of the way of that ridiculous war the King's wagin', so e' did. An' there'll be a lot o' wives an' children an' all who'll thank 'im too, if they ever knew who 'e was. Hidin' us up in the North Vale, behind the Wall an' never lettin' anyone else in. 'E doesn't get a lot o' appreciation, I'll wager, wherever 'e' goes now, but mark my words, mind; mark 'em: the man's a hero. I'll not have it said otherwise, an' those bloomin' Royalists, always stopping this country from movin' forwards, tellin' everyone they'll yet get young Cuiron up and running things again once they've broken the curse. Fighting a war no one remembers what for, against the Mertosians and Khubroni who live hundreds of leagues away, that by most accounts just want to be left alone. Well, just ridiculous is all I can say. Talk to anyone in the real world who've got their heads on right an' you'll see what I mean. We don't need those in-bred warmongers back in place. We needs to move forwards, to get this country going once more. 'S like an old abandoned 'ouse, is the Shale Valley, 's terrible. Just waiting for the dustsheets to be thrown off once more. Well, Lodger was the man that did all that for me; lestways, 'e tried in his time, and can't be faulted for it.'

Tig and Tangle paused in confusion. They felt their whole world revolve and were momentarily lost. In a flash they had both had something resolved; the cause of the strange sense they had always had about their father but had never been able to identify had suddenly become clear.

'That's as may be,' weighed in Kjerros, unwilling to allow Sirephus to get off the back foot, 'but what can you tell us about this Fetlock? He's a cold-blooded murderer, from what we hear. What are you doing giving him and his men lodgings?'

'E came with Lodger,' said Sirephus, subdued. 'I durstn't be knowin' anything about 'im apart from 'e's running things now. Takin' over from Lodger's replacement, Captain Rumé. Seems like they didn't get on, but now it seems this Rumé's been involved in the murder of one of the Great Ones from over the seas, or some twins he was helping were. Good as dead he is now, even if Fetlock didn't do away with him as 'e reckons.'

'And now they've gone to Khubron?' asked Feran.

'What's it to you, sonny?' retorted Sirephus, but returned a less sneering look when Paequat lifted the edge of his sword up into the man's neck. 'Err, y-yes, yes, that's what they said, but, well, what does that mean?' simpered Sirephus. He looked at them, carefully, each in turn in supplication. 'They could go anywhere; it's just what they told poor old me. 'Ere, you two,' he added, pointing to Tig and Tangle, 'you're not 'e's daughters, are yer?'

'We have to catch them up,' said Tig. 'Do you have any horses left?'

'Horses? No dear,' replied Sirephus. 'I don't have any horses. The stables? Well, they're a bit of a legacy, but there aren't any horses left in Rhal, I can assure you of that.' At this, Feran, who had stayed by the door, turned away back into the courtyard. He kicked out in disappointment at a bucket that had been left out following the rider's swift departure. It banged into one of the doors of the set of stables lining the yard at right angles to the set they held Sirephus in. A fleeting sound of rustling was heard, although he thought nothing of it. 'Just birds,' Feran said to himself as he came back to the doorway at which the rest remained gathered.

'Wha'd'ya expect to do even if you caught them, may I ask?' Sirephus was continuing.

'We'd punish them for killing our friends, the twins,' spoke Feran.

'And how exactly could you four children with your scarecrow take on the eight of them?' quizzed Sirephus, amused by the thought. Since Feran had been away, he'd gathered his wits together.

But Kjerros had had enough.

'Ah, he's no help to us!' he cried in frustration. 'Only a hindrance. Tie him up and leave him; we'll have to think of another way to catch up with those villains.'

Paequat backed Sirephus, step by step, towards a set of chains hanging down from the rear wall, further and further away from the light cast through the doorway. Outside, within the other set of stables, the disturbance caused by Feran continued. Sirephus' breath came in nervous gulps and he started to sweat. He began to cower and held his hands out in front of him in plea but Paequat continued his advance and Sirephus continued to be pushed back. Tig passed to Kjerros a bind of rope that had tethered the horses earlier that morning, and he advanced on Sirephus.

There was no exit from the stable yard except back past Paequat and Kjerros, who were armed, and then through the girls and the other boy, and then the gate. Sirephus, a seasoned old campaigner, seemed to know the low odds of escape that faced him. He didn't try to flee.

'Hands up,' commanded Paequat, and Kjerros bound Sirephus' hands together in the dark corner before running the rest of the tether through the large iron chain links set in the wall. Then Paequat and Kjerros retreated and, as they all moved outside into the courtyard, Paequat closed and bolted both parts of the stable door shut from the outside.

'Keep quiet and stay still,' Kjerros warned through the closed door.

But it was as he did so they all heard a curious noise. It sounded like a coarse scream.

'Shut up, old man, or I'll get my friend to demonstrate his aptitude with hardened steel,' said Kjerros, as carelessly as he could. But the call sounded like it was coming from somewhere other than Sirephus.

'What is that noise?' enquired Tig. In her distraction, she picked up the bucket that Feran had kicked over, and stopped it from rolling in semi-circles in the wind by the second set of stables. 'You know, it sounds like there's something in these,' she told the others.

'Maybe its more horses,' suggested Feran. 'I wouldn't believe a word that doddery old codger's said.'

Kjerros walked up to the first doorway and pulled back the lock of the upper section. He took a good grip on the handle and swung it open quickly.

As everyone met up with Kjerros they saw he was staring in wonder at a pair of eyes.

'It's a mothmag!' cried Tig.

'Not just one, either,' said Kjerros, as he opened the lower stable door to release four of the creatures. Feran checked the gate to the road outside was shut.

The mothmags that emerged were sandy brown and, for birds, had strange facial features, more akin to waterfowl than sky-bound hunters. The backs of their long necks were mained with downy dark-brown feathers, and they could raise their shiny black spoon-shaped bills up to Paequat's head height. Their eyes were like black pearls, glossy and huge, but with yellow circles within their depths that gave them an unerring avian stare. Even so, they behaved in a friendly, mischievous manner. Their legs were like those of a wading bird but were stronger, more like a horse's hind legs. The knee joint flexed towards their rear but, instead of webbed feet, they had long powerful talons with short stumpy claws and thick pads under each toe. These were highly developed so that, as the mothmags trotted and wandered, their upper bodies didn't jerk or bob but were propelled forwards smoothly. From the waist upward, they glided as swans crossing the surface of a calm lake. Tig and Tangle warmed to them immediately and sought to capture an appreciation of each of their personalities as they watched them walking and strutting about the yard.

'Blimey,' said Feran. 'They're huge!'

'And fast too,' added Kjerros. 'Look at their legs! These must be racers!'

'They won't fly away will they?' asked Tangle.

'No, they're flightless,' replied Tig. 'Their wings won't lift them into the sky. They can flap them pretty fast, which makes them lighter so as they can run like the wind, but they won't be able to get over this fence.'

The mothmags didn't seem to know this, however, and would every now and then dart around the courtyard, looking to pick up speed. They beat their small wings furiously in an attempt to follow their smaller cousins into the air, screeching and crowing with their heads held up tall. But they had no success, as Tig had predicted.

'They've got bridals and saddles on,' Kjerros spotted. 'Quick, before they get too excited. Everyone, find a mount!'

'Paequat, you'll ride with me,' said Tangle.

'Is someone going to let me out of here?' cried Sirephus, whom everyone had momentarily forgotten about. 'I would ye measure the loss of my four precious mothmags sufficient recompense for an old man's freedom!'

'Only on one condition!' shouted Kjerros, as he ran behind a mothmag, struggling to get anywhere near it. 'What's the word you use to calm them down?'

'Isn't it obvious?' Kjerros heard Sirephus say aloud in amused wonder. 'It's "Behave!"'

As Sirephus shouted the word, all the mothmags stopped on the spot and started looking around on the ground for anything interesting to eat. Everyone was then suddenly able to climb upon their backs as though they were cows grazing in a pasture. The stirrups were lower to the ground than they would have been for a horse, as the backs of the mothmags were only as high as that of a young pony. Then, true to his word, as Feran unlocked the main yard gate, Kjerros rode back to the middle stable and unlocked the upper section of the door.

'You're not tied to the wall,' he explained to Sirephus. 'It's not a real knot. But stay in there until we're gone!' Kjerros goaded his mothmag forwards to the main gate. He led them out and onto the road.

As the light grew in the white sky they each leaned forwards following the example of Kjerros. Paequat sat behind Tangle and held on to his hat with his spare hand. Feran made sure he was right behind his cousin. Tig's mothmag, unwilling to wait, began to claw at the ground. Once Kjerros was satisfied they were all holding on to the reigns of their mounts tightly, he cried out: "Away!"

Like lightning from a clear sky, the mothmags pounced forwards, accelerating rapidly, scrambling the road underclaw. In their prints they left a trail of flying stones and chippings ripped up from underneath them. The faster they moved, the more they pushed their necks forwards and, the more they streamlined their bodies, the faster their small wings beat.

Lighter and lighter they pressed the ground until everyone sat upon their backs felt they were flying instead of running; flying over the road and close to each other, flocked together at twice the speed of a galloping horse. The mothmags' calls to each other grew brief and exacting; only the barest instructions seemed to be exchanged around them, so as to keep their heady formation. They rotated the lead amongst them, as it is in the skies, to share the work and the benefits of being either in front or following behind in the group.

None of their riders had any previous experience of being on the back of a mothmag, although Kjerros' father Kewyn had told him all about the creatures and how they should be ridden after once seeing them raced, in Cambwall. But even so, Kjerros was not ready for the dizzying speeds at which they travelled. Neither was anyone else. Tangle was aware at how smooth and steady the journey was, but only sheer concentration kept her panic under control as she clung on to the reins and Paequat clung on to her waist from behind. Feran saw Kjerros and Tig swapping smiling glances, clearly thrilled by the experience, but he himself could only grimace in mock happiness. He yearned for the ground, though it was but four feet below him, and did not serve their purpose at walking pace.

They had raced along the road for the first part of the morning when Tig had a concern. She waited until the mothmag she rode had rotated in the flock next to Kjerros' mount.

'Kjerros, don't we stand a chance of being seen by Grodel?' she asked. 'We're going at such great speed, we're probably catching them up quickly.'

'You're right, Tig,' replied Kjerros, a similar wave of concern then crossing his face. 'But I don't know how to slow them down without asking them to stop!'

'But there must be a way of getting them to the equivalent of a trot!' said Tig, as her bird moved ahead, leaving Kjerros to consider how he could solve the problem.

As he thought, Tangle's mothmag then came alongside, on its way to the front of the group.

'Tangle!' said Kjerros. 'Do you know any way to slow these down? We don't want to be seen by Grodel or Fetlock yet!'

'Why not?' responded Tangle, as her mothmag passed ahead and Kjerros found himself at the back with only Feran immediately in front.

Her comment made Kjerros think again and he saw the potential wisdom of it.

'Of course,' he mused. After a few moments, as his mothmag made for the front, he explained his plan to everyone one-by-one. They all agreed and relaxed on their rides for the first time, feeling they couldn't travel fast enough.

They saw Grodel's carriage first and then perceived the cloaked riders about it in the distance. It was nearly noon and the sun once again was hidden in high white and grey clouds that threatened neither rain nor blue sky, but allowed the pursuers to see well ahead down the road. From where they followed they were at the brink of a swell that dove downward to trough half a mile ahead of them, only to rise again slowly afterward. The road wound through it all in a reasonably straight line, but was obscured at each small twist by low rocks that had been revealed by the excavation of shale that had occurred in the area for many years. As the carriage approached the lowest point in the road ahead they put Kjerros' plan into action. They each wore the hood of their cloak up so that they would not be recognised, and Paequat wore the handkerchief, that usually lay about his neck, tied up around his face. If anything, the mothmags speeded up as they headed downhill with glee and approached the horse riders silently. Then, as they rounded the last corner in the road that lay between them and Fetlock's men, they split themselves into two pairs by each turning the reins either left or right. The mothmags let out a screech, which was unplanned but very helpful, as they sped through the company and disturbed the horses. Paequat shrieked fearsomely as he snatched a dark wooden crossbow from the hands of one astonished rider, turned and fired off a bolt that smashed into the axle of the carriage. As it fell off its wheels, Tig threw something inside its small window and Kjerros relieved the last rider he passed of the wine skin he had dangling off his saddle.

They passed in a whirl of flying dust and, as suddenly as they had appeared, they were through and gone ahead. One or two errant bow-shots were fired but the riders were in no position to aim accurately, their horses spooked by the rush and birds. Quickly after Tig had passed the carriage there was a booming command to: "Cease firing!" The strangeness of the mothmags and Paequat's inanimate screeching sent the horses running wild and leading the riders off the road. Grodel and Fetlock were forced to jump out of the carriage as it was dragged out of the ruts, off the edge of the road and perched precariously on top of loose rocks above a drop down into a shale quarry.

With the comfort of the distance advantage and the threat of being caught overcome, Kjerros was able to put into action the second part of the plan. Together they re-grouped and then, before they had reached the summit of the swell and they could still be clearly seen, they veered sharply off to the left, onto the grass and headed southeastward, as accurately as Paequat advised towards the Fords of Netheign. The friends had in the past travelled in fear of pursuit, or in doubt of where their enemy lay. Now they sought to signpost their whereabouts and their destination, and hoped this would lend them an advantage.

They travelled as quickly as they could over the grass but the going was slower. Still they kept up their efforts and rode on, through clumpy tussocks that crunched under the press of the mothmags' claws. The layer of turf was thin under which was packed layers of shale. The mothmags were now tiring and had less joy searching for a steady foothold to be had in the ground. They decided that, if the mothmags had problems, it would be as nothing in comparison with how awkward it would be to try to bring horses out over the terrain. Therefore they continued as long as they could, until they could see the winding way of the Highborn. Then they dismounted from their birds of burden after commanding them to 'Behave!' within the shelter of a brief copse of scrawny elm that was surrounded by low-growing rowan and unkempt hedges with thin, dark green leaves. From where they stood they had a view down to the river and away south to the Pinch.

Upon feeling the ground beneath her feet after a full day of riding, Tangle felt queasy, as though the oddity of how she had just travelled abruptly caught up with her, or her feet wanted to punish her for their disuse in such matters.

'What was that you managed to snatch, Kjerros?' asked Feran breathlessly, noticing the leather water skin hanging over his cousin's shoulder.

'I'm not sure. I'd better have a taste!' answered Kjerros. He unplugged it and took a long swig before re-sealing it and then slowly falling onto his back. Alarmed, everyone quickly ran to his aid and dropped to his side, fearing that he had imbibed some deadly poison. But Kjerros then cracked a wide smile.

'Thass'a best gnastia I've e'er had!' he slurred, looking only very roughly in the direction of the faces that were peering in on him.

'Gnastia!' cried Tangle delightedly, as Tig felt in her pockets and found a few leaves left of the rockflower plant. The thrill of having raced past their pursuers and put a day's distance between them went straight to her head. 'It's been ages since I scaled. We've got to have a party tonight!' She came over to Feran and gave him a serious kiss.

'Do you want to come to my party tonight?' she asked into his ear softly.

'Hey, is someone looking after those?' asked Tig. Upon averting her eyes she'd noticed how the mothmags were wandering about randomly. Between her and Paequat they were able to round them up once more by saying 'Behave!' a number of times, but each needed a person to control it properly. They seemed unwilling to move on in any direction they didn't chose.

'Oh, Kjerros; you're useless,' complained Tig, as she tried to get him to stand up and take the reins of his mothmag. All he would do was smile at Tig and try to hug her.

Tig and Paequat then set about tying the mothmags to the trunks of the trees. Tig decided to keep their saddles attached in case of any emergency.

'Well, we must be well ahead of them by now,' she said to Feran. 'Why don't you go about and collect some branches up and see if we can get a good fire going?'

'I just hope they don't catch us up until we get to the Fords,' said Feran.

'They'll have to go the long way round if they stick to the road, and that's if they can even get the carriage mended and back onto the road again,' answered Tangle, arriving at Feran's side after setting Kjerros down onto his cloak. 'Or they'll have to abandon it and share horses if they try our short-cut.'

'What was it you threw inside the carriage?' asked Feran. 'I know that Kjerros explained it needed to be something to make Grodel think of us as your kidnappers holding you hostage, but what was it?'

'It was a lock of my hair,' Tig explained, 'wrapped in one of

Tangle's handkerchiefs. Well, I say 'lock', but it was more like whatever I could pull out whilst riding on the back of Windwing.'

Feran gave her a blank look.

'You mean you didn't name yours?' Tig answered.

'Do you think it'll work?' Feran asked, getting to the point. 'Are we safe? Will Grodel follow us for definite?'

'He can't go to Cambwall, now,' said Tig. 'You heard him back at Rhal say he was looking for us. So now they all think we're racing off to the Pass before them, Grodel has to come along, too. He can't leave Fetlock's side if he knows they're chasing after us. And if he's with them if we do get caught, he won't let anything happen to us.'

'Tig! That's genius!' Feran approved.

'Well, it was Kjerros' idea. Now then,' she said, turning around to Kjerros and Tangle. 'What about that fire, you two?'

The day drew to a close and darkness fell slowly. But once it was up, the campfire flung out dancing shadows and threw up glinting sparks to the low clouds. A fair wind from the east brought with it the rumour of rains to come and the sound of the approaching Highborn. What had seemed in daylight as a circle of low bushes seemed at night to be looming confusions of twisted briars, animated by the breeze as though filled by a coven of unseen creatures. It made the friends cluster together around the fire.

To calm her mind, Tangle had given her sister the task of grinding the remaining rockflower leaves into a powder for that evening's festivities. Kjerros, now mostly sober having had the remainder of the gnastia removed from him and given over to Paequat, who, Tangle announced, was the 'only one who could be trusted with it,' had busied himself with the task of making up a hot meal for them. He used up some of the provisions they kept in reserve for when the occasion required something more than their usual fare of bread, rice or very chewy cake.

Once they had eaten, Tangle discovered she still had in her bag Tig's sea-chelys; she'd brought it out with her the morning she and Tig had discovered Paequat. This surprised everyone, most of all Tig.

'I thought I'd lost it!' she said.

'All the more reason for celebration, then,' Tangle encouraged. 'For besting of the riders from the North! For the continued hope we have for the twins! And for the theft of an entire flagon's worth of gnastia! To our feet, everyone! Tig, can you play 'Though It Be Night' for us? I want to dance!' and Tangle spun to her bare feet and flowed around everyone until they were all standing up, except Tig, who said she'd get too dizzy if she stood.

'What are you all standing about like that for?' asked Tangle, piqued at the distinct lack of movement coming for the direction of the boys. 'You have to dance!'

'Tig's not playing yet,' said Kjerros, feeling very self-conscious. Feran hung around awkwardly, gazing at Tangle. She seemed to him as a woodsprite or fairy, bewitching him with every skip and turn, life shining out from her.

'Well,' Tangle replied, grabbing onto Kjerros' hands and dragging him out around the fire, 'you'll just have to sing the words then, won't you!'

As Tig began to play a piping, low rhythmic chant that supported every step of Tangle's as though it was the dancer that led the musician, Tangle came around to Paequat and showed him how to clap in time with the music. To help, Tig nodded her head each time, so that Paequat could follow her or Tangle to keep up. Tangle also removed the gnastia and took it around to Feran, but as she did so, she started singing the words and looking at Kjerros as though she would only lead him through them for so long until he would have to sing them himself. She sung them plainly and yet delicately, and each time she'd finish a verse, Tig would intone a gentle rise in the music, which would lilt and flow seamlessly with Tangle's lyric and dancing. As the song built, and she passed the wine skin around, Feran and Kjerros joined in. Once she had been around three times, Kjerros was confident in every word and Tangle was able to stop singing and concentrate on her dancing as she twined her way about them all. But Kjerros was able to keep the song going, supported by Tig's playing and Tangle's dancing and Paequat's clapping.

Kjerros quite surprised himself as he sang, for although Feran was comfortable performing, playing as he had on numerous times in front of the whole village, he had never sung in front of anyone before. But he felt himself soar as he danced around the fire, watching Tangle leading Feran in her steps, and seeing Paequat grinning as he clapped along and took the occasional swig of gnastia himself. Tig began to wind the song down as gently as a feather falling from the sky until it came to a rest and they all fell into a great giggling heap together, heads spinning from the motion, bodies one on top of the other.

'Get off you lot!' laughed Tig, at the bottom of the pile. 'You're crushing them!'

'Crushing what?' asked Feran, before guessing. 'Oh, you've made up some blasters? Fantastic!' he exclaimed, rolling off the group of them and ending up on his back, his hands feeling out for the ground.

'I hope you've not bent them Kjerros, you lump,' teased Tig, as Kjerros stood up and wandered over to Paequat to steady himself. Paequat, though, didn't seem the most balanced either. He turned to grin at Kjerros, who grinned back, and they both fell over together.

'Boys! Get up!' commanded Tangle. 'You've not done this before, so watch Tig and me first. Paequat, I don't know if this'll work for you, but you're very welcome to try.'

Tig produced five rolled up leaves from her pocket. They recognised them as the last of the rockflower leaves Feran and Kjerros had picked over by the roadside before Rhal Springs Castle. They each took one. Tangle then placed hers between her lips and sucked in sharply through the leaf as though through a straw. For a moment it looked like she would cough. Then she swallowed, removed the leaf from her lips, took a swig of Gnastia and then ate the leaf. Tig followed suit, and then Feran and Kjerros. Paequat, who seemed distracted and who had drunk the most Gnastia, just ate all of his in one go.

Feran and Kjerros sat still a moment, alive to any change, when suddenly the world melted.

They saw fireworks behind their eyes and the surrounding bushes turned into drops of green rain. The floor became a blanket and the fire a huge sun half buried in the ground. Feran sought Tangle, who appeared as a beacon of pleasure, and as they blended into each other he lost himself in her. Kjerros wandered away from the fire as it threatened him with taunting hands, each footstep splashing up arcs of colour and rippling out across the ground. He found fascination lying on his back as he watched the dancing shadows of the bushes spell out strange words in the air until he knew no more.

Tig had always found she was less susceptible to rockflower than her sister because, she had eventually reckoned, she was afraid of losing control. Therefore, although she would never admit to such a fear, her resistance meant the effects for her were diminished. She sat still with her legs crossed and her head level, not seeing clearly but still able to understand what was going on around her. She was finding Kjerros' childish attraction to the surrounding shrubs amusing and was making a note to speak to her sister about what she was up to in the morning, when she saw a gold figure arise. She realised it was Paequat but wondered at the way he moved. He seemed cautious about being seen. She wondered if he'd noticed someone in the bushes, perhaps one of Fetlock's men.

The thought when it hit nearly overwhelmed her: 'We've been so stupid! What on earth were we thinking?' Then a darker thought entered her mind: 'What if Paequat has seen them first? What if he moves to kill this person, thinking it is one of the pursuers, and it's someone else?' She remembered how much Paequat had been drinking. 'I must stop him!'

Tig stood up and sought her balance. It wasn't easy. Carefully, she picked her way forward, following the golden lines left in the air where Paequat had passed and dismissing from her mind the visual cacophony generated by her movement. 'It's not real,' she kept telling herself, as five pink bubbles floated up from her toes each time she placed them down in a step. Ahead there was a buzzing noise. It seemed to radiate from a large tree, the trunk of which kept trying to wink and nod in her direction, but she wouldn't allow it. Harsh red stars flowed out from where she suspected Paequat to be and it was confirmed when she saw a golden arm flash momentarily from behind the trunk. Then there was a sharp snap of metal and the red stars ceased.

'Paequat? Are you there?' asked Tig, regretting it immediately as her words swam out of her mouth. They wreathed themselves about her neck in the form of a scarf before turning to powder and falling to the ground.

There was no answer, but Tig now heard low laughter as she circled around the trunk to find a glowing Paequat on his knees, swiping his hand through the air and describing different shapes that floated off gently like illuminated smoke rings. He shone so brightly that Tig could hardly bear to look in his direction.

'Paequat makes little suns!' he screeched delightedly, as he dotted the air and left golden spots that hung around like stars, before standing up very suddenly and disturbing everything. He pulled something to his shoulder, something which Tig couldn't make out because it was hidden in his glow, but gave off little red sparks of lightening that she didn't like. She wanted to ask him what he was doing, but didn't want to confuse things by speaking again.

Instead she looked out over to where she guessed Paequat was watching and tried to see something that could help her understand what it was that had brought him out here. She could see he was excited as he not only glowed but pulsed as well, but she didn't like the sense she was getting from whatever it was that he was carrying.

Then she heard a faint noise, away beyond the open patch of grassland that lay in front of them, from a distance that spanned all the way to the hidden Highborn River. The low cloud cover closed the space in and made it seem smaller than it was. But whatever it was that had made the noise was moving very quickly, for by the time Tig heard the next sound it made, it was nearly upon them. She was alarmed because she was looking straight ahead towards the woods opposite her and couldn't see any rumour of its advance. Then it swung from the clouds, enormous and swift, a huge white bird that Tig and Paequat watched encircle their camp and swoop below the level of the tree tops. Then it was that Tig guessed the contraption Paequat held, cocked and ready. It was the crossbow he had snatched from the guardsman as he passed through Fetlock's company. She saw how the bird circled her friends, but felt no fear because it gave off a maternal, protective aura and seemed beautiful and graceful. It was then with a lurch of horror she realised Paequat had been taking aim, using a low stump of a branch to rest the crossbow on.

'No, Paequat! No, don't shoot it! Don't shoot!' she cried, and made to wrest the crossbow from his arms, but in doing so Paequat was startled. The short bolt flew out straight and true. He had not even been looking at the bird, but fate or some other force guided his aim so that it could not escape. The sound of the bolt leaving the bow left a thin blue trail behind it, as though the shot was on a string. The white falcon gave a pitiful cry as the bolt pierced through its wing close to the body and wounded it dreadfully. It fell, tumbling to the ground in anguish and shock until it hit the ground with a sickening sound. It fluttered continually with its uninjured wing until it had exhausted itself and lay still, dead to all waking torment.

Chapter 11

THE CHILDREN OF HUD

'Are you sure you can do this?' Behvyn asked his brother. He regretted his words as soon as they had left him. He had hoped it wouldn't sound like a challenge. He had hoped it wouldn't sound like he was at all worried about Behleth. He had hoped it would come out sounding nicer. He was wrong.

'If she can, I can,' Behleth replied, as quick as a flash, his pride rising up to the surface. 'I'm not sure about you, though,' he added.

Behvyn gave Behleth a narrow-eyed look of incorrigibility. This was another of those times where it was his decision what they would do. Whatever he chose, it would affect them both. He could shout out and ask for aid. Behleth had been unconscious for the best part of a day and his time for recovery had been short. He seemed to be fit, but blood would still coalesce around the corners of his mouth whenever he spoke more than a few sentences.

'Perhaps there is harm in it,' he said to himself, 'but there is more harm, I think, in treating him like a child.' Then Behvyn simply dived into the river that wound up beside them and began to swim. Behleth jumped in straight after, howling his surprise and the two started their challenge.

Both went off hard. The river was of the same strange substance as the Lightwater, so Behvyn found he could breathe under the surface. After becoming comfortable with this, he discovered it was more efficient to swim inside the river instead of along the top, but in the time it took Behleth to cotton on to this, Behvyn had gained a large advantage. At one point, he even had Yinko and Rumé in his sights ahead of him. Behleth was barely visible behind. But his brother, irked by memories of how he had needed rescuing by Rumé on the Highborn, and from being incapacitated by the verse on the discus, drew upon a well of determination not to be bested. He also wanted to shake off his brother's concerns for his well-being. He loved his brother but didn't want his coddling. He found a steady rhythm that he could to settle into and began to close the gap on Behvyn.

Behvyn, intrigued by what he was doing, focused towards the surface and saw the plants, trees and the edges of the rocky horn that climbed in the ever-growing light. At the base it had been dark but now that he estimated he had reached about a third of the overall height it was noticeably lighter, even though it could not equate to more than a pre-dawn glowering. The river seemed to respond to the light differently to how it behaved in the dark. It had pulsed in the tunnel from the Lightwater, it had glimmered at the base, but now it had none of that luminescence about it. Instead, it seemed to feed on the sun and the feel of the river changed. It was less fluid, more physical and harder to swim through, but at the same time the current grew in strength and because of this Behvyn was able to keep up the same pace as before using fewer strokes. He wondered if it would be even more soupy progress further upwards.

Behind him, but closing down the gap, toiled Behleth, still competitive and now more so that he could see his brother slowing. Earlier, the river had been dark but clear enough to see through. Now it was more difficult because of the thin light and how it refracted through the swells near the surface, but he noticed how he gained and this provided him with fresh effort. In addition, feeling how the current pulled him up and along more urgently, he positioned himself where he felt it strongest and drove with his arms and legs all the more.

Having lost sight of Yinko and Rumé before rising into the early light, Behvyn had no way to pace his progress. He felt a degree of ignominy at being slower than a girl pulling a man at the same task, even if she was used to such travail and he was not. He wondered how many times he had twined around the White Horn. He could not be sure but reckoned on either two or three times, which would have put him some little distance above half the height overall, or so he measured from his recollection of the horn from its foundations. He didn't know if he could give the same again.

As Behvyn focused on getting to the summit and the glory of victory filled his mind, his brother focused on Behvyn's slowing action and benefited from having a pacemaker ahead of him. He was able to measure his effort and all the while keep doing just that little bit more to close the gap. As he passed around again, Behleth's eyes were dazzled by direct sunlight and the constituency of the river again changed. The current grew stronger once again. He had not noticed anything above the surface of the river in his climb except the repeating sides of the sheer cliffs that defined the chasm in which the kingdom lay, but now Behleth decided he could race Behvyn from the surface of the river better than from inside it. Behvyn seemed confident the stronger current would keep his advantage over his brother, but Behleth was now nearly in striking distance.

Sensing his closeness, Behvyn kicked on again and the two began an almighty climax to their contest. Finally, the river stopped rising and straightened out ahead. Behvyn saw them first: steps rising out of the river in front of them and Rumé's boots climbing up and out. There were little more than a hundred strokes left to reach them as, from his peripheral vision, Behvyn could see Behleth moving up to him from above. Ahead, Yinko reappeared, her face still glowing with delight and watching the race conclude. She sat on one of the lower steps under the surface and held out her hands. The first to touch her would win, both brothers understood.

Behvyn's pains from having rowed about the Gathering came back to him; his shoulders flamed in agony. Behleth was endlessly determined but less efficient in his efforts. Still, the gap closed further. Faces that looked similar to Yinko then appeared at either side of the top of the river and the boys both noticed they were being stared at in wonder. It was now clear daylight and the sun shone through the river, gleaming off the bone-white riverbed and banks. Both brothers could hear their audience's voices, raised in excitement, encouraging them to their fullest efforts at the last. There was nothing to separate them now. Behvyn's lead had been eaten away, but Behleth had not been allowed to form any advantage himself. To the final few strokes they applied themselves and then all sensed the shockwave that accompanies the arrival of an eminent individual. Behvyn saw Yinko look behind her in added excitement. It was possible for the twins to sense among the crowd that had gathered that this was now a special moment.

'Are they going to do it?' some said.

'Yes, of course they will, but who will be Champion?' others asked.

'The one near the surface gains most!' said a younger voice close to Yinko.

At hearing the voices, both Behvyn and Behleth tried desperately to out do the other and they strove equally to touch the hand of Yinko first, swimming one above the other. With a final launch both stretched out for the win as the eminent figure came down to join Yinko in the river. Yinko cried encouragement to both and their hands touched at the precise moment the figure reached her side. Yinko clasped their hands tightly as she turned to look at the eyes of the one she most loved and feared in the world.

'They met at exactly the same time, my Dal-Hirovo,' she said, both in marvel and elation, as the brothers found their feet on the steps and stood, breathing heavily, surrounded by the crowd that had grown to see them.

'Honours shared! It is a tie!' declared Dal-Hirovo, and the satisfied cheers of the crowd rang in the brothers' ears as they continued to be viewed in long but polite stares of wonderment.

Behvyn and Behleth, though instinctively frustrated not to have won, were appeased by their reception as a phenomenon and became curious about just what they had achieved in addition to tiring themselves out. They found it strangely comforting to be encircled by families of water-people behaving so similarly to how the families in Muscle Oaks would have at one of their routine competitions about the main square or in the north field.

It was also with great inquisitiveness that they turned to look at the eminent figure that had called the match. They saw how, even though his cloudy blue eyes and his dry, clipped voice betrayed his age, that he was still hale and vigorous. Yinko drew them out of the river onto a dry platform of stone and they again had the strange sensation of not being wet when they would have expected to be. Both brothers found their legs still felt the sensation of water and it was some time before their muscles forgot it and remembered they were on land once more.

'You two are fit beyond any others we have had visit us for

many centuries,' spoke Dal-Hirovo, 'but you are now also travel weary and will benefit from rest. So, Yinko will show you to a place of comfort and we shall have an audience later at sunset. But I extend to you my welcome now, Behvyn and Behleth Hahn of the North Vale. I am Dal-Hirovo, King of the Hudron. Welcome to the Citadel of Hudros!'

At that, Dal-Hirovo walked into the wide waters that surrounded them outside of the river. The platform was merely that, and the buildings and architecture that described the skyline were all partially submerged. The vista was one of a city whose white rooftops only stood out into the air and where the majority of life was conducted under the surface of the sea that ran through the streets. As the crowd of interested faces melted away back into the channels that ran between the homes and halls, Yinko led them to a nearby home that protruded out of the waters higher than most. Once inside, they found Rumé at the balcony of their own chambers prepared for them.

'I will return at sunset for you all,' said Yinko, and gave the boys each an affectionate caress before diving off the balcony and into the depths to rejoin the rest of her kind, leaving them all with a sense of jubilation at being where they were.

'Daymen! We're actually in their city!' cried Behleth, on the edge of belief.

'I thought they were all just myth and legend,' agreed Behvyn.

'Imagine what they're saying right now about you two,' replied Rumé. They both looked at him in curiosity.

'Yinko seemed quite impressed with you both as well,' Rumé added. 'Not surprising. As she brought me up here she told me they had sent down the helpers to the halfway point expecting you to stop there in exhaustion. No manling who wasn't a Hudron has ever made the swim to the top, and there you were, battling it out to the very finish. And Behleth,' he said pertinently with a note of caution, 'they prefer the term "Hudron" to "Daymen".'

Behleth blushed in embarrassed wonder.

"So they are Day-' Behleth began before stopping himself. 'It doesn't seem to suit them, anyway. They're not nearly as ill-mannered as I thought they would be.'

In their weariness, the brothers assuaged their curiosity of their new surroundings by standing at the balcony and looking out across the expanse of the citadel. Among the many spires that furled their way out of the waters, they could not but have their gaze return to the tallest. This was a vast, wide dome topped by a towering, thin spire, whose shadow acted as a measure of the time to the citizens who flocked to different areas at different times of the day. The Hudron could be glimpsed under the surface if the sun was not directly upon it, moving in great shoals as fish in a deep sea, clearly discussing the events of the morning with those that had not been fortunate enough to be there. They went along channels and chutes, between buildings and rocks, above and below each other at great speed, and their languid swimming style made it look so natural and easy. Behvyn found it calming to watch them and not a few times was tempted to dive in to join them.

'Yinko told me there will be a meeting of their council this evening, young Masters,' advised Rumé, as they ate the meal provided later that afternoon. They overlooked a land covered in shadow and only dimly lit by the fading pink-orange light in the sky, and the walls of the great fissure in which the White Horn improbably rose seemed more stern and lofty than before.

'They look like they would snap together and eat us all,' remarked Behleth, turning his glance away from them.

It was as they stood there that all direct sunlight to the Citadel of Hudros winked out and in the same moment a bell tolled from the roof of the great chamber they had admired earlier on that now dominated the view ominously.

'It is time,' said Rumé, hearing the bell, and as he did so, Yinko could be seen swimming up to their house. 'But remember,' he cautioned, as Behleth told of her approach, 'although honesty wins friends quicker than naïveté, take my lead in what you reveal. I do not yet see why we have been so welcomed for disturbing them. They will certainly need something from us, but what it may be I have not yet learned.'

Yinko took them through the submerged streets after hearing they were well, leading Rumé by hand and setting a gentle pace for the boys. In the darkness she and the other Hudron they passed had a more solid presence than in strong sunlight. But because she had spoken to them with the smallest ounce of fear in her voice, Behvyn went alert for danger. His brother was enjoying the attention of Yinko and he used the opportunity to show her with what minimal effort he could propel himself alongside. As they reached the steps of the great chamber, Yinko held back and did not touch them with her feet. Rather, she genuflected and became grave. Behvyn and Behleth looked so surprised that she was not coming in with them, she explained quickly to put their minds at rest.

'You alone are summoned to the great Chamber of Debate within the Palace of Talviani,' said Yinko. 'It is where the 'Mirovi', our Council, meets, and then only rarely, but I am not one of them. That does not make me sad, for they can be long in debate and I am not so inclined! I would rather swim about the rocks and the pools and make display, for my spirit does not want to be bound in considered reason. But I have seen the face of our beloved Dal-Hirovo since he saw you this morning and something is laid upon his brow that I would have removed. I do not know if you can help, or if you are indeed the cause of this concern. But as I love life itself, I love the Dal in every way I can imagine. It would make every Hudron eternally grateful to you if you could put his mind at ease. So that you can keep your minds on what matters most, know I will look for you until you are done inside and need me to take you back to your chambers.' Yinko finished and withdrew, long holding her stare at the twins before melting away into the dark waters.

'We should go inside,' said Rumé, as the twins came either side to lead him. 'We are expected.'

Together all three walked up a long sequence of watery steps. Behvyn no longer gave any thought to how they had been swimming only moments ago but were yet perfectly dry, as their footsteps began to ring inside the long ante-chamber they found at the top of the flight. Instead of being long and narrow ahead of them, it was broad and curved away to each side, encircling the room within in a great ring. It was thirty paces from entrance to the door opposite them.

As they covered the distance, Behvyn noticed how the flooring was set in overlapping tiles as would be found on a roof, or rather as scales on a fish, so that the grain of entry was with them and the grain of exit against. At regular intervals in the cambered ceiling were set paintings of past events, some of which the twins could interpret as scenes from the history of the Shale Valley and others they did not recognise. He saw that light came from strange lanterns that did not burn in flame but seemed illuminated by some intrinsic quality of the waters they held, as though they had caught the memory of the sun and retold of it's brilliance as trapped messengers of day.

At the interior door, they were ushered through quickly by two guards who asked them their full names. Finding no cause to grudge them this information, they entered into the main chamber of debate as the circle of Mirovi stood and listened to the door guards' introduction.

'May it please your grace Dal-Hirovo,' the guard burbled, 'and those here assembled that we herein execute your orders to admit Behvyn and Behleth Hahn of Muscle Oaks in the North Vale and Captain Rumé of the King's Guard, Champion of King Cuiron.'

They were ushered towards the circle of Mirovi where they found there were three seats for them, next to each other and to the left of the simple throne upon which sat Dal-Hirovo. As they were motioned to sit, Behvyn noticed two strange sights. The first was that the inside of the great dome of Talviani glowed about its structure in the same way as the lanterns positioned outside of the room did, so that the light inside was as strong at night as it was in day. The second were the two manlings, looking very similar to each other, sitting to the right of Dal-Hirovo.

'As you have been kind enough to make your introduction,' began Dal-Hirovo, rising once everyone had been seated and turning to the brothers and Rumé, 'then let me extend the same courtesy to you. My council of Mirovi consists of seven advisors. To your left are the Issin-Valenzi, Issina-Chinido and Issin-Unjidé-Tuo, who together advise me on matters of state. Further around are the Yessin-Tach, Yessina-Yinsho and Yessina-Qhik who advise me on matters outside of this kingdom. To my right I have my Hinasta, the venerable Lol Teneth, who unites and illuminates us all with the wisdom of Hud, our true guide through life.' As each

Hudron was introduced, he or she (the females' formal title ended in an 'a') stood for the benefit of being seen more clearly and, before sitting again, smiled and held out their hands in a gesture of giving.

'To my immediate right,' continued Dal-Hirovo, 'I also have two further guests of the Citadel.' At this, Rumé became alert. 'Could you introduce yourselves to this assembly?'

They both stood. Behvyn noticed how short they were in comparison not only to himself but also to the Mirovi, who were seldom shorter than he.

'I am Avi Lindacre,' said the manling on the right. He looked keenly around the other faces in the room. Avi had an old face with little colour in it but his intelligent eyes gave away the vigour of his mind. He spoke as a manling with a high degree of confidence.

'This is my twin brother Santi,' Avi said, with his hand on his brother's shoulder. Santi nodded about the room, brushing out of his deep-set eyes the long straight brown hair he shared with his brother. Santi was almost identical to Avi save for the hunch in his shoulders that spoke of his brothers' dominance. He gave a look ever so briefly to Behvyn that said to him that whilst his brother spoke, he would send his mind off to other things, in the way that someone who is less concerned with specific matters but pressed more by the urgency to do great things will. As his brother talked, Santi remained unsettled, not sure whether to sit again or to remain standing until he had finished.

'We are once of the Shale Valley,' continued Avi, seemingly aware of his brother's predicament but unwilling to guide him in the matter, 'so our wise ones taught us, but we are now cursed to be an ever-travelling people. Cursed, I say, for it is today we have learned that we have now truly lost all contact with our people. There is nowhere else to continue our fruitless search, now that we have finally reached this glorious Citadel after endless years of travelling to many strange and wonderful places upon this fair continent. But seldom have we been so welcomed or so fortunate in our discoveries as to meet with the gracious people of the Hudron, or to make the acquaintance of so majestic a ruler as the Dal-Hirovo, in whose presence and wisdom we humbly place our services and our fate.'

Avi and Santi sat down and Behleth gave them both a sympathetic look, which Avi returned graciously.

'Thank you, Avi Lindacre and brother Santi,' said Dal-Hirovo, now seated along with everyone else and keen to begin the matters for discussion. 'I have called this meeting, but it is not through any design of mine that five of you are here. We will look to understand why it is so later, but for now, knowing that for you the Hudron existence and way of life is a topic of childhood mythology or complete mystery, I will first explain ourselves and our culture. Do not worry that there are those assembled here that might feel they know this already. It is only in the telling of ourselves to others that we may most fully know ourselves. In this you may see how we can help you and also how you may help us.

'Of the five races of manling created by the Axumé we are both the most and the least populous. Our children live all about us but rarely do any of them grow into maturity, so painful and unkind a procedure it is. Each full-grown Hudron has passed through a mighty challenge and many more that we would have loved to have joined us in adulthood have not come with us. You see, we are as any other manling in that we are the same shape and size, the same weight and have the same faculties as you, Master Behleth, or you, Santi Lindacre. But we do not have a skeleton inside us and we do not have as protective a skin as you do to keep us from the harmful effects of the elements outside of water, such as wind and extremes of temperature. We are liquid and in our health we are totally transparent; indeed we would find it hard to see our own kind save for the natural effect water has on light and how we refract it through ourselves.

'This may still make us sound so very alien to you, but consider this further. You are mostly liquid, too. Think! If you did not drink water regularly, how quickly would you desire it above all else? You would last two or three days at most, before dying of thirst. If you were cut you would bleed pints; if you died and were buried, think how light your body would be after it had dried. Water is in our shared make-up. Though our surface appearances are very different, in every other aspect we are alike. We speak the same language of the Axumé; we live in communities and love our

198

families and friends. We seek peace and happiness and freedom to live, as and how we will.

'In one aspect, though, because of our own unique and wondrous design, we Hudron differ to all other manlings. Behleth,' said Dal-Hirovo, now standing and walking over inside the circle towards him. 'You have swum in the Lightwater. But it is not as other rivers in the Shale Valley. How is it different?'

Behleth responded quickly.

'It is dry, and I can breathe in it like I can the air,' he replied, standing to do so.

'Exactly!' responded Dal-Hirovo, enthusiastically, causing Behleth to smuggle his beaming smile and flushing face down towards the floor. 'That is because it is not a river of water, but a river of our young. Long they have lived there, as long as I have been alive, and possibly for many eons before. We do not know how they were born, for that is one secret our beloved Hud does not reveal to us.' Dal-Hirovo smiled at Lol Teneth, who steepled his hands up towards his vaporous lips. 'And yet the river is there, and any Hudron you see about this Citadel is from it.

'As I said earlier, it is not an easy path from the river to adulthood for the Hudron, and not an easy choice for anyone to make. As I am now, and the Issinas and Issin, the Yessinas and Yessin, and the Hinasta himself, too; we are sundered from our kin in the river. Yes, we can care for them, but we are no longer like them. We cannot communicate with them, so wholly different are we to them that they cannot recognise us. We speak to them and hope it brings them comfort, but we do not know if it does.

'But some make the transition, knowing the loss to come. Few but steadily have we emerged, first by growing more than the others, so that we have weight and awaken to our surroundings. Then by feeding on our kin so that, though their numbers diminish imperceptibly, we grow until we can choose to be born. Choose, I say, for it is at this juncture a decision must be made that fewer still take. The choice is a hard one, between dissolving back into the collective, losing one's being and maintaining the river, or forming the many into the one in permanence. To choose the latter path can be seen as an ultimate act of selfishness, balanced with the desire to know and to be. It is an aspect of our lives that the guilt of this decision weighs heavily on each of us at times. Knowing that we selected the fate of millions and in that moment of decision all other possibilities ceased for those who went into making up us. It is something our Hinasta helps us each with.'

Behvyn couldn't fail to notice the reverence Dal-Hirovo showed to Lol Teneth in front of them all. However, he found himself wondering if the attention in this specific instance seemed to be more obligatory than natural, as though the Dal-Hirovo tired of such observations and would rather the Hinasta would sustain the memory of his earlier appreciations for the rest of the meeting.

'Once the choice is made there is no turning back,' continued Dal-Hirovo. 'The young Hudron must climb newly formed from the Lightwater at first light and bare themselves to the elements of air, wind, rain, and most terrifying of all, sun. It is this last element that sears us and causes our 'skin' to form. For one whole day, we must suffer in the agony of formation until the sun recedes behind the Uspheron. It is only during this one rare day that others may come upon us unlooked for. Master Behleth, it is this reason why, through grim bedside stories, children in your land know us as "Daymen", and also why our tempers are least in check. But, as we leave our old lives behind, we feel like murderers.'

Behleth nodded an appreciation of the kindness of Dal-Hirovo in explaining this to him but Behvyn saw he now felt ashamed at having needed to know. Yet his awkwardness was not an uncommon sight about the circle as the Mirovi each recalled, through Dal-Hirovo's explanation, their own birthing. Though they kept perfectly still, their consciousness seemed momentarily elsewhere and inside they seemed to shudder.

'At night, we return to the Lightwater,' spoke Dal-Hirovo, now more softly, 'but it does not accept us as it's own any more. Though it birthed us, there is nothing left for us there and our guilt overcomes us too strongly if we seek to stay. So, we move on to the White Horn, through the very same tunnels the likes of which all of you have travelled to reach here. In the darkness of the mighty chasm we recover from our ordeal and collect to each other. Friendships form and teaching is given to any new arrival. Those with special talents are encouraged to develop them to imbue their own sense of individuality. Coming from an identity of millions to become a personality in one's own right needs reinforcement. And in the darkness we are safe from direct sunlight, which we fear above all else then.

'But we do not need fear it any longer, as we all discover over time. The skies are in reach if the White Horn of Hudros is climbed, and as a consequence of our origins we are comfortable swimmers. It is a natural tendency to take to rivers and as we move out of the darkness we come to love the light. It hurts us no more and shows us how we can delight in the air. Our community splits its time between the darkness and the sun, between land and water and between hope and despair. Despair at sacrifices made by others and the responsibility this means we carry; hope at what we can achieve for all our kin in our highest form.'

Dal-Hirovo, satisfied at the extent of his own words, then sat down and looked to his right as if he were about to invite Avi or Santi to answer a question he had. However, the Hinasta then stood sharply, but not so sharply that he could not then turn his motion into a flowing bow.

'And one more thing, if the Dal will permit me?' He paused until Dal-Hirovo nodded his consent. 'It is of course by the will of Hud that we are given this opportunity to reach for such greatness, and that we are blessed by him.'

Lol Teneth bowed low once more and stayed down until Dal-Hirovo echoed the blessing. Now satisfied, the Hinasta returned to his seat and allowed proceedings to continue. Behvyn again caught the sense that Dal-Hirovo found such observations a burden, and also from Lol Teneth, that the Hinasta knew this of his king.

Dal-Hirovo now moved on to call upon the Mirovi, not speaking with Avi or Santi as he had earlier planned.

'Issina-Chinido, how flow the lands of the Hudron at this time?'

The Issina, seeming pretty to Behvyn and Behleth, although more conditioned in her words and poise than Yinko, spoke of the state of the Lightwater and of the White Horn; of the waters about the chasm; of the playfulness of the young adults in the rivers, and of the morale of the kingdom, which was good. She spoke of the arrangements for the forthcoming Exumé gathering at the next full moon, of the health of the Hudron and of the quietness of the skies and airs. Of this, she concluded this winter would be a harsh one and that the living-line on the horn, above which the Hudron should not sleep at night, should be set to half-height no later than the next Ul-Tay of the moon, 'lest freezing be risked,' she added. Behvyn understood this to be only about six to seven weeks away and momentarily imagined how terrible it would be for a Hudron to freeze in the cold. He thought of how his skin was so much more protective of him in comparison and understood from this the limits the Hudron faced in helping anyone other than themselves.

As Issina-Chinido concluded, Dal-Hirovo thanked her and the other present interior Mirovi for the report, and noticed how Rumé sat stone still in his seat. All evidence suggesting to everyone else about the circle a man of endless patience, but to the eyes of the wise Dal it was seen through.

'I fear we have attended to our own insular matters now for too long,' said the Dal. 'Instead of coming to the Yessin next,' who all nodded at their mention, 'could Captain Rumé focus us on the matters most pressing to him and the brothers Hahn to my left. It may be,' he added, looking over towards Avi and Santi specifically, 'we can find the root reason why three races of manling find themselves all in one chamber tonight and help us to each know our next moves. Maybe your paths lie together?' added Dal-Hirovo, delicately.

'Your Highness,' began Rumé. 'You honour us with your hospitality and your consideration. As you have said, it is not by any clear design that we are all here in this room, but I would encourage us all to use it to our mutual benefit. The Issina has laid before you the state of your land and said it is hale. But yet it dies.' At this statement from Rumé, Behleth noticed there was a marked drop in the comfort of the Mirovi, though the Dal-Hirovo did not stir and offered nothing in his face.

'If you wonder how I have come to reach this conclusion,' continued Rumé, 'it was from the carefully picked words of your Issina. You are as our youngest babies in the effect the changing elements can have upon you and every winter you lose more of your number. As for your young, no more chose adulthood and you do not know why. You cannot encourage it yourself and you do not know what the solution is. Yet time runs out each year as you dwindle. Issina-Chinido, may I ask: how many winters have the youngest of your adults now seen since forming?'

'Yinko is our youngest, Captain,' answered the Issina. She sought to hide her discomfort in her voice but spoke in a less conditioned manner than before; as she used to speak as a young-ster herself, before her parents together passed away during a hot summer and she devoted herself to the Mirovi. 'She has gloried in the Exumé over a thousand times.'

'I thank the Issina,' said Rumé, and nodded unerringly towards her. 'Over eighty-three years since the last Hudron chose the path to adulthood. Within what span of time does the Hinasta predict the end of the highest form of the Hudron? Perhaps you take com-fort that your race may resurrect itself as long as the Lightwater flows. But if not, then you may well wonder if Hud has abandoned you.'

'The Captain goes too far!' responded Lol Teneth, heatedly. 'The Hudron will never pass! That is not the plan the great Hud has for us! We are beloved, and we are mighty. Our Dal is now over seven hundred years old and can live that time again. The oldest among us, I am fifteen hundred and twenty-four! We can endure for it is our path to do so. We have a grasp on life that we need not relinquish. It is in our hands to survive and in time to see again the emergence of new adults up to the horn-lands of Hudros and into the Palace of Talviani for their blessing. We have no need to think such things, and to do so only poisons our minds to defeat.'

At the end of Lol Teneth's outburst, the Mirovi were highly unsettled, but Rumé did not relinquish the floor. He pressed onward.

'The Hinasta is of course right to say that such negative thoughts should not be allowed to dominate the psyche of such a nation. I agree, they need not. But they must not remain entirely out of mind, if only within this caucus. Compare your earliest days with these, Hinasta, and you will undoubtedly see the difference is as that which exists between growth and decay. The dying leaf,' he said more gently, 'may cling to the branch stubbornly through a whole winter, but it does not help the tree by doing so.

I do not stand here in front of you solely to reflect your own concerns that you yourselves know only too well. The Dal-Hirovo is correct in assessing we are needy as well. So I shall say simply that we too are in transit, and both flee from our enemies and chase others that in turn endanger our friends. We are in direst need of swift passage to the pass of Ithed and Antheon. In return, knowing your jeopardy, I submit to you that we will help the children of Hud in whichever way it becomes possible to do so.'

Rumé sat back down to much ensuing questioning. In each answer, about those that chased them from the North Vale, and those they chased, those they sought and those he had met upon his way, he mentioned all that he had mentioned to Behvyn and Behleth, but not a word of the discus. This he kept back. Dal-Hirovo showed pleasure at each response Rumé gave to the questions that came in from the Mirovi, but seemed more frustrated as it continued that he was still not aware of what was controlling the overall events. It was obvious to Behvyn that, as time passed well into the evening, the King of the Hudron began to doubt they were being told the fullest truth, so he was not surprised when the Dal-Hirovo sought to ask more questions himself.

'Would Captain Rumé explain,' asked Dal-Hirovo, 'why three groups of individuals would all be travelling to the same pass at the same time? What do you expect to find there?'

'The outcome of meeting each other, my Lord,' answered Rumé.

'Smartly said, Captain, but why there? Are there not enough opportunities to confront each other within the Shale Valley?'

'Such was I told of Fetlock's intentions just before I would be slain,' answered Rumé. 'He did not think at the time I would escape and use this information. As I am driven by the memory of those words, so Fetlock's men drive our friends ahead of them towards that same passage.'

'Yet what could you do once there?' asked Yessin-Tach, speaking for the first time. 'You are blind, are you not? A mighty warrior and leader of manlings as you seem, you are still only three in number and they are without such disadvantage. Therefore, I do not find myself convinced you journey towards a fight. And your friends have fended off attack so far, as you advise. Why could they not use similar cunning to outwit their pursuers once again? Your aid may even weaken them with the added responsibility to look after you. I believe there is something else to it, Dal Hirovo, that we are not being told.'

But instead of demanding an answer from Rumé at that point, Dal-Hirovo diverted the discussion to the two old-looking twins to his right.

'Masters Lindacre,' he asked, standing, 'it may now be opportune to hear from yourselves how you come to us as well. By the sounds of it, there are many matters affecting the Valley at this time. Please add your own for the benefit of the Mirovi and our other honoured guests.'

Avi stood for the twins and paused in choosing where to start his story, following on from the picture Rumé had drawn for them all.

'We have heard much already at this gathering of three kinds of manling, and I thank you all who have spoken in our company. We are honoured. As we are the shortest of the three races, I shall keep my comments the briefest also.'

At these gracious and self-deprecating words, the sense among the room became less defensive. Behvyn felt more comfortable now that the concerns behind the diplomatic façades faded as everyone listened. It was, however, only a brief respite.

'May I make three comments only,' said Avi. 'Firstly, I would make a comparison. The race of manlings represented by Rumé regenerates at will but wastes its offspring, as we all know full well the Shale Valley is engaged in an eternal war with Mertos that also embroils Khubron. The Hudron do not reproduce as adults and, it is to be much lamented, their potential young are not being born to them. And we, who call ourselves men also but are separate as a race to you both, now find ourselves dying out entirely, without the luxury of glorying in war and no hope for young.

'Secondly, I should make a statement of fact. When our race was last together we numbered some twenty individuals, from a once proud nation that has been almost utterly destroyed by the war in Mertos. It is our eventual death as a people which calls the Lady Alcabell to these lands, as the most powerful of the Axumé, and the only one who would be capable of resurrecting us.'

'Thirdly, I will have a guess at the future. As the Lady Alcabell approaches, so together our joint hope should grow for the remedy of all our earthly ills. We should again be made whole as a people and the Hudron may again know the wonder of the arrival of children to their homes. Even the war with Mertos could end, too, and the Shale Valley peopled in peace rather than emptied by baseless war. That is the succour I carry with me and pass to you believing it to be true.'

Avi had spoken with such calm assuredness that it was some few moments before the room had noticed Rumé standing once more.

'Captain Rumé, you have something else to remark?' asked Lol Teneth haughtily.

'I thank Avi Lindacre for his words of hope and again cede the floor to Captain Rumé,' said Dal-Hirovo.

'You are kind, Dal-Hirovo. In the light of the words of Avi, these words will seem heavy: Alcabell is dead.'

At this there was an outbreak of consternation and Santi cried aloud: 'It isn't so!'

But at one glance towards Rumé's face, they all saw the truth of it written there.

'What is the worst of it is that she was killed. Dal-Hirovo, if I may apologise, I am sure my earlier explanations will have caused some of the Mirovi vexation as without this information, which I was loathe to give out unless it be expressly required as now, our actions may have seemed puzzling. The young masters that accompany me saw her moments after the fatal attack and were able to rescue her body from the icy cold of the Highborn. Yet she lived no more.'

The Mirovi looked in alarm at Behvyn and Behleth and even Dal-Hirovo, who until now had not betrayed any internal surprise, raised a long stare at the twins.

'Your Highness,' concluded Rumé, 'indeed there is more to my need to reach the pass of the mountain ranges. I believe I am on the trail of the very killer of the world's only hope for its continued existence.'

Rumé again took his seat and this time the silence was long.

Eventually, without standing, Dal-Hirovo sought to bring all matters to a conclusion.

'Now I begin to see more clearly what challenges we face. What horror it brings us to hear of the death of one of the Undying Ones. Indeed our language cannot even bring itself to accommodate it in logical terms. For your experiences, young Masters,' said the Dal, turning to Behvyn and Behleth, 'forever have our condolences.

'Yet, though the Hudron cannot leave here, tied as we are to our rivers, action must be taken. Though it is an empty retribution, we must do all that we can to support those who would avenge Lady Alcabell's death. Avi has spoken of how he and Santi cannot find their own kind about these lands here. From that perspective, further travel should be encouraged. Rumé endeavours to track and defeat an enemy all of us share. But he has little help, save from two brave youngsters. Therefore, Avi and Santi, I urge you to go with Rumé, the better to pursue our joint justice. If it is the last great achievement of your race, you will forever have the thanks of us all. The task may even take you to those who yet remain.

'As for how you may reach Ithed, there is a way among the roots of the mountains we will show to you. It is underground and very dark. The Lightwater is not the only river our young yet live in. There is another also. It is called the Darkwater, and the route to it stems from here. There has never emerged from it one of our young in living memory, though we maintain the living tissue within the tunnel just in case. The way slopes away from us and you can slide along it at speed on what we call a 'hirass'. It will take you to the foothills of Ithed in no more than two days. From there, you only have to crest a pathway to reach the passage through to Khubron and the revenge that you seek.'

Behvyn's eyes sparkled at the thought of completing the rest of their journey to the pass in great ease and the desire to see his friends once again came flooding back to him. Suddenly, they were no longer a week or two behind, and even had the chance of catching them. Avi and Santi looked pleased, and the Mirovi also. The formality of the meeting then dissolved with a wave of the hand from Dal-Hirovo and Yessina-Qhik came over to them offering clothes and food and provisions, along with advice.

'I am one of the Yessin, the external advisors of the Mirovi,' she said, 'and have cause to travel to the Darkwater upon occasion. I can tell you about the passageway and how you can take the hirass along it.'

They each thanked her as Avi and Santi came over to Behvyn, Behleth and Rumé.

'It looks like we will have an adventure together,' said Santi, expressing a kind of stilted keenness in his face, if not his voice.

Avi was, in contrast, quite obviously infused with a spirit of purpose by the outcome.

'It would be our honour,' he said to Behvyn and Behleth, 'to help you catch the killers of Alcabell. Our honour indeed.'

Behvyn then noticed the doors open and, outside in the encircling hallway, heard that Yinko awaited to collect them.

He then sought Rumé but did not immediately find him. After he had extracted himself from Avi's conversation, however, Rumé appeared from behind him, the Dal leaving his side and emptying the Palace with the rest of the Mirovi.

'There you are, Rumé,' Behvyn said.

'Is Yinko here for us?' he asked.

'Yes,' answered Behvyn. 'She's waiting for us now.' At this news, Behleth went on ahead.

'Then let us go. We will meet the Yessina in the morning from here to be taken to the route of the Darkwater.'

'Rumé, did this evening go well for us? I have the feeling that they don't think we told them the whole truth.'

'Behvyn,' smiled Rumé. 'We told more of our truth in here than did the others of theirs. But as for how it went, it could not have gone much better. Now there are other things to worry about of greater concern.'

'Such as, what?'

'Such as, what your brother thinks he is up to with that young Hudron. Now, lead me on.'

When they reached the outside, having crossed the interior floor with more care than before because the scales were now against them, Behvyn could see Behleth was performing dives and splashes off the hallowed steps of the Palace of Talviani for the amusement of the Mirovi on their way out, and also much to the rapt entertainment of Yinko.

Chapter 12

THE CARES OF KJERROS

Tangle could tell that it was only in the spirit of reconciliation that Tig finally let herself ride alongside her and Paequat, four days after the wounding of the white falcon. But although this outward sign gave comfort to the others, Tangle knew Tig had not yet forgiven Paequat for the attack.

What was worse was that she and her sister were still at loggerheads. Tangle had protested vehemently that such a malicious act would never have occurred to Paequat had he not been scaling, and she steadfastly believed it to have been an accident, albeit borne of an irresponsibility that they all took an equal share in. Fate, she had argued, had intervened for whatever reason, and Paequat could no more have avoided doing what he had done than he could have avoided being brought to life by Alcabell. But Tig was not having it.

It had meant that, for an awkward first few days, Tig rode almost entirely alone, until she had allowed Kjerros to accompany her. He, in the meantime, was trying to escape from bearing the burden of Feran's sole company, as his cousin, unwilling to contradict any degree of Tangle's conviction, but not providing her with the outright support she expected, was cold shouldered by her for days.

'How can you be so sure?' he had once ventured to ask Tangle, only to receive silence in return.

'Well, I'm not,' he continued. 'First, a pile of bodies racked up at the top of the twin's back garden. Now a harmless falcon, with a mangled wing, shot down in idle fun? Think, Tangle! You know what we're like when we're on gnastia; we're still ourselves, only without control. Paequat's revealed that an instinct for killing lives inside of him!' He looked up at the straw man sitting behind Tangle and smiled meekly. 'No offence.'

'Why don't you just run along now?' Tangle seethed and slowed her mothmag down to move away from him.

Feran coasted up to Tig, but had received short shrift from her too.

'Do you believe what Paequat did was wrong, Feran?' Tig asked without looking at him, her eyes steadfastly held to the eastern horizon ahead of them. 'The thing is, we both seem to disagree with my sister over this, but I do wonder how long you'll be able to keep that point of view before you swallow it and run back to her arms.'

Kjerros, on the other hand, had reacted in quite the opposite way to that in which Tangle would have predicted.

'Give it time, Feran,' he counseled. 'Tangle knows you love her and Tig won't let her high principles get in the way of our friendship for ever.'

'How about you?' asked Feran. 'You don't seem to have taken a stand one way or another. I don't think they respect you for that.'

This seemed to have a profound impact on Kjerros, and Feran wondered for a moment if he'd just lost the company of his cousin as well.

'I'm naturally cautious, I'll admit it,' said Kjerros, turning around. 'I despise this about myself, Feran. It's the element that keeps me back. The debate the girls are having over Paequat's guilt simply disinterests me. But ever since your reckless dash to the side of Sirephus' house in Rhal Springs, I've been looking for an opportunity to, well, if not throw myself into harm's way, then to make a contribution towards our goal in some other way. So, after the 'event with the cross bow', as we now all seem to be calling it, my thoughts go to the welfare of the falcon.'

Kjerros uncovered the lifeless bird contained warmly inside the cage he now carried upon the back of the mothmag with him and smiled.

'She'll be better soon,' said Feran, and kept his doubts to himself.

After four day's travel, Kjerros' devotion had reached such a level that the others felt they could not assist in the falcon's recovery without his permission, so overbearing had become his attention to the task he had assumed upon himself.

'Where's that blanket gone now?' Kjerros fumed upon the

back of the mothmag. It had fallen once more, much to his annoyance. He looked around in the decaying blue-yellow light at the end of a mild, wet day and could see it some twenty yards away behind him. It was hanging in the moody breeze, draped above the ground; caught upon the moist heads of the marsh reeds that lined their course down to the Fords of Netheign. He cried out to the others to slow down, which surprised them all as it had been a rarity for him to speak to anyone other than Feran for days, and circled his mothmag around. He tried to collect up the blanket again, but it proved difficult; the mothmags tended to move fast or not at all. Kjerros became noticeably desperate to cosset it once more over the top of the wicker cage that had been fashioned by Feran to allow him to carry the lifeless falcon along with him.

Once, on the first day out from the clearing after Rhal Springs, Kjerros had dropped the cage with the falcon inside it onto the ground from off the back of the mothmag. Mortified, he sat in tears by the cage gently turning it the right-side up, having to watch how the great bird inside of it moved solidly and ever so slowly down the sides. Wincing each time a feather had got caught on the coarseness of its rough construction, he continued correcting the cage until, with a last grim movement, the falcon slid back into place. As a result, he now kept the cage firmly under the crook of his left arm and shoulder and only rode with his right hand. It was the act of having to control the mothmag and collect the blanket all with the same hand that was now proving to be the problem.

'Kjerros need help?' asked Paequat, from the front of the group.

'No thanks, Paequat,' answered Kjerros, and smiled at the straw man until Paequat looked away from him again. 'You've done enough,' he then muttered beneath his breath.

'Kjerros!' chided Tangle, overhearing him. 'How dare you! It's gone to your head, looking after this bloody bird!'

'Well, it is a bloody bird, isn't it? That's just the point!' he responded angrily. 'And somebody's got to get it well again!'

'Well, that's rich. It's not like we haven't offered!' replied Tangle, confounded.

'Oh, exactly when?' retorted Kjerros, finally gathering the blanket up and quickly covering the cage over. 'Was it during the time you two,' nodding at Feran, 'went off into the woods back there to 'gather berries' or when you last said a word to your sister, or-'

'Oi, enough!' enjoined Feran from next to Tangle. For this, he received a sharp dig in the ribs from Tangle who then rode off, leaving Tig in limbo between the unmoving cousins and the slowly vanishing Tangle. They began to move on to keep her in sight.

'Come on, you two,' called Tig, as her ride jogged away from Kjerros and Feran. 'It's not much further now to the Fords. We can make it before nightfall.'

'Now what did I say?' Feran wondered after Tangle.

'I think it was deviating from the phrase: "The world revolves around you, my love", wasn't it?' needled Kjerros.

'Push off, you selfish sod' replied Feran. 'And that diversion into the berries wasn't fun for me. Tangle threw just about everything I ever did for her back in my face and I have absolutely no idea why!'

Feran tried to look sternly at his cousin, who was busy reorganizing himself with the reins, but instead smiled.

'Look, you have to understand her,' said Kjerros. 'She's just found out her father could be some renegade captain, with a past he's never told either of them anything about. She probably just wants to know you're all you seem to be.'

'Huh?' came back his cousin's reply.

'Oh, come on Feran, look at us all now,' explained Kjerros with forced patience as they again got going. They started to close the gap on Tig. 'It's only been two weeks since we set out on this trail, but there have been some big changes already. The girls have just lost the father they thought they knew for him to be replaced by a stranger. How can they go back? What's in Muscle Oaks for them now? Us? We're here. Behvyn and Behleth? We will never stop hoping we'll see them at the Pass. Paequat still feels they are alive and I don't believe Fetlock. But there's nothing for the sisters back home now. Tangle must be so badly disoriented. She's been away for a year and will have expected to come back, carry on from where she had left off, like with you, and make real all her hopes and dreams for the future. Now none of that seems possible, the only thing in her life that is still on track is you.'

'She's got Tig as well,' said Feran, already feeling the pressure of this new responsibility.

'That's not the point!' replied Kjerros, instinctively. 'Tig is her sister. As long as they can, the two of them'll be there for each other, but you must be able to see how Tangle's bursting to make her own way?'

'Well, that's no excuse to terrorize me!' bemoaned Feran. 'I'm quite happy being with her and we love each other. Why would she have to go and complicate it all for us?'

'She's just reacting to what's going on around her. This is not easy. Anyway, I've got no interest in being your confidant. Just take notice of it, is all I'm saying, and you might escape more 'chats' like the one you had the other day. Just be there for her; it's everything she needs in the world right now.'

They rode on in silence with Kjerros attending to the cage and Feran seeming most concerned with perfecting a scowl. They could just see Tig in front. Tangle was so far ahead that they had no idea where she was.

'How's "Flappy"?' asked Feran, as the night started to come down in earnest.

'Don't call her that! Or the "Wingless Wonder,"' Kjerros anticipated. 'I wish she would 'flap' again, but she hasn't moved.'

'What, not at all? It's been a while now.'

'Not since I found her on the ground,' replied Kjerros. 'I've thought she was dead several times but she's still warm. Just doesn't move.'

'How's the wing doing?'

'I've still got the bandage on, but that's the strange thing. It bled awfully in the early stages but after I changed the bandage yesterday it looked almost fully mended. The wing, I mean. The skin had grown back and the bones and ligaments seemed knitted together already.'

'But they'd been torn to shreds,' said Feran, doubtfully. 'They couldn't recover this quickly, it would take weeks.'

'I know it should, but it hasn't.'

'That's weird!'

'You're telling me! And that's not the only thing; here, look at this,' said Kjerros. 'I found it around her neck only this morning, covered up by layers of feathers.'

He held up a short, delicate silver chain, no longer in circumference than a ladies' wrist might be, about which hung a small black gem set in a pendant of silver.

'Strange to name-tag a bird,' replied Feran.

'I know. I wondered at first if someone owned her. But either way, I'm not too happy with the idea of her having it about her neck,' Kjerros explained. 'She could get throttled by it. If she's recovering well, I don't see that she'll miss it.'

'More than well! But what would a bird be doing with that?' asked Feran, watching the jewelry glinting in the strong moonlight.

'I don't know. It's nice though. Why don't you give it to Tangle as a bracelet?' Kjerros passed it across to Feran who grasped it between his fingers and dangled it in front of his face. 'It might, you know, ease things along between you,' he added as an afterthought.

Feran, suddenly seeing it as his best opportunity to be allowed back into Tangle's company, joyfully thrust it into his pocket and thanked Kjerros heartily. Kjerros, realising his cousin's mind would now be ceaselessly imagining and re-imagining the splendor of his reunion with Tangle, returned his own thoughts to the unnatural speed of the falcon's recovery. She had eaten and drank nothing, despite his efforts, but to no detriment. Indeed, everything he had expected to be necessary to return her to health had proved impossible to provide. He now wondered if he should even try to give her food, given her astonishing progress. She looked quite well, but with the one major exception: she had not moved, and he didn't know when she would.

Until then, he decided, he would continue to support and monitor her recovery, even if she didn't need his help in achieving it.

'We'll stop here for the night!' cried Tig ahead of them. 'Tangle and Feran, you two make the fire tonight. Paequat and I will get water. Kjerros, do whatever it is you intend to with the falcon.'

'You are so strong and brave,' Kjerros said to the falcon in the cradle of his arm as they slowed, still in wonderment at her progress.

'Blimey, thanks!' replied Feran, dismounting for his evening meal. Kjerros said nothing, although he looked fit to burst.

The five companions, once seated around the campfire and sated of their appetites for the day, sat in relaxed mood, only disturbed by occasional squabbles between the mothmags secured to the trees around them. The mothmags with their curious ways had become like pets to them and were a constant source of entertainment, like young children at a party. They sat in each other's company comfortably until Feran, always the first to feel the need for speech when there was none, raised a question that was foremost in his mind. He would not have had the confidence to do so had Tangle not taken to holding his hand as they'd sought firewood earlier that evening.

'How far ahead of them do you think we are?' he asked quickly.

'Did anyone see anything today?' asked Tig, giving Feran an approving look.

'We've been going downhill all the time and I didn't spot anything,' replied Kjerros.

'We've been going on mothmags and they've only got horses,' added Tangle. 'We must be half a day's ride ahead of them by now.'

'I agree,' said Tig, 'but that does assume they've kept with horses.'

'But they also had a carriage,' added Kjerros. 'That would slow them if they mended it and continued to use it. With that coming along as well, they would have had to keep to the road if they wanted to follow us, and that's a long detour. We left them in no doubt about where we're going and they'll be sure it's us from the locket of hair you left with them. We must be well ahead of them now.'

'Paequat see something.'

'When?' asked Tig.

'Paequat see something now,' he said, and pointed ahead of them, through the night, towards the direction they had been heading all day.

'What? What do you see Paequat?' Tangle asked. 'Is it the twins?'

215

Paequat shook his head so quickly that his hat stayed still.

'The Fords? Do you see those?' asked Kjerros, speaking directly to Paequat for the first time in many days.

'Yes!' answered Paequat. 'Paequat sees Netheign Fords.'

'The Fords already! We've made fantastic progress!' cried Tangle excitedly, in part pleased at how she had forced the pace earlier in the day. She put her head on Feran's shoulder, whose spirits soared that moment.

'Listen, you can hear the river against it as well,' added Tig.

'Can you see the bad men, Paequat?' asked Feran. 'Are they there?'

Everyone looked to Paequat in concern. Tangle raised her head off Feran and gave him an annoyed stare and again his heart plummeted. Paequat stood up and walked away from the fire to have a better look.

'Why'd you have to ask a question like that?' asked Tangle. 'We've just agreed we must have been moving much faster than them. They can't be in front of us!'

Feran thought desperately.

'We've been travelling really quickly,' Feran said, 'but we also stopped each night to rest the mothmags.'

'So?' challenged Tangle.

'So I just remember hearing a story once,' began Feran cautiously, 'where these two men flogged their horses remorselessly and rode at a gallop incessantly for three days. At the end of it, six horses were dead, but they'd made the journey in half the time it would have taken them normally.'

'That's so cruel!' said Tangle.

'Yes, but the men riding the horses were scouts for the King and had seen invaders coming up over the Green Mountains. I remember now, it was Crowther Dogwood that told me, earlier this year, through a lot of grumbles about being taken advantage of. He'd learned all about this battle that had happened recently and how close it had been, from one of the King's Guards whose horse he'd been asked to re-shoe for free. This Guard had explained to him that everyone had been so surprised by the direction from which the attack had come that they had to bring an army out from Cambwall itself to defeat them.'

'Who did they turn out to be?' asked Tangle, only the potential for forgiveness in her voice. She was more interested than she sounded, though.

'Dogwood didn't seem sure,' replied Feran. 'I don't think he listened to the Guard's story too closely; he must've been too annoyed about giving somebody something for nothing. But that was the same night as there was some attempted coup or other, in Cambwall. I remember him mentioning that.'

'I remember!' cried Tangle.

'What? How?' asked Feran, bewildered.

'I was there! Well, we were there!' Tangle said to Tig and invited her over to their side of the fire. Kjerros moved in to Feran's side to listen as well but kept an eye on Paequat, who continued to scan the darkness ahead.

'It's not much of a story, but, well; we were in the forecourt to the Palace, performing in front of a few groups of courtiers and merchants. Then we were suddenly shouted at to make way and from inside the Palace gates there galloped out all these knights, aiming straight for the arsenal. Everyone was in alarm.'

'Except Tangle, here,' added Tig. 'As quick as a flash, the first thing she said was: "We must get back inside the Palace!" as though we'd ever been inside before. But as we were surrounded by courtiers who assumed we were in the habit of performing in front of the Prince, they gathered us within their huddle and we all headed inside the East Wing.' Tig looked with pride towards her younger sister. 'We hadn't been invited to play for the Prince by that stage and we'd been desperately awaiting our chance.'

'Once inside, though, there was more going on,' continued Tangle. 'Someone had found a drugged guardsman in front of the King's chamber and Prince Idren couldn't be found. They kept looking for this other Prince whom we hadn't met at that time, and there was lots of dashing around. We didn't know our way around back then, but in order to get out of the way, we slipped down some stairs at the back of an ante-chamber, more to stay out of sight than anything else.'

'That was the only route that didn't have guards all around it,' added Tig.

'We wanted to keep moving,' explained Tangle, 'and to look

like we knew our way around. So we went down the staircase, which led to another and then another, more winding set of steps. At the bottom of that there was a corridor running left and right, so we just followed it off to the left and got further and further into what we thought were servants quarters.'

'We had, by that time, become horribly lost,' mentioned Tig, at which they all laughed.

'What did you do then,' asked Kjerros, enthralled.

'The only thing I could think of,' replied Tangle. 'I started to sing; "The Measure of Life's Success", I think.'

Tig raised an eyebrow. 'You think? Hmm. Well, it was definitely that. Only the most romantic song in our entire repertoire she could think of! I started playing along on my sea-chelys.'

'And then a door opened and out walked Prince Idren,' said Tangle.

'Just like that?' asked Feran, thrilled but uncomfortable. The revelation distanced him from Tangle.

'Pretty much,' she replied, and then noticed Feran's face. 'Don't worry, sweetie. He didn't look all that different from Behleth. Anyway, he said he heard our music and wondered who we were and what was going on. I explained that there was something going on upstairs with people rushing about and he said he'd not heard anything and I replied, "Well you're not going to all the way down here, are you?" He then agreed and thanked us for the music and then made his way to the stairs.'

'What did you do?' asked Kjerros.

'We followed him, of course!' replied Tangle. 'It's not every day you get a chance to get close to a Prince, and he was the only one who could show us how to get out of there; there was nobody else around. He seemed to realise this after we'd been following him for some little while; I think he even slowed his pace once to make sure we knew the route. Anyway, once the Royal Guards had found him everything calmed down and we were able to find our way back through the Hall of Victories, to the East Wing exit. Then we got out of there as quickly as we could!'

'We didn't want to hang around,' said Tig, 'in case the Prince discovered we shouldn't have been there, although I think he guessed that much, anyway. We wondered what he had been doing in the servants quarters at that time of night as well.'

'The next day there was an announcement that the attack had been repelled and every last enemy killed,' concluded Tangle, 'but at enormous loss. There were also rumours among the courtiers that the drugged guard had died protecting the sleeping King Cuiron from being given a deadly poison. Then rumours grew that the attack had been part of a plot to leave the Palace defenceless, but that the plotters had not reckoned with a certain Prince Kinithor. It was he that had come to the rescue of the crown with an army of his own, up from the southwest, unlooked for, that replaced every lost man with one from his own brigade and fortified the numbers around the Royal family twice over. It was then that Kinithor was welcomed by Prince Idren as a brother and given many high honours. Though not of the same line, Kinithor was admitted to Prince Idren's company when he would see no other. Now they are the best of friends, as far as I know.'

They all still had questions, but seeing Paequat returning towards them, they steeled themselves for what he would say.

'Paequat not see bad men,' he announced. 'But Paequat see what they did.'

'What? They've already been here? What is it?' demanded Kjerros, impatiently.

'Fords brokened,' said Paequat.

Tangle again grasped for Feran's shoulder and Feran this time put his arm around her.

'So, let me get this straight,' said Kjerros. 'We ride like the wind only to find we're a day late. And now, even if we do find a way to cross the river, because the Fords are now broken, armed riders led by the man who boasts of our friends' death could then descend upon us. And I have to care for a bird we shot down with a crossbow because it seemed like a good idea at the time. Am I about right? Am I? I'm never scaling again. And neither are any of you!'

~ || ~

Behleth was not enjoying the training. He had been as keen as a youngling on Charion's Morn when he had first seen the devices;

219

the idea of 'shooting along like a rat in a drainpipe', as he called it, had held enormous appeal for him. But as the operation of the underwaterway craft was further explained to them his enthusiasm began to wane.

'We really travel backwards?' he asked, astonished.

'That's not a problem, is it?' asked Yinko.

They all now stood together about the entrance to a short tunnel which lay at the eastward foot of the towering White Horn of the Hudron. They had descended from the Citadel very early that morning (in a very leisurely manner compared to their arrival) so that they could learn the art of controlling the craft along the practice tunnel before they needed to leave for the Darkwater.

'What are these things called again?' Behleth asked Yessina-Qhik in as polite a way as he could manage at the time. After his first few attempts with Avi, he had more bumps and bangs in more places than he cared to acknowledge.

'They are called "hirass", Master Behleth,' the Yessina replied. 'You are not enjoying riding them?'

Behleth, dusting himself off, looked over to Yinko who was now helping Avi back on to the hirass from which they had both just fallen.

'Not at all,' he replied, smiling gamely. 'I'm having six kinds of fun, really. I just don't see why we have to travel backwards, is all. It makes it so much more difficult.' Avi nodded in support.

'It is the traditional way,' responded Yessina-Qhik, with her voice burbling more strongly than before. Her manner reminded them all of the ways of mentors they had each had in the past. 'The underwaterway will make its turns and runs as it will, and there is no controlling or changing it. So why the need to face frontward? The hirass will not turn you over, only your fear. By facing back the way you have come, you do not see that which approaches and so cannot be alarmed.' She broke off to look at Avi; whose crossed arms and cocked head spoke volumes of doubt. 'Hirass are not designed to be driven, Master Avi, only ridden upon. They need your faith.' She looked up at them all. 'We are possibly trying to do too much. We must each dispel our concerns and let the hirass do the work. Now,' she concluded encouragingly, 'lets try again.'

After this, she felt she had finally broken through to those two who had been having most difficulty. Santi, Behvyn and Rumé had collapsed at the end of their first trial run in a great mangle of bodies, but had all emerged in great fits of laughter. Their second attempt was perfect. Now, having satisfied the Yessina with three further perfect rides, they entertained themselves by watching the other's learning curve.

'Come on, I think we've cracked it now,' said Avi to Behleth under his breath in front of the expectant audience, and they picked up the small hirass once again to take it back to the start of the practice run.

'I can't think how to switch off, though,' replied Behleth, as they again seated themselves into the hirass.

'Just shut your eyes, then,' suggested Avi. 'It's what I fully intend to do this time. Let's try it.'

They both did and, after so much failure, they performed the craft without incident all the way to the end of the practice run.

'Wonderful!' exclaimed Yinko in delight, and she ran over to them and lifted them out of the hirass one by one, congratulating them both with an affectionate hug. Behleth was momentarily lost in a haze of bliss. He noted Behvyn's sour look with deep satisfaction as he walked over to him, unable to suppress a victorious grin.

'You just get your head back on getting yourself down to the Darkwater,' said Behvyn.

'Just because you're jealous,' replied Behleth.

'I am not!' snapped Behvyn, giving his brother a very hurt look. 'It might be very nice for Feran to be able to catch up with Tangle all this time, but don't think it doesn't eat into me every moment that Tig is goodness knows where and I can't look after her from here.'

'I didn't mean it like that,' Behleth said, downwardly.

'For crying out loud, just have some consideration for once!' Behvyn snapped.

While they spoke, the Yessina and Yinko had conferred, although 'argued' may have been closer to the truth. Then it was announced, by the now flustered Yessina, that there would indeed be two hirass to make the 'descent' to the Darkwater. The first to leave, she explained, would carry Rumé, Behvyn and Santi. The second would carry Avi and Behleth, and Yinko.

Behleth, surprised, smiled at Yinko, who then came over literally bubbling with excitement. Behleth could see small butterfly-shapes rising and evaporating inside Yinko's body.

'I didn't think anyone except the Yessin were allowed outside the call of the tower, Yinko?' Avi asked, though clearly pleased at the prospect of being accompanied by a Hudron on what he expected to be a challenging journey.

'I have just been made an honourable Yessina,' Yinko replied to them both, as they watched the other three being taken over to the entranceway of the underwaterway that would lead them to the Darkwater. 'For me, it is a great honour to represent my people to you, yourselves representatives of two different kinds also.' She let her gaze linger on Behleth a moment or two longer than either of them felt to be inconspicuous.

'Isn't it dangerous, though?' asked Avi, oblivious. 'I mean, to you, Yessina-Yinko, if I may be the first to call you that. You are safe here, but the cold of winter approaches; if those whom we pursue trap us, the weather outside may become too harsh for your own safety. Forgive me, Yinko, but without shelter or warmth you could perish.'

'Then we shall make all cares for you, Yinko,' responded Behleth, as the reality of Avi's well-meant words caused Yinko's enthusiasm to waiver. 'Do not worry; I will not let you freeze!' She looked at Behleth gratefully before encouraging them both to 'make quick steps', determined not to be shaken from her own hasty resolve. They walked over to watch the leaving of the first hirass.

Behvyn sat facing towards Yessina-Qhik, on the outside right of the hirass, with Rumé next to him and Santi on the leftward side. He was pleased to see the face of his brother approach as they went through a final sequence of checking that they had everything with them and that it was all secured. This included the buffering braces to slow their progress to a stop for when they must eat and rest. This would be possible at a point halfway along the full distance of the underwaterway which flattened out for half a league of so before heading down more sharply once again. Next to the braces, which looked like oars with circular balls of padding at the blade end, were stored their food for the journey, water and their packs.

Then, as an additional honour, Dal-Hirovo, unaccompanied by the Mirovi, approached to wish them the highest good fortune. Wordlessly, his presence reminded them of their additional responsibility to the Hudron.

With everything ready, Yessina-Qhik made one final suggestion. 'The journey is two days; leaving now you will enter into the Darkwater at sundown tomorrow. I suggest you drag the hirass into the river with you; they will not be seen by any above the surface, and it may encourage-'

The Dal placed his hand on her shoulder to comfort the Yessina who at this moment seemed overcome with sadness, and nodded slightly at the two Hudron that held the chocks in place at the front of the hirass. They removed them and the hirass, with Rumé, Santi and Behvyn upon it, began to move slowly away from those that stood by to watch the first moments of its long descent. Nothing was said and, within a short while, they were engulfed in a complete darkness.

Behvyn knew that his brother must surely be behind him, travelling as quickly as he; but he was not wholly confident. He supposed the rate at which he felt they travelled was increased by the darkness. But as he sat there, letting the hirass take them along the underwaterway, he became astonished at how fast they would need to be travelling to reach the pass of Ithed and Antheon in only two days instead of fourteen.

'Rumé?' he asked. 'How far could we walk in a day?'

'We would make eight leagues in the open ground of the North Vale, maybe nine. In the forest we barely made three,' he replied.

'That is how I measured it!' said Behvyn, pleased. 'But this cannot be right. If it were to have taken us two weeks to get to the pass, at say seven leagues a day, then that is very nearly a hundred leagues; and yet we are now going to make that distance in less than two days? That is fifty leagues a day; excluding a third of the time spent eating food and sleeping!'

'We move at a mighty pace; yet may it be faster still! For we are behind, and far. Until we are ahead in this race to the Pass, I do not feel comfort in the prospect of rest. We are too disadvantaged already. But to travel at this pace is only the same as if we were on horseback. Our enemies chose well to keep their mounts, though they had to ride half the length of the Valley on them. We take a more direct route, but from what I last saw, Fetlock was six day's ride out from the Fords of Netheign if he planned to stop, or four days away if he didn't. That was four days ago. Once over the Fords, he could make the pass in three days, or less if he is particularly cruel to the horses. He has not seen us dead; so he will not assume that we are. Given the speed he travels, he believes the race is on. It is close, Behvyn; do not wish for any progress slower than this.'

'My dear Rumé,' replied Behvyn, lightheartedly, 'you can consider me duly alarmed.'

At this, Santi laughed quietly from Rumé's other side, at the notice of Behvyn.

'Master Lindacre, can you now see what I meant by my earlier words?' said Behvyn.

'What's all this?' asked Rumé.

'Nothing,' replied Santi. 'Just that I asked Behvyn what you were like, as it was agreed we would be sharing this journey together. He said you reminded him of two things. Firstly, the moon; in that your thoughts can be as high as the stars yet shed little light to those that dwell on the ground.'

'Did he now?' said Rumé.

'Yes, I did, but in all affection,' appeased Behvyn.

'And the second?' Rumé enquired.

'The second was an empty ale barrel,' replied Santi.

'Really? And how so?'

'Sobering,' said Behvyn.

Rumé said no more, but rumbled to himself for a while, much to Behvyn's amusement. Santi returned to his previous state of alertness, though less tense than before. Behvyn listened to the slither of the runs that were close beneath them as they moved efficiently over the soft jelly lining of the twisting underwaterway. The lining did not pulse and glow as the passageway from the Lightwater had. Instead, inside the night of the tunnel, Behvyn let the motion and the sound carry his mind off far outside, to a warm fireside from the past, inside the Poachers' Inn; and to a late evening around its glow shared with Tig. Without noticing, he fell fast asleep.

At the same time, Behleth had never felt so awake. His whole body felt like it was on fire. His heart popped and flinched with every sudden brush made against Yinko's electric velvet skin. Their legs were wedged together, with Behleth on the outside left, Yinko in the middle and Avi on the outside right. Behleth found himself leaning out leftward to avoid pressing into Yinko's side, but it was having an unbalancing effect.

'Move in closer, Master Behleth,' Yinko would say with polite encouragement, at which Behleth's heart would pound again nervously. He would fill with bewildering emotions that made the world unreal. As his mind grasped for normalacy again, he would again lean away, quite insensible of doing so. Eventually, having done so too many times, Yinko reached for his arm in the darkness, and linked hers through his so as to keep him in place. As she did so, Behleth felt a thrill wash through her. He began to have the first realisation that he was not alone in being swept up in a wave of emotion he didn't understand. As they felt the pull of the earth each time they swung low and sudden around a long, downward curve in the underwaterway, Behleth mused belatedly on Yinko's nervousness before the journey. At the time, he had thought it was to do with the honour of the assignment, as she herself had explained. Now he wondered.

'Master Behleth,' said Avi, 'have you, I wonder, ever been outside of your own Kingdom before? That now seems to be the path ahead of you, and possibly yourself also, Yessina. I can remember the first time I left mine. I was just a young man at the time. Quite the most terrifying aspect of leaving home is the saying of 'goodbye' to everything that is familiar to you and seeing it replaced by sights that you never imagined possible. Why now, take those trees upon the heights of the White Horn, Yessina; or the Cold Falls of the North Vale, Master Behleth. The most wondrous sights may await you, after you say 'goodbye'. True, there are other sights that may not be so inspirational. Like the inside of this chute we are flushing through.'

'Where are you from, Avi?' asked Behleth. 'I know that over the mountain pass there is the Kingdom of Khubron and that through it northwards lay the battle plains towards cold Mertos. But where did you begin your journey?'

'You know of Mertos; good, good,' replied Avi. 'Well, I was born there, so they tell me. But I do not remember it. It has always been the lot of our race to move about. Behleth, you have a kingdom; the length and breadth of the Shale Valley. You can walk in it and be of it. The rivers, the mountains, the coast, the winds, the clouds and mists, the grass and the rocks; it is yours and you are of it.

'But imagine one day, at the end of an age during which your achievements rivaled even those of the Undying Ones, the land beneath you being ripped and torn and crumpled like paper. Imagine the Highborn drying in a moment; the trees in Muscle Oaks blasted into fiery atoms and falling to the earth like a rain of black snow. Imagine seeing all your towers of worship, your buildings and craft and homes brought down to the ground to turn to dust and ashes only to then be covered by a river of molten rock. Imagine the re-direction of your rivers away to feed life in other kingdoms, the darkening of the skies and the migration of the stars to point elsewhere, leaving not even nothingness but a total absence of everything.

'My forebears were left for dead, abandoned in a non-place, eons ago, where there once was a great realm. Since then, they gathered together; the last unwanted remnants of our race. They were forced on as unwilling cuckoos, obliged to foist themselves upon the kindness of others for a place to live. Our numbers diminished first by a deadly red flood through our old lands, then by despair, and then by assaults led upon us by hosts who eventually tired of our presence. Our hope has only been held in place by adhering to one thought; that if our great civilisation be not re-built, that the memory of it be preserved for all eternity.'

'And is that why you travelled here? To look for a way in which that worthy goal may be achieved?' asked Yinko, the sorrow in her voice tempered by caution; Avi was controlled in his speech but both Behleth and Yinko could hear how his blood boiled in its telling. Neither of them felt they could blame him.

'Yes, lady,' he replied simply.

'Are you so sure it was not, well, fate?' asked Behleth, unwisely. 'Sometimes things just happen that can't be avoided.'

'Do not be sure fate has no name,' responded Avi, once more aflame. 'We were not made to suffer idly. The Great Ones deigned it, though we cannot guess at their purpose. Why, even the minions of the Gulkrylith were said to have looked in pity at our destruction, as another page in the Red Book might be written.'

At the mention of the Gulkrylith, Yinko shrank over to Behleth. Avi's soft apologies to Yinko went unheard by Behleth, whose ears pounded now that Yinko's head lay on his shoulder and her arms about his neck. He thought to himself that he might never sleep again.

The morning of the 22nd of October, 3817, was the chilliest yet, as tendrils of fog from the Highborn rose like frozen spirits and cast about the dozing forms by the river. It draped them in a fine layer of icy droplets. Kjerros was the first to wake. Ill tempered by a thin diet and shivering from the cold, he made his way down to the riverside to wash the sleep out of his eyes and then to stand perplexed, staring out at the destroyed Fords, seeing them for the first time.

The Fords of Netheign were more substantial than he had imagined. They were constructed of giant-sized squat boulders that had been flattened off at the tops. The water and algae that coated them had combined to given them a brown-green look, so that they reminded him of the strangest of things – pickled walnuts. The boulders – or giant walnuts; his early morning mind was prepared to consider both options – had been fitted together so expertly that the Highborn passed through the gaps between them with very little fuss; while the tops looked like a continuation of the narrow road that swung up from the south to meet it. The road itself passed through the village of Netheign, itself long left desolate since the early days of the war. Kjerros could see through the mists that the road back here was much less well maintained than the Kings Way; even in comparison with it as far up north as he was from. It was not lined along either edge with white stone to define it; neither was it repaired of pot-holes or cambered to encourage the run off of rains to gutters delved into either side. The pools of water upon it looked stagnant and deep; the carriage tracks gored into it knotted and twisting. In comparison, the Fords looked like a floor, smooth as wet glass. With one obvious exception, he noted in dismay.

The Fords were complete for two thirds of their span over the rushing river. But the final third had been attacked in a manner of which Kjerros had no guess. The giant boulders had been smashed to half their height and the water flowed deep above them. Only a jagged tooth here and there pierced the surface; shards of rock up to the size of a man littered the riverbed and the eastern bank. It was as he stood staring at the water pouring over the destruction, hoping for an idea that would allow them to cross, that he found he now had company. It was Paequat.

'Good morning,' Kjerros said, tiredly. He no longer had the effort to keep up his fury towards the straw man.

'Kjerros awake early,' said Paequat. 'Have things on mind? Paequat very sorry for falcon.'

'Yes,' Kjerros answered. 'I was trying to think what made such a mess of the Fords.'

'Bad men with fire powder,' said Paequat.

Kjerros was thrown. 'How do you know these things Paequat?'

'I see ghosts of actions,' replied Paequat.

'It was the same men as those we thought we were in front of?'

'Yes.'

'Well, it doesn't help us get across, does it?'

'Paequat knows way.'

'What, to cross the river? With the mothmags?' replied Kjerros cautiously. 'It doesn't involve killing anything, does it?'

'No. Paequat can talk to Him. He may let us cross.' And with that, Paequat walked off, down towards the river, much to Kjerros' bemusement.

Unsure whether to follow Paequat or to see how the others were, Kjerros eventually decided to see if anyone else was awake. When he got back, Tangle was sitting up, yawning into her hands.

She caught his puzzled look and the uncertainty of his stride.

'Well, talk to me Kjerros,' she said. 'And help me up. Have you seen a ghost?'

'Funny you should ask,' Kjerros explained as he brought her to her feet.

'What? Who is 'He', I wonder? Well, we'd better get back to him,' she said, full of business. 'There two are still fast off. We can let them sleep on a little more. Come on, then.' She led Kjerros down to the riverside once more, where they paused a little distance away from Paequat, who they saw talking loudly with his hands and feet in the river. He chanted solemnly, making his usual thin, high voice sound sonorous and commanding.

Tangle was astounded; she even forgot to let go of Kjerros.

'He's talking in strange language! I wonder if it's the old tongue of the Graces?' she managed to utter.

'What, the Voice of the Immortals?' asked Kjerros. 'He can't be! No one knows that language. Who would have taught it to him!'

'But listen, Kjerros!' implored Tangle. 'Uromo is the original name for the Ruler of Waters, that we call 'Hud' now. I remember seeing statues of him in Cambwall. He must be trying to speak to Him!'

'He's actually trying to talk to one of the Great Ones?' murmured Kjerros in disbelief.

'I can't believe it either!' said Tangle, as excited as she could be having just woken up. Only then did she realise how cold it was and she sought the warmth of Kjerros' cloak; uninvited, she wrapped herself inside it, and stood on Kjerros' toes.

'Sorry, but the ground is freezing,' she said to him, looking at Paequat.

They both thought of suggesting to the other that they quickly go back to fetch the others. But neither of them spoke it.

They stood there, sharing the same cloak; Tangle up on Kjerros' booted feet, deep in the mists that clothed the land, and there they waited. As they did, Paequat's sonorous chant became more abrupt and more urgent. It sounded less like a request and more like a call. His words began to change. Instead of 'Uromo' it was now 'Uromo-can' and they heard a new phrase, 'Yalké fir'ennieth!'

almost as though Paequat was asking the Water King to recall something from his long past.

A wind got up. Tussles of Tangle's hair began first to float and wander like snakes to a charmers' song; and then, as the wind grew in strength, as it plunged and swirled, it streamed about her. It whipped into Kjerros' face; it was pulled out in front of her; it was driven into bangs. As the wind rose so it became colder, and so harsh that Tangle could no longer face into the wind. The mists were shredded. She turned around and faced Kjerros. Responding to a look she gave, Kjerros turned his back to the wind and locked his arms around her. Together they had a sideways view down to the river and the strangest sight either of them had yet seen. They both gasped in fear.

Paequat was reaching a crescendo with his chant:

'Aureth naur,

Umovo-can Gancalcian!

Alcabelliath Taer! Taer!'

As he spoke a last great 'Taer!' all about him the waters were lowering. Slowly, but definitely the Highborn was weakening. First, Paequat's arms could once again be seen. Then, as the waters receded, his legs began to show.

'I'm afraid,' said Tangle, looking away from Paequat into Kjerros' frozen face. Tears of cold were drawn from his eyes by the wind so that he couldn't see her clearly; but he could feel her shaking, not with cold but in terror. He looked at her, kissed her delicately on the forehead and whispered to her that he wouldn't let anything happen to her. She hugged him again to stay warm and continued to shudder at each word Paequat said.

'What is he?' she asked aloud, her breath coming in gasps, speaking through the cold and the fright.

'He's your son, Tangle,' said Kjerros, unsure of where he gathered the strength to withstand the elements and to watch Paequat conquer the river. 'You must not fear him, or the power he possesses. Remember how he told us how he was brought to life?'

Kjerros heard a sobbing 'Alcabell?' from within the cloak.

'Alcabell,' said Kjerros, confirming Tangle's answer. 'It isn't Paequat, Tangle. It must be Alcabell. He is Her gift to us all. None of us, not even he, knows what to expect he is capable of.

I'm sure that on the inside he is as frightened as you are at what he is doing, even now.'

But as quickly as Kjerros' confidence had grown, it shrank into nothingness. For just then, through streaming eyes, he saw an arm of incomparable size. It emerged fleetingly from the river, upstream from Paequat, who was now fully revealed though he stood upon the riverbed, and scooped back the waters so that they ran down in only a trickle over Paequat's feet.

From whipping storm to stilled breeze, the wind lay down once more and Tangle's hair came to rest. Kjerros and Tangle loosened their clutch on each other and stood looking at Paequat, who beckoned them to fetch the others.

'We cross now,' Paequat said enthusiastically, walking up and down and playing with the fish that flipped and juggled themselves on the riverbed.

Tangle moved out from under Kjerros' cloak and ran back over to where Feran and Tig still lay asleep. Wordlessly, she woke them, gathered up their belongings and handed them to them. Kjerros went over to the falcon, which still lay in the same heartbreaking pose as ever and took up the cage in his arms, once he had placed his pack across his shoulders. As he did so, he couldn't help watching Tangle. She caught his eye on her and gave him a concerned, distracted look.

Feran was the least aware of the circumstances, but was eventually quieted once his usual barrage of questions met with no answer. Tig immediately sensed something very strange was happening, but did not ask. She saw the look on her sister's face as she went about corralling the mothmags and noticed neither Tangle nor Kjerros made any move to mount the birds. She wondered where Paequat was and whether he was in trouble. The night before, they had reached no conclusion as to how they could get across and had determined to sleep on it. Now that they had, she could not imagine what solution had been found. She made sure Feran kept up with them and, in no time, they were all on the move, dragging their mothmags behind them, down to the river.

Or, to what had been a river. Tig and Feran were knocked stiff by the sight that met them and it was only with the tugging of Kjerros and Tangle that they were capable of moving again. Tig found it easiest to focus on Paequat, whose clear enjoyment of the circumstances distracted her mind from the waters that were still held back by an unseen force within the Highborn. Since leaving Paequat, Tangle noticed that the height of the waters to their left, up towards the North Vale, had grown. Instead of approximating the normal level of the Highborn, they had swelled to such an extent that the banks were already beginning to flood. If they had not moved sooner, Tig and Feran would have been swamped where they lay.

They made as to walk down to meet Paequat, but none of them could. They all feared a sudden breaking of the tide; a quick reversion to what had been there only a short while ago; the strong, lithe flow of a mighty river.

'He promises he won't let go,' said Paequat, and ran back up to them. Tig let herself get drawn down by him as he offered his gloved straw hand out, to screams from Tangle. Feran went to her, but she wouldn't be touched. Instead, as if in a haze, she let her mothmag drag her down onto the riverbed, her face an unhealthy sallow colour. Feran followed directly behind, jittering with fear at the mounting wave to their left, forcing his feet to move, his whole body feeling nerveless.

Kjerros was the last to leave the bank, with Tig nearly the full way across. He waited until Feran had made it halfway across, released his mothmag ahead of him and then dashed for it. He ran down the side of the bank, the falcon lifted as high as his head, and strode as faithfully as he could manage over the smooth stones that dotted the riverbed. Each step sank a few inches into the oozing silt, but he pretended not to notice. He was a third of the way across when the first of the waters hit him. They took his footing out from under him and caused him to fall, face forward, with the cage held out in front of him.

He rose to his feet. His clothes, face and hands were now covered in thick, pungent soil. He looked behind him. The river was being loosed as he went. He dashed again, a blind panic stinging his body back into life. But he could find no rhythm on the uneven ground. He would build up an unstable momentum only to come crashing down again not twenty paces further on. He yelped in terror, and this time he lost control of the cage. He dropped the falcon as he splashed into the fast running water that was now a foot in depth. He was only halfway across. Upon hearing his cries he saw Paequat run down into the water from the far bank. Feran had made it and was watching Kjerros with Tig and Tangle, their mothmags dancing with pleasure as his own met up with them. Paequat's look of delight fast turned to alarm.

Kjerros could hear them all shouting from the bank, and as he again found his feet, saw Tangle struggle from Tig's grasp and begin to climb down into the river. But Paequat saw this and screamed at her in a terrible way. She stopped, long enough to come to her senses, and let Tig take her back up to safety. Meanwhile, Kjerros looked around frantically for the falcon. The cage had gone missing. It was gone. Floating down the river to the sea! Then he saw it. It was rolling off to his right, up against the giant boulders that made up the Ford. He strode in large, exaggerated steps over to it and grasped it triumphantly, only to discover with a sickening lurch that it was empty. It was smashed, and there was nothing inside.

'Kjerros must come to Paequat!' he heard dimly through the sudden anguish that smote his heart to the core. He was so distraught he didn't care for the mounting waters and could only stand like a lost child at a fair, helpless and deadened to everything except the grief that now overwhelmed him.

'I killed her,' he said to himself. 'I killed her!' he screamed, and thrashed at the river, now up to his waist. His action threw him off balance and sent him spiralling along the river's foaming surface, straight into the boulders where he caught like a grain in a filter. But the force of the water was now such that he could not place his feet down from where he was pinned. The current had taken him closer to Paequat and the far bank, but there was still a quarter of the distance left to go.

Then Paequat reached him, and just in time. As they caught each other, Kjerros was pushed by another sudden gush as more of the held-back waters were released and they were both taken over the low part of the Ford, over the ruined teeth of the boulders that had been destroyed by Fetlock's men. As these were much lower in the water than the others, so they were swept clear over them, and into the southern flow of the Highborn. Here, though, the water was less strong, slowed as it was by the barrier formed by the Fords, and the water level was lower. Just low enough so that they could both once again place their feet down and make their way jointly over to the east bank, where their friends waited.

Feran held out a hand for Kjerros and hauled him out of the water; Tig and Tangle were able to lift Paequat up without any struggle. Only his waterlogged boots gave him any weight what-soever, and they marvelled at how he had not been borne away by the water more easily.

As Kjerros hit the ground, he was sobbing.

'I killed her!' he cried. 'Washed away; smashed against the rocks by the current!' No one could snap him out of his grief.

Meanwhile, Paequat was still full of purpose. He strode off back further up the river and started calling in the strange tongue again.

'Ai Ifurvo can Tulset,
A wer'goviran kinesset,
Lovabrium Umovore,
Cabelliath tuo viandrice!
Meandum Gulkrylith atteni!'

These last few words were shouted so loudly that the others all had to cover their ears; even Kjerros was shaken from his misery. Knowing what had happened the last time Paequat had spoken so, they all stared at the creature, berating the river and expected the unusual. What they then saw surprised them all.

Like a shot, something burst from the surface of the river at the point at which it was being held back and it sped so fast into the sky none of them saw what it was. They all looked up and saw nothing until Tig saw movement, so high above them that she struggled to mark it out to the others. But she followed it and it became clearer.

'Look, there! There!' she pointed. They looked and saw a sight they had all wished for over the last five days. It was the falcon, and she was describing fast, wide arcs in the morning sunshine, until she saw them. Then she swooped down to sit with the one who had cared for her most.

As Kjerros swapped his tears of woe for tears of joy, Paequat made a final announcement into the Highborn.

'Umovo un calibreth, te ne Rathiel an!' he said and at that very moment the pent up waters that had yet to be released were let go. They crashed upon the Fords and engulfed them, first in furious torrents and then, as their cacophony died down, in heavy flows, and the Highborn went on once more.

Paequat then came over to Kjerros.

'Kjerros is nearly drowned. Umovo says sorry. Says, just having fun!' Paequat was clearly concerned at having placed Kjerros in such danger. But Kjerros was not thinking about it.

'Paequat?' said Kjerros, watching the white falcon greedily eating up some of the small fish that littered the bank side. 'I'm sorry.'

'Kjerros need no sorry,' replied Paequat happily, draining the water out of his boots before turning away eastward to face the last stretch of the journey to the pass of Ithed and Antheon.

It now looked so much closer than before with the river crossed. The snaking of the road led to foothills and then the sides of the mountain. The twin peaks of Ithed and Antheon were clothed in snow; the Pass that lay between them sat inestimably high. But they all knew they had less time than ever to get there. It would be a race, with Fetlock and his men on horseback and they on moth-mags.

Kjerros discarded the cage ceremoniously and they took up the reins of their mounts, as the white falcon followed them over-head. Then they began the last charge openly along the road, with Behvyn and Behleth at the forefront of their minds.

Chapter 13

ITHED AND ANTHEON

Behvyn thought the first stage of the journey to the Darkwater had passed more slowly than any other single day he could remember. Not that he didn't appreciate how quickly they had been travelling, but that as it required no thought or action on his part to cover the necessary distance, he found himself at a loss over what to do, in addition to simply sitting as still as he could.

Rumé was close up against him, so they had ample opportunity to talk comfortably above the low level of sound made by the runs below them; but because they shared the hirass with the stranger, Santi, neither felt comfortable making casual conversation.

Behvyn longed to know Rumé's views of the Hudron and the twins they'd met in the Citadel. He wondered if he let himself dwell on the fate of the falcon or if he spent his time instead musing on what he would do if they caught Fetlock. But the grim man mentioned very little aloud. Behvyn understood that he didn't want Santi benefiting from his council. In his own mind Behvyn mistrusted the stranger for there remained much unspoken.

He remembered well how awkward he had been upon meeting the other twins and wondering how they had come to be in the Palace of Talviani at the very same time that they themselves had reached there by chance. He assumed it was they who had tricked him into looking away as two figures had dived into the Lightwater two nights ago in the woods, but if he were right, then it raised a number of presently unanswerable questions. For this reason, Behvyn realised, he had believed little or nothing of anything said by either Avi or Santi. He determined to keep vigilant in their company, in his words as well as his actions; but vowed also, inwardly, not to be rude to them for no reason. One act of secrecy did not necessarily make them criminals.

To fight off further sleep, which would be dangerous given their speed, Behvyn tried to guess what might lie ahead for them. Although the discus had shown them their destination, they did not yet know what it was specifically leading them to. It was a fear of what it could be that drove them so hard to it, a fear of something powerful falling into the wrong hands. For Behvyn, this fear was real, but he found himself able to face it with the knowledge that his friends also followed the route to the Pass. It was their hope of finding him and Behleth there that spurred Behvyn on. Indeed, so consumed was he by the desire to see Tig once more that he would occasionally forget the danger they all raced towards. Then his left arm gave him a shot of pain and it would all come flooding back; the memory of the explosions on the sail barge, with his brother still on board and being left for dead by Fetlock.

'He'd better ride hard,' Behvyn said aloud.

'Hmm, did you say something?' asked Rumé, stirring.

'I'm sorry Rumé. I didn't realise I spoke. I was just thinking, about, you know, him.'

'So was I,' Rumé answered, quietly. 'About what is to come. We have a way to go but I think, at the stopping point, we should discuss it in depth.'

'That would be good,' agreed Behvyn. 'I've got no idea what to expect.'

'None at all? Well, that won't do!' replied Rumé. 'I should give you some idea at least before then!'

Rumé paused for a short while as though struggling to remember something specific before he began telling Behvyn of the rich history that lay between the lands of Khubron and the Shale Valley. He talked of the 'First Finding' of the route out to Khubron; not by a great explorer, as one might have thought, but by a simple man named Eldren, who had been forced many ages ago high up the eastern sides of Mount Ithed when the hunting had been poor.

He told how in tracking the local creatures on whose meat his family and village relied upon to see them through the approaching winter, Eldren had become short of breath at such an elevation. In a near faint he had seen between two vast mountains over to the other side of the range; the first Shalean to see into western Khubron. He had managed to gather himself and investigate the Pass, but he had not been able to progress any further once he had reached the summit. He later told his villagers it had been as though there were a wall in front of him through which he could see where his next step would have landed if he had had but strength enough to make it; but that he famously 'did not own it' within him.

'From the village in the east Vale,' Rumé continued, 'the story filtered only very slowly southward, as these were the days of the Early Kings and the network of roads and the greatness of Cambwall were but seeds in men's minds. Eventually, well after Eldren's day had passed, it reached the ears of an ambitious merchant sailor who was re-fitting his ship in Cambwall Town, and who saw in the story the prospect of new markets without the inherent dangers of the sea, or the growing taxes being levied on such routes. He secretly enlisted the backing of a member of the Royal Court to mount an expedition into the newly discovered lands.

'With instructions received from his sponsor, a chief opponent of King Gathlon, and with a cavalry regiment collected twenty leagues outside of the capital, the merchant, whose name is not remembered, made for the Pass.

'Riding horses up to the foothills, the hundred-strong expedition then swapped these for their own feet and a dozen or so pack-horses at Spoburn, which was the last village they came to before the upward expanse of the mountains. If they'd known it,' Rumé confided, 'they were at the very village Eldren himself had lived in.

'At first light the following day they set out up the side of the foothills and climbed steadily across the lower face of the mountain, describing a route similar to the road that is now carved into it. Up they went until no villager or keen-eyed sentinel could see them and the only rumour of their passage to remain was the ghostly chatter of loosed stones descending from above. But from that cold morning to this the merchant and the riders were never seen again; only a few of the doughty horses returned back to the village, still loaded with most of their last owners' provisions.

'From this strange event, most of the stories of evil portents and of mythical creatures that come descending from the skies to protect the secrets of the 'land over the mountain' have stemmed. But then an old wise man who had lived in Spoburn had later recalled the tale of two lovers, Ithed and Antheon, and the outrage of King Gathlon at the loss of his own men – who had been tricked into going by the courtier – was turned to amazement.

'It is said,' Rumé continued, 'that the King called the old man to his Court and had conversation with him. Thereafter the King's temptation to send more men to the Pass was quelled and for many long years, whenever curiosity was sparked regarding lands to the east of the Valley, the reply was always: 'Remember the wrath of Ithed!'

'Then Ithed was a man of old?' asked Behvyn. He was surprised by the reply.

'Indeed, Master Hahn. There was none like him in history. Perhaps the greatest man ever to have lived on this land,' spoke Santi.

'Santi! You know this tale too?' asked Behvyn.

'Aye, Behvyn. If I may, Captain?' Santi asked.

'Of course,' Rumé smiled.

'If I can remember it at all, most of Ithed's story is best told in verse,' he explained before beginning in a soft, low voice:

> Ithed stood upon the prow
> of his mighty ship a-sailing,
> and in the mortal light did he
> from far see lands in making.
> That forceful toil of Gods embroiled
> in coupling seas and earth
> Did cease upon the winding song
> And flashing brow
> of Ithed Alcalerion
>
> Said he to vast Myoniad
> and at the ear of Elieth,
> On whose nurturing hands did lay
> The slough and slime of creation,
> 'Be you here a-leaving!
> For to populate that place I shall;
> Lead to ways unfollowing,
> And fulfill your works I will!'

The wake of Hud was mighty
leaving deepening trails;
The forming of all rivers led
and waters in the Vales,
And Hameld did land a throw'n fist
So forcing out the lands;
Snow-capped points met low-hung skies
Night-shod then punctured white

Yet Alcabell was she who stood alone
And before she went untimely,
Did pause to see that safely so
All peoples were residing.
Ithed adjoined fair Antheon,
Though hand was in such chance,
For Alcabell would see his eyes
Alight in love solitary

A firesome heart and vital pulse
Did rage within Ithed,
And stag'ring thru unfinished forms
Did seek too soon paths wakening,
Not for caution would Ithed care
To set Antheon above all other
Yet straddled on the mountain tops
Did they sink to scorch'd oblivion

Lost amid the rocks' embrace
Did their separation start
Though close forever they would be,
Twin beating mountains' heart;
Yet such was Ithed's scorn for others:
Never to be mournéd,
And bitter as their fate did wend
So their railings sweep the environs

'There's more to it than that, about the beauty of Antheon and
how Ithed allocated each of the peoples of the world a land to live

in but that is all I can remember,' said Santi as he drew to a close.

Behvyn was rapt.

'You recall it well,' congratulated Rumé. 'It is said that the five peoples were drawn together at a central point by Ithed and four of them were given realms within this continent. A fifth race were then obliged to retrace Ithed's progress from the east and find the island he remembered unclearly passing by on his way to these lands.'

'Would that be Laummeth?' asked Behvyn.

'Very good,' answered Rumé.

'But there is no record of anyone having reached there,' answered Santi, 'and Ithed had no maps and would not leave Antheon to guide the others there. It is assumed they all perished at sea.'

'That is a sad tale,' said Behvyn.

'The ending of a race of people cannot be otherwise,' replied Santi, his voice bitter. No one spoke for a long time afterwards, but Behvyn's imagination was now filled by the ideas of the creation of the lands and the first great peoples to populate them.

Yinko was asleep. Behleth was sure of it. He could feel her breathing steadily. Yet it now presented him with a problem. He was in high arcs of pleasure that she'd seemingly drifted off to sleep resting on him. But the angle of descent was levelling off and they were running horizontally. Avi had noticed as well. This was the stopping point, they were both sure, and Behleth needed to use the brakes along his side to slow the hirass. Only, he couldn't bring himself to wake Yinko.

'Master Hahn,' warned Avi, finally, 'if you don't work the buffer on your side, she'll surely wake up when we come smashing into your brother's hirass!' he said.

Behleth started, embarrassed, which woke Yinko. She quickly removed herself from him in drowsy confusion. He grabbed several times at the handle of the buffer until he caught it in a grip. Then he raised it as he had been shown by Yessina-Qhik, above his head first and then ahead of him and out to the side, as, together, both he and Avi touched the sides of the underwaterway.

Rather than a gentle slowing as expected, the result was sudden, with the buffers working much more effectively than guessed at. The walls of the tunnel nearly wrenched the buffers out of their hands and it was all they could do to stay seated and grip onto them as the hirass slowed sharply to run at a gentle rate. Unable to see ahead, busy as they were, Behleth asked Yinko if she could see anything in their approach.

'Nothing, it's just dark,' she replied, in her lightly burbling voice as they lost further momentum. Then: 'Wait: I see a light, I think. Yes!'

Moving at what they guessed to be only a walking pace now, Behleth and Avi withdrew the buffers and stowed them as the hirass glided towards a stop precisely where all three of them could now see where the light was. It was a lit torch held by Santi, and he was waving it vigorously from the very left of the tunnel. They could see Rumé and Behvyn off to the other extreme on their right, leaving as wide a space as possible in between them and the path of the hirass.

'They think we would arrive on them too fast!' said Behleth, as though this was the unlikeliest of events. Avi bit back a remark.

'We're here!' they cried in unison, waving their hands as their hirass came to a restful stop five yards short of the other. They saw that this had been parked with its runs pointing towards the walls of the underwaterway, sideways on to the direction of travel, and so they did the same with theirs before walking carefully on the tunnel lining over to the others.

After a meal and a short rest (both held off to the side of the underwaterway, just in case) Avi continued the topic of where they were going. As Rumé, Avi and Santi had seen the Pass, they did most of the talking.

'The Wrath of Ithed blows hard all year round,' explained Avi. 'Even if his eye moves to Antheon and lets us through, the opportunity may be brief. Approaching the Pass for which ever purpose we may find the way blocked.'

'You are right, Avi,' replied Rumé, 'and I do owe you and your brother more of an explanation of who we track as well. I did not say too much in the Citadel with the Mirovi around, for the crime committed does not encourage a rational response. To those few who can bear it, and included in this I name Dal-Hirovo and

Yinko as well, I say to thee: a man called Fetlock killed the Lady Alcabell, and did so most traitorously. It is our retribution we seek to lay upon him; his still-living body we target; his life we must extinguish lest the remaining light of it incense the Axumé to cause our utter destruction. That is the burden of our task, as we sit here now, that we must achieve; for in failure do we fail everyone left living and every life yet to run behind them.'

Rumé's words had an overwhelming effect. Yinko stood and shouted a pledge from the Hudron and Avi and Santi offered a promise to fight alongside Rumé, to the death if necessary. Behvyn and Behleth, caught up in the wave of emotion that flooded through the camp, raised their daggers and shouted: 'For Alcabell!' Energised beyond their expectations, they raced over to the hirass and set them in line with the tunnel, keen spirited to begin the second part of their journey through the underwaterway. But even as Avi and Santi and Yinko moved to settle back onto the hirass, Rumé spoke, remaining at the side of the tunnel.

'I must tell you of a new danger now, that all who take the road will face, and why the road is more treacherous than the elements alone can make it.'

Behvyn and Behleth exchanged a look of deep concern.

'The last of the armies to leave this land,' continued Rumé, 'was little more than a legion of farmers enlisted in desperation by King Xiomes upon hearing of a long list of heavy defeats in Upper Khubron. Every well-trained man had been spent. Yes, the war goes very ill for the Shaleans, and we should not be surprised to see the line of battle on this side of the Ice Mountains if our view at the Pass is a cloudless one.

'It was with rumour of this desperate situation that the troops were sent out to fight, but their thin courage was not trusted to. To maintain discipline Xiomes ordered his Captains to see to it that their nerve couldn't falter. Traps were set following their progress, making any retreat impossible. I would not be surprised if the approach to the Pass, even within the Shale Valley, were littered with traps on either side of the road. I only hope I am wrong or that your friends discover this in time.'

The silence that followed Rumé's words lasted until they had reloaded their hirass and moved on their way towards the

Darkwater and the gateway to the Pass, in a very different frame of mind to that in which they had been only moments earlier.

Tangle blinked. The darkness was nearly complete, save for a subtle silver-grey cast on each leaf that faced the waxing moon. Only their progress disturbed the lands around them, their passing shaking the late-evening dew from the goose grass, or sending up the small hard stones of the road surface and scattering them downhill.

The mothmags had proven to be tireless runners, their tenacity comparable only to sea birds that spend their whole life on the wing. The five friends would stop and rest them, not through any sign of slowing, but from their own fatigue; but the breaks were short and the rides long. The race was nearing its finish, though Paequat had not scouted the horse-riders they followed. The Pass of Ithed and Antheon was no longer in sight, so close were they to it that the first ridges of the mountain reaching above them obscured their view of the peaks that had loomed over them in the preceding days. Only the short way ahead was clear. The road continued its winding way up the side of the mountain in long diagonal sweeps; first northward, then southward, now northward once again.

Feran had told Tangle how its broad ascent had been carefully re-designed in the first days of the war to maximize the number of men that could walk abreast along it. Another legacy of which was that there was a series of low turrets that held a perfect view of the way before and after each turn. Through disuse, these had been covered over by ivy and were now encroached upon by ugly, angular trees covered with black-green thorns; once cut back, but now re-claiming their old dominion. They were on the road to the Pass, and each hidden corner presented its own danger.

The tension had become so oppressive that even Feran had stopped talking. Tig led with Paequat sat behind her on the same mothmag and Tangle followed directly behind, with Kjerros bringing up the rear and Feran sandwiched in between. They stayed close, riding closer together than they had on the flats of the grasslands extending back to the Fords. This was so that if Tig whispered an instruction to those behind her, she knew all including Kjerros could hear. Tangle imagined at any moment they would be seized upon by Fetlock's men, and loathed to remove her attention from the crumbling turrets at each corner they passed until they had to refocus on the next. Looking up, as Paequat spent plenty of his time in so doing, she had counted roughly forty turns in the road that they would need to navigate, each with its potential as an ambush point. They trusted much to Paequat.

The dew and an earlier unseen rain had dampened all sound save for the occasional splashes made by the mothmags in small shallow puddles as they trotted along, always uphill. The bird's spirits, if no-one else's, seemed undiminished, Tangle thought, lest it seemed they held back their usual playfulness with each other so as not to upset their riders' uncommon quiet.

As they rounded their tenth corner, Kjerros, who had been keeping count, made mention of it.

'We must be a quarter of the way there now,' he said in a whisper.

'Yes,' came back the terse reply from Tig.

Tangle glanced behind her and noticed Feran's face was haunted white and his movements were small or jerky.

'I guess you're not used to this sort of thing,' she said.

'On the contrary,' his pride springing to his defence, then suddenly leaving him with only his wits to finish the sentence, 'I-I was concerned about something else.'

Tangle couldn't think what and was confused.

'You see,' Feran continued, 'I've been more terrified only once before, and it was when I asked you if you wanted to dance with me, at that Longest Day party those few years ago.'

She let her expression change, but wondered what had brought all this on.

'I thought my life would end if you said 'no', but you didn't. From that day, I've never forgotten how that made me feel.' Feran looked up. Tangle had decided she would drift in next to him. 'It seems we're going into a place where I don't know what will happen next without warning and I wanted to let you know I will do everything to make sure nothing happens to you.'

She moved to speak but Feran wasn't finished.

'But it was in the telling of that I wasn't sure of, because I don't want to sound like someone who would smother you. I know that's at least part of why you took away from home for that time. Anyway, so that you know, that was what I was thinking about. And, well, just so that you know I mean it.' Feran reached into his pocket, as everyone else who had found it impossible not to listen in watched him. He pulled out his fist and dangling down from it in the still moonlight was the most delicate and beautiful bracelet Tangle had ever seen.

'This is something I got for you,' Feran announced, aware now of the looks he was getting. 'I'd like you to have it, if you would; and to wear it, if you like.'

Tangle leant over the space between them and embraced him, still moving as they were. With a shiny tear rolling down her cheek, she let Feran give her the bracelet and she placed it around her left wrist tightly before letting him go. As she did so she saw Kjerros ride past them towards Tig. Instead of a smile her sister wore a look of pity.

'Paequat,' asked Kjerros, 'have you seen anything yet?'

'Paequat not see riders,' Paequat replied, 'but begins to hear river.'

'A river?'

'Yes, to the northward side,' added Tig, who had also heard it. 'Paequat says it is called the 'Darkwater' for it's born underground, within the mountainside before it emerges.'

'But doesn't it run down to the Highborn?' asked Kjerros. 'How come we didn't see it as we approached here?'

'Apparently it dives underground again before it even reaches here,' answered Tig.

'A strange river indeed,' mused Kjerros. 'Would it be a place to slake the thirst of horses driven almost to their death?'

Tig understood Kjerros' meaning and immediately warned the others behind them. They bunched together again and continued their progress with their senses peeled towards the sound of running water and what it might mask. Kjerros remained near to Tig.

'You know,' she said to him after they had made another five or six turns, with the chill oppression of what may be around each corner drifting down upon them like a fog, 'I can ride one of these.'

'But how well can you use one of these?' Kjerros responded, flourishing his sword energetically.

'I have my man to do that,' she answered, and gave Paequat a pat on the arm. Kjerros remembered the ghoulish way Paequat stored his sword and the limitless skill he seemed to have with a blade. He conceded the point.

'Then, if I cannot protect you, what would you with me, my Lady?' Kjerros taunted lightheartedly. But the impact of his jest was more serious than he expected.

'Don't, Kjerros,' Tig replied, flashing an apologetic smile. She rode on purposefully ahead, leaving Kjerros behind and a little abashed as Tangle and Feran passed him, asking after what he had said to her.

'I don't know,' he answered. 'I must've touched a nerve.'

'Tig's got nerves of steel,' answered Feran.

'But they needn't act as a cage upon her,' replied Kjerros.

'Some cages can be opened,' said Tangle, 'but beware what lies within.'

The sound of the river grew imperceptibly as the night reached its peak and their progress along the road to the Pass reached the halfway mark. The splashing and scattering noises made by the mothmags changed to a rhythmical but dull pattering as the road dried out. Their ascent was already high.

On looking down, over the way they had come, Tangle could barely make out the detail of the ground and saw no lights on in the direction she guessed lay Spoburn, which they had passed through in the hours before dawn. All looked peaceful and the valley stretched out dramatically in front of her. From where she was she could see a long stretch of the Highborn, framed by two rivers: the Jostling to the north, and the Spo to the south running away from them, heading westward. There was only rumour of the Manton rivers further south, but the Fords could still be seen, once again bearing the full brunt of the Highborn and the white froth that cast itself above the level of the broken walkway was just visible in the moonlight.

Although the view grew more breathtaking, Tangle noticed the air began to feel thinner and less wholesome. At the same time, a new scent was borne upon it that was refreshing and encouraged her progress. Though she thought little of it, it was the scent of the Darkwater calling them up, invigorating them all like a song in the night. As the air thinned, so Tangle's warmth drained away from her and the snow-peaked mountains above them radiated out a cold wave that she could do little to shelter from. They each drew up their cloaks and covered their heads with their hoods and moved along the road faster than before to get themselves going again. But then they met with the first gusts of 'Ithed's Wrath' descending from the northeast; a wind that would only grow stronger and more invasive. Tangle shuddered atop her mothmag that seemed impervious to the growing cold and ever keen to walk on. Her mount gave her heart and spurred her onward, to steel herself not only against the elements that rose in chorus against them, but against the growing sense that they were not far away from the inevitable confrontation that would ensue. She trusted to Grodel's influence that they would be safe, but past that, she couldn't guess.

At last, the moon was lost behind Ithed's peak, no longer able to cast its light upon the road they travelled along. The switch to total darkness was sudden. The impact was large. Now the mothmags struggled to find the way. Although the road had been carved in straight lines lower down it had necessarily begun to curve about the edges of the rock, which grew more rounded as they climbed their way up. They did not begin to approach the peak, however. The Pass lay at only half the overall height of the mountains either side of it, at the point at which Ithed and Antheon met. In this new darkness and from Kjerros' continued counting of the turns they had made, Tangle believed they were three-quarters of the way to the Pass. Which was why the mothmags' sudden disorientation proved so frustrating.

'Hoy, there!' she cried to her mount, as it sidled towards the edge of the road away from the rock side. 'Back! This way!' she commanded, kicking into its sides and jerking the reins leftward.

'They're all doing it!' said Kjerros, as his mothmag turned upon the spot and tried to descend.

'We'll have to get off and lead them!' announced Tig. It had become clear the mothmags could no longer be ridden.

'I don't understand,' said Tangle to Feran. 'We rode them all night last night, no problem,' the memory of which caused her to yawn. By doing so she then set off everyone else.

'It was a clear night last night, with the moon out all of the time,' replied Feran, wiping his eyes and in so doing stinging the weight of sleep into them.

'What?' asked Tangle, and Feran repeated himself, this time successfully over the noise of the Darkwater.

'It's getting loud now,' Tangle replied. 'I guess once we're past that river, we'll be nearly there.'

'I'm sure of it,' replied Feran confidently.

Dismounting, they took the mothmags' reins in hand and began leading them along the way, making much slower progress than they had been making before. This Tangle found unsettling, for they no longer had the comfort of knowing they could all ride away quickly if trouble came upon them.

Furthermore, at walking height her view of things was diminished, and it was less easy to scout out a corner turret with the same confidence that no one was holed in within it. As they began each new stretch ahead of them, she imagined all the places they had passed that they had not been sure about, and creeping out from within them, a crouched form, clad in black, unsheathing a weapon, to stand up against them if they should seek to flee back the way they had come.

The wind began to grow against them, always pushing at their sides, and the rush of the river above them filled their cold ears. It grew so loud that it began to echo among the cracks and crevices that the road now zigzagged around. In addition, the road was no longer paved with small stones, or tended in any fashion. The coarseness of the rocky sides overshadowed a road roughly hewn from the solid mountainside, narrower than before, and edged only with a thin layer of grey soil no more than two yards wide that held in it a sorry-looking collection of low shrubs and dead briars. The air continued to thin, but as Tangle grew used to it, she no longer smelled the sweetness of the Darkwater and forgot its nourishing pleasantness. Instead, she began to doubt she saw things, and struggled to keep her mind on what she was doing. She wasn't the only one.

'Tw-twenty e-eight, nine, eight? Eight?' said Kjerros, who was struggling against the pull of his mothmag in one direction, the wind in another and the gradient in another still.

'You said that last time, Behvyn, my darling,' said Tig. 'It must be twenty-nine now.'

'Twenty-nine,' Kjerros repeated, as his mothmag's behaviour grew even more out of control. 'Twenty-nine, twenty-nine,' he continued with every step towards the next turn.

'Ithed's W-w-w-wrath!' Tangle shivered at her mothmag. 'It'll be mine you'll get before long, if you – don't – calm – down!' But her ride saw things differently and launched itself about in a throe of confusion.

'Don't let it go!' cried Tig, and Tangle held on to the reins as best as she could. But the bird was witless and would not calm. It dashed suddenly to the side of the road and jumped around among the briars, cutting its legs and feet as it did so, dragging Tangle about with it in fits and starts when: 'SNAP!' A trap was sprung.

So fast did it raise its huge, rusted, fierce jaws up out of the earth that for a moment no one realised what had happened, including the mothmag that had set it off. Its body continued to dart madly about as its head landed in the dirt, severed perfectly from its neck.

'Let go of it, Tangle!' cried Kjerros, as Tig stood speechless and the rest of the mothmags, instead of startling further, behaved more calmly than before, as though they wanted to take their minds away from what had just happened.

Tangle released her grip just in time with a cry, and she stared at her hand. As the bird flailed its way along the edge of the road-side, it tipped another trap, which caught it, half through the body. Dead, but still pummelling its legs in a hectic dance of denial, it sent itself and the trap lodged into it over the brink and down two levels of the road beneath. A third trap was sprung as it landed and held it in a final mortal lock. As they looked carefully down, making sure not to leave the edge of the road, they could see the wind cast itself upon the carcass and blow its feathers against the grain of its body in a final dismissive gesture.

'Twenty-seven,' said Kjerros sadly.

'Someone told me to take my hand off the rein!' said Tangle, as Feran picked her up off the ground where she lay.

'It was me, didn't you hear?' said Kjerros.

'No. I mean, I couldn't hear a thing, what with the wind. It sounded like it came from inside of me. It was really loud!'

'It was probably your common sense,' suggested Tig, as she looked over her sister. 'It's nice to know you have some.'

Tangle had a few scratches on her face and hands, one of which looked quite nasty across the bridge of her nose but which had stopped bleeding quickly.

Kjerros, holding Tig's and his own mothmag, was still incensed. 'What is this place? Traps? Why would anyone put traps all the way up here?' He went gingerly over to where the first sprung trap still lay; the one that had beheaded 'Windwing'.

He couldn't see the device very well in the darkness, but the longer he stared down at it, the more he could make out. About its hinges wound a coil half-an-inch thick, and its teeth, rusty but still sharp, had smashed into each other with such power that they had become bent out of shape.

'About one and a half yards, do you think?' asked Tangle, coming up to him. 'I mean, in height.'

'Just tall enough to embed itself into the chest of a man,' Kjerros concurred. 'It feels old,' he said once he had plucked up enough courage to lean down and touch it.

'Did Kewyn teach you much in his workshop? You used to spend your days there.'

'Yes, about iron and steel and how it can be turned into anything anyone asked us for. I'd say that these were made in Cambwall. They must have been laid down thirty years ago, given the way they've rusted since,' he said. 'And they're not to trap animals; they're far too strong for that. They're expressly designed to kill men; ones that wear armour.'

'That doesn't make sense,' replied Tangle. She looked down in the darkness. 'Why set them here when this is the only way in and out of the Shale Valley? We've got soldiers in Khubron.'

'Perhaps it's to make sure they stay there,' suggested Tig,

gathering up the reins of her mothmag out from Kjerros' hand. Momentarily, he didn't let go. Tig raised her hand to his face and caressed it. Then she took the reins from Kjerros' frozen hand and went on ahead.

'Kjerros,' warned Tangle.

'I know,' he replied.

They took stock now that they had a new problem. They had one fewer mount, meaning that two more of them would have to share a mothmag, if it would bear the weight. But they were not sure it would. Tangle had carried with her much of Tig's provisions to compensate Tig's bird for the additional weight of Paequat (and his boots). These provisions had nearly been lost, but had fortuitously been released from Tangle's mothmag before it had plunged over the edge; the second trap having severed the securing belt that ran beneath its body. While this was good news, they doubted they could now escape quickly, should the need arise. This acted like a stone in their shoe. In the terror of what had happened, much of Tangle's dread had been forgotten about, as a toothache may be when facing the point of a sword. But now it crept back into consciousness and insinuated itself in amongst her concerns once again.

As Kjerros counted 'thirty-seven' the wind strengthened noticeably. They had reached a crest of sorts and the road wound less steeply, making its way in towards the mountain. Tangle could see a little better, for although the moon could not show itself directly here, and Ithed rose above blocking it out, it reflected coldly off the snow-cast peaks of the Mizzle Mountains to the north and Antheon to the south. Powdery snow covered the road and settled in amongst the rocks they walked past, just as dust collects in a basement. It hadn't snowed here, she realised; it had been blown down by the gale from the lower reaches of Ithed's peak. It was cold enough that it hadn't melted where it collected.

'N-no wonder there isn't any cloud here,' muttered Feran. 'It's so windy!'

'Then the only thing to do is just keep going!' called Tig from ahead.

Tangle noticed the mothmags responded to the extra light and plucked themselves up from the strange cast that had befallen them in the dark. Soon Kjerros was able to count 'thirty-eight', and this time there was no turret to worry about. She could see in advance how the road wound ahead of them and for the first time since they had begun their ascent up the mountain, she felt comforted by the view. Also, she could now see the mountain river.

It met the road at the thirty-ninth corner, almost spilling over into it, rushing fast down a deep channel that had its beginnings in the side of Mount Ithed only some hundred yards higher up. Once it passed the road, it snaked away due west and then turned northwestward further down. Eventually, it ran back inside the mountain, chilled and hungry for warmth.

'Darkwater,' said Paequat. 'Do not drink!' he added, just as Kjerros was minded to rush towards it and do that very same thing.

'Is it deadly?' he asked.

'Too cold for Kjerros,' Paequat replied.

'"Too cold for Kjerros" is right!' Kjerros repeated as the wind continued to pound them from their right.

Tangle turned directly into it to catch a glimpse of the final ascent that would be laid out ahead of them once they had rounded the final bend in the road. The last few steps would need to be taken along a short road south that was sheltered from the wind by a wall of solid rock to its left and then, once its corner had been turned, eastward up a wide and snow covered pathway that led straight to the top of the ridge that separated Ithed from Antheon. A fell wind smote itself upon it, sharpening it like a blade and rushing up a storm of snow. The ice-specked wind blurred Tangle's eyes instantly, but as she looked away she thought she caught a glimpse of a figure stood upon the ridge. She tried to look back but the icy air wouldn't let her see again.

They stayed together as they moved on for the final stage of their climb and approached the last corner. As they neared it, Tangle could see that the Darkwater encroached onto the road. The river came into their path, or rather over it. For where the two met, the road suddenly drilled downward by way of a snow-dusted stairway into a brief tunnel that rounded the corner to emerge some fifty yards later, by way of another set of stairs carved into the rock, opposite where she now stood.

For a moment they hesitated. They looked about in every direction for a sign they could see of footprints in the snow or a breath of steam from a horse, but saw nothing. Then a brash sense of adventure once again overcame Feran and he made for the wide steps, leading his mothmag behind him.

Tangle followed him down, then Tig with Kjerros close behind. Paequat joined them last. They were in the tunnel and untouched. They were nervous, however. Amid the loud rushing of the Darkwater above them, which echoed around the chamber they found themselves in, they caught their breath again and slowed their racing heartbeats.

'Does this mean we overtook them, somehow?' asked Feran. 'They're not here.'

'I don't know, Feran,' replied Tig. 'We haven't seen them, but that doesn't mean they're not hidden from us. It's best to expect the worst.'

'We're so close to the top now and we haven't seen anything,' said Tangle, her words coming slowly though gasps for air.

'Don't speak, sis,' said Tig.

'Ready?' asked Kjerros. They all nodded. Feran went to stride off again, but this time Kjerros was having none of it.

'Oh, no you don't,' he said. 'It's my turn this time. Everyone stays close!' As a precaution, Kjerros held his sword out in front of him and Paequat reached into himself to produce the other. There was little room for maneuver in the tunnel if it was to come to a fight. The mothmags had not been left behind and they blocked everyone's vision except Kjerros'.

They reached the turn in the tunnel and Kjerros inched his face around the corner to catch a glimpse of the other half that awaited them. Nothing; at least that he could see in the darkness. He looked down and thought he saw spots of blood in the half-light, but couldn't be sure. There was a faint light that showed the awaiting steps at the end but lit nothing else. He motioned them all forwards.

'Here,' he heard, and felt a soft hand take his mothmag's reins from him. It was Tig. 'We'll leave them in here, just for now.'

Kjerros kept focused, now able to hold his sword in two hands. Step by step, they made their way forwards towards the opening.

Their feet began to press beneath them a fine layer of snow that became deeper and drifted up to the first stair. Kjerros began the ascent, keeping as quiet as he could. The voice of the wind and the rattling of the river helped. He tried to keep his movements as steady as possible. His head became level with the road again, then his shoulders and his arms. He looked about him. It was still dark, but slightly lighter than it had been in the tunnel. Only a few paces ahead of him on the road he could see the cast of the moon-light once again, falling direct and bright. He made it up the final steps and began to move along, encouraging the others up and out with his hand.

They filed out slowly and deliberately, leaving the mothmags behind. The road advanced them southwards only another thirty paces before the high rocky wall to their left ended and the road turned to the east, to the Pass.

'Come on!' cried Kjerros, elated after one final glance around. 'We've made it! We're here!'

'We're here!' cried Feran.

'Don't move!' said a sharp voice. 'One more step and you'll be dead!'

Chapter 14

THE WINDOW OF THE DARKWATER

Behvyn noticed it first. The hirass had begun to slow for the second time in their journey. The gradient that propelled them through the underwaterway had become shallow. He now rode with Rumé and Behleth; they had decided to swap around for the last leg to allow both sets of brothers to travel together.

Avi had been the one to suggest it. He had said, rather too openly to Behvyn's mind, that it might make the journey go faster if they were to cycle the occupants in this way. Yet no one disagreed and only Yinko seemed put out when it became clear she would have to ride separate from Behleth. He hugged her many times before setting out on the first hirass and promised her many more once they had finished their journey to the Darkwater. Now, Behvyn realised, it was not far away. They would soon need to raise the brakes. He made to make mention of it to the others, just as soon as he could get a word in, for they were deep in conversation.

'But if there are five of these verses, as you say there could be,' said Behleth, 'and we have one, then doesn't it mean he could only get the other four? I mean, why not destroy this one, or throw it in the sea? That would end anyone's hopes of getting all five.'

'Not forever. If you threw the discus into the sea, it would be the most irresponsible and dangerous act in the history of your people. Think! If it was found by a total stranger, washed up on a beach a thousand leagues away and managed to tempt them to read it! And it will not be in Fetlock's plans to let another possess similar power. He and his master must have them all. If you kept it, you would be hunted until found. As for destroying it, well; let us see. Would you like to bet the Graces thought of that?'

Rumé took out his dagger, removed the discus from his cloak and asked the boys to watch carefully. He plunged the blade deep into its middle, released his grip on the handle and waited.

Behvyn watched in amazement as Rumé's dagger popped up

out of the discus so fast that Behleth had to catch it in mid air. There was no mark left on the smooth metal face that had been rent open only moments earlier.

'A temporal defense; any act aimed at destroying it will simply reverse time around it back to the point at which it was whole again.'

'Well, fair enough,' rallied Behleth, as Rumé hid the discus within his bag. 'I will not steal from you in the night and attempt to destroy the discus! But to find two others, let alone four, given where this was located; that's not going to be easy!'

'No, I agree, and it makes me wonder at it. How to do it without trusting to chance? They must know something. But now let me think. The discus showed the way to another point. If it is known that it shows the way to where the next verse may be found, therein lies your hope. The second may well show the way to the third, and so on. In this way Fetlock could have faith that he can achieve his task for his master, as long as he gets to each first. The fatal verses for each race have lain dormant through all ages of man. Yet one is found and points to another. Why should they be revealed, now of all times? A force I do not yet understand is at work, but will hope that more is revealed to me in time.'

'Now you make me suspicious,' said Behleth.

'About what?' asked Behvyn.

'About the war with Mertos. We wage it but from all I've heard it doesn't sound like the Shalean attack will win. For every soldier we send in, how many are there to greet them, Rumé?'

'Ten, maybe twenty on the battlefields. You're right. It's pointless with only one outcome: the total defeat of the Shale Valley. Unless.'

'Unless you had the verses of Mertos and Khubron!' said Behleth. 'But how to search for them in such huge countries without notice?'

'Start a war there?' answered Behvyn.

'Start a war there, indeed,' responded Rumé. 'As long as it continues we know the verses have not been found. If we can end the war, we reduce the chance of Fetlock's success of finding them; but ours, too. We would still need to find them. We cannot let them be collected by others who do not know either their provenance or power.'

'I think we're coming towards the end of the tunnel,' exclaimed Behvyn after a pause, the thought having been almost driven out of his mind.

'Can you see anything?' asked Rumé.

'I- wait!' Behvyn looked behind him, for as the Yessina had taught them, they travelled on the hirass facing back towards the way they had come. 'Yes! Yes, it is lighter ahead. We need to get ready with the braces!'

They slowed quickly, their heads forced back in a way they'd not experienced since being spun around as children, and came to rest only a little way short of the end of the glistening tunnel. The twins removed Rumé and then the hirass off the main running way over to the left side of the tunnel in case there was anyone outside looking in. The Darkwater lay on the other side of a tall, diaphanous membrane that sparkled ahead of them. Although the thin grey evening light was only a rumour of direct sunshine, to their eyes, used as they were to near-perfect night for two days, it was a painful window in whose direction they could not stare at for long. But stare at it they did, in appreciation of the majesty of sight's return, for the light was broken into colours like temple glass whose shards were forever evolving. A kaleidoscopic array of crossing beams, gold, white, blue, deep indigo and green-yellow, played upon the glowing, pulsing floor, reaching out towards their feet.

'Let's keep quiet. We'll need to hear the others approaching,' suggested Behvyn, to which the others agreed.

'It's so bright, and yet, I know it can't be more than dusk!' whispered Behleth, fascinated. The underwaterway itself seemed to respond to the light's warm refractions with closer and brighter bands of energy, so slow moving and dim in the heart of the passage and yet here so fast moving and alive. The pulses shot back down the way they had come like lightening flashes.

'Do you see anything within the light?' asked Rumé, after they had waited a while. 'We are now where the second verse could be. It may be on the riverbed, or in the walls of the tunnel, or outside at this extent of the Pass into Khubron. It might be on a discus or a different object. We will not venture out there until the others arrive behind us, and then only speak of our search in direst need, for this matter does not concern everyone we travel with. Search around here now and quickly, and I will continue listening for their arrival.'

Behvyn and Behleth did just that. Sliding and slipping as they went, for the gelatinous covering to the underwaterway was thick here, they searched for such an object as they both feared to find.

'Where exactly are we meant to be looking?' asked Behleth, somewhat disconsolately. 'It's a tunnel, a dark one, with no holes other than one long round one in which anything placed would find its way to the bottom and be picked up by the very first visitor to it.'

As they neared the membrane, their eyes adjusted enough to look into the fractured light without pain. 'Now I can see properly, I can't see anything,' added Behvyn ruefully.

'No Hudron children, either,' said Behleth sadly. 'Unless. What's that? A patch where the light doesn't shine through so readily,' he began, but the moment after he spoke, they both heard Rumé shout out: 'I hear them coming! They arrive too fast! To the sides!'

The twins had a moment to look into the darkness behind them, but couldn't see anything. Then they had one more moment to gather their wits together and throw themselves to the side walls before the second hirass pitched suddenly out of the void and into view, travelling at full speed.

Before the twins knew, it was past them. Only then did the blurred cries of Avi, Santi and Yinko catch up with them. At full tilt, the runaway hirass plunged through the membrane in front of it and passed wholly into the Darkwater outside, where, as it merged into the flow, it was pushed upwards, towards the surface. It took everything on it with it.

Yinko's cries were the most painful to hear. Through the window onto the Darkwater, Behvyn and Behleth could see what ensued. Avi and Santi found each other and swam over to the young Hudron, who would have been impossible to see in her own element had she not been wearing a cloak to spare her the cold of the tunnel. The hirass was taken by the strong current away, off west and downwards, along with everything else that had been secured upon it. But that was forgotten. Yinko screamed in such agony and this would be heard if she broke above the surface of the water, which she now seemed to be driving for as though chased by flames from below. But Avi reached her in time and brought her back, and together with Santi, they were able to re-enter, with some difficulty, through the entranceway back into the tunnel set into the side of the river from whence they had come.

As Yinko collapsed weakly into Behleth's arms, he looked around, bewildered and angry.

'What were you doing?' Behleth demanded from Avi and Santi. 'Weren't you paying attention?'

'We lost control!' replied Santi. 'We didn't see the light behind us growing, and then, when we did, it was too late.'

'Everything is swept away, except this,' said Avi. He handed a piece of parchment he held in his hand over to Behvyn. 'I don't know what it means but, as we passed through the membrane, it plastered itself to my face and it was all I could do to remove it from my eyes and stash it in my pocket before the current bore it off away with everything else.'

'It is a message,' explained Behvyn.

'Read it aloud, provided it is in a language you understand,' said Rumé.

'"To anyone that doth seek the end to a six-starred rainbow, let it be known that here it did endeth; and that such gold as was promised is now here no more."'

'Then Fetlock has been here already,' said Behleth, dejectedly.

'The race is lost,' added Behleth.

The look on Avi and Santi's faces showed their dejection also.

'Our attempt to capture the killer of Alcabell has met with failure!' bemoaned Santi.

'The murderer has escaped us? Then let this be his last victory and our last defeat!' said Avi, whose words, strung through with vehemence, gave the others heart. 'And there is this. I saw the shapes of figures outside, as we neared the surface of the Darkwater. Would they be those we pursue?' At this, fresh hope spread through the group.

'Or our friends who seek us,' suggested Behvyn, adrenaline rushing through him. 'Rumé, we must know if they are out there.'

'I can't go out there again!' cried Yinko suddenly, and fell to her knees.

'What is it, Yinko?' asked Behleth, still holding her and now sitting with her on the tunnel floor. 'What's distressed you? Let me understand.'

'T-the D-D-Darkwater,' she was eventually able to say. 'Full of bodies. Dead bodies!'

'I didn't see anything myself, Yessina,' added Avi. 'I didn't see the, ah, bodies?'

'H-Hudron children,' she replied. 'So small!'

'Rumé,' added Behvyn, quietly so as not to be overheard by the others, 'there must have been the Hudron verse, here, in the membrane. Suspended like that, it would have warded off the Daymen children from coming inside the tunnel. That would explain why no more children made their way up to the Citadel. They wouldn't want to touch it. Instead they would go back into the river and, well...'

'And deconstruct, back into fragments of themselves once again, but now with the painful memory of what it was like, just for one day, to be a whole being,' finished Rumé. 'Behleth, wait here with Yinko. Behvyn, Avi and Santi: go back inside the river at once and hear what you can, but be extremely careful. Stay within the water! It looks like Fetlock has beaten us here and he may have posted lookouts above or inside the river. Go in vigilance and go now! There is no time to lose.'

With that, the three of them disappeared through the membrane and into the flow of the Darkwater, leaving Rumé, Behleth and Yinko alone. Behvyn swam into the Darkwater taking care to stay as close to the riverbed as possible as the far bank approached. He rose towards the surface slowly and, as he did so, he could clearly hear voices above him.

'Is that the way we must now go, Captain Fetlock?'

'Our road lies clear before us once again, men! A gift from the river has seen to it. First sunlight and now moonlight come to aid us: truly, you can know our cause is blessed. Now, listen you two. Remain here for three days. Do not reveal yourself in that time, unless you have the chance of knocking off the heads of any who follow us. That's if they can even make it up the hill. I might leave someone else back as well.'

Then Behvyn heard mutterings of "No need" and "We can take care of things". Then Fetlock continued.

'Either way, at the end of that time, travel to Olamude. We'll take the road steady. Grodel and I will meet the five Marshalls and catch up on the progress we've made in Terreplatte and the Gales of Woe whilst we wait for you. But we'll leave it in 3 weeks' time, whether you're with us or not.'

Behvyn turned to Avi and Santi and motioned at them to return to the tunnel. They nodded in assent and together rejoined the others.

'It is sound intelligence, and I am thankful for it, Behvyn,' replied Rumé. 'Now there is something I have to tell you: I know where your friends are.'

Behvyn had to be stopped from running straight out through the membrane and taking on the swordsmen left behind by Fetlock. It was only in a great deal of frustration he agreed to consider their options.

'We will remove them, Behvyn, only not like that!' commanded Rumé. 'Come here!' and Behvyn ran over to Rumé who held him in a grasp and whispered quickly in his ear: 'I can see again, Behvyn, just now. I can see through Tangle, so Behleth advises. She's wearing the falcon's gemstone. Now keep calm!' Then he coughed. 'Now pull yourself together,' he said, much more publicly. 'I have a much better plan.'

'You, men! Yes, you! Hear me and come out from your crouching place! Tell me who he has left behind?' Behvyn saw Rumé command through the howl of the wind. Though he had shouted, it barely travelled. The dusk was deepening and the day's warmth had already been sucked out of the air by the snow-filled gale of Ithed's Wrath. Rumé was stood outside the Darkwater, on the snow-covered road, just past the exit of the tunnel from where the way rose up above ground. Behvyn watched from his hiding place inside the river with his head just poking up through the surface. He knew Rumé couldn't see a thing where he stood but that in his mind's eye he was watching his friends move up the mountain road below them. The last thing Rumé advised him before he had walked out into the snowstorm had been that he'd just seen Kjerros mouth 'twenty-nine'.

'Is that you, Narrow? Gilliant?' Rumé continued.

No response.

'You were ever my best blades. Did he leave you here in this forsaken place, among the cold bones that forever separate Ithed from Antheon? Show yourselves! I am alone!'

Behvyn saw movement away to the left and two men appear. They were running up the gradient and came to a halt just short of the lower entranceway to the tunnel steps, which lead underneath the river as it flowed vociferously.

'Is that you, Rumé?' the taller of the two asked, amazed. 'Fetlock must have left him for us to play with, don't you think, Gilliant?'

'I think it's a trap,' replied Gilliant. 'You come here instead!' he cried over to his former Captain.

'I can't do that, Gilliant,' Rumé replied. 'You know I cannot see. Some things will not mend, though I give you this chance to give over your ways and join me in stopping Fetlock.'

'Thank you Captain, but no,' replied Gilliant.

'We'll come to you, but you'll pay for your defiance,' announced Narrow. But just as he was about to walk down the steps leading into the dark tunnel, Gilliant caught his partner by the arm.

'You imbecile,' he said. 'He can't have found his way here alone. There must be someone in the tunnel. We'll go across the ground instead.'

'Yes, yes!' agreed Narrow, and together they jumped up, off the road and onto the snow-covered ledge that led straight to Rumé. 'As ever, old Captain, your plans go awry! Fetlock was wise to show us the danger you are to others around you. And now you have led yourself into your last dead end!'

They advanced, swords unsheathed and held out ahead of them in readiness to strike down their old Captain, who had been turned traitor to them through the words of Fetlock. The wind hurled down and the icy flakes stung their eyes, but they kept them fixed on Rumé. Step after step they drew nearer.

'Keep your blade sharp, Narrow; there's more to do after this,' explained Gilliant, as they came within striking distance, when there came a large, echoing: 'SNAP!'

Narrow had set off one of Xiomes' ancient traps, and its twin-toothed wings rose out of the ground like the giant jaws of a raven-ous shark rising up from the deeps. He and Gilliant both collapsed dead to the floor; their swords, like their chests, cleaved in twain.

'Well, give us a chance!' complained Behleth, an arrow still fixed to the bow in his hand. He emerged out of the river from next to Behvyn and stared at the remains of Fetlock's soldiers that now lay in front of him; not in horror but in the way someone does at the theft of a much-anticipated mouthful of food. 'I had them all the way, but you said don't shoot until they reached you!'

'It was a calculation,' replied Rumé, in some relief. 'I assumed the most likely place for anyone to put a trap would be beneath the short-cut way that would avoid the tunnel for a fast exit. Knowing Gilliant's desire always to second-guess an opponent, I am afraid I played him off against himself. Sorry, Behleth. At the least, you will not now have their deaths on your conscience. They can count their own regrets in eternity, but you have been saved one.'

'Regrets? Why would I ever regret killing someone who would happily kill my friends?' Behleth asked.

'I hope you never learn,' replied Rumé.

'Come,' said Behvyn next to him, 'let's bring Rumé back inside the underwaterway. The snow will cover the bodies outside in no time; it would not be right to place them in the Darkwater. Let us leave them to Ithed to do with as he will.'

But as they came up to guide Rumé back inside, the Captain bent suddenly in anguish.

'Let go!' he said. He held his hands up to his face as his legs buckled. The brothers didn't know what was happening but caught Rumé by the elbows as he fell to stop him hitting the road.

'Let go!' he said again, and the twins did as he asked, although in a shock of confusion.

'R-Rumé?' asked Behleth.

'Who was that?' said Rumé.

'It was me; Behleth.'

'Then let's get inside! Darkness is falling along with the snow and it's not a night to be sitting around outside!' said Rumé, back to full strength once again as suddenly as the new moon's appearance through the high running clouds above.

Unsettled but dutiful, Behvyn and Behleth helped Rumé along the road once more and into the flow of the Darkwater, as breathable as the Lightwater, and on inside the underwaterway, to where it was warm and they could await the arrival of their friends.

~ || ~

They each filed out slowly and deliberately, with the mothmags left behind them in the tunnel behaving themselves well and keeping silent now they could see in the clear moonlight once again. The road advanced them southwards only another thirty paces before the high rocky wall to their left ended and the road turned to the east, to face towards the fullest height of the Pass and the approach into Khubron. They were at the waist of Ithed and Antheon and had completed the ascent of the road.

'Forty. Come on!' cried Kjerros, elated after one final glance around. 'We've made it! We're here!'

'Don't move!' came a voice none of them could see but all of them knew. 'One more step and you'll all be dead!'

For a moment, it didn't register. Tangle looked puzzled.

'Was that…?'

'Behvyn?' Tig finished.

'Well, you never know,' said Behvyn, emerging from the river and walking towards them all, out of mystery and into moonlight. A widely beaming Behleth followed him closely. 'We haven't checked that part of the road, yet.' He cracked a huge grin and began to laugh.

'Behvyn! Behleth!' they all cried with joy and raced towards them both.

'You made it!' said Feran in wonder.

'We thought you were dead!' exclaimed Tig, not letting go of Behvyn. Tangle was similarly limpet-like as she clung to Behleth. He immediately noticed the scratches on her face but held back his comment as Tangle clearly had little care for them.

'We didn't know where you were! But now you're here!' said Tangle. The cold, the snow, the driven ice-specks and the wind were utterly forgotten in an endless moment of sheer happiness.

Then Behvyn and Behleth introduced Rumé whom they brought to join them outside, and as they did so, they noticed the moth-mags for the first time, poking their heads out from the tunnel from which their friends had emerged. They all laughed at how strange the creatures looked but were told also in many praiseworthy ways by Kjerros how they were the best of travelling companions and wonderful beasts of burden.

It was while they were at the height of humour together that Paequat finally showed himself to them and the twins looked to the sisters in recognition and confusion. Paequat took the occasion very seriously and was awed to meet his other two parents, his fathers, for the first time. For their part, surprised and disoriented as they were, Behvyn and Behleth extended their warmest greetings and made the largest of efforts to calm Paequat down from his nervous state, talking of how well his hat suited him and how thankful they were that he had looked after their friends so well. Paequat in return looked eternally grateful.

So, there, in the worst of elements, did the friends make their sweetest reunion, the first time they had been back all together since the Autumnfalls celebration weeks before. So joyous a moment was it that they strove to keep as clear a memory of it as they could, among those that remained; for never were they to have such a meeting again. They held each other, laughed, joked, and spent tears of joy, though mostly they would just glance at each other while others talked, and smile satisfyingly in each other's company once again.

Eventually, the cold and the elements would not be ignored and steadily the talk turned around toward more practical matters.

'How did you find us?' asked Tig.

'It's a long story, but we knew where you were some of the time,' said Behvyn. 'We just wanted to get here as quickly as we could, so that you didn't get here without us.' He gave a smile that was so worn with relief that Tig suddenly burst into hot tears.

'I was so worried about you,' she sobbed.

'I'm here now,' was all Behvyn could say without his voice cracking.

'Come on,' said Behleth, finally, once Tangle had become reattached to Feran and Kjerros had wandered a little way down the road to catch a close-up glimpse of the Pass they had seen so often in their journey, and where he assumed they would now be heading. 'We should get inside now.'

'Inside?' asked Kjerros. 'Inside where? The river?'

'Ah, well, you're not going to believe this,' began Behleth, enjoyably, but found his words cut short by a strange, whining sound. The next thing he knew, Kjerros had been thrown backwards and spun down onto the edge of the road, as though tugged sharply on his right shoulder. He stayed down and didn't move.

'Kjerros!' Tig screamed. Behvyn's blood froze. Feran immediately ran over to his cousin and dragged him around the corner behind the rock face that hid the Pass from the road. He moved him just in time; a second shot lodged itself in the ground within a footprint of his that he had made only a second earlier.

'That was a crossbow!' exclaimed Behleth in bewilderment. Kjerros was in shock, the agony of the short-feathered stave of the bolt impaled deep in his shoulder fast dwindling as his body sought unconsciousness.

'It must be someone at the top of the Pass!' said Behleth.

'Is that you, Fetlock?' cried Rumé.

'If you want something done, you just have to do it yourself these days!' Fetlock's voice came from high on the Pass.

'Quick, everyone get back behind the wall! You too, Paequat. It's dangerous.'

'I don't think he'll be worried,' whispered Tangle. Paequat knelt down to Kjerros who was writhing fitfully, his eyes glazed.

'You'll never do this, Fetlock. We know what you seek,' warned Rumé.

'On the contrary, you blind fool. We have one each, and you're just about to hand over yours to me!' replied Fetlock.

'Doro maiure, Ni elieth' chanted Paequat, and pulled the bolt from out of the back of Kjerros' shoulder. Kjerros shuddered silently. 'Doro maiure, Ni elieth!' Paequat repeated once again, and Kjerros fell into a sudden and peaceful sleep. He then placed his hand over the wound and repeated the same words.

'What's he doing?' asked Behvyn, alarmed. He remembered how Rumé had told them about the figure who had attacked the white falcon and realised it would have been Paequat.

'If you don't,' continued Fetlock, 'I'll read the Verse of the Hudron.'

'Don't worry, Behvyn. Paequat won't do anything to hurt Kjerros,' said Tig.

'What does he mean, he'll read it?' asked Behleth. 'He can't, can he? He wouldn't. He'd kill Yinko, the Dal; they'd all die!'

'He will sleep now,' said the straw man and stood up.

'Don't be ridiculous,' shouted Rumé. 'Your master would never let you.'

'I don't think he'd begrudge me the fun of consigning a couple of hundred Daymen to their eternal river, do you? Now. The verse, Rumé, or I start reading,' said Fetlock.

'Never!' cried Rumé.

'What?' said Behleth, horrified. 'But he could kill Yinko! You can't risk her!'

'He knows what he's doing!' barked Behvyn, getting control of his brother. 'Behleth, we can't give him the discus. He'd only destroy us too!'

'You will never have this verse!' shouted Rumé.

'How can you be sure he isn't bluffing?' asked Tangle, alarmed.

'What's happening?' someone else asked, emerging from the river, wrapped heavily in Behleth's spare cloak. 'Oh, are these all your friends?'

'Yinko? Yinko, get back inside! Quick! It's not safe for you out here!' Behleth cried.

'I warned you. This is your fault, Rumé!'

Fetlock started to read.

Yinko collapsed to the floor from where she stood.

'No, Paequat, you'll get hurt!' yelled Behvyn.

But Paequat didn't listen and instead Behvyn watched in fear as the straw man rounded the corner of the rock face and began a slow advance against the gale-force wind that ran down from the height of the Pass. As he lost sight of Paequat, Fetlock's voice carried out over the storm, conjuring strange words. Then he heard another cruel sound as before and saw Paequat fly back past them, over his own footsteps, to land several feet off the far side of the road. Behvyn winced in case he set off another trap that he guessed littered the area off the road.

At the same time, Behleth went to Yinko's side to see if there was any way he could help, but was warded off by flames that sprouted up from the snow and forced him back. The cloak she wore began to burn and she held her head tightly between her hands. She shook as through crying. He knew just what she was going through and that she was helpless unless Paequat could stop Fetlock.

Behvyn watched as the straw man straightened himself up quickly, punched his hat into shape again, and plucked from out of his stomach the crossbow bolt that had struck him. He threw it down to his side and walked forwards.

This time he was lost to view for longer until the now familiar sound reached them again. The cruel 'zip' made another smacking noise and Paequat was again thrown back the way he had come. The wind caught more of him and sent him further off the edge of the road. There was a gruesome 'SNAP'. Another trap had been set off. Everyone hidden around the wall jumped in fright and could hear a cry of success from above them over the wind as Paequat stayed down.

A minute went past. Then another.

Footsteps were heard approaching and the voice of Fetlock was coming closer. First one guard, then another, then a third turned the corner from the Pass and, behind them, finally, came Fetlock. He wore a flamboyant white cloak, fastened high up onto his left shoulder with a brass clasp, and tall black boots. His face looked tired but his eyes burned. Behvyn felt a surge of anger rise within him. He was barely able to control himself as the guards filed out and aimed their freshly loaded crossbows at him and his friends. The soldier's hands looked frozen as they shivered; they were not so warmly dressed as Fetlock. Behvyn worried they would fire off a shot just from the cold. Kjerros lay still as death on the ground and Behleth stayed down on his knees at Yinko's side.

Behvyn saw that Fetlock held a curious object in his hands. It was shaped like a fish, was about a foot in length, and was transparent as though made of glass. He continued to read from it in the moonlight, strange words that Behvyn could not guess how they may have been spelled but sounded like the code for life. The sounds had no power over Behvyn but seemed to crush Yinko, who still lay with her head in her hands surrounded by flame. Fetlock disgusted him as he continued to read. All he could think about was how the people he had met in the Citadel of the Hudron would all be doing the same as Yinko. Crawling around in agony and knowing they would die. He feared the completion of the verse; he hoped there was still time.

As Fetlock continued, a sound akin to that of a taut string being cut echoed around them. Rumé seemed alert to it. Then Behvyn watched Paequat rise again.

The trap had virtually severed off the straw man's left leg from just above the knee. He reached down for it and pulled it the full way off. Then he removed himself from the trap and, hopping, rejoined his leg back into him, as the sisters had seen him do before in the twins' back garden. A moment later, to the sound of two more 'twangs', he was whole again.

Fetlock stopped reading.

'There, all finished,' he said, luxuriating in the power he had commanded. He glowered into the faces of the sisters, who had done nothing but stare at him in hatred as he'd read in front of them, before he caught the look in Behvyn's face. Confused, Fetlock turned to see Paequat advancing once again and gave a howl of disbelief. He smashed the Hudron Verse on the ground and ran off.

'Men! Shoot him!' Fetlock commanded as he reached the top of the Pass. 'Behind us! He comes again!'

Paequat tossed the last bolt to have pierced him behind him nonchalantly, and stopped.

'Paequat?' said Behvyn. 'Will you not chase them?'

'Paequat won't attack if men are leaving,' he said.

Behvyn stalled as he wondered what to do next when suddenly Rumé nudged him and handed him his sword.

'After them!' he commanded. 'The pulleys on their bows are snapped in the cold; they won't work again. Chase them over the Pass! Be quick, press the advantage! You have them on the run!'

Without thinking, Behvyn started to run forward as fast as he could and chased after the guards, waving the heavy sword in front of him as he went.

As they ran behind Fetlock, the guards had no time to turn and aim accurately in the strong gale. Two tried to fire off shots but both weapons failed. They threw them at Behvyn who dodged them easily and ran so fast he caught the third guard who hadn't yet managed to take a shot. He threw Rumé's sword down, grabbed the crossbow from him ferociously and aimed it back into the man's face. The guard couldn't get away fast enough as he went over the top of the Pass calling after the others and Fetlock to let him catch up with them. Then Ithed's Wrath rose up so strongly that Behvyn could barely climb high enough to see over the ridge. He caught a quick glimpse of the guards and Fetlock being blown heavily down the other side into Khubron, falling and slipping in disarray towards a large number of horsemen that awaited them below, before he was himself thrown back down the way he had come. He was just able to gather Rumé's sword as he skidded along the treacherous slope and was grateful to Feran who stopped him from falling further back into the dangerous ground that had trapped Paequat.

When he returned to the others he shook with excitement, but quickly got on top of himself.

'We can't chase after him,' he said. 'It's too steep on the other side and there's a brigade of cavalry at the foot of Ithed waiting to take him off to Olamude. We have to see what can be done for Kjerros and Yinko first!'

His foot crunched on something. It was a piece of glass, part of the smashed Hudron Verse. However, as he looked down, he saw the pieces were moving towards each other. They were collecting themselves back into the whole again and fitting seamlessly together. He bent down and brought it up, once again formed into the fashion of a fish.

'It mends itself just like the discus!' he said. After studying it quickly, he held it out. 'Who will look after this?' he asked.

Paequat offered his hand. Behvyn gave it to him and watched in surprise as Paequat absorbed it inside his chest.

'What can we do for Yinko?' asked Behleth, who feared to go near her though the flames had by now died down. His eyes were filled with tears. Tangle ran over to him.

Paequat also came over and placed his hand very gently onto

Yinko's shoulder. Her cloak smoldered in the cold.

'Awake, awake once more, child of the Hudron.'

Yinko began to move. She slowly lifted her head up and looked through her hands at them. Then she let her arms drop to her sides and showed them all how blissfully happy she was.

'I don't understand,' said Behvyn. 'She was crying.'

'She is overcome by love,' explained Paequat. 'By the love of Hud. The love he has for his children.'

'I still don't see,' said Behvyn.

'Rumé can guess?' asked Paequat.

'Fetlock read all of the Hudron Verse. But he did it wrong?'

'Correct!' cried Paequat, excitedly.

'But how could he do something like that?' asked Behvyn. 'Surely the words only read in one direction?'

'No!' said Paequat. 'Words read in many directions! What are Hudron Verses are written onto?'

'It's see-through!' exclaimed Behvyn. 'He read it inside out!'

'So, Fetlock read it wrong,' said Behleth. 'But why the flames? They looked so terrifying,' he said, as Yinko hugged him tightly.

'Powerful verses. Destroy life. Also bring life!'

'How do you mean, Paequat?' asked Tangle.

'See tomorrow. Now we get inside.'

'Inside? Inside where?' asked Feran.

'This way. Follow me!' cried Paequat, and he led them all over to the edge of the Darkwater. It filled their noses with its fair scent and their ears with its noisome flurry.

It took some persuasion of those who were unused to it, but eventually they were all able to make it into the river, and then inside it into the underwaterway. They would have found it more fascinating had they not been so deadly fatigued or concerned about Kjerros. Tangle was the last through, allowing herself to be guided by Behleth. She was concerned about the mothmags that they were keeping outside. But once they had checked that the creatures were secure within the shelter of the roadway tunnel, untethered but content, she agreed to pass through the strange environment with faith.

Once inside, Paequat laid Kjerros, pallid and cold, down in the middle of the tunnel. The display from the window of the

Darkwater had now been lost. The others gathered around him but were ushered away by Rumé, who instead called Tangle to his side.

Then Behvyn raised the alarm.

'They've left!' he cried.

After hours of searching they eventually gave up and met once again, inside the tunnel by the resting form of Kjerros.

'I don't understand,' said Behleth. 'Why would they do this to us?'

'I don't know,' said Behvyn, 'but they've completely gone. Rumé, have they definitely taken the Shalean Verse with them?'

'It's gone,' he confirmed.

'Avi and Santi! I knew there was something wrong with those creepy twins!' lamented Behleth.

'Did you say: "twins"?' asked Tangle.

'Yes, they were twins,' replied Behvyn.

'They even looked like each other,' added Behleth.

'I don't know, I can see the resemblance between you sometimes,' added Tig.

'Where did you find them? I mean, how did you meet up?'

'Well, it was back at the Hudron kingdom,' said Behleth. 'In the Palace of Talviani,' he added, hugging Yinko.

'That's where we saw them first,' added Behvyn, 'although, we were sure they followed us through the North Vale before.'

'That's funny,' said Behleth, 'because now I come to think of it, Avi did say something odd as we set off yesterday.'

'What was that?' asked Tangle.

'He was talking about great sights he'd seen since leaving his country. He mentioned the Cold Falls.'

'Really?' asked Behvyn, astonished. 'They'd been there?'

'Are you sure?' asked Tangle, 'because Paequat told us that Alcabell had been killed by twins! Only, we thought he was referring to you two, so we thought he was wrong.'

'They killed Alcabell?' asked Tig.

'And now they've escaped with our Verse?' cried Feran.

'And we didn't do a thing to stop them? By the Graces!' exclaimed Behleth. At that, consternation broke out among the friends. 'There are two brothers out there somewhere who could write us straight into history without a moment's warning! We have to get the discus back!'

'We shall,' called Rumé.

'We must!' urged Behleth, readying to leave.

'We will!' replied Behvyn. 'But right now, I don't care!' he added, quieting them down instantly. 'I really don't, not right now. Not about them, or about Fetlock. We'll get them; we'll stop them. But for now, Rumé: tell me how Kjerros is.'

Although the others stayed on the edge of wakefulness for as long as they could, eventually Tig, Yinko and Behleth fell asleep and Feran was told to get some rest by Tangle, as he couldn't stay awake without yawning. Behvyn stayed up to help Rumé and Tangle with Kjerros.

Tangle, though deeply fatigued, had declared to Behvyn that she felt an immediate bond with the blind leader and, though she did not know his purpose in needing her, she felt proud to be able to help Kjerros in whichever way she could. She watched eagerly as Rumé investigated the extent of Kjerros' injury with his hands. Each time she looked into the grim man's face he asked if she could look at Kjerros. He would say: 'I feel something here, what is it?' and Tangle would need to return her gaze to an article of Kjerros' clothing, or his hands, or neck or hair or face. Behvyn knew why Rumé needed her but didn't let on. Tangle had been so attentive in doing what she had been asked that it was not long before Rumé had his diagnosis, though he was confused by it.

He quietly asked Tangle to get Paequat and waited until she had brought the straw man to his side.

'This young man's shoulder has been shattered in many places,' he explained. Tangle flinched. 'It was an unlucky shot that hit the socket joint and went through to splinter the blade behind. I have seen two wounds of this kind before and know that neither man I saw take such a hit ever had use of their arm or shoulder again, though one was still able afterwards to make a grasp with his hand, of sorts. But here the bolt is removed and yet there is no bleeding and the entry and exit wounds are already covered over. And the bones that should be confused are moved back into place as I have never known before. Is this your doing, Master Paequat?'

'Paequat want to help Kjerros,' he answered, defensively.

'Help him?' replied Rumé. 'You nearly cured him!' At which news, Tangle gave out a large sigh of relief and hugged Paequat many times. 'You have a gift, Paequat, one that is not earthbound, I deem; to transcend some problems that nature herself would otherwise be hard-put to fix.'

'Then Kjerros will be all right?' Tangle asked, unwilling to get ahead of things.

'He will mend in a fashion he had no hope of doing so before Paequat lent forth his remedy,' replied Rumé. 'He must not move his shoulder for the bones must re-set, and he will be in a great deal of pain for weeks. I will now make up a bandage about his shoulder to keep it fixed in place and a sling also to bind the arm across his chest. It may be that he can move with us in a few days' time.'

'Then we could be here that long?' asked Behvyn.

'Yes, but we have time,' assured Rumé.

They sat in silence together while Rumé worked and the others slept as the torches about them guttered and grew dim. Then Tangle asked the foremost question in her mind.

'Were you the one who told me to "let go" back when the moth-mag dragged me off towards the edge of the road?'

'I am sorry. It was an invasion to have done so,' replied Rumé.

'You saved my life! Don't apologise!' cried Tangle. 'I don't know how you did it, but I am ever thankful. If there is anything you would ask of me, only speak of it and I will do it!'

'You have no obligation to me, Tangle. Only this will I ask. That you let me explain our connection and think no less of him that caused it.' So Rumé told Tangle of how she was his sight and of the bracelet and its history as he knew it, and he showed her the necklace he wore and how the black stones were twinned, as she extended her wrist forward to compare them.

'I am not an idiot,' replied Tangle. 'I knew Feran had come into the bracelet in some fashion. But now I know its origins I don't see the gift in any lesser light. It was given to me in love and I know that the love is there with or without such a token. But you need not worry, Rumé. I won't set down this responsibility that I know you did not place upon me. It looks like you've travelled in darkness for too long,' she said, looking down the tunnel. 'Tomorrow you will see in the thick of day through me, with Feran at my side! And who knows,' Tangle added with a glint, 'should we ever come to Cambwall, the Queen may congratulate her King's Champion upon the rescue of the fair Lady Tangly!'

'Lady?' coughed Behvyn.

'Then you know of me?' replied Rumé, astonished.

'What else would you have expected? For you are the Champion of his King! Of the heroics of Captain Rumé, Behvyn, the stories about Court are legion. But,' she added, as she went over to her sister's side and settled down for the night, 'I thought they were all invented, like the tales of Daymen. But now I see it isn't so. Goodnight.'

Behvyn showed Rumé to the edge of the tunnel and was about to turn in himself when something caught in his mind. He went over to Paequat, who was stood in front of the window of the Darkwater.

'Father Behvyn has question?' the straw man asked.

'Yes Paequat. It was from when I saw the Lady Alcabell. It was so sad being there as she lay. But she said something to me with her last breath.'

Paequat said nothing.

'She told me I had to do something.'

Still Paequat was silent.

'Do you know what it was that she asked of me?'

'She say find surrogate,' said Paequat.

'Yes, she did,' replied Behvyn, relieved. 'You are her surrogate?'

'I am.'

Behvyn slept a deeper sleep than any through the remainder of that night, with many questions answered and the happy knowledge that, between them, Paequat and Rumé had drawn from Kjerros much of the poison of the attack he had suffered so shockingly, and now gave him every chance of a full recovery.

The next morning grew old before anyone stirred, even Rumé, but it made its presence known inside the underwaterway. The cold white light of the sun reached down through the river and broke into a chorus of many-hued rays as it passed through the membrane that held back the water's flow to play on the floor where they each lay. The Darkwater again had a wholesome look about it.

Kjerros was the last to stir as the others were into the full swing of having breakfast; a limited one given what they had lost on the hirass the previous day.

'No! Stay down,' said Feran, as he noticed Kjerros trying to sit upright.

'I'm all right,' Kjerros began, but the others wouldn't have it.

Tangle led Rumé to his side once more and she looked into Kjerros' face.

'Kjerros,' she said, 'Captain Rumé here is just going to check on you. You need to lie down and stay still. Relax.' But she couldn't help smiling as Kjerros flashed an amused, impatient look.

Rumé felt over the wound in deep puzzlement. 'I don't understand it,' was all he said for some time before addressing Kjerros directly. 'How do you feel, Kjerros son of Kewyn?'

'I feel slightly concerned that you know my father's name. Putting that aside, there's a throbbing coming from my shoulder from where you've just prodded it,' he answered. 'But otherwise I'm fine.'

To prove it he stood up and walked around, feeling a little foolish at why everyone was staring at him so.

Tig noticed his discomfort and came over to him.

'Do you remember what happened last night?' she asked him.

'Well, yes, and no,' he replied. The others stood around him in surprise. 'I can remember meeting up with the twins,' he said, and looked around to smile at them again, 'and then waking up here. I can't remember how I got here, or where we are now, in fact. I don't know. But that's all. It's not a problem is it?' he asked Tig, who smoothed his back, kissed the hand of his good arm and shook her head in silence.

Rumé had stayed down at where Kjerros had lain. Behvyn noticed he seemed caught in two minds about something.

'What is it, Rumé,' he asked. 'I don't know how it happened, but Kjerros is fine again, it seems. You helped him get well.'

'No, not I. Paequat. And it is astonishing, to take someone in such a state through convalescence so quickly. It makes me think on.'

Over the sound of Kjerros professing to a ravening hunger and the joy of the others in seeing him up and about, eating and joking with them, Behvyn worried over what Rumé now saw a chance for, and whether it would break up the greater company only just established after much trial.

As the excitement of the morning ran its course and the weather outside grew ever sunnier, it was decided at last to leave the comfort of the underwaterway behind and continue into Khubron and the chase of Fetlock. Without a sign of Avi or Santi having been found about the Valley side of the Pass, Rumé had argued this as their only choice.

'At least we know where he's gone, and we may find rumour of the others as we go, too. Now they have the Shalean Verse, Fetlock will be as interested in them as us, now.'

'But what if-' Behleth had begun.

'We won't chase "what if's",' he'd said in reply. And that had been that.

For once, they had time on their side. But when they moved to go, Yinko was once again distressed at the thought of passing through the dead of the Darkwater. Eventually, it was Paequat who was trusted by the beautiful Hudron to place her in a spell that sent her to sleep. She did not know any more until they had taken her through the river and into the warm sunlight where she awoke for the second time that day in Behleth's arms. The others went to search out the mothmags.

They found them where they had left them. Though their feathers were dusted with snow, they seemed to have passed the night well enough, sheltered as they had been in the very centre of the tunnel. Here, too, they found the remains of their provisions. Though they had lost half of them to the Darkwater, the Hudron had stocked the travellers up so well in the Citadel that it did not cause an urgent problem. They loaded enough food for a month onto the willing backs of one of the mothmags. Onto another they placed Yinko, bound about with much clothing around her arms and legs and their warmest and greatest coat was put about her, for of them all she was the most delicate by far.

They strode along the road that led the short way up to the Pass out of the Shale Valley. The wind had stilled from the gale of the previous night and the change was welcomed heartily. In scanning around, Behvyn saw that the bodies of the two swordsmen, Narrow and Gilliant, had been swept away. Where to? Only Ithed knew. Then he noticed a crossbow bolt still lodged in the road from where it had nearly hit Feran as he'd rescued Kjerros.

'That was a close one,' he said to Feran, who nodded in relief, picked up the bolt and pocketed it.

'That's my good fortune,' he said.

'Hey!' complained Tangle.

'And here's more good fortune,' Feran agreed, reaching for her and holding her hand.

'And more still!' cried Tig. It took a moment for the others to understand what she'd meant. Behvyn followed her eyes up to the sky and then to the great bird that circled about them in joyous loops high above. As Tig had cried out it began to swoop down to run close, skillful rings around them, and dazzle them with the brightness of its white feathers in the sharp light.

'The falcon!' cried Kjerros, and watched in amazement as she swung around to settle quickly onto his uninjured shoulder and graze the side of his face with her golden-orange beak.

'She's not forgotten how you looked after her,' said Feran.

'Both your wings are mended,' suggested Tangle.

'This is the best of tidings,' announced Rumé, 'and well met, for now we are complete, and can view our course together. Come, look at the edge of one land and at the beginning of another.'

As the sun reached its highest point, they walked with care up the short stretch to the top of the Pass and saw about them the lands laid out below. Behvyn glanced cautiously about close-by, expecting to see Fetlock's guardsman but he saw nothing; no rumour of the night's activity. Then he lifted his eyes and drank in a view that overran his wildest imaginings for many long moments.

The Mizzle Mountains to his left stretched on away northward, their huge peaks cloaked in a soft shimmer of mist until the curve of the world lost them to sight. But at the point they began to disappear, steering eastwards from out of them was a lesser, darker range that reached only half their height but looked deeper and more treacherous. These, Rumé explained with the help of Tangle, were called the 'Alyn Martyrs' by the Khubroni, or the 'Bear's Tooth Ranges' by the Shalean troops that had been sent there. Southward wandered the Eruna. On the eastern side that Behvyn saw now for the first time there was no similar carpet of blue-green trees about it as within the Shale Valley, for they were desolate and unwelcoming. About their feet lay a vast lake, ten times the size of Tieco. But two further features inside Khubron dwarfed it. Behvyn barely believed what he saw.

The road ahead led down steeply over rock and then over dark earth, laden with drifts of fallen scree, into a mighty jungle burgeoning with life. A new rain fell over vibrant green trees, swaying in a circling wind. Hills and waters lay within the jungle's scope and not a few small settlements were scattered within its depths, between which there ran only a thin and wandering path. Behvyn's eyes were taken from one wonder to the next by the flight of a thousand colourful birds, each taking off and flying hurriedly only to settle again a short distance away and to call out sharply once they had done so. These sounds mixed with countless others, some high like birdcalls, others low like growls that shook the air. From his vantage point Behvyn could see it all laid out in front of him, in all its unfathomable complexity. But he could also see past its edge and away further into a different landscape.

This he did not dwell on for long as the land reaching out past the jungle's edge looked barren save for a distant smudge of smoke rising from it and dark marks drawn upon its white plains. Framed by the jungle to its south and west and the Alyn Martyrs to the north, it was obvious that this was the war zone that had stood contested for an age.

'Do not assume the war that looks so distant is not at our feet as well,' warned Rumé, reading Behvyn's thoughts. 'We must be vigilant when we go beneath the high canopy of Chyalis Calambria, the forest that awaits us. For though we enter the wide lands of Khubron outside of the conflict, you will find how every step forward will seek to embroil us in it. Be warned! We will not pass through this land untouched. As for our course, Olamude is directly eastward of us, and you can see from here the heights of the three temples toward the outer edge of the jungle that mark its location. However, Terreplatte is far northward, under the gaze of the Alyn Martyrs. Though we pursue Fetlock,' he added, 'and predict he will tread that road next, we mustn't gamble on it. We will look to build our surety in Olamude. But for now, we must make our own way there and search for the key that will unlock peace in this land.'

As they were about to begin their march for the day there was a noise behind them. Behvyn, still with Rumé's sword, went with Paequat to investigate and quickly returned, excited.

'Yinko,' said Behvyn, 'you must come and see this.'

They all made a short journey back to the edge of the Darkwater where they each stood in awed silence as, slowly but steadily, the water took form to break the surface and reach out over the sides. Away to the far side of the river was a figure stood in an extended stretch, as though freshly uncurled and keen to bask in as much sun as it could expose itself to, though it seemed also to cause it to flinch in some pain. It was almost perfectly transparent and the moment she saw it, Yinko shuddered with an enormous release of stress. She broke into laughter.

'A new awakening!' she cried, a sumptuous wave of happiness flowing through her. 'It will be the first in many decades to make it through the underwaterway!'

'And not alone, it seems,' added Behleth. As he spoke, another form emerged from the river and began its slow process of rising to a stand in front of them.

'The Dal will praise you, Yinko,' said Rumé. 'The Mirovi will honour your name.'

'They have more naming ceremonies to arrange now. The last, my own, was too long ago. That is enough to sustain me now, through any hardship we may face.'

They did not hurry away from the scene. Once they had each had their fill of the spectacle, they gradually came back to the top of the Pass to face the east once more.

As they came to join him, Behvyn looked around at the faces of the others to gauge how each was feeling about the next stage of their journey. Behleth was determined, refreshed by a long sleep, and invigorated by the chance at last to travel with his friends.

Feran seemed calm now that Tangle was in a playful mood. He wondered how long that would last. Kjerros looked uncomfortable at the prospect of the descent and embarrassed at the need to ride but, despite his recovery, the others had reassured him they still felt it was necessary. Tig lead his mothmag up to the top of the Pass. Behvyn held the reins of another, the one they had loaded with their packs, and the last was lead by the inscrutable Paequat and ridden upon by the heavily cosseted Yinko.

'Well?' asked Tangle. 'Are you going to ask me, Lord Rumé, brother of Her Majesty, Champion of Champions, or would you make me offer?' She glanced around conspiratorially.

'Court speak,' explained Tig.

'Lady Tangly,' said Rumé, 'would you do me the honour of placing the bracelet you wear upon your most delicate wrist about the neck of the white falcon?'

'And why, might I ask, would you desire me to do such a thing?' she teased.

'Why, so that I may see the one most beautiful thing in this world I could never see without you doing so,' he parried.

'Which is?' asked Tangle, a little confused.

'Your very Ladyship, of course,' he replied.

'In that case, one would be absolutely delighted,' she said, blushing.

'They don't really speak like that in Cambwall, do they?' asked Kjerros.

'Oh, you wouldn't believe it,' replied Tig.

'Remind me never to go there,' he added.

'Her Majesty's brother?' asked Behvyn in wonder.

'That is a story for later, Master Hahn,' said Rumé, as he sent up the falcon into the sky.

The drop down into Khubron was so steep that Behvyn could watch the falcon from above as it scanned their way forwards.

'Behleth?' asked Rumé. 'How hard do you think it is to find two brothers running madly through a jungle?'

'Not hard for a falcon, I imagine,' Behleth replied, perking up.

'Quite so. I've found them already,' smiled Rumé.

At this news, Behvyn's hopes rose up for the adventure that lay ahead. 'We go at once!' cried Rumé.